STRIKE
and
BURN

STRIKE
and
BURN

TAYLOR HUTTON

BERKLEY

NEW YORK

BERKLEY
An imprint of Penguin Random House LLC
penguinrandomhouse.com

Library of Congress Cataloging-in-Publication Data

Names: Hutton, Taylor, author.
Title: Strike and burn / Taylor Hutton.
Description: First edition. | New York: Berkley, 2025. |
Identifiers: LCCN 2024021974 (print) | LCCN 2024021975 (ebook) |
ISBN 9780593817759 (trade paperback) | ISBN 9780593817766 (epub)
Subjects: LCGFT: Romance fiction. | Thrillers (Fiction) | Novels.
Classification: LCC PS3608.U93 S77 2025 (print) | LCC PS3608.U93 (ebook) |
DDC 813/.6—dc23/eng/20240513
LC record available at https://lccn.loc.gov/2024021974
LC ebook record available at https://lccn.loc.gov/2024021975

First Edition: January 2025

Printed in the United States of America
1st Printing

For Sarah Mlynowski.
Thank you for being our favorite matchmaker.

AUTHOR'S NOTE

This book contains a variety of topics that may be difficult for some readers, including adult themes, stalking, violence, child abuse, domestic abuse, suicide, and explicit sexual content. Please exercise your own discretion.

STRIKE

and

BURN

ONE

HONOR

Six Months Ago

It's a truth universally acknowledged that a woman should meet men on the apps and not in the morgue. Yet here I am, in the saddest place I've ever been, at the worst moment of my life, while also trying not to notice the stranger across the room.

I can't do this. I need to leave.

The first time I came to this morgue I said goodbye to my parents.

The second time was to say goodbye to my little brother.

This time is unquestionably the worst.

There should be a word for those who have lost everyone they have ever loved.

When I leave this windowless jail of a room, I will be entirely alone in this world. It will be the first day of the rest of my life without my favorite person, my best friend, my identical twin, Grace.

I'm only eyeing the guy in here because he's so conspicuously distracting, obnoxiously intruding on my grief. Who wears a tux and a dark cashmere overcoat *to the morgue*? Who takes a call *at the morgue*? Anger heats my skin. For the past ten minutes, I've been sitting alone with my sister's body, trying to process the horror of it. I did not anticipate that this final moment would be interrupted by someone who has absolutely no consideration for anyone, dead or alive, other than himself.

What's he doing here, anyway? He's obviously not grieving anyone.

My twin was three minutes and twenty-seven seconds older than me, and now, for the first time in my life, I'm older than her. How can that be true? I feel trapped in one of those nightmares where you want to scream but you can't.

Gracie and I used to stand next to each other in the mirror and play Spot the Difference. Our own parents often mixed us up, which always seemed ridiculous to me. We moved through the world like complete opposites. I once read a quote that one sister is always the dancer, the other the watcher.

Gracie was my dancer.

And yet it's my twin's face that I now look at on a metal slab. So this is what it's like to have someone scoop out your heart. This is what it's like to have nothing left to lose.

What happens when the person who shares your secrets dies? Do the secrets die, too?

That could be one mercy.

The guy looks over but doesn't break his conversation. He's got the kind of arrogant good looks that probably let him get away with everything. Eyes as dark gray as the midnight sky. Thick, wavy hair, and a jaw sharp enough to slice ham. Gracie would have loved him.

How could he not see me? What could he possibly be talking about that is worth disturbing my last—my *final* goodbye? As he starts wrapping up his call, he sweeps past me as if I don't even exist. Like I've dissolved into vapor.

Except I am right here, under these flickering fluorescent lights. I have not disappeared, and neither has my grief.

On his way out the door, he accidentally hip-checks Gracie's gurney, bumping it.

Last straw. I wheel on him.

"What the fuck is wrong with you?" I snap. "That's my sister that you just pushed out of the way like a—like a shopping cart! What are you even doing here?"

To his credit, he turns. Stares at me as if seeing me for the very first time. Then slides his phone into his coat pocket. His eyes linger, taking measure. Then he nods, finally apologetic, and with what looks like a wave of compassion, he holds up his hands as if in surrender.

"Breathe," he says. "Please. Just breathe."

TWO

STRIKE

Six Months Ago

The first thing I notice is that she's hot—but more like a sunbeam than a thunderstorm. The second, that she's so teary and enraged, she looks like she might deck me.

Fair enough.

I'm so used to this place, I forget that for other people, any time spent in the morgue rates as one of the shittiest days of their lives.

I look back at the gurney I bumped. A toe-tagged girl.

This fucking world.

I should let this woman punch me. It would probably make her feel better.

"I'm not kidding," I say. "There's literally no air circulation down here. You got to breathe. In and out."

Her nostrils flare, but she inhales and exhales along with me. In my pocket, I hear Axe still talking, his distinct accent clipped and low. I tap the button to end the call without taking my eyes off her. I've got a dozen things that need to be handled right now, starting with identifying the body of Esperanza Martinez and finding out who put her here (no doubt her abusive ex-husband) and ending with the sort of gala that is so dull it makes me want to carve my own eyes out.

But I can't do anything more than contemplate this furious young woman standing in front of me.

She's got a smudge of bright green—paint, maybe?—streaked across the edge of her chin. And some on her neck? Like a kid who got a little overly excited with the finger paints.

"Sorry for being disrespectful," I say sincerely. "And I'm sorry for not making what I hope is your first and last trip to this hell-scape any easier."

"It's my third time here, actually," she says, her chin lifting in defiance, her voice trembling slightly.

Oof. "Sorry. That's . . . a lot."

"Yeah, well. Reluctant return client," she says. A tear breaks and slips down her cheek. She brushes it away. She hates that she's crying, and suddenly all I want more than anything is to cheer up this heartbroken girl.

"Tell me more," I say. "I see a lot of . . . this type of thing . . . in my line of work." Not a complete lie. Plus she's got the saddest eyes I've ever seen. And I get the sense she needs to talk.

She presses her lips together. I can feel her loneliness joining forces with her need to say something about her sister. I remain stock-still. During my basic training for the CIA's Special Ops Group down in Virginia, I learned to hold a position for hours without betraying a moment of restlessness.

But in this case, it's not an assignment. I want to know. "Please," I say. "I'm . . . here."

"Gracie went missing over a week ago," she says, her words coming in a tumble. "Troy, her boyfriend, returned from their camping trip without her, claiming that she'd run off into the night after an argument. He said he'd searched for her for hours, and he was worried she'd fallen off a cliff." She seems to remember my advice as she pauses and takes a long, shaking breath. "So for ten days I've lived in this nightmare of not knowing—except I *did* know. I did." She looks at me, her eyes electric with fury. "I knew that whatever happened to Gracie, it was Troy. This afternoon, they found her at the bottom of a ravine. He must have pushed her. But now I've got some . . ." She swallows hard as her shoulders lift and drop in a sigh.

"Some confirmation," I say.

She nods, closes her eyes, but when I offer her a handkerchief, she half laughs. "Seriously?" she asks. "You're going to let me use that beautiful handkerchief for my snot?"

"Oh, it's not mine. It's property of the morgue," I say deadpan, hoping the joke will brighten her up. I'd do anything to coax a lighter mood out of her, trigger a sense of connection, if only for a moment. Even though that's not my usual MO. "It's part of their new hospitality revamp."

She blinks, but then nods, takes the handkerchief, and blows her nose, hard. Then she doesn't seem to know what to do with it.

"Keep it," I say. "They're doing a whole line of morgue souvenirs. Nice touch, yes?" I stroke my jawline, like I'm thinking it through.

"I mean, it's useful, at least," she says. "Better than a shot glass that says *Last Shot*, right?" She sniffles and blows again.

"Or a mini-flashlight that says *Lights Out*."

She shakes her head—but I can feel that the dark humor is also wringing out some tension.

"And," I add, "the parking lot is pretty well-lit. Four stars for that, right?"

The reward of her laugh feels like a sliver of sun through this gruesome room. "Three stars," she says, and then takes a beat. "Because they really should offer valet."

"On the upside, a friendly, courteous staff."

She glances around.

"Staff?"

True, the place is deserted. The people who work here tend to keep to themselves.

"Just a skeleton crew," I say, and then groan. "Morgue pun, sorry. In all honesty, I do wish they had a coffee machine."

"A coffee machine might bump the place up half a star," she says gamely. "Or complimentary pumpkin spice lattes."

"Or lottery tickets. Back massages. A goldfish in a plastic bag. The thing about a morgue is the bar is just so low."

"Agree." She nods and sighs, but while she might still be close to tears, she's no longer standing on the edge of them.

"So what did they book him on?" I ask. "Second degree? Manslaughter?"

"Troy? No," she says. "Troy hasn't been charged with anything."

Every muscle of my body tenses with that all-too-familiar rage, like liquid fire inside me. I forcibly unclench my fists.

"Then I hope you get some kind of justice," I say carefully. "Or at least some closure."

"Justice," she repeats, like the concept is alien to her. "Right."

I can't let myself think about some sociopathic murdering fuckhead named Troy walking free or I will punch this wall until I break every bone in my fist.

"Strike Madden," I say, extending my hand instead. I suddenly crave contact with her skin, and when she places her palm in mine, I am calmed. She feels delicate. I spy half-moons of green paint under her fingernails. Artist's hands.

"Honor Stone," she says. "Sorry if I can't add 'nice to meet you,' because I'm not sure it has been nice, exactly, to meet under these circumstances." She shrugs.

She's right. Electric, maybe. But not nice.

"You've got some . . ." I use the side of my thumb to rub at the green paint and show her.

"Oh!" She takes her handkerchief to the place I've touched. "I'm such a mess."

"You paint?"

She nods. "I do."

"Hang on, let me . . ." She stands still—and with just the press of my fingers to her peach-soft cheek, I'm rock hard, like I'm sixteen again, alone with my hot new crush behind the schoolyard wall.

"You never said why you're here." She's got me focused in her gaze. "I guess I'm not on my best morgue behavior. But then again . . ." She pauses. "Neither were you."

"I'm sorry. I'm doing some work for a friend who was assigned to this case. The details are confidential out of respect to the victim's family."

"Oh, so you're like . . . a private social worker?" she asks. "Or a PI?"

"Something like that." Less is more in this situation; best to deflect. "It never gets easier."

"This fucking world," she says fiercely, softly—the exact phrase that crossed my mind only minutes ago. I can't mask my surprise. There's something so unusual and intense about this woman.

I take a step closer to her; the thought rises like a tsunami—all I want is to crush her body against mine, to feel that softness, to catch the scent of her hair. The intensity sweeps through me, wild and thrilling.

I could throw her against the wall, pin her mouth with mine, hike up her dress—

She's still watching me, curiously.

"Let's get some fresh air," I say. "We don't need one more second down here." My voice is neutral—it's not a line. Honor Stone is sexy as hell, but I don't want her to think for a moment that I'm moving in on her, taking advantage of her vulnerability.

I step forward and push open the exit so she can walk through it. Outside, it's dark, and I'm late. But I don't want to leave her. Not yet.

"Where's your car?" I ask. "I'll walk you to it."

"Oh, uh, I Ubered," she says as she slides out her phone to call another ride. She's moving like she's underwater. She's likely in shock.

"I'll wait with you." The freezing wind is like a slap in the face, and all she's got on is a paper-thin denim jacket. I slide out of my coat, place it over her shoulders. The coat swamps her; it's so heavy I feel like she could topple from its weight. She must have rushed over here as soon as she got the call. It's a miracle she's even wearing shoes.

"Thanks," Honor says. "Wow, it feels like it could snow any minute, right?" Her teeth are chattering—she's got no gloves, no stockings. She's like the Little Match Girl. After another minute, my hands automatically move to rub her shoulders and arms.

I feel her startle and then relax.

A phone buzzes. Hers. She snaps to life as she pulls it out of her pocket, flustered.

"My Uber just canceled," she says. "Ugh, and the next guy is seventeen minutes away." She looks up at me, takes a step away. "Listen, you've been very kind, but you should probably go back to . . ." She waves a hand at my bow tie. "The grand ball . . . or whatever you came from. I'll take the bus."

I grin. "Who do you think I am, Prince Charming?"

"I don't know. I don't know anything about you," she says, her uncertainty hanging in the air like a question I'm supposed to answer.

"I'm just the guy who'll get you home safe," I answer.

THREE

HONOR

Six Months Ago

As I follow Strike down one long block into the heart of Shelton, I work very hard to dismiss the thought that maybe he's leading me into a dark alley to murder me.

Nah, whispers Gracie. *Statistically impossible that we'd both get killed the same week. Also, Strike's too handsome to be a murderer.*

Wild as it is, I hope Gracie's voice will always sound so clear to me.

But as soon as we turn the corner, back onto a main street, I see why Strike's dressed like James Bond, and I relax. The Keystone, a luxury high-rise hotel that went up last year, is having some kind of bash. It's like a Hollywood movie set right in front of me. Women in bright silks and men in tailored black-tie pose on the red carpet in front of a strategically placed graphic logo backdrop, but I don't recognize the company.

"What's the event for?" I ask. I forget that there's a whole other Shelton than the one I know—a city that's been struggling and in decline since I can remember. But there are some parts of Shelton where people get dressed up and clink glasses and don't eat supermarket ramen for dinner on the regular.

"It's for Game On. I'm in tech—" Strike breaks off as a large black SUV slows to stop in front of us. "Your ride." His fingers deliberately brush the space between my shoulder blades, setting my skin ablaze at the point of contact. My back arches slightly, and I turn to look at him. I don't want to leave him. Not just yet.

Is he also feeling captive inside this moment?

Under normal circumstances, I am not a risk-taker: I don't gamble. I don't sleep around. I certainly don't fantasize about meeting Prince Charming at the morgue.

I am, in fact, currently wearing granny panties.

But there is something about this man that makes me want to be rash. I give myself a couple of seconds to really take him in— Strike's tall and trim, with strength in his symmetrical face. Scruffy cheeks offset his good looks, a dark stubble that's the good kind of abrasive. I imagine its scratchy softness against my own skin, and my face goes hot with an impulsive desire to bury my nose in his neck.

The way he's holding my gaze, I wonder if he's keeping any impulses of his own in check. He doesn't seem like the type to lose control of anything.

A crawling unease plays in the back of my mind—I get that Strike might not be at liberty to talk about his business, especially if it involves NDAs and dead bodies in a morgue, but he doesn't really remind me of a private investigator. Not the ones in the movies, anyway. He's too . . . what? Hot? Rich?

Anyway, my chariot is waiting, I guess.

Shyly, I slip off the overcoat and hand it over. Strike takes it, then wraps it around me again.

"It's freezing," he says in answer to my questioning eyes. "You need it."

"If you're sure . . ." But I'm already sliding my arms inside, and he's buttoning me in like I'm a small child about to head out to play in the snow. He's so close I can hardly breathe as he places a hand on each of my shoulders and draws me in closer for a hug.

"You're going to be okay," he whispers in my ear.

I make the decision without even realizing it. Actually, it's not even a decision at all. It's like a reflex. I stand up on my tippy toes, and surprise myself by bringing my lips to his. He doesn't kiss me back at first, but I'm beyond worrying about embarrassment tonight. I can feel he wants me and so I decide to screw everything else. I have nothing left.

And then he's kissing me back, his mouth against mine, testing whether I will give him what he wants, and when I open my mouth, his tongue finds mine, and a match is lit between us; our chemistry is as fierce as a burst of flame, sharp and crackling. He pushes me up against the car and grips the back of my head. I moan into his mouth and grind myself against him. He trails a hand up my thigh and under my skirt and grips my hip. I feel the hard length of him against me, and I shiver. His touch feels cold and hot at the same time—my flesh sizzles—and all I want is *more, more, more*. To keep feeling him instead of the desperate sadness. This, whatever this is, is working.

More, more, more, I think, or maybe whisper—it's all happening so fast.

I hear a click and realize the event's photographer has turned his camera toward us.

Strike springs back, and then smooths down his clothes. Shakes his head a few times as if to clear it.

"Goodbye, Honor Stone," he says, an emotionless mask falling into place, as if we weren't eating each other's faces moments ago. "Stay safe."

This feels like a warning. Of what, I'm not sure, but now my skin prickles in a very different way than it did when he had his hands on me.

Our moment is over.

"Listen, I really appreciate your . . ." I don't know how to finish.

"My . . . ?" Strike prompts, a brow raised, that hint of smile again.

"Your kindness," I say. "Five stars for your kindness."

His laughter is more like a shout of surprise. A slow uneasiness moves through me. Who is this guy, for real? Is it safe for me to get into this car? Except that something about the way Strike is opening the SUV's passenger-side door feels less like being abducted and more like being efficiently dismissed.

"Thanks for everything," I say. "Really. I mean it."

"It's been an honor, Honor." Immediately, he looks rueful. "Christ, did I say that out loud? Bet you've never heard that one before."

"Never." I shake my head. "Not even once." The car's interior is so cavernous that once I'm inside, it feels like it's swallowed me whole.

"Well, I hope this gets you home safe to your loved ones."

"Home alone, actually," I say.

"Good movie."

"*Home Alone Three* is my favorite." I bite my lip and then decide to go for it. He's made no attempt to get my number. "Listen, can I get your info—to return the coat? It's too beautiful to keep. Feels wrong."

He sweeps away my words with a hand.

"Consider it the kindness of strangers."

I don't argue—while this coat is probably as valuable as a mortgage payment to me, to him, it likely has the worth of a cup of coffee.

"Okay . . ." I buckle in and relax into the soft, prewarmed leather seats. I needed that reminder. We are *strangers*.

Strike keeps the door open as he grins mischievously. "Also, I have to respectfully disagree," he says. "*Home Alone: The Holiday Heist* for the win. Better showdowns."

"Who would have thought you'd have such strong holiday movie opinions?"

"Ah, I take my holiday movies very seriously, my friend," he says. I can't look away from the unfathomable darkness of his eyes.

"See you around this fucking world, Honor," he says with a finality that knifes through my heart as he shuts my door.

I shiver again, but this time it's not because I'm cold.

In my last sight of Strike, he's crossing the street against traffic, head bowed and serious. I press my fingers to my cheeks, now burning-hot to the touch, as I try to steady myself. That was a crash-collision, and it's over now.

Wrong place, wrong time, wrong everything.

FOUR

HONOR

Now

"You're kidding me, right?" asks the bank manager.

I shift in my chair, nervous. Her name tag reads *Blake*, which feels like a friendly name. Rhymes with cake? But this Blake isn't sweet. She's cranky. Maybe because she's so pregnant she looks like she might go into labor any second. In fact, every part of this woman looks way too swollen to be working, and whatever I say only seems to make her crankier.

"Um, no," I say. "Not kidding. I'd like to take out a small-business loan. Or a personal loan. Or get a second mortgage?"

"A second mortgage?" Her round cheeks puff in disbelief.

"If I can? See, the shop ran well enough through the holidays, but last week, after I woke up to find it was raining in my bedroom, a contractor confirmed I needed to get my whole roof reshingled ASAP." I clear my throat. "Because of the leak," I explain into the grumpy silence, "that's on its way to being a waterpark."

"Yeah, that's not how this works," says Blake. "We don't just hand out money."

"I know. That's why I'm asking for a loan." I try to keep my voice calm. I will not cry. I will not cry. "Business is actually pretty good, so—"

"But you already have a loan. In fact," she says, "you have . . . four."

"That's impossible."

"It's right here on my screen." Blake shrugs and rests her hands over her bowling ball of a stomach as if to guard her unborn child from my financial failure. As if how pathetic I am is contagious.

"There must be some mistake."

"I can print your records."

I rub my eyes. I haven't been sleeping well lately. Ever since Gracie died, there are too many nights when I don't sleep at all. I had one evening with a mysterious Prince Charming, albeit in the morgue, but since then, I've been living the Cinderella life.

Shelton Savings and Loan, situated on the edge of town, looks like one of those cute banks where picture-book animals might stash their assets. It made Gracie and me feel safe when, three years ago, we pooled all our savings for a down payment on a small mixed-use building out on Maple Drive.

Sure, it wasn't the best part of town, but we had a grand vision about how we'd make it work. We'd use the downstairs to open our dream store, Grace & Honor, where we'd sell affordable, snuggle-worthy blankets, mood-setting candles, and an elegant assortment of bath and beauty products. But that was just the tip of the iceberg. On the far wall, we'd discreetly display what our clients really came for—our collection of oils and rubs, masks, ticklers, and other covert adult delights. A rechargeable vibrating panty. A Bluetooth-operated couples massager. A tassel flogger. Nipple-play gel.

Our wager paid off in spades. As it turns out, the secretly spicy women of Shelton needed a place where they could dip in and purchase eye masks along with battery-operated gadgets for their nightstands—all without having to visit a sex shop. I became an internet sleuth extraordinaire, scouring the web for packaging so inconspicuous it could get past the snoopiest mail carrier, along with wink-wink Instagram posts so that our buyers knew exactly what to pick out without having to ask.

Upstairs, Gracie and I created a home. Sure, it was a little unique, since we decorated mostly with our purchased stock misfires. A floor lamp shaped like an octopus. Pink plates printed with the words *Mama Needs Rosé*. The couch we rescued from the sidewalk, reupholstered with tablecloth fabric in a pattern of eggplant and peach emojis that we kept after a canceled bachelorette party order. (This is also why we drank from penis-shaped straws.)

We'd have done better if Gracie hadn't stocked our inventory with expensive things that she wanted herself—like that silk bathrobe that she "borrowed" and then stained with peanut butter. Or when she scooped funds to pay for car repairs. Or whenever she bought rounds of drinks during her nights out with Troy. But we kept our heads above water—also thanks to Gracie. She was useless with taxes, inventory, and payroll, but Gracie could sell sand in the desert.

Sales have slumped without her. I'm still trying to catch up from the month when I didn't work at all and let my one sales assistant, Josie, run the shop part-time. I struggled to keep it open over the trauma-trigger of the holidays, especially the run-up to Christmas.

Even now I fight the urge to close early. Last week, Jo told me that my sad energy was scaring away the customers.

She might be right.

Blake is still clicking away at the keyboard. Her cheeks look extra puffed with smugness. My heart sinks.

Four loans? *How?* Behind her chair, her printer whirs.

"Business is hard," she says as she hands over the sheaf of printed papers. "How old are you, anyway? Twenty-two? Twenty-three?"

"Twenty-six," I say, and then kick myself. The question was rhetorical. Blake was serving me a put-down. She thinks I'm inexperienced and stupid.

"Well, then, hon, you're old enough to understand that when you take out a loan, you gotta pay it back."

I simmer. Wow, what a bitch. I've never been good at being bitchy. Gracie was the fiery half in our dynamic duo. She handled the confrontations. I was the peacemaker. When it comes to co-running a small business, it's all about finding that perfect balance, and Gracie and I had it like two wheels on a bike.

Silently, I count to ten as I look at the technical blur of single-spaced printed pages.

"Yes. I totally get what a loan is," I say. "Are you sure this is about one-one—"

"One-one-eight Maple Drive." Blake's eyes flash with exasperation. "It's all there. I printed you the original mortgage, and then the second and third mortgages. And the small-business loan."

"But I don't know anything about . . ." I'm riffling through the papers, a note of panic edging up my voice.

She squints at me. "So, you aren't Grace Stone?"

My stomach is a sudden free fall of fear. Aha. "I'm her sister. I'm Honor. Gracie . . . died." It's so hard to say. "I'm not responsible for her debt."

"Look. You cosigned it." Bank Bitch Blake turns her screen to show me, and there it is, cosigned: *Honor Sunday Stone*. "It's also in the printout. Last page."

I stare. Fuck. Me. Gracie forged my signatures and used Troy's address to route the statements. That's why I never saw them.

While I can't even describe how much I love my sister, this news hits me like a Mack truck. For Gracie, money was a childish pleasure, something she felt she wasn't allowed to keep. She had no guilt about having light fingers, either, lifting twenties from my wallet and trading them for drugstore makeup or gas station snacks.

These loans would be play money to her, not a real legal obligation.

But still. To leave me like this. *How could you, Gracie?*

I'm almost too scared to ask. "How much do I owe?"

Her eyebrows raise. "With back payments and the monthly interest compounding . . ."

I don't hear the rest. Suddenly there's a loud and angry buzzing in my ears. I feel winded, sick, frightened, furious—capsized in feelings. They consume my whole body. Not only have I lost Gracie, am I really going to lose the store, too? Our apartment is the only place I've ever felt safe enough to call home. Gracie and I dreamed about it since we were little girls. It's been our haven.

I think of Strike, who pops into my head way too often and at the strangest of times—usually at my bleakest. (And sure, a lot of times at my thirstiest.) *Breathe*, I remember.

Those dark eyes, holding me to a sense that I was stronger than I knew.

I take a long breath and wonder for the millionth time where he is. What he's doing. If he ever thinks of me.

A few minutes later, I leave the bank, stunned and humiliated. My heart is battered by the thought of our store being flushed down the toilet. I have three weeks to come up with back payments before the start of foreclosure proceedings.

Three weeks.

I'll need to find a sizable chunk of money. Like, tomorrow. And I just don't have it. No solution is obvious. Sublet Gracie's bedroom? Sell my plasma?

I try to let the cold spring air seep into my mood.

There's got to be a solution to this mess.

Breathe.

I've held on to his word since that night. It's helped me—even if Strike himself vanished without a trace. At first, I was optimistic that I'd find him somewhere, somehow. For a few weeks, I was as deep down the internet rabbit hole as a person can wriggle, even though my midnight online searches pulled up next to nothing. I had such brain fog that night, I couldn't—and still can't—remember his last name, and searches for "Strike wealthy age 30s Shelton, PA" got me exactly nowhere. There wasn't a record of anyone named Strike attending that fancy Game On event at the Keystone, either—though I did learn about a labor dispute with the kitchen staff there.

Gradually, as time passed and it became clear to me that I couldn't locate Strike anywhere, I forced myself to release my grip.

Breathe.

Just as I'm crossing State and Main, a familiar-looking man exits a nearby building, and my body is plunged into ice and terror. No.

No. No. NO.

It's him. Troy Simpson.

A small, strangled cry tears from my throat. I heard he left town months ago. I thought he was gone. That I was safe.

Why is he here? What does he want?

He's already taken what I loved most. For a moment, I'm trembling and completely immobile, watching Troy's graceless, stompy walk—like if a sadist was a wind-up toy. He used to march exactly like that down the halls of our high school, not stopping until he'd rammed his body into mine or Gracie's, pretending he couldn't tell us apart. Like it was inconsequential that we were separate people.

Even before Troy wormed his way into Gracie's life as her roller-coaster on-again, off-again boyfriend, he was a horrible kid. In elementary school, he'd play Catch and Kiss during playground tag, pushing his chapped lips into girls' faces and pinning us hard against the chain-link fence. By sixth grade, Troy found a new game, standing on a toilet in the girls' room and peeking over the stall.

"I'm on Poo Patrol," he'd tell everyone and triumphantly rattle off the bathroom habits of girls in the class; how long they took, if they flushed more than once. It was awful.

Back then, Gracie never seemed bothered by Troy. But I despised him, especially when I was on the toilet in the girls' room stall and looked up to see Troy staring down at me, grunting and obviously masturbating. I never used the school bathroom again.

Years later, when Grace and I both worked as waitresses at the Open Barrel, a beer garden that liked to brag about its fifty-two different lagers on tap, Troy would come in looking for Gracie. By then I had graduated high school, though Gracie had never gone back after tenth grade.

At first, their relationship seemed harmless enough. But soon, Troy turned into a pouter and then a shouter if Gracie so much as looked at another guy.

At some point, the shouts turned to punches.

Toward the end, I always knew when Gracie had spent a weekend with Troy because she'd be wearing long sleeves and pants to cover the marks he'd left.

You know Troy's got that flash temper, she would remind me, a bag of frozen peas held to her black eye. *But he always feels so bad about it, and mostly he's as sweet as a kitten. Also, the breakup sex? Chef's kiss. We get rough in bed, too, you know. I'm not the* only *one with bruises.*

It wasn't Gracie's fault that nobody'd taught us about love. No matter how hard I tried to make her see reason, Troy was her way of reliving the worst patterns of our childhood.

You're better at being alone than I am, Sunday, she'd say, using my middle name. And I'd think, *But I'm not alone, because I have you.*

They broke up after Troy fractured her rib. But they got back together a year later after Troy declared his love with a necklace that he swore was his grandmother's but I'm sure he'd stolen from some retiree's house while he was fixing their clogged toilet.

It wasn't long before new bruises appeared on her arms, her neck.

Gracie knew I'd do anything to free her. I offered to pack up and go with her anywhere, anytime. We could leave in the dead of night and figure out a new life. I'd tell her my plans, and then she'd smile with her mouth, but her eyes would be distant. "That's sweet. But I have to stay here. I love him."

Troy was quicksand, and I lost Gracie inch by inch until one day she was gone.

I didn't even get so much as a warning from the police that Troy was back. Figures. But Troy hasn't seen me yet, and for a moment I watch him stride along like he owns this town. His fried-egg eyes remind me of a cartoon Rugrat all grown up. He acts like people still think he's cute and full of mischief, when he's actually disgusting, spoiled by a life of getting exactly what he wants. Example: even though he's barely qualified to be a plumber, he'll never be out of a job since his dad owns the company.

But in the next moment, I'm pretty sure Troy's got me in his eyeline, and I feel my insides collapse as my panic buttons finally activate: *Run, run, run.*

I duck behind a mom pushing a stroller, and then I veer off into a side street. My stomach cramps, but I don't let that slow me down as I start sprinting. I try to imagine I'm in a video game, the last survivor of a zombie apocalypse—even though what I really want to do is pivot, track him down, crush his skull. Obliterate him. Bank Bitch Blake deserves a taste of retribution, too. My heart is pumping like a fist and sweat stings my eyes. I'm running, but I'm raging, imagining that I'm sprinting forward.

Not retreating.

Except that I am retreating. As fast as I can.

Why am I always the prey?

FIVE

STRIKE

Now

"Buuuuullllllshiiiiiiite, my friend," Axe growls in his Scottish brogue as we sit on opposite ends of his conference table in his office in downtown Shelton. He raises his glass. "It's all about the water. One drop. Opens up the peat." There's an energy here at SynthoTech that feels different from my company, DME. For one, it's an industrial loft space. Steel-framed windows. Exposed brick and concrete. Fridge full of Red Bull for his hyped-up interns.

We run two kinds of ships—if DME's a yacht, SynthoTech's a catamaran. DME is more established, and our gaming arm has created revenue for us for the past ten years. Whereas SynthoTech, less than a year old and specializing in AI apps, is the new kid in town with everything to prove. Axe is ready. He's not only got a head for business—he sold his last tech start-up for eight figures—he's got the guts for it.

He's dead wrong about scotch, though. "I'd rather add ketchup to a filet than douse a beautiful drink of Macallan with tap water," I tell him.

"Buuuuullllllshiiiiiiite, Strike. Buuuuullllllshiiiiiiite."

I hold up a hand. "I heard you on the first bullshite, and I feel sorry for your dull, inept taste buds, which could lick a campfire and call it s'mores."

At that, Axe laughs, impossible to insult. We've known each other for over twenty years, meeting first online as dorky teenage hackers, up all night toying around with the dark web, then as young recruits for the CIA, where my specialty was covert operations while Axe did cybersecurity and cryptography. Later we worked together in private military contracting. My joke used to be that I was the brawn to his brains, but that was before Axe traded his taped-together glasses for LASIK surgery and took up off-road motocross. Lately the asshole has been upping his game in the gym, and he might even be more ripped than me.

Also, let's be honest: I've always been pretty fucking smart, too.

We've built our careers in tandem through the years, leaning on each other for expertise and enjoying the company in our downtime. This afternoon, after a day's work, he's decided to pick up an argument (scotch: undiluted or with water?) that we've been having for years.

The fact that the bastard is Scottish makes him think he's an expert on this.

"Call me a gentleman, but I like to savor it neat," I add, just to piss him off. "Are we done here?"

Axe taps the copy of Brené Brown's *The Power of Vulnerability* next to his bottle of Macallan. "Our next pick."

We meet twice a week for books and scotch—either my office or Axe's. On both of our calendars, it's marked as DND—Do Not Disturb—and our assistants know not to touch it. It started back in Libya, on a private security detail. We were both reading *A Problem from Hell*, and since then, Axe has created an intricate algorithm—which he's patented—to choose our next read from a diverse selection of books.

But I'm cranky as shit today. I don't even need Axe to call me out on it. I've been off for months, and I pin it to the night I met Honor Stone. Not that I've ever slept particularly well. You don't lead the kind of life I've led and get to enjoy a solid eight hours.

That first night, she slid into my dream like a melody, lingering in my sleeping mind. Since then I've touched the edge of her cheek a thousand times. Remembered the curve of her hip. Her limpid brown eyes like the color of this scotch at the bottom of my glass. I've seen Honor twice in person since that bizarre evening. (I don't count the times I've googled her.) Of course, she's never seen me. She has a cute shop in a not-so-cute part of town, and on two different occasions, I've found myself parked across the street, fixated on the front window as if under a hypnotic spell.

I've never gone in.

It's an irrational urge. I have no idea what compels me to squander time from my packed schedule to sit in the front seat of my car, like a cop on a stake-out—though I did run a check on that piece of shit, Troy Simpson, who at least knew to get the hell out of Shelton and who will feel the law of my fists if he ever shows his face in that shop again.

Mentally, I'm there all the time. I can't stop thinking about her.

This is not something I do.

All I know is that she's most beautiful woman I've ever seen, the most intriguing woman I've ever spent time with, and had she been at the morgue for a reason less distressing than identifying her dead twin sister, I would have bent her over and fucked her on one of those cold steel tables.

"Strike!" Axe calls, and I look up. "Where are you?"

I was far away, pressed against an SUV, my hands gripping Honor's thighs.

"Sorry. Right here."

He squints at me but doesn't push.

"I was saying that no one on my team wants to switch over now. They are all too excited about AI. It's the future, old man. Get on board," Axe says.

"Fuck AI and fuck you, too. AI is going to destroy humanity."

"Or save it," Axe says. We enjoy this argument, and though I play devil's advocate to Axe's all-in position on artificial intelligence, I know where I stand—in the spot where I can make the most money.

"Did you get the info I needed on Martinez?" I ask.

"'Course." Axe scoffs. "Is next week still go time?"

"Just ask one of your all-knowing AI systems. I'm sure it can tell you."

"I did, and it said, 'Strike Madden is an arsehole.'" Axe slides the file across the table. I flip it open, remain blank-faced as I read the dossier. Axe always clips the coroner's photos of the dead body to the first page—on purpose, I know. To provoke me.

"Sunday night," I say.

He nods. "I'll schedule accordingly. Be careful with this one, Strike," he says.

"Always," I say, and then have to join in when he laughs straight in my face, because of course that's some pretty obvious buuuuulllllshiiiiiite.

SIX

HONOR

Now

I do not stop sprinting until I'm safe in my apartment, my back pushed flat against the door, panting. Oh my God.

My body is slick and my skin burns with heat. I feel eyes on the back of my neck, like I'm being watched.

Did Troy really see me? Was he following me? I'm gasping so hard for breath I think I might pass out. I guzzle water straight from the kitchen tap, listening to my heart pounding like a drumbeat in my ears.

Troy is back in Shelton.

How could I have been so stupid, to think he was out of my life?

Once I've recovered my breath, I head back downstairs to double-check the locks.

Of course, with four loans, I might not even have a store next month.

How am I supposed to keep going? How do I live in a world where Gracie is dead but Troy Simpson could be lurking around every corner? I have no safety net. No family. There's a real chance I might find myself homeless. What would happen to me and Keeper—the best chunky Calico cat in the universe—if I lost the leaky roof over our heads?

Six months ago, I shut the door to Gracie's bedroom, unable even to peek in. Today, when I slip inside, it feels different. It looks the same, of course: walls painted lilac and plastered with posters of Taylor Swift and Garth Brooks. On her ruffled pink bed, her collection of Pokémon plushies sits in a perfect line. A little girl's room for a woman who never had a childhood.

"Goddammit, Gracie!" I pick up Pikachu, Gracie's favorite stuffie, and I throw it against the wall. It bops softly to the floor.

The last time I saw my sister, her backpack was up on her shoulders, ready for her camping trip with Troy. She had her hair tied up in a blue bandanna, a smear of sunblock on her nose, and a nervous energy as she studied her phone, breathless for Troy's next message.

"What's so funny?" I asked.

"Troy's texting if you want to come with us," she said, laughing in that skittish way she had when Troy made her feel uncomfortable. "He says you, me, and him should have a threesome under the open skies."

"Oh my God, that's so gross!" Though unsurprising. Troy described our theoretical threesomes constantly, especially when he was drunk.

"Chillax, why don't you? It's a joke." She wouldn't look at me as she tapped away at her phone.

"Gracie," I said, my voice a warning, my skin tingling with the fear and disgust I felt whenever we discussed Troy, "don't you see how completely fucked-up that is? Everything he says belittles you. He's being disgusting and cruel and trying to drive a wedge between us. Why can't you understand that?"

"Why can't *you* understand that you're just jealous because I've found someone to love me and you haven't?" she shot back. "He'd do anything for me—he would. I'm sorry you're the one alone and left behind—but stop blaming Troy."

"That's not love, Gracie." I said it softly, but I couldn't help the desperation that crept in. I knew the camping trip was a bad idea. Nothing good could come of Troy and Gracie alone in the woods with a couple of cases of beer. I grabbed the strap of her backpack, and she yanked away, hard.

"Stop trying to keep me here," she said, holding up her hand like a traffic cop. "Stop ruining everything!"

"You don't think I want you to be happy? Of course I do!" I was openly crying now. "We've lost our whole family, and I can't bear to lose you, too—especially to him. But every day, you turn away from me a little more, and I can't—"

"Sunday, this isn't about you! I don't tell you how to live your life!" Gracie erupted. "You don't get to tell me how to live mine!" A car horn beeped, long, impatient, and she jumped to attention.

"Please—" I was begging her, my eyes hot, my voice quavering, giving up all pretense. "Stay here with me this weekend. Don't go camping, please? Please? We can make popcorn and watch movies and do pedicures and—"

"Stop it!" she shouted, her voice shrill with rage, her finger stabbing my chest. "Just—stop it!" And then Gracie walked out the front door and slammed it behind her.

Those were the last words Gracie said to me: *Stop it.*

That was the last time I saw my sister alive.

I sit on the end of her bed and fold over in pain. My face is drenched with tears. As I go to retrieve Pikachu, I spy a photo of us wedged into the mirror above her dresser. Summertime at Lackawanna Lake. We're sixteen. We're both smiling, both in bikinis. Mirror images. Identical opposites.

Oh, Gracie. I'm so angry that I'm not allowed to be angry with her. It's hard to hate the one person you'd do anything to bring back to life.

I don't often let myself think that I'll never get a chance to say goodbye properly. If I couldn't have stopped her from going on that camping trip, the least I could have done was hug her before she left. Told her I loved her. Told her that I couldn't live without her. I still can't believe I hadn't already learned my lesson on that front—how often we don't get a warning before the final goodbye.

My love for her fills the room, an infinity of shared laughter and all those hugs we did give each other. My love for her fills me with an aching longing for one more evening on the couch together.

This is all a cruel mistake, right? She'll be home tonight, calling my name, charming me into making her a toaster oven pizza.

Gracie, come back to me.

I'm living in so much silence. So much loneliness.

The only person left in my life who I can talk to is Josie.

And tomorrow I have to fire her.

SEVEN

HONOR

Now

Up before dawn, I get out of bed and bring my mug of instant coffee with me downstairs to the shop to sit in what used to be a closet until we took off the door and nailed a slab of scrap pinewood to the wall to make a floating desk.

When I check the business line voicemail, Gracie's voice fills the shop, reminding Jo that the new boxes of tutti-frutti bath bombs are in. It's my painful ritual, my daily punch to the stomach. I can't bring myself to delete her voice.

One of the most excruciating things about losing the person you love is that other people stop saying their name. Everyone else moves on. Business as usual. No matter that there's one less person in the world.

Gracie, Gracie, Gracie. What should I do?

Every time I imagine firing Josie, I feel sick.

I look up at the framed painting above my desk. Trees ablaze like so many ruby-red-tipped matches. Gracie always swore it was one of my best.

"Honor, you're a frigging artist," she used to say. "Let's sell your paintings at the store! It's a crime to waste your humongous talent!"

The answer is suddenly clear. While I'd be too shy to sell my paintings at the store, maybe I could . . .

I pull up Etsy and hit Get Started.

A few more prompts, and I've got a profile. So far, easier than I thought. But when it asks me for a name for the storefront, I hesitate.

I want to be anonymous. *Need* to be anonymous.

Firefly! I smile as it comes to me. Yes, the shop will be named in tribute to one of my favorite childhood pastimes with Gracie. We used to catch fireflies in jars. Tiny lanterns to light our darkest nights.

You'd be happy about this, wouldn't you, Gracie?

When the site brings me to the Upload Images button, I run upstairs to the apartment and pull out a stack of canvases from where I've stashed them in the back of my closet. I take photos on my phone.

My face is hot and flushed as I envision other people seeing these. It's one thing to keep a corner of our store devoted to edible undies and slippery, cherry-scented lubricants. It's a whole other feeling to expose my decidedly sexual paintings to the world.

I've spent my entire life with a sketchbook in hand, but I've got no formal training. The closest I ever came was when Gracie found a job working as a model at the Artist's Annex in town. Local artists and designers met there to talk about the latest exhibition downstairs at the Willis-Holmes Gallery. I'd occasionally dare to visit it, slinking around the edges of its daunting white vertical space, shivering in its refrigerated air, soaking in the sculptures and paintings stretched on canvases so large I couldn't imagine a house big enough to hang them. And always, always holding on to a wild dream that someone would see me and believe I was an artist, too.

Over the years, with help from YouTube video essays, I patched together a solid education. Even if real art school was above my reach, there's a ton you can learn as an outsider.

I know I've got an eye and a knack for capturing the female form in oils. I have my own style—a way of saturating the colors and exaggerating the proportions. I imagine men with ropy muscles and raised veins and intent. And then, eventually, men and women, men and men, women and women, in every combination came together on my canvas, their naked bodies entangled and ecstatic.

I'm gnawing my bottom lip raw as I watch each of the six images that I've selected upload to my storefront. I give them titles and set modest prices.

When I'm done, my heart won't stop pattering. Firefly looks great—but have I lost my mind? Pretending my work is anything but amateur? Will people think I'm a pervert?

Losing my shop and apartment would be worse. Risk hits you differently when you've already lost what you love most.

The shop bell jingles just as I'm adding my bank wire information.

"Hey, you! Good morning!" Josie Greene is one of those bright and bubbly if-sunshine-were-a-person people who can find a silver lining even in a day of thunderstorms. She looks the part, too—she's all eye-pleasing curves, with a thicket of strawberry blonde waves, a scattering of freckles, and a chronic condition of resting smiley face. It's not an act, either. "I'm a Cancer rising, but it's my Sagittarius moon that keeps me feeling like a million bucks" is what she earnestly tells everyone.

"Whatcha doing?" she asks now as she plonks down her tote,

covered in cartoon hedgehogs and overstuffed with her weekly supply of cozy mysteries from the Shelton Public Library.

"Running numbers," I say as I quickly log off Etsy. I love Jo, and hiring her part-time was one of the best business decisions I ever made—but I still don't want her to know that I'm selling my paintings. She'd ask to see them, and even though Jo is no prude, I can't imagine letting her peek into my private subconscious.

"So, get this. My insulin went up another fifty bucks a month. Fifty! Can you believe it?" Jo crinkles her forehead, the closest she comes to a frown. "I mean, what the actual F, you know? Like we need it to be any clearer that Mercury is in retrograde? Between tuition and now this insulin thing? I'd seriously be up a creek without my little paycheck paddle." She smiles at me gratefully.

And my stomach drops. Jo makes light of life when she can, but she has type 1 diabetes and wears an insulin pump. Of course, hers is zebra-patterned and bedazzled, because according to Jo, "something that keeps me alive should be at least half as cute as me."

If the shop went under, I'd figure out a way to live off M&M's and Happy Meals, but Jo could literally die without her medication.

I can't fire her. I won't.

"You okay?" she asks. "You've got worried eyes."

I shake my head, force a smile. "I'm good. Maybe just a little chilly."

"Here ya go. Catch." Jo opens the coat closet by the front door, finds and then tosses me what at first I think is a blanket.

It's not. It's Strike's cashmere coat. I hung it up so carefully that first night, like it was a king's coronation robe. It's too beautiful to wear—though sometimes I visit it just to run my finger up and down the sleeve, or a few times to sniff the fabric. Now it all comes rushing back, how the coat feels like him—gorgeous, tailored, perfectly designed.

Imagining the man in it catapults my body back to all those feelings I had that strange night at the morgue. Strike's allure burns so hot in my head I can practically conjure him in front of me. Every detail is seared into my mind. I've touched myself between my legs more times than I can count, my hands taking over whenever my daydreaming got too intense.

In all my fantasies, that stupid photographer doesn't interrupt us. Instead, Strike takes me right there, on the street, tucking us away into a dark corner and pushing my body against a hard brick wall.

I don't let myself dwell on it too much. But how could the trauma of identifying my sister's body have occurred within the same hour of such molten desire?

Obviously, there is something *very* wrong with me.

While Strike went up in smoke, Troy is all too real.

And right now, I'm terrified to tell Jo that I saw him.

I draw the coat around me like a shield to protect myself from Troy. For a moment, it does feel like a superpower, as if Strike has given me a buffer between me and everything that scares me most.

"Thank you," I whisper.

EIGHT

HONOR

Then
(Age 6)

The matches look harmless, tiny soldiers tucked into their beds. We've never been told not to play with them, much like we have never been told not to touch the hot stove or stick our fingers in the outlets. In our house, lessons are learned the hard way, and if we're left with scars, so be it.

Maybe this is better. This way we'll never forget.

Last year, two accidents. Gracie put her hand straight on the burner. I spilled boiling water onto my feet.

We know the pain of sizzling flesh.

Now we are six. We are smarter, more careful. Less accident-prone.

Gracie holds up the matchbook. It has a bright green cover and the name of a bar written in elegant script across the top.

"Fancy," I say. We are out in the woods behind our house, far enough away that we can't hear the shouting. We sit on the trunk of a fallen tree, knees touching, our bare feet blackened by dirt and leaves. "You think the spell will work?"

"Dunno. We're missing the candle part," Gracie says, and shrugs. "But if one more kid says we have fleas, I'm going to punch them. We need to fix it."

Gracie and I are covered head to toe in swollen bites, and we can't help but scratch them till we bleed. Even marking them with Xs from our fingernails doesn't help the itching. The mosquitoes feast on us like they're starving. Still, it's better out here, together and alone, far from the reach of our parents, than inside and at their mercy.

"We can try." I take the matches from her hand, and I rip one out like I've seen Daddy do a thousand times before he lights his cigarette.

I turn the cover over, sandwich the match between the flaps, and pull.

Nothing happens.

"Let me." Gracie takes her turn, and still there's no flame. Only the faintest smell of burn. "Shit."

We've started cussing this year, and the words feel good tumbling from our lips. Like our language finally caught up with our lives. The curses make us powerful, like we're little witches, casting spells.

I take the matches back, pull out another, and flick its red tip.

"Hear ye, hear ye! Thy matches will now be litten, and the mosquitoes shall fry!" I swipe the match again, and its head erupts into a bright orange flame. I squeal in excitement. "I did it!"

I touch my match to the one Gracie is holding between her fingertips, and that, too, erupts.

"Now what?" Gracie asks, the tiniest note of panic in her voice. "It's gonna burn my fingers."

Of course, she's right. I hadn't thought of that. Hadn't anticipated the way the fire would quickly lick its way down the stick.

"Drop it!" I yell, but when she does, it sets a pile of leaves at her feet aflame.

"Fuckity fuck fuck," she squeaks when a piece of ash singes her big toe. Luckily the ground is wet, and the fire peters out quickly.

I'm still holding my match, watching the fire inch closer and closer to my fingertips. How long can I hold on before I get too scared and drop it? At what point would burning my fingers still be considered an "accident"?

Gracie is the risk-taker between us, the one who is unafraid of the boys at school, the one who just last week took a candy bar from the 7-Eleven and slipped it into her pocket, the one who sticks her tongue out behind our teacher's back.

And yet there's something about the fire, its fierce yet calming orange glow, that speaks to me. I think about how good it feels to be the one who lights the match, the one who controls how it burns.

It's so close now, too close. Gracie screams for me to drop it. I don't.

Instead, I blow it out.

Watch as the wind carries the smoke up into the sky like a prayer.

I tuck the matchbook back into my pocket to play with later.

NINE

HONOR

Now

It all happens fast. Too fast. Suspiciously fast? My computer dings. I rush over to check. Yup, it's an email on my new Firefly account, and one new message from a pgdelgado titled: YOUR ART.

Just those two words together feel so presumptive. My face goes warm. Also, who is pgdelgado? Is this a trap? My Etsy business is only three hours old.

YOUR ART. I'm tingling with conflicting thoughts:

Is someone really interested in my paintings?

I feel too shy to open the message. What if it's an angry note about "Your Art" violating decency standards?

It feels like something scary is hiding behind every door lately.

Come on. You can do it.

I take a breath and click.

> Hello, Ms. Firefly.
>
> Your paintings are so vibrant and mesmerizing. I'm looking to hire a head artist for my production studio, and when I came across your page, I realized you'd be perfect for the job.

Would you be willing to interview? According to Etsy, your
studio is located in Shelton—my office is half an hour away. I
look forward to hearing from you soon.

Whoa! What? This is incredible. I press my fingers to my
cheeks, which are burning with surprise. My eyes briefly flicker
heavenward. Perhaps Gracie is somewhere, a guardian angel looking out for me—or feeling guilty about the mess she left behind.

What should I write back?

No way will I go interview for a job. Head of a production studio? It sounds like a scam. They'll need to buy some art for real
dollars before I take them seriously.

I click over to my paintings. These're not my most graphic, but
they're hot. *Afternoon Ritual* stars a naked woman, sprawled on
a couch on a hot summer day, robe open, eyes closed, hands behind her head. Another painting, *Blue Room*, I painted from a
photo of myself, bare-breasted and staring out the window. Shar-
ing my art pushes me way outside my comfort zone.

Gracie was the only person I showed my more risqué pieces
to, and she flipped out. *These are my favorite, Honor! They belong
in a museum.* No matter that Gracie had probably never set foot
in a museum herself.

In the few paintings I've made of Gracie, she vibrates with
energy. In one, she's come off a day on the lake and is tipped back
in the kitchen chair, sunburned, drinking a Bud Light. In another,
she's in her ratty bra and thong, eating from a bag of Flamin' Hot
Cheetos on the back porch, the afternoon light on her face and
Keeper in her lap. After she died, I put those paintings away.
Gracie is so *alive* in them. They hurt worse than looking at pho-
tographs. But they also affirm something in me that I know to be
true—I've got talent.

When Josie goes up to the apartment to make herself another cup of coffee, I jump back onto Etsy to answer my new pen pal.

> Hi there! With my gallery show coming up, my pieces are in pretty high demand. But let me know if you want to buy something from my collection and I'll get my assistant to send it. As for the job interview offer, thank you but I'm afraid I must decline.

I hit send before I can chicken out. Then I sit back, my hands pressed to my cheeks. Can they tell I'm lying about having a legit show? Though I've dreamed of having my work hung in the Willis-Holmes Gallery since the first time I tiptoed through it.

I bet pgdelgado isn't even real. I'm being catfished. It happens all the time. *Squash those hopes.* Gracie used to tell me to aim higher, which always felt ironic, since Gracie aimed so low and expected even less.

I grab a rag to stop my overthinking. Wipe away the words *clean me* that I'd written in dust on my desk. The second my computer dings, I rush back to the screen.

> Name your price for all six pieces.

I set the cost of each piece at between three and four hundred dollars—a fair price, especially since they're all pretty small. Six pieces equals $2,400 tops. I've never made such a big lump sum of money in one day.

It takes every last bit of bravado in me to type: $2500.

I hit send—just as the next message comes through.

> Only catch: you interview for the job.

TEN

HONOR

Now

Interview? No way. I'm being trolled. Lured. Duped.
My fingers fly across the keyboard.

> This feels too . . . easy.
> If this is some elaborate plan to steal my identity, then while you're at it, feel free to pay down my Visa.

Less than a minute later, the reply pops in.

> You're a funny one, Firefly.
> But really, I'm a gentleman of honor.
> (Did I mention I am a foreign prince who needs a small fee to claim my rightful inheritance?)

Honor? Does he know who I am? The prince joke is funny—but it could be a way to butter me up.

> Just let me know if you want to buy, thnx.

Then I log off, put my laptop to sleep.

The bell above the front door tinkles.

My first two customers are married regulars. One pretends she's here for eucalyptus body butter for her eczema, but soon enough she's in the back section looking at newly stocked toys. She and her wife, who always buys from our bath section, leave with a green apple–scented body wash and a pointy little hummingbird of a massager that Jo cheerfully explained "is excellent for anyone with wrist tendonitis. You don't want to have to worry about carpal tunnel when you're exploring . . . tunnels."

I rang up the sale with a smile.

A few new faces wander into the shop and buy some small things—a leather keychain, decorative mugs. It's the sort of brisk spring day when the weather turns warm and brings out foot traffic. I almost feel a stirring of optimism. But before I can, a terrifying thought suddenly claws its way out of my subconscious.

What if this anonymous buyer isn't some harmless, lonely old guy but Troy Simpson?

No, I'm being paranoid. There's no way Troy can trace my Etsy storefront to me—my name doesn't appear anywhere, and he's never seen any of my art—not to mention, Troy's hardly the type to browse arts and crafts online.

Seeing Troy on the street was a jarring reminder that he can cross into my life whenever he wants. He could be at the door the next time I open it to sign for a package. He could surprise me by the dumpster when I take the garbage out at night.

Just because he hasn't yet, doesn't mean he won't. When Gracie was alive, Troy would often linger outside the shop for extended periods. On occasions when she and I went out for ice cream or to the movies, I'd sense his presence, as if he were concealed just beyond our sight, hidden in the shadows, observing us.

And so when Josie comes bouncing back in with her coffee, I know I've got to tell her Troy's back, too.

"Hey, Jo, before you start changing the window display, I need to let you know—" A cash-machine sound from my phone interrupts us.

It's the sound of a Zelle transaction.

I check my notification.

No. Way.

"What?" Josie is next to me in a flash, craning her neck over my shoulder to see the message on my phone. "Holy crap! Who sent you five thousand dollars?"

"Nobody—it's a credit card reversal," I lie automatically. I'm in shock. The sale is linked to my Firefly account. My heart is thumping. Is this real?

The bell jingles, and a woman with a fluffy white dog to match her fluffy white hair sweeps in, beelining right to the back section. Jo hurries to help her.

Five thousand dollars. It's a windfall. The store's never sold such a big-ticket item. The priciest thing in Grace & Honor is $250 for a hand-loomed Mojave blanket that's been sitting unpurchased by the door since I first opened the shop.

In contrast, the nineteen-dollar clit massagers in the shape of a lipstick tube will need to be restocked, since the white-haired woman is buying all of them.

"Little sorority sisters' get-together," she says to Jo with a wink. "Never too old to be naughty. Hope there's no hidden cameras back there!"

Once the fluffy lady and her lipsticks have gleefully departed,

Jo turns to me, uncharacteristically serious. "Speaking of cameras, I think we need security cameras installed up front."

Goose bumps prickle up and down my skin. "You think?"

"I know," says Josie. "I hate to tell you this, but I saw Troy at the CVS yesterday. I left—I couldn't handle it."

"I saw him in town yesterday, too," I admit.

One of my main motivations for creating Grace & Honor in the first place was to give my sister a truly safe space. To pull her interests in a different direction, away from Troy. A place to lock him out—and yet Gracie ended up handing Troy the spare key.

He was always here, hanging around like a bad smell.

"I really, truly thought he'd moved," I say.

"Actually," says Josie, her face in a rare sorrowful expression, "even before I saw him, I've been getting a weird vibe that he might be . . . around." She shivers. "Maybe it's just PTSD. But remember last year when he barged in here and sneaked up behind you and grabbed your ass? Then pretended he thought you were Gracie?"

I nod, tight-lipped. No need to mention that Troy's been grabbing my ass and boobs since middle school. Or that my own sixth sense lines up with Josie's.

"We don't know his next move," says Jo. "Especially if he's not lying so low anymore. I don't want to feel like a sitting duck, calling in my complaints to the Shelton police."

We trade a meaningful look. The Simpson family—led by Troy's uncle Charlie, the chief of police—has the kind of power that could make Shelton turn a blind eye to Troy's violent streak. The bar fights, the fender benders, the DUIs—Troy's record is long, but it wasn't until Gracie was killed that I learned how powerfully he's been shielded.

Josie was there the morning Charlie came over to the house in person to notify me that my sister's body was found. He sheepishly chalked it up to "one of those freak tragedies." But I know better. So does Josie.

Most critically, so does Troy.

Charlie couldn't even look me in the eye that day. Just acted like it was a matter of course that disposable women like my sister have a way of falling off cliffs.

"I'll work on getting cameras," I tell her, even though I'm not sure how we'll pay for them. "And we've already got new locks and the alarm system."

"Yeah, I *really* appreciate it." Jo blows out a long exhale. "Because if Troy starts hanging around like he used to . . ."

"Troy only hung around here because of Gracie. And now she's gone. So why would he come back?" My voice is shrill with anxiety.

"Because you're her identical twin," says Jo quietly.

The truth is sharper than a blade.

"I'll figure it out," I say finally. "I'll make it my top priority to get those cameras."

"Thanks, Honor." Jo floats out her arms, resetting herself. "Okay! I'm gonna switch in the new spring scents. And maybe you should use a bit of that lemongrass calming oil on your wrists? You're giving off some stress . . ." She waves a hand as she makes her way to the front of the store.

Once she's moved off, I sit back at my desk and catch a glance of the painting above it. *Fire.* My nostrils flare with black smoke and burning ash. A wall of heat, the sting of smoke in my eyes, the slow lick of a flame.

Even though she loved it, Gracie used to say it was bad karma to hang that specific painting in a spot where I'd see it every day.

Should I switch it out for a painting of Gracie?

That would be painful, too.

When the shop bell jangles, my memory has such a hold on me, I don't even turn around. I should know better than to keep my back to the door.

ELEVEN

HONOR

Then
(Age 10)

"It looks worse than it is," I tell Gracie when she sees the blood trickling out of my nose. We push deeper into the thicket behind our house. "Nature," we call this place that feels miles away from the destructive aftermath of Daddy's last bender. "It's not broken, just busted."

I've got some tissues stuck in each nostril to stanch the blooming blood as Gracie paces in front of our favorite old oak tree. It has a hollow base where we curl in like bunnies. We've spent many nights held in its womb, knowing that no one has noticed we're gone.

My sister looks fragile in the filtered sunlight, her face so mottled I can't tell what's shadow and what's black-and-blue. "He stores up too much energy when he's between jobs." I squint. "Looks like it's your eye that caught the worst of his fist," I tell her.

"Do you ever think Daddy could hurt us?" she asks.

I laugh. Point from her face to mine. "He kind of already does?"

"No, I mean . . . like, bad bad."

"Nah . . . Daddy's rough on us," I say, "but he knows when to stop." I'm talking nonsense. The punch I took only minutes ago made me see stars. When I fell to the floor, howling in pain, Daddy's response was "Quit your crying, I've belted you worse. You're lucky I'm not in fighting shape these days."

"Think Rusty's okay?" she asks.

"He'll be fine so long as he stays with TJ," I say. Our little brother has a way of dodging the worst of what happens around here by staying at the Brewers' house down the street. TJ's mom serves her five kids three square meals plus snacks, and the Brewers don't seem to mind if there's one more mouth to feed. Rusty's good at sneaking his way over to their place.

At home, we're lucky if there's anything but leftover McDonald's in the fridge. Thank God for free lunch at school. Sometimes Daddy brings home a big sack of food, mostly for himself, but then he gets so high he nods off before he can eat it. Gracie and I call those "McRoyal Nights," since we eat like queens.

I have no idea what Mama eats. She lives on cigarettes and little green pills and spends her days lying in bed watching epi-sodes of The Bold and the Beautiful.

"We could run away," Gracie says. "Hitchhike to Philly or Bal-timore."

"Sure," I say. My tissues are now blood-soaked, so I switch to my sleeve. Which sucks, because I like this sweatshirt. "Except for the part where we land in social services or get sold into a child slavery ring."

"You read too much, Honor."

"We're kids. No one helps kids," I say. Gracie nods in agreement. At school, the teachers are strict and nervous with us, like we're undomesticated beasts in a zoo. To be fair, we kind of are. Our big eyes and knotted hair and stained, outgrown clothes make us seem *feral. When we fall asleep at our desks—because we've been kept up all night by our parents' fighting or Daddy blasting the TV— they get angry about our disrespect.*

When we come to school with bruises, they turn a blind eye. It's not like foster kids are guaranteed to have it any better. And no one wants to be responsible for breaking up a family, even one as messed-up as ours.

No one wants to make our problems their problems.

"Rusty should go live with TJ forever. Mrs. Brewer's so nice, she wouldn't mind," Gracie says. "Then me and you could run away, just us two. We can figure it out as we go, and we wouldn't have to take care of a little baby."

Rusty isn't a baby anymore—he's four—but we were the ones who rocked him when he cried and fed him from a bottle. We were the ones who snuck formula under our shirts at the CVS when there was no cash left to pay for it. We were the ones who shielded him with our own bodies when Daddy took out the belt. Mama can barely get herself out of bed and remember to brush her teeth before nightfall. She was no help with an infant.

Sure, Rusty ties his own shoes and pours his own milk now, but he'll always be our baby.

Even if, at age ten, Gracie and I have lots of baby steps ahead, too.

"Where, Gracie? Where do you think we can run off to?" I ask, frustrated now. I check my nose. The bleeding has stopped. "There's nowhere to go!"

Funny how when you're a kid the world can be as small as where your legs will take you. This place, on the forgotten outskirts of Shelton, sometimes feels like it's surrounded by barbed wire, and we're too little to scale it.

"Then let's play Rapunzel," Gracie says. On days like this, when the fear subsides, thinking about our long-term survival doesn't

*seem worth the effort. A little bit of daydreaming and playacting
can be all the escape we need.*

*We should be coming up with a plan in the moments when we're
most convinced that we need one. Like now. Because we won't do
it on the good days, like when Mama lets us in her room and combs
our hair and calls us sweetheart or when Daddy shares his french
fries willingly.*

*But when we've run to Nature to lick our wounds, we can't help
but be kids. We play pretend, like we're princesses stuck in an enchanted garden or locked in an ivory tower.*

Though, even in our imaginative play, we are trapped.

TWELVE

STRIKE

Now

"I like it," I say as I walk into Grace & Honor and survey the small store. I watch as Honor Stone swivels around and jumps up from her desk chair like a startled deer. "Smells good in here, too."

The place doesn't look like much from the outside, a two-story saltbox in the ass-crack of town, but inside it's clean, inviting, and strangely homey.

"It's lavender," says the curly-haired, smiling shopgirl who's been standing near the door stacking a linens shelf. She serves me an even more oversized grin. My dossier says her name is Josie Greene, age twenty-five, and that she's worked here for eighteen months. "That candle's called Into the Garden, and it's half off. Right over there."

"I'll take three," I say to the woman, though my gaze has barely flickered from Honor's face. The sight of her up close, after all these months, feels like a gut punch. Somehow, she's both exactly the same and even more beautiful than I remembered. A bit more cautious, maybe.

I told myself that I wouldn't come here. Or that I wouldn't come inside, at least. Too intense, too complicated, too dangerous. A really fucking bad idea. And yet today I found myself parked across the street. Again.

Over the past few months, I've tried to bury myself in work. I've had meetings for DME across Asia, Europe, and the Middle East, and still, memories of the few minutes I spent with this random woman have chased me all around the globe. In a beer garden in Berlin, I was sure I'd heard Honor's laugh. Midnight on a street corner in Paris, I thought I caught the scent of her skin, light and clean, soap with a hint of honeysuckle. On a date in London with yet another forgettable fixup, thanks to my assistant, Paula, I'd randomly asked her thoughts on *Home Alone: The Holiday Heist.*

I'm not proud of my fixation. I despise the fact that ten minutes in the morgue got me so whipped. Seeing her now, I have no idea what the hell I'm doing here. Axe would laugh his ass off if he knew—then call me a stupid motherfucker.

He wouldn't be wrong. I want nothing to do with this woman. And yet. Here I am.

"Hey," says Honor, as she walks halfway to meet me, arms crossed.

"Hey," I echo. She's dressed in a green-flecked sweater and faded, ripped jeans that hug her curves. My eyes are hungry as I give her a once-over. "I kept thinking I'd run into you at a haunted house or a funeral parlor."

"But you found me here." I can feel her trying to play it cool, and yet I can tell I've rattled her by showing up.

"Well, yeah. Eventually. Thanks to Yelp," I say. "Looks like this shop has some excellent reviews. So I figured when I had a

chance, I'd come check it out for myself. How've you been doing?"
I'm keeping it casual, though my mind is firing up memories of
that night. My hands on her cold, shivering body.

"I'm . . . okay." She tilts her head and finally, finally offers a
tentative smile. "How can I help you?"

Right. I am in her store, which sells girly home goods and sex
toys in the sort of neighborhood I'd never accidentally find myself
in. Yeah, not at all a weird place for a thirty-five-year-old single
man to shop. I spent years being trained in counterterrorism operations, surveillance, reconnaissance missions, and yet it didn't
occur to me to think of a cover story before walking in here. What
the actual fuck is wrong with me?

"I need a gift for my sister," I say.

Her face flashes with disappointment even as she smiles. "Of
course!"

"We've got gifts," chirps the shopgirl. "Look around! You're
free as a bird here."

"This is Josie," says Honor.

"Uh-huh." I don't bother to break my gaze away from Honor.
Does her brain also play us on an endless reel of mouths, hands,
skin, touch? Does she remember that sudden all-encompassing
hunger?

"We got some flannel button-downs, right, Jo? That's always a
solid gift."

"Uh, sure," Josie says. She makes no move to get me anything.
Instead, she stands, watching us like she has front-row seats at
Wimbledon.

"Josie. The shirts?" Honor prods.

"Right," Josie says, and she starts to walk off. "You know, I'm
sensing really good vibes here."

Two spots of pink appear on Honor's cheeks, but she remains

cool, almost standoffish. I probably should have called first. Then again, what would I have said? *Hi, Honor. It's Strike. So sorry about your sister, but I do still wish I could have fucked you right there in the morgue. Let's meet up?*

"This place is five stars, promise. Take your time and let me know if you need any help," Honor says.

"Great." I'm already roaming the shop, pulling items, and within minutes, I've got a pile for the register counter.

"This Mojave blanket's my fave," she says. "Your sister's lucky."

Oh, right. My "sister." I nod. "Yup."

When Jo returns, I take the soft pile of shirts in her arms and add them to the stack.

"Is it a milestone birthday?" asks Honor.

"Um . . . yeah. Thirty." Only because that was my last milestone birthday, five years ago. "They call thirty the end of youth, right? A few gifts might soften the blow."

"End of youth?" She laughs. "That seems a bit dramatic."

"Agree. I think getting older is great." I inspect a shelf of curiosities—water carafes, pocket watches, a Swiss Army knife with a bone handle. I could be wrong about this place. Not all girlie. I like the knife. "There are some major perks. You know yourself better. What you like and dislike . . ."

"Travel," she says. "Cold lemonade. Autumn leaves."

I put down the knife with the slightest bit of regret and turn to her. "Vintage cars. The feel of silk. That exact shade of green."

I mean her green sweater. Is this where I add *your soft eyes, your candy mouth*?

Again, what the actual fuck is wrong with me?

We stare at each other like we invented dirty thoughts. Holy shit. What is it about this girl? How does she make the air between us hum when we haven't even touched?

"Um, do you think your sister needs multiple sizes of the same shirt?"

"Not sure of her size. Figured I can't go wrong this way." I start prowling again, picking up picture frames, ceramic bowls, some sea glass. A cute, janky starfish that I hold up, questioning.

"Jo found it at the beach, and I stuck a price tag on it, because why not?"

I nod. "I'll take it." With every loop, I add more items to the pile by the register. Everything I touch is something she picked, a tiny piece of her. I select another beach find, a conch shell bedazzled with fake gems and sequins.

"Ah," I say. "I've looked everywhere for one of these. Very rare, the Barbie Conch."

"That's the one-of-a-kind Ariel of Atlantica edition," she tells me, then drops her voice. "Actually, it's Jo's handiwork. She took a crafting class this summer, and I didn't have the heart to trash it. She was so proud. Please, whatever you do, don't tell her about the candle-making course at the Y."

I laugh. "You're just the kind of boss I'd figured you'd be. I'm guessing she's also the mastermind behind the sparkly picture frames?"

She gives me a guilty grin. "Fifteen percent off with the code ALLTHATGLITTERS."

But now something's really caught my eye. Half-hidden by a high shelf, it's a canvas painting of a girl standing in long grass, her head tipped up as if to enjoy a late-afternoon beam of sunshine.

"Now, that's beautiful," I turn to catch Honor's gaze. "Did you paint it?"

"I did."

"Tell me it's for sale."

She bites her lip. "I'm not sure," she says, looking stricken. "I mean that's not why it's here."

"It's of Gracie, right?" I say.

"Yeah." She's chewing her cuticles, tears glinting in her eyes. "That's why I don't know if I want to sell. She was happiest when she was in nature. That was where we used to chase fireflies." She sighs, clearing her throat. "I assume talking about Gracie will eventually get easier. But that feels a long way away."

"If you don't sell it to me, you should place it somewhere people can look at it. At her. This beautiful person you loved. This beautiful piece of art. Hiding it feels wrong."

Her eyes snap to connect with mine. "You think?"

"I do."

"Then it's yours. Consider it my gift to you for helping me out. The kindness of strangers." She exhales a soft, nervous laugh. "I'm trying to get out of my own way lately with my art."

"I'm glad. But I need to buy it from you. If we don't support artists, then the world will never have enough art. And this world needs art." I can hear the vehemence in my voice, surprising even myself.

Jo looks over, confused. I don't blame her. Something strange is happening between Honor and me—not just the banter or even this quiet moment of grief, but there is also tension. I once had this same feeling during psyops parachute training in Langley. Standing on the edge of that plane, my heart racing, ready to leap out into the uncharted unknown—it all comes back to me in a roar of uncertainty and adrenaline. Being here is a really fucking bad idea, and yet I can feel myself dragging this thing out. I fill the counter with dozens of items from around the store—even that corny conch.

To Jo, I say kindly but with authority, "Please gift wrap all of this."

"You bet," she says, hopping to attention.

Swiftly, Honor tallies the purchases as Jo finds tissue paper, boxes, and twine in the lower cupboard.

When I hand off my card, Honor looks shocked.

"Something wrong?"

"Oh, it's just . . . I've never seen an American Express Black Card." She laughs nervously. "It even feels different? Like a brick of gold with numbers on it. Willy Wonka's magic ticket!"

"It's made from titanium, actually." I try to suppress a smile. She wears her innocence without any cover-up. And yet she's running this shop like a badass.

As she rings up the items, I glance out the storefront window. This place is a huge security problem. A fucking fishbowl. Not safe. As I walk the perimeter, I push up the sleeves of my sweater to my elbows and notice Honor not-so-subtly trying to catch a better look at my half-exposed tattoos.

"Curiosity killed the cat," I say with a wink when I return to the front.

She ducks her head, mortified. "This is yours," she says, returning the card. "And thank you so much for coming here today. Please wish your sister a happy birthday from me. Are you doing anything special?"

"Sister?" A smile tugs at my mouth. "I misspoke. I'm an only child." Watching her confusion delights me. I feel like a kid about to stick my finger in a cake. The buzz cranks up and spreads into a full-body tingle.

"Wait, what?" A laugh catches in the back of her throat. "But then who's all this for?"

"People who need blankets, of course," I say cryptically. "Great

to see you doing well. And I promise to take care of this painting."
I reach my hand across the counter for her to shake—a formal
gesture to match my promise—but I relish capturing her soft,
small hand in mine. Like an animal in a trap. I imagine my hands
on her shoulders again. Circling her waist. Other thoughts press
in, unbidden. I hate how much I want her—hate that I've come
here mostly to make sure she's out of my system, only to find that
she feels like the one thing that could restore my faith in something good and pure and real in this fucking world.

"Thanks," she says softly.

"You've got a knack for leaving a lasting impression." I'm
squeezing her fingers in mine. Too tightly, maybe. But she's allowing it. Her eyes are filled with unspoken words.

Before I go, I find myself walking to the farthest wall to look
at another painting, semi-obscured by the back area where they
keep their spicier products. A glance at the image and my cock
twitches. "Another hidden treasure. You're full of surprises, aren't
you?"

"It's one of my favorites."

"And yet so personal that you keep it tucked away for your
eyes only?"

"Something like that. Gracie used to ask why I would bother
pouring so much of my time into my art when I only end up hiding it."

"She had a point, no?" I ask.

Honor comes around from behind the counter to stand next
to me. Takes a moment to think before she speaks. "Art is my
diary," she says. "A way to explore the corners of me that I never
knew existed."

"In your mind," I say, "where the rules don't apply."

The painting is extremely erotic, even though there are no

exposed body parts, no entangled limbs. It's a single foot, only the hint of a leg, but the toes are the focus. Curled tightly, with red-painted nails.

A private moment, captured just before release.

She returns to the register, but I sense her stealing quick, flickering glances from beneath her lowered lids. This is strangely sensual. Watching her watch me as I look at her painting. Because we both know what she's painted here. I lean in closer.

Trace my forefinger along the foot's arch without actually touching it.

Then, in a smooth and decisive gesture, I take it off the wall and bring it to her at the register.

"I want this," I tell her. "Please."

"That's not for sale," she says.

"Because it's of Gracie?"

"No, because . . ."

She and I both know it's her. Mid-orgasm. My mouth goes dry.

"Where would you even hang it?"

"Oh, my house has the space." I lean across the counter so we are mere inches apart. All I want is to press my fingertips against her soft lips. "Because here's the thing," I say forcefully. My voice, low, turns husky. "I *need* this painting."

"No," she whispers, but I sense her nervousness, see the subtle rise of color in her cheeks as she leans slightly closer to me.

"Don't do that," I whisper.

"Do what?" she whispers back.

I raise a finger just millimeters from her lips. The anticipation of touching her stiffens my cock again. As I slowly press and then brush the tip of my finger against her bottom lip, I feel the tremble in her skin. One long, rolling shiver. The moment is fleeting, as quick as a flash, but the intensity of the sensation lingers and leaves me craving more.

"Don't make me beg," I mutter, leaning to whisper the words in her ear.

"Why do you want it?"

"I don't want it. I *need* it. How much?"

"I . . . I don't know," she says. "First you need to tell me if you're opening a store next door to mine and stocking it up with my inventory. Who is all this really for, anyway?" She lifts a bottle of massage oil from the counter and waves it, shy, flirtatious.

Just then Jo appears, her arms laden with tissue paper and ribbons. Honor sets down the massage oil with a small, embarrassed laugh. The spell is broken. I don't know if I'm grateful or furious.

"Here's the truth," I say. "Do you know Turning Point?"

"Of course I know it," says Jo, merrily interrupting as she comes over to grab the tape dispenser. "It's the shelter over on Greenpoint for women and their children who've faced domestic abuse."

I nod. "I usually donate money. But there's always birthdays, sobriety anniversaries—days worth celebrating. And a gift can bring a smile, you know?"

"Wait—so you're giving all this to Turning Point? That's incredibly kind of you," Honor presses a hand to her heart. "Gracie and I were so grateful for Turning Point back when we were little. It was how we got school shoes, raincoats, and our sixth-grade graduation dresses. That place saved us. Or saved our pride, anyway." She strikes an awkward pose, arms in the air, like a beauty pageant contestant showing off her baton twirl. "They even got us dentist visits." She doesn't look like a kid whose parents didn't get her to the dentist. Then again, I do know how easy it is to hide trauma behind pearly white veneers.

"I'll take everything in the store. No need to wrap any more." I withdraw my wallet again. "All of it."

"As in, the whole place?" Honor squeaks like a mouse.

"For Turning Point. Everyone there could use some comfort. And that's what this place is all about, right?"

"Whoa," says Josie. "Are you a Sagittarius? This is, like, intense social impact. I want to call the *Shelton Herald*!"

"Scorpio," I say. "And you better be joking about calling the *Herald*."

"Scorpio," Josie says. "Interesting."

Honor's eyes sparkle. "This is really generous of you."

"Ah, I don't think I'm totally selfless." I lower my voice. "The painting," I remind her.

"The painting?"

"Yes. The one of *your foot*?" I grin. I might as well have torn her clothes off, she looks so shocked and exposed. "That one is just for me."

THIRTEEN

HONOR

Now

After Strike leaves, my entire body is still buzzing with impact. After months of fantasizing about our reunion, here I am, encountering him in the last place I'd expect. I might not have been date-ready—or even regular ready—but at least I wasn't raw with grief. Strike himself was mostly just the way I remembered—same intoxicating aura of mystery, same hall-of-fame jawline—but I also loved discovering a deeper layer of his personality, especially when he talked about my art and Turning Point.

When Jo finally comes back from the stockroom, she and I dance around the nearly empty store, reveling in our change in luck. She's brought up enough in overstock to replenish the floor and will put in a reorder on all the staples that Strike (and the team he summoned) carried out the door.

Along with some very real problems.

As in, I can hold off foreclosure. As in, I don't need to lay off Jo today.

"Dude was *fire*," Jo says when we stop jumping and start hauling out our boxes of *Welcome to Shelton* mugs and hoodies from the back room—leftovers that a travel agency ordered in bulk from our shop for a convention here that got canceled.

"You think?"

"Honor! Did you even see that? He swooped in here like Superman. Actually, no—Superman is too earnest. That guy was giving full-on Batman. Dark and mysterious and that black AmEx. Holy shit, and that jaw!" Josie fans her face. "You are one cold little icicle if that guy didn't put a purr in your panties."

"Josie!" I laugh, self-conscious. "Let's figure out how to even out these empty shelves."

My brain is replaying every moment of our interaction. Strike's magnetic pull. His finger tracing the arch of my foot. That tattoo I only got a glimpse of. It was a series of lines, like a bar code.

He's like a thousand-piece puzzle, and I've only got the corners.

He also now owns two of my paintings. I wish he'd answered when I asked where he planned to hang them.

"Earth to Honor." Jo jabs me with the end of a hanger. "Where did you go?" Her eyes glint, knowing.

"Nowhere." No need to mention I was remembering Strike's mouth when he spoke those words: *Don't make me beg.* The feel of his breath on my ear. The delicious hunger in his words.

"All I know," says Jo, "is your and Strike's love lines were brewing up an electrical storm. I don't think I've ever felt such blistering energy." She stops to survey our work. "Okay. I'm heading home. Here's what I think you should do."

"Nope. Not calling your pal the virtual reiki guy for a massage," I say.

"Fine. Then take one of our luxury 'massagers,' go upstairs, and rub out some of that sexual tension that's steaming up this joint."

"Jo! Stop!"

"Because tomorrow, when I come back, the air better be a little less . . ."

I fold my arms and stare. "Less what?"

"Less . . . *moist*," she says, and she walks out the door. I can hear her cackling all the way to her car.

Upstairs, Keeper jumps into my arms and nuzzles my armpit, reminding me to feed him. Then I open a bottle of cold, cheap white wine, give myself a nice healthy pour, sit at my laptop, and pull Strike's receipt from my jeans pocket.

I want to know everything about this man.

Strike Madden. DME LLC.

Starting with: What is up with his strangely vague business name?

My search results for "DME" lead me to a couple of Getty Images stock photos of Strike on red carpets; one is for the Vets Gala, the other a photo from the night we met. Neither of them with a plus-one.

I don't get any hits when I type "DME" in combo with Strike's name, either. DME apparently stands for "durable medical equipment," but something tells me this is not Strike's line of work.

His identity has been highly scrubbed. I wonder why.

Why am I not surprised? After all, one look at Strike and you can tell he doesn't let anyone learn one more damn fact than what he cares to show.

I log on to my Firefly account.

Ah.

Relief and pure pleasure spike through me to see that five-thousand-dollar receipt again.

Better than a reiki massage!

Thank you, P. G. Delgado, for buying my paintings, even if you're some random lonely old—

I sit up ramrod straight and nearly choke on my gulp of wine.

Could P. G. be an alias for Strike? So weird that they both showed up on the same day, right?

My fingers fly over the keyboard. I look up the names Peter, Paul, and Paolo Delgado. Patrick, Phillip, Preston, Palmer.

Delgado. Madden.

Nope, nope, nope.

Ping.

I'm staring at my screen when the chime of my Etsy Messages notification sounds.

Ping.

It's pgdelgado.

> Looking forward to filling my home with your art.
> My favorite is Rainy Day Girl.

Whoa. Was not expecting that. I painted it of Gracie last year when she had a really painful bout of vaginal strep, worse than the usual UTIs that plagued her. She never took care of herself, but would wait it out, hoping it would heal itself, and I'd be the one racing to the Walgreen's to grab antibiotics and a gallon of cranberry juice. In this painting, Gracie is lying on the couch holding her Pikachu stuffy. It's one of my favorites, too.

> What do you like about it?

For a moment I feel pathetic that I'm asking this random buyer for compliments.

Her body is bruised by life's wounds. Still, hope: cradled lovingly in her arms is an object of love and comfort. Who will she become?

Bruised. They used the word *bruised.*

Delgaldo has a sharp eye to catch the faint smudge of greenblue on her forearm, another at her neck. Troy's bruises. Apparently, Troy likes rough sex. Gracie told me she used to pretend to like it, but mostly, while she satisfied him with her body, she'd disassociate. Let her mind drift.

"Gracie! The whole reason for sex is to find pleasure in your body," I told her. "To feel the most pleasure you can." Not that I've ever found a partner particularly skilled at doing that.

"It's not like that with Troy and me," she'd answered simply, like that wasn't the saddest sentence ever uttered.

Ping.

I'd like to schedule an interview. I really believe your art style and skill set will be perfect for a project with my production studio.

Ha. I don't want to explain all the ways I'm not qualified—
Ping.

I've been looking for a truly original figurative artist like you for a while. Come tour my studio. Half an hour, tops. I think you'll be very interested.

Oh my God. They're actually serious.

I type fast to stay ahead of second thoughts: Send me the details.

And then I slam shut my laptop.

I know Shelton inside and out. If the address turns out to be a Motel 6, I can just block the sender, assume I sold my painting to a perv, and call it a bittersweet win. Five thousand dollars' payment for my art changes my life big time. Meanwhile, I'm tired, and it's dark out, and Keeper must have slipped outside while I was taking out the trash. I call for him, clap my hands, and whistle. Typical indoor-outdoor cat, he doesn't come running.

"Keeper!"

I give up when I'm sure that Keep is deliberately ignoring my call and has chosen to prowl for the night.

I check in with Etsy one last time. Delgado's sent me an address to a studio called Ashburn, plus the time: 10 a.m. tomorrow.

The address is in an extremely good zip code.

And Ashburn comes up on Wikipedia and Google Maps as exactly what Delgado says it is: an art animation and production studio. There are no additional details, just an image of a modern building, all steel and glass and solar panels.

It's all happened lightning-fast.

Still, a tiny part of me is whispering: *Why not you, Honor? Fortune favors the bold! And since you don't have a fortune, what have you got to lose?*

With a pounding heart, I tell them I'll be there—Looking forward to it!—and as soon as I log off, the exhaustion hits me like a truck. The money, Strike's visit—it's mind-blowing. The moment my head touches the pillow, I fall asleep, dreaming of Strike staring at my painting.

All these months, and he chose today to resurface.

When a sound startles me, I'm so groggy I think it's Strike. I was dreaming about him so deeply . . . a dream where we're back at the Keystone hotel, only now I'm all dressed up and Strike is leaning in, whispering in my ear, but I also hear music. It's too loud; I can't hear what Strike's saying—

The tinkle of chimes.

It's my phone.

My eyes open as I grope for it in the darkness.

Maybe it's Delgado, changing the time—or reneging on the meeting.

The words are a blur. I blink.

For a moment I just stare, as if I've been shot by a tranquilizer dart.

The fear now rises in me like a flash flood. I sit up.

I miss her

Troy fucking Simpson.

My heart is a nine-pound hammer. Every hair on my body is raised.

With icy fingers, I type back.

> Don't you dare say that to me. Don't you
> fucking dare.

But Troy is not the sort of man to back down from a fight. Warning him *don't you fucking dare* probably excites him. This realization hits too late. His reply is quick.

Her death was an ACCIDENT. You gotta
believe me on that. Everyone else does! But
when I saw you on the street, I thought

Grace was here again. I wanted to grab her
and kiss her mouth and take her home—and
when I realized it was you, my heart crashed.
So fucked up, right? She made me so
goddamn happy. Seeing you was the first
time I felt good since my beautiful girl died.
Gracie wouldn't want me to hurt this
bad. She wouldn't want you to be alone
either. She'd want us

No, no, no. Troy, you evil, manipulative piece of shit.

I power down my phone, my heart in my throat. Terror curls like a tidal wave over me. My thoughts are racing. My hand gropes, an instinctual urge to gather Keeper close—but of course, he's not at the bottom of the bed.

He never came inside.

In a flash, I'm downstairs, throwing open the door, shouting: "Here, kitty-kitty. Come on, Keep! Come back to me, sweet pea." My voice is pleading.

No answer. Only blackness. Only stillness.

A bone-deep shiver rolls through me from my toes to my scalp. Troy is out there somewhere. Waiting for me. His eyes on his next, identical prize. His dick probably rock-hard at the prospect of cornering me, owning me, possessing me the same way he assaulted and overpowered Gracie. We are one and the same to him; I've just got more fight in me, that's all.

In Troy's mind, I'll bet that's called foreplay.

Troy is stronger than Gracie and me put together. It would take nothing for him to break in here and attack me. I've heard too many stories from Gracie. I hear them now, the whisper of a ghost. Warning me.

I can't stand here with the door open like this.

Tonight I'll sleep with an ear out, listening for Keep's meowing. In the meantime, I shut the door hard, bolt it, check the locks, and return to my bedroom, wild-eyed, with an inescapable sense of dread.

FOURTEEN

HONOR

Now

The next morning, no Keep. I leave him his breakfast by the back door, shower and blow-dry my hair, and then stand in front of my meager closet. I reach for my favorite black sweater and remember that's what I wore the day Gracie didn't come home. With an ache in my heart, I ball it up and stuff it in the back of my closet. At some point, I'll donate it to the Salvation Army.

Better yet, I'll burn it.

According to Waze, the studio is about twenty-five minutes away, out by Elmhurst Golf Club. The fancy part of town, with mansions and long green lawns and gates with intercoms. The side of Shelton that doesn't look like a broken promise.

Jo texts that she'll be over in ten with her car for me to borrow. As I lock my front door, I feel the first stirrings of hope—

"Good morning, beautiful."

A soft scream escapes my lips as I jump and turn.

Troy Simpson, in grease-stained jeans, a thin T-shirt, and a trucker cap, is standing on the bottom step, a longneck in hand, a paper bag in the other. His eyes are unblinking lust.

"You aren't supposed to be here." I can hear my blood beating in my ears. "You need to go. Right now. I mean it, Troy. Get off this property. And stop fucking texting me."

"Jesus, Honor. What is your problem? I was clearing out some stuff, and I found a bunch of Gracie's shit, and I came over to drop it off." He lifts the bag, then drops it down on the step between us.

"You could have mailed this to me."

He shrugs. "I felt like looking at your pretty face. Which is also her pretty face, you know?"

"Ironic," I snap, "considering how much you liked to punch it."

Anger is a sudden spark in his eyes, though he keeps his easy sneer in place. "Aw, Honor. You gotta stop blaming me. Just ask the cops. She's the one who went off on her own that night. She knew those woods were dangerous. I was sound asleep in our tent."

I stay silent. Every molecule of my being wills him to leave.

Troy rearranges his face into what he must think is a sympathetic smile, but really, it only makes him look more deranged.

"I get it. You're grieving. I'm grieving, too. But we should really grieve together, don't you think? Want me to come by and see you sometime? I'll bring you flowers. Peonies. Gracie's favorite." His thumb and forefinger snap out like pincers to grab my chin.

"Don't touch me," I say, but he's got me clamped tight.

"I'm just looking at you. Soaking you all up. Those eyes. Same but different. You have to let go of your hang-ups, Honor. You want it—look at all the slutty things you sell at the store. Ever thought about what it's like when a real man takes charge with a riding crop? I could do things to you that you'd learn to enjoy. Just like Grace did."

"Troy, I don't think this is funny."

"That's because I'm not joking. Not ready for the whip? No

problem. We can ease in. Start with nipple clamps. You sell those, right? Next time I come back, maybe I'll bring you something special from my personal collection."

"No thank you," I grit out. His breath is hot on my face. Disgusting. What I want to say is that there won't be a next time. That I never want to see him again. That I wish him dead.

"You've always been more uptight than your sister. As if whatever was good enough for her couldn't be good enough for you."

I'm silent. I smell tobacco and gasoline on Troy's hands. The hands that killed Gracie. He's not letting go. His grip on my chin is as tight as forceps, and I imagine spending the rest of the week rubbing concealer over these two small bruises, like commas, he's marking on me.

When I don't speak, Troy lets go of my chin and hocks a wad of spit on my black pumps.

"You were always so bitchy, Honor. So stuck up. You know what you need?" I can't answer. I'm shaking so hard, my teeth are chattering.

"You need someone to get right in there and pull out that stick that's stuck so high up your tight, sexy ass."

And then he turns on his heel and strides across the lawn, kicking up clumps of green, before hurling himself into his truck.

It takes the whole drive to get my breath reset, and my palms are damp on the steering wheel of Jo's Volkswagen Beetle, a vintage clunker with a scrapbook's worth of faded bumper stickers. I find the private road that not even Waze could geolocate.

But somehow, by the time I turn up the winding driveway—as steeply curved as a castle staircase—that marks the entrance to Ashburn, I've got Troy Simpson pushed to the back of my mind. He might be the devil incarnate, but his phone call and visit will not hijack this interview. I'm not going to give him the satisfaction of taking more from my life. He's taken too much already.

Breathe.

One last turn.

Whoa. This isn't the cool corporate building photo off Wikipedia. It's a private residence. A great big fancy house.

With its own name. Another first for me.

You're a real artist, Honor. You're a real artist, Honor.

The private road is at least a quarter mile long, banked by white ash trees. Along the way, I catch glimpses of other buildings—a stable, a carriage house—as the magnificent stone manor comes into view.

There's a fork in the drive where I could pull right up to the front, but I stay to the left, which takes me around to what seems like the staff parking lot—and that's when I see the large steel-and-glass modern building from online, connected to the house by sprawling green lawns and intersecting concrete paths, almost like a school campus for engineering or tech.

Whatever this interview has in store for me, I need to keep my composure. Even if I'm not right for the job, Delgado is impressed enough with my art that I could make a strategic professional connection.

"We've got plenty of Grace and Honor," Gracie used to say. "But not much Opportunity."

No shit, Gracie. But look at me now. Making the most of this moon shot—for both of us.

Troy's repulsive presence—the heat of his breath and the stink off his fingers—lingers in my memory, but I know how to manage my panic. When life gets real, I get calm. As if I can clone myself and let a whole other Zen Honor take over. It's my best survival instinct, one I honed the hard way as a kid. My childhood sucked, but I can thank my parents for one thing: poise under pressure.

I smooth down my skirt and my hair, then recheck my lipstick one last time in my compact mirror. Miraculously, there are no Troy finger bruises on my chin.

I've got half an hour to make a killer impression.

"You got this, Honor," I declare to my reflection in the compact. No matter how much I secretly doubt it.

FIFTEEN

HONOR

Now

I approach the front doorbell with my shoulders tensed and my back straight, as if braced for impact. I'm not sure what to expect. The facade of this house is so imposing, with its large windows and a grand doorway that's embellished with carvings and banked by thick stone columns. The doorbell is one of those video ones with loud ringing chimes that echo. I squint into its eye and then step back. I imagine Delgado, whoever they are, looking at their camera and right up my nose.

As soon as the door opens, I am taken aback.

"Paula Delgado," says the fashionable silver-haired woman in the doorway. "Nice to *officially* meet you, Honor Stone." She extends a hand.

Huh. Definitely not who I pictured. She's impeccably dressed, too, in one of those power suits that female lawyers wear on television that look impossible to sit in.

"Hi." I shake her hand, doing my best to channel all my self-confidence, and then I follow her inside.

"Can I get you anything? Water? A cup of coffee?" I barely

hear her, I'm so nervous. I really want to impress this lady, even if she looks a little bit like Bank Bitch all grown up. Like she knows she holds my future in her hands.

"No thank you," I say.

"Then follow me," she says, brisk and impersonal.

We're only at the entrance, and I'm overwhelmed. It feels like that time when we went on a school field trip to the state capitol: everything scaled for giants. Mutely, I follow her glossy silver bob. When I look up, I gasp at the giant chandelier—it's as beautiful as it is terrifying, constructed with crystals sharpened to knife points, all angled in downward concentric circles.

If that thing fell, I'd be sliced and diced.

Paula flips a glance back at me. "It's quite something, isn't it? Strike had it custom made." Her voice is rich with admiration.

Strike.

Did she just say Strike? Oh crap, crap, crap.

I am in Strike Madden's house.

What the actual fuck?

"Yes, it's beautiful," I say, trying to keep the tremor out of my voice. "Is *all* of this Ashburn?"

She nods. "Yes—but he occasionally conducts first interviews in the library." She smiles. "People are so curious about this residence because it's got history and character. Strike also likes to give a sense of being accessible."

"Right." How could I be so stupid? How could I not have realized I'm about to be interviewed by Strike Madden in his giant house/corporation?

He's set this whole thing up. I want to laugh and scream. Mostly I want to run away. It's so horrifically unfair to be caught by this much surprise.

Stop it, Sunday. This job could be the opportunity of a lifetime.

If it were anyone else's life, I'd assume Gracie was right. But like my twin, I'm a chaos magnet. I take one last look at the chandelier—now it just looks like a weapon.

If there even is a job.

Paula leads me down one long corridor after another. There are rooms on either side. All doors closed. As much as I want to bolt, I can't help it—I'm curious to get a peek into Strike's life. *Curiosity killed the cat*, I remember Strike saying yesterday when I was trying to decipher those mysterious lines of his tattoo.

I've never been in any of the big houses in Elmhurst, though Gracie briefly went out with a finance bro from around here. He bought her a nice watch, and when she found out he was married, she sold it on eBay and used the money to take us to Atlantic City, where we played the slots and drank lemon drops until the room spun and the money was gone. It was a very Gracie-style bender, turning lemons into limoncello and ending the night with empty pockets.

"You'll wait in the library. Strike's dealing with a last-minute production snafu," Paula says. "You sure I can't get you coffee?"

Any doubt I had that she said anything other than *Strike* is wiped clean. For a second, I try to convince myself that it's a different guy with the same name, but no way are there two Strikes.

"I'm jittery enough," I blurt. She arches a finely shaped eyebrow.

"You'll be fine. The fact that you're here at all is promising. He doesn't waste his time on candidates he's unsure about."

Then Paula opens the door of a room that feels like something out of *Beauty and the Beast*. Soaring bookshelves, buttery leather couches, and glass lamps. Fine textures everywhere. I want to roll around in it the way little kids do in snow. But then I remember

Strike pacing my store, buying all my fuzzy slippers, compliment-
ing my sweet and semi-worthless knickknacks—when all the
while he was living in this palace?! My cheeks burn.

There's an oversized ivory chessboard on a game table. When
I lift the knight, it's as heavy as the dumbbells I use for my You-
Tube workouts and twice as big. There's a glass-fronted cabinet
filled with beautiful old objects that look like they've been cu-
rated from someone like Charles Darwin or the King of England.
Cigar humidors, horn-handled magnifying glasses, an antique
globe. I wasn't so far off imagining him invited to the Met Gala.

The room reminds me of the movie *Clue*.

It was Strike in the library with the bishop.

"Please, sit," says Paula—as in *don't snoop*. She points to one
of the couches near a giant picture window. I nod, sit, and am
immediately aware that my thong is riding up, my stomach is
cramped, and my clasped palms are slick with sweat. But with
Paula's eyes on me, I sit up straighter, cross my legs a little tighter.
I'll need tweezers to pick this wedgie.

I am a professional. This is a real interview (maybe). Although
I might have just peed a little. As soon as Paula's gone, I jump up.
What in the hell is this place, anyway? I pull back the heavy cur-
tain on a view of the grounds—the paths and outbuildings, the
corporate headquarters, the hills on the horizon. Is that a lake in
the distance? It's not quite real. More like something out of one
of those British shows on PBS.

And who are these people, anyway, striding in and out of the
main office building, crossing the green, or huddled together on
the benches? They do look legit, as if they are showing up for
their workday, papers tucked under their arms.

I turn my attention to the room. Strike's everywhere. In the confident and sensual masculinity, the understated opulence, even the smell—a rich and intoxicating woodsmoke.

I read once in *Us Weekly* that rich people hire interior designers to fill their libraries. But that doesn't seem to be the case here. The paneled floor-to-ceiling bookshelves are overcrowded and obviously frequently used. Paperbacks and hardcovers from every sort of genre, though Strike's even got a stash of the kind of thrillers they sell in the drugstore.

A couple of shelves are dedicated to everything food, from vintage-style cookbooks to glossy coffee-table books penned by new star chefs. There's a book called *The Guide for the Home Butcher: How to Slice Any Animal for the Dinner Table*. There are books on medieval roads and ruins, Greek myths, and sports, as well as classics. And an entire bookcase dedicated to art. Old Masters. Impressionists. Surrealists. Warhol. Japanese anime. Comic books.

There's also a complete shelf of anatomy textbooks.

It's all so fascinating. I walk slowly, reading the spines like Jo's tarot cards, searching for insights. But Strike's collection is too varied—both broad and randomly hyperspecific. On a shelf dedicated to medicine and healing, both traditional and alternative, there's a book titled *The Colon Is Sixty Inches*.

Wow, you learn something new every day. I slide the book from the shelf.

"Honor Stone," says a voice from behind me.

SIXTEEN

STRIKE

Now

When the book falls out of her hands, I can't help but laugh.

"Sorry," I say, though I'm not in the least bit sorry—she didn't see me slip into the library, and it's been as captivating watching her browse the room for several minutes as it is fun seeing her flushed and caught off guard. I pick the book up off the floor. "I thought about knocking. But then I remembered this is my house."

"What the hell, Strike? Please explain what I'm doing here!"

I ignore her anger, which, to be honest, is adorable. "Out of my entire collection, you pick *The Colon Is Sixty Inches*?" I ask, trying to tease a smile out of her. She doesn't answer. Instead she folds her arms in front of her chest. "Guess it's better than you finding my *Twilight* box set."

When she doesn't laugh, I add, "Okay, you don't look particularly thrilled to see me."

"How could I be so gullible?" Honor asks, and her fists clench at her sides. "I can't believe I thought any of this was real. I hope this prank was fun for you. I thought—"

Her voice catches, and the energy in the room shifts, and for a second, I'm terrified she's going to cry. Shit. This wasn't what I wanted at all. Anger I can handle. Tears are my kryptonite.

"Wait, Honor. No, you have it wrong. This isn't a joke." I take a step toward her, and she takes a step back. Then another.

"Then could you explain? Because I don't get it. What's this game you're playing? Because you sure as hell haven't let me in on the rules."

"This is not a game. Obviously, you could have left the moment Paula—very deliberately—mentioned my name." I keep my voice flat, calm. Professional.

"I almost did go!"

"Yet here you are," I say.

"Why did you have her invite me? What is this?" I notice the slightest tremble in her voice. Could she really be scared? Of me? Honor Stone's only concern should be her sister's killer—and if she wants to stay safe, she should stick with me. Here, I can protect her against whatever that psychopath might think up next.

"I thought reaching out online was a way to have a conversation without any of . . . *this*," I admit, the brush of one hand indicating the space between us. I'd like to be as completely honest with her as I can. I want to openly acknowledge the undeniable magnetism that exists between us every time we meet—a powerful force that is so strange and new to me—and also make clear that an "us" will never, ever happen. Hiring Honor Stone is the quickest and smartest way I know to take control of this situation: I'll extinguish my infatuation, keep her out of danger, snuff a local threat to the community, and also get DME the best figurative artist around.

She'll be an asset to the company, and having her as an employee will put an immediate stop to this madness. Two birds with one Stone.

"My idea was to create a neutral space to get to know you," I say. "I can't help but be curious. Your art is incredible and fascinates me—and this job is real and available."

This is all one hundred percent true.

I do want to hire her. I *need* to hire her.

"How is *this* a neutral space?" Honor asks. She's still standing, and I wish she wasn't so close to the door.

"Ha, okay. Maybe not neutral. This is my house. But it's connected to my workspace and DME's corporate headquarters. Right now, on the property, between staff, talent, and admin, I've got about two hundred and fifty people on the payroll. And since you came all this way, I'd appreciate it if you'd please hear me out."

Now I sit at the edge of the leather couch with my hands loosely folded. As much as I'm enjoying that cute, angry little crease between her eyebrows, I don't want her to leave. We have real business to attend to. I finally found my artist. I'm not letting her go.

"I had to leave work, borrow a car—so if this was only a pretext to let me know you have a weird fetish for my painting hobby, then you've really wasted my time," she says.

"No."

"No?"

"Sorry. Hobby? Is that what you call it? My God. People would kill for your talent. This is a real interview," I say, relaxing back into the couch. I try to look as harmless and nonthreatening as possible, which isn't easy, seeing as I'm six foot three. "Sit. I mean it."

When she hesitates, I add a softer "Please."

She sits in the chair facing me, but keeps her hands balled in her lap and her posture rigid.

"Let's lay down our weapons and start over. Hi, I'm Strike Madden, CEO of Dark Matter Entertainment, also known as

DME, an international gaming and multimedia company that I founded ten years ago. Thank you for coming in for this interview. Based on what I've seen of your paintings, I think we'd work well together."

She doesn't reintroduce herself, but she also doesn't leave. I take it as a win. She cocks her head to the side, and I see the slightest kindling of curiosity. Many thanks to the God I definitely do not fucking believe in.

"Work together how? Also, just so you know, Jo has this address. I gave it to her before I came."

Her voice is tight. She's scared. For real.

Okay, maybe not so surprising. We did meet in the morgue. I did buy out her paintings, and then her shop—and she probably considers that money a small fortune.

Suddenly I feel like a real asshole. Which, to be fair, isn't a new sensation, but it's not one I particularly relish.

"Listen, if it makes you feel safer, I'll get Paula to come in here with us."

"No." She shakes her head. "I'm okay. I'm listening."

Our gazes lock. I can feel how much she wants it all to make sense. "When I saw you that first night, I was deeply curious about you. I did some sleuthing—"

"Stalking. Also known as stalking," she interrupts.

I lift an eyebrow. A challenge. "You didn't try to find me, too?" I ask, and she can't hide her own guilty expression. "I found your shop in town, and the Etsy account connected to your shop. Firefly is connected to that account, too. It wasn't hard. If I'm a stalker, I'm a lazy stalker."

"No. My Etsy account is separate from the shop," she says.

"You have two different virtual storefronts, but they have the same proprietor. It switches right over," I explain calmly. "That night, you seemed so sensitive yet brave and, of course, beautiful. Same as your art. I couldn't look away." I take her in—I can't help but stare—and then I shake my head. Back to business. She's too easy to get lost in. "You should work for me."

"Should?"

"I *want* you to work for me," I counter. "Please. And I mean that in the least stalkery way possible." I've said *please* more times in this conversation than I have in an entire year. Maybe my lifetime. What is it about this woman?

"I give this explanation two stars. Lacks clarity."

"Then let me be clear. I need someone who can head up my design and storyboard team for the gaming production branch of my company. And I think that someone is you. Actually, I know it is."

"Why me?" she asks.

"Because your work matches the sensibility of my new venture. Because you're really fucking good at what you do, Honor." Our eyes hold for a beat. *Because you being my employee means I can't touch you.*

"I'd like to see your studio," she says, and relief rolls through my entire body. "It's my turn to see if you're for real."

"Great." I stand up, about to offer her my hand, and then think better of it. Instead, I head toward the door. "Follow me."

SEVENTEEN

HONOR

Now

I'm quaking as Strike leads me from the library and up the staircase. He gives me some background on the house as we walk. It
belonged to an old railway baron, and he bought it a few years
ago for a "steal"—whatever that means in millionaire talk.

The house is beyond incredible. Between the silk carpets, the
hand-painted wallpaper, and above all, the stunning paintings on
the walls, I don't know where to rest my eyes. Just like Strike's
bookshelf, the art explores a wide range of mediums, but each
piece feels personally chosen, not just picked by a designer to
match the colors of the room. Strike does exactly what he likes.

At the top of the stairs, my knees buckle, and I grip the ban-
ister. I'm in Strike Madden's mansion, interviewing for a job I'm
unqualified for.

Get it together, Sunday! whispers Gracie. *Fake it till you make
it! If this really is a legit job interview, you've got to behave like it's
one, dammit. Also—he's more likely a billionaire.*

I hear my voice, way calmer than I feel, ask Strike how he got
into gaming. "Have you expanded internationally?" (Yes, it's a

global brand.) "Do you want to take the company public?" (Not this year.) I stop just short of calling him Mr. Madden.

I can feel Gracie's approval giving me extra sprinkles of confidence.

Strike is respectful of my questions. He has some impressive answers, too. About how he put together the plan after reading a bunch of books about entrepreneurship, details on how he raised capital and found angel investors. He exudes such composure that his success feels like a foregone conclusion.

We head back down the stairs on the other side of the house and exit through a side door to the outside, cutting across the green to the office headquarters. I'm still in an issue of *Elle Decor*, but we've moved from the Gilded Age into a Silicon Valley crypto billionaire's workday.

The lobby is gigantic, flooded with sunlight and sleek with digital touch screens displaying DME announcements and updates.

Somehow, it puts me more at ease.

"This compound is like Frankenstein, but in the best way," I tell him.

"What do you mean?" Strike gives me a teasing look. "Overbuilt and heartless?"

I smile, shaking my head. "I only meant that it has so many components. I want to sip a mug of hot chocolate at your cozy library fire. The residential hallways feel like a New York art gallery." Not that I'd know. "While this—" I open my arms to encompass the vastness of the space—"feels futuristic."

Strike nods. "A hundred years ago, back when Shelton was thriving, there were fox hunts on this property. But when I bought the place, I definitely didn't need all that land. It seemed like a better idea to design my workspace." He winks. "Plus, you can't beat the commute. And I liked designing it all to my specifications."

"Gracie used to say if she ever built a mansion, she'd install four ovens and a Skittles machine. Which, if you knew her, was very Gracie."

"I like that. A house can be many things," says Strike. We leave the lobby, heading down a glass-walled passage and up a flight of stairs.

"So can a person."

Strike flashes a grin. I sense he's glad that I noticed this about him.

"I bet you chose every last piece of art and furniture yourself, too."

His smile widens. "Right again. No decorators. Here we are. The studio screening room." On the second floor, we walk down another skylighted hallway, stopping front of a double-wide door. Strike enters a code into a small panel, and I hear the snick as the door unlocks.

I can't help it. I gasp.

The media studio is a huge masterpiece of technology, with ergonomic furniture, flexible workstations, and integrated smart lighting. Even more amazingly, the walls are all made of screens. Projected onto one of them is what looks to be a graphic artist's work in progress.

I blink. It takes me a second to process the image itself.

A young woman—hand-drawn, in boots, with a long sheathed sword at her naked hip—straddles a man who kneels between her legs.

"She is very, very naked," I blurt out.

"Now how can one be 'very, very naked'? Isn't it like being pregnant?" Strike folds his arms at his chest. "You either are or you aren't?"

"I don't know, but she definitely is—one hundred percent naked." I laugh nervously. She is not real. She's a spicy drawing. I never blush when I'm standing in front of one of my own paintings, but this feels different. Drops of sweat bead at my temples. "This is not what I was expecting," I admit.

"This is my specialty," explains Strike. He clicks a remote. The image changes. The woman is now kissing another woman as the man watches. The nakedness has been replaced with barely there spiderweb-lace lingerie covering the women's impossibly large breasts. "See? Not naked."

"But this is . . ." My voice trails off. What is it, exactly? I'm transfixed and slightly ashamed by the tingling in my body—the moving images are so sensual and erotic. Unlike anything I've ever seen before. Yes, they're animations, but they're also beautiful, and in no way childish. Something wholly new to me.

"The images are risqué. Fascinating, too," I say as I step closer to one of the screens to get a better view.

"Aren't they?" Strike's voice is amiable. As we watch the drawings shift, my cheeks flame, and I'm shocked that I feel wetness between my legs. From a sexy *drawing*. Or maybe from Strike's proximity. To be honest, both are equally enticing. Every time I'm around this man, the background falls away and my inhibitions go up in smoke. But I don't want to abandon myself and my boundaries—usually so strong they can feel like I'm behind a stone wall. This feels gravely dangerous. Nothing has ever kicked down that wall.

Strike—and considering this possible job offer—might be the worst idea I've ever had.

"What am I looking at here exactly?" I keep my voice neutral.

"It's a mashup. A pinch of erotica, a scoop of hentai—that's a loanword from Japan. It translates to 'sexual perversion.' Though, of course, that's not what this is, either, exactly. Anime is growing fast with American audiences, especially Gen Z, who have been raised on animation along with their gaming. So it was only a matter of time before we combined chocolate and peanut butter to make something different and tasty." The word *tasty*, from Strike's mouth, sends a *ping* straight up the back of my neck. "We can go anywhere with erotic gaming. As long as we get away from making it—"

"Too explicit?" I ask. He laughs.

"Ha, *all* of it is explicit. I meant misogynistic. You can do anything you want in gaming and animation. You're not restricted by the limits of actors. But it tends to lean hard on the male fantasy." A thoughtful frown cuts the space between his brows, as he moves a half step closer to me so that we can watch the screen together. The scent of his skin floods me with memories of the night we met, and I feel weak. When Strike glances at me, I'm conscious of my nipples, erect little points under the fabric of my clothes. If he notices, he doesn't acknowledge it. "My competitors want to explore the darkest corners of these fantasies."

On the screen, a brunette wearing sparkly pink stilettos, her body glistening in oil, now stands before an audience of barely clothed men and women. I find myself debating whether the stilettos make her look *less* naked.

Or does the oil make her look *more* naked?

Clearly, I'm incapable of rational thought around Strike.

"But that's not what you want?" I ask.

"No. Absolutely not. My fantasies—at DME, I mean"—he quickly catches himself—"are designed to be arousing, sure. But also beautiful. I want this studio to focus on erotic gaming as storytelling in a sex-positive way."

"Feminist erotic gaming," I say.

"Yup. Exactly. I want to center women's pleasure. And I've proven that it can be profitable. Keep your eye on the screen."

A story unfolds in front of me. A young woman is pursued by a man, and at first it seems as if he is the hunter and she is the hunted, until we see she's been leading him all along. They meet up in a tiled bathhouse filled with dappled sunlight and a number of women, of all shapes and sizes, who overpower him. I don't know where to feast my eyes. There are so many mouths and hands and curious, wriggling fingers. As water cascades over the man's body, the women peel away the scraps of his clothing as they pull and bend him into every conceivable position. As he takes one woman from behind, he is kissing another, then another—

I let out a trembling breath.

"It's . . . delicious," I say, genuinely stunned. "It's role reversal set in paradise. I love it." My fingers are tingling with the same itch I get when I'm on the verge of creating art. It's a little bit naughty, but also new and thrilling.

Gracie's in my head again.

Why are you such a badass with your paintbrush and such a prude in real life?

I am not a prude. I'm . . . careful, I retort.

Could I do this? I feel rocked to my core. I want to jump in and see what I can create.

"So, this is the creative epicenter, Honor. This is my newest developmental arm of DME. We started in classic video games. Single-shooters. Zombie apocalypse. Military psyops stuff," he says. "And we struck gold early with those kinds of games because I was able to leverage my personal military experience. Now I'm taking the company in a one-eighty. A whole new direction."

"Female-centered sexy stuff?" I can't help but think that if I were drawing what I see on-screen, I'd add another man. There are too many women testing that one man's stamina.

That's certainly not *my* fantasy.

"Yes. I want the opposite of violence," he says. "No more gore. No more war. I want to gamify art, lust—all the ways we desire."

I stare at the moving images. I see why Strike would think I might be a fit for this work. There's something soft and feminine happening. Like my foot painting. Exaggerated proportions. Almost caricature-like.

"And here I thought I was coming to interview for a studio that might want me to draw a gecko," I say.

"Like for car insurance?" He laughs, and I love that I can win that burst of joy from him, like sudden sunshine across his face. "Yeah, we're a little spicier than reptiles," he says. "Right now, you're an outsider in this world. That helps. I want you to imagine original characters and storylines. The technology is here. Next, we level up to virtual reality."

"The erotic metaverse," I say. "Exciting," I add, and I feel my cheeks go pink when Strike's lips quirk in a smile.

"Most digital sex feels like a bad date with benefits, so someone's got to build it better. And it's not going to be the bros. We need women. I think you'd be completely fucking luscious at this."

As much as I love the way Strike says the words *fucking luscious*—come to think of it, Strike saying dirty words to me would be a VR game I'd sign up for—it also feels like too much. My stomach plummets and my thighs clench.

No, no, no. I can't work with this guy. There's too much that I don't know about him. I'm already compromised by his money. He can't buy me. I can't do this.

No way.

I take a step back, expanding the space between us. His magnetic pull is too strong for me to remain clear-headed. This shit is weird, yes. But also . . . beautiful? This is a potential job opportunity. There's no chance I'll actually take it, right? And yet I'm still here.

"Why do you think I could do this?"

His eyes narrow as his chin raises. He dominates so instinctively. He'd be a demanding boss; already I can see that. "When I saw the painting of your foot, I knew you'd painted a woman mid-orgasm."

"I . . . didn't . . . it . . . wasn't . . ."

But of course he's right. Even if I can't admit it to him. Instead, I glance down at my own feet, which, thank God, are tucked away safely in heels. My toes curl with desire.

"Or what about *Girl on the Bed*?" Strike presses. "You can feel everything in that painting. The rain outside. The sense that perhaps she's waiting for her partner to come back to her since we see a hand around her ankle. Or what about *Night Snack*—that couple, naked in the kitchen, where she's biting his shoulder? You paint desire better than anyone, Honor. You might not even consciously recognize it in yourself, but you're already playing out full stories."

"I make single images," I protest. "Not entire movies or animations."

"Poets often turn out to be great novelists. They bring their knowledge of the specific to a bigger canvas. We need an intoxicating female vision." Strike shrugs. "I'd give you free rein. Make the hours you need. You would bring us your concepts. We've got storyboarders and inkers and even 3D printers to flesh out your vision. So to speak."

I smile at him; the smile he sends me back is so devastating it hurts. I need to bring us back to neutral ground, though I take one hundred percent responsibility for this detour.

"Even if I could pull it off? I'm not sure I'd want to," I say.

He stares at me, unblinking. I notice that Strike does this whenever he's processing information.

"Why not?" he asks.

"My art feels . . ." I pause and collect my thoughts. "My art feels more like . . . a secret self." I laugh, nervous. "I guess I feel a little bit shy?"

"Don't be," says Strike. "We should never hide our truest selves. And how secret can it be when you'd hung two paintings in your shop? He looks at me intently. "Step out of the shadow. Step into the light. You know you want to."

He's right. I don't like to feel any shame about my art. Instead, when I allow myself, I feel shame's exact opposite: pride.

My hands are twisting into a knot. I truly cannot tell if I'm about to walk away from a once-in-a-lifetime opportunity—and my chance to save the store—or if I'm escaping from some sort of elaborate trap. "I'm very sorry if I've wasted your time," I tell him, "but I think I should go."

Strike raises a finger. "You promised to tour the art studio as well. I insist you see it. As I would insist that any job candidate tour it."

His professional demeanor has become steely. As if we barely know each other—which, of course, we don't.

And yet, to walk away—that's completely irrational. This job could pay off my debts and free me in a way that the shop's revenue never could. The memory of Troy's visit sends a sickening shudder through me.

This job would be protection from Troy. Because protection takes money.

I nod. "Sure, of course," I say. "I'd love to see the studio."

EIGHTEEN

HONOR

Now

We leave the media room to continue down the hallway.

"Ah, good. Some privacy. Looks like the team is out to lunch," he says as he codes in the key to open a large white door.

And then he serves me another moment of *Holy crap.*

It's a wide space, drenched in sunlight, as big as a tennis court and stocked with tools and equipment. Everything imaginable in Costco sizes. It's like I'm staring right into the world of my favorite Instagram page. What Gracie used to call my "art nerd porn." I used to salivate over those #ArtStudio and #ArtistsOnInstagram photos.

It's an artist's paradise. Everything I could possibly need is here. Plus a few things I wouldn't know what to do with.

Like a pottery kiln.

There's even an espresso bar.

I walk around the room as if in a daze, entranced by the shelves and cabinets of brushes and paints—oils, acrylics, watercolors. Paint tubes and boxes, pastels and charcoals. I run my finger along the edges of the easels and stretched canvases. I stare in frank admiration at the shelf of sketch pads arranged by paper thickness and texture, from onionskin to watercolor.

It even smells the way I imagined: lemony citrus and a hint of turpentine. It's supply heaven. I feel my creative energy tugging at me. Willing me to stay.

There are no monsters from my past here. No nightmares, no evil.

This place—its pure creative potential—lights a match in my soul.

Oh no. I've fallen in love. With this room.

Well, well, well, who knew you'd be the Picasso of porn? I hear Gracie joke.

"What do you think?" Strike's voice is almost a growl, breaking through my reverie. I have to physically restrain myself from reaching out and spinning a paintbrush between my fingers.

"I think . . ." I clear my throat, which has gone froggy with emotion. When I was a teenager, I dreamed I could be a very different Honor Stone, a happy rebel in Dr. Martens and cute pink-tinted hair who came from a family that could take me places—figuratively and literally. A girl who went to Europe, to museums, to art school. A girl who was given endless giant helpings of love and support and, yes, art supplies. "I think it's my dream space."

"So, you'll take the job?"

Now that I've seen this place, there's no way to unsee it. I rub my skin to make the hairs stand down.

"As an artist, it's like my wildest fantasy."

"Wildest fantasy, huh?" he says teasingly. Before I can think it through, I swat at his arm. At the contact, I feel the zap in my fingers—and between my legs.

Nope, won't be doing that again.

"Seriously, I can't believe this place exists. I can't even imagine having the privilege to work in this room every day," I say.

"Welcome to the fantasy business," says Strike as his smile breaks like sunlight across his face. "I'll have Paula send the contract."

"Contract?"

"Standard issue. Health insurance, salary, vacation days, tax forms."

"Oh, right." I nod, as if I'm someone who signs contracts all day. Inside I'm turning cartwheels. I'm so giddy I don't want to address any of the doubts gnawing at the back of my brain. Last week I was in tears sitting at my local bank. Today this strange, exhilarating man has swept in with what could be the solution to all my financial problems.

Too strange, maybe? Does Strike see me as a charity case? Does he think he needs to be my savior? Is that the piece of the story I'm missing here? "You still haven't told me exactly what you were doing at the morgue that night," I say.

"Identifying the body of a woman, Esperanza Martinez," he says. "She'd come from an abusive situation to Turning Point using another name. We'd planned to put her into a safe house. But her husband found her first."

"Oh." I hadn't quite expected that answer. I'd assumed his connection to Turning Point started and ended with donations. "I'm sorry."

"I didn't know her well, though I spend a lot of time at the Point. But it's the same old fucking story. As you know."

"So you're obviously a giving, charitable type. And you've seen me at my lowest." I lift and drop my shoulders self-consciously. "I feel like you're doing a nice thing for me because you're a nice person. But I can take care of myself."

As he seems to consider this, the thoughts behind his gray eyes are as enigmatic as a winter sky.

"No one has ever called me nice, Honor," he says. "Because I'm not nice. Not particularly. You should know that sooner rather than later. But I'm good at recognizing talent, and I recognize yours. If you can accept that and you'll consider the contract, then I hope we have a deal."

"I need some time to think," I say. "It would be a big change."

"If you take the job, please bring in your other paintings. I bet you have a basement full of them," he says. Inwardly, I do a double take. How could he know that? Does Strike have some sort of dossier on me with all sorts of information? Does he also know I keep my art supplies in the oven?

"I might have a few," I admit.

"Great. The storyboarders and animators need to see what you can do. We like to keep a consistent house style, and I want you to set the tone."

"I'm not classically trained," I say. "Your team won't . . . respect me." It's so hard to say it out loud. But if I don't speak one of my worst fears about this job right now, I never will.

Strike looks a touch impatient. That steely businessman is back, brushing aside my concerns. "Of course they'll respect you. Sure, they're all experienced in animation and coding, and they're all trained to create from a vision. *You* are the vision. You're the quintessential original content." He stops, as if weighing whether or not he should continue, then says quietly, "You're what I've been looking for."

"Okay," I say after a pause.

"Okay?"

I nod. "Send the contract." My heart is beating like a jackhammer.

"I'll get Paula on it," he says. "She's also going to send you home with a VR set and passcodes. We've been beta testing a game. I'd like your thoughts."

"Great." I reach out my hand to shake his, trying to project confident girlboss vibes, but as soon as our skin makes contact, I feel that jolt of electricity shoot straight to my nether regions again. In the reaches of my memory, Grace's hot take is loud and clear. *Buckle in, Sunday! Working with Strike Madden is going to be one wild ride.*

NINETEEN

HONOR

Now

Alone in the car, I press the heels of my hands to my eyes. *Breathe.* I've lived through so much. I've taken countless knocks without ever letting anyone see my pain. I'm usually able to keep my emotions in check.

But this bolt from the blue—in the form of Strike's totally unexpected faith in my talent—actually has me teary.

Kindness. That's what's undoing me.

I wish Gracie were here so I could tell her everything.

"Health insurance, Gracie," I say. "Imagine that." A proper medical checkup, somewhere other than the ER, for the first time in my entire life.

You would *think about the practical stuff,* Gracie tells me. *Girl, did you see that coffee bar and drinks fridge? Free lattes and La Croix all day!*

The thirty-one-page contract hits my inbox before I'm home—we've exchanged telephone numbers and email addresses—and it's even more generous than I optimistically imagined.

I sit in the car and google "401(k)." Ohmygod I'm quadrupling my earnings. Nothing in the contract jumps out at me as a problem. If I had any extra money, I'd hire a lawyer to go over it with a fine-tooth comb, but since I don't, I'll just reread it carefully over the weekend. Make sure I'm not selling my soul in the fine print.

No need to jump to a yes too quickly.

According to the contract, Strike wants me to work only three afternoons a week. I choose which days. Part-time, technically.

He's still putting me on his health insurance.

I've got over one thousand people on my payroll around the globe, he texts back when I ask if it's a typo. You're a rounding error, Miss Firefly.

"Cheese and crackers, you got it!" Jo is already hopping as I walk into the shop. "You're taking the job?"

"I might," I say. "But . . . there's a catch. Remember Strike Madden, DME? Mr. American Express Black?"

"Of course." Jo looks at me, her eyes wide and head cocked like a labradoodle.

"It's his company. Dark Matter Entertainment. He wants me to work as a designer."

"Cue the record scratch!" yelps Jo. "That is the best thing I've heard all week. That guy is, like, Hemsworth brother hot. He is so fine—"

"He's also so hard to find online," I interrupt. "Could you do a little digital digging on him before I say yes?"

"You know I love to go all Nancy Drew."

"If he checks out and I do take it, I'd love to give you a few more hours at the shop if you want them."

Jo beams. "I knew it! I knew my luck was changing! When I pulled an upright Wheel of Fortune card this morning, I felt so tingly, and I said to Bryan, 'Something is shifting from bad to good.' I thought it'd be a lead on a new home—but this is even better!" Jo lives with her boyfriend in the garage loft behind her mom's house, and all she wants is to move out. She spends half her time on her phone planning her theoretical wedding and the other half looking at tiny houses.

"It's just on a trial basis," I say. But one that will put off the bank and allow me to see Strike three times a week. I'm only starting to let that sink in. I blow out a breath. *Focus on the health insurance, Honor. Not on the hot, off-limits boss.*

"The way you're smiling, I have a feeling you'll be working your ass off to level up into something permanent," says Jo.

I knock wood. If I can make this job work, we both win.

"Hope so."

"By the way, when you get a chance, please look at those links I sent about farmhouse wedding ideas, okay?" She sighs. "Bryan would get married on a hockey rink, so I really need your opinion."

"You realize you're not technically engaged yet?" I say gently. I dislike Bryan as much as I love Josie, though I've never had the heart to tell her. He's not the worst guy—he's certainly no Troy—but he's lazy and undermining, and Josie, who is sweet and kind and loyal, deserves someone who loves her wholeheartedly, woo-woo and all. Bryan seems to think she's . . . fine. In the meantime, the boy—and though he's twenty-four, Bryan is most definitely a boy in my eyes—is currently jobless and spends most of his days on Jo's couch watching replays of his precious Philadelphia Flyers, even though he himself never made it past junior varsity ice hockey and spent all his time benched.

"The cards don't lie, my friend," Josie says, as optimistic as ever.

As soon as she leaves, I'm back on my phone, scrolling through this contract on DME letterhead. Over a thousand employees. Strike is serious about this. He really thinks I could—

My head snaps up.

I'd know the sound of those boots anywhere.

The same footfall as Daddy.

I'm up out of my chair in a second, sprinting to fasten the bolt. But I slip on my way and skin my knee against a display table. I'm too late.

Troy throws open the door like a punch. Thank God Jo's gone so I don't have to worry about us both. My whole body shakes with fear.

"I've been thinking about this morning. I went about it all wrong," Troy says as he plows inside the shop. He's changed into one of his "good" Hawaiian shirts, and he's holding a heart-shaped box of chocolates. The cheap drugstore brand, with an *On Sale* sticker.

"Stay. The. Fu—" But Troy cuts me off by pressing his finger to my lips. We're so close I can smell the Aqua Velva on his skin.

"I think you need me to woo you, Honor. So that's what I came to do." He removes his finger; I want to wipe my mouth. I want to gag. "After all, I already know what you look like naked, kinda."

"For God's sake, Troy, don't—""

"Sorry, sorry. I get that you're old-fashioned. A little bit of a different flavor from Gracie." His smile is so knowing I want to scratch it off his face. "I remember that about you. How in high school you used to wear that pink headband with the flowers?" His eyes won't let me look away. "All I'm here to say is I can get fancy with you if that's what you want. Footloose and fancy-pants. Have dinner with me at Wagon Wheel Grille this Saturday night? For our Gracie."

Our Gracie.

Bile climbs my throat.

There are so many things I want to scream at Troy—that he's a monster, that he made Gracie's life a living hell, that I would shove a knife into his chest before I went anywhere with him. But even his smile is dangerous, like a sprinkle of sugar on top of a cup of poison. I force myself to push all those words down, to squeeze them into a fist and compress them like charcoal.

Yelling this morning didn't work. Time for a new strategy.

"I'd like to, um, sit with that idea awhile, Troy," I say neutrally. Borderline sweetly. "Respect for my sister and all. I need some time. Not sure Gracie would want either of us to move on so quick, you know?"

I hate my placating tone. I hate that I'm essentially eating shit out of fear. Obviously, I'd much rather bash his brains in with a baseball bat, but if I actually reject him, who knows what revenge his bruised ego would be capable of?

"I knew Gracie best," he says in that same knowing voice. "She'd want you to be happy. And since I made her happy . . ." Troy moves to give me the chocolate box. He's way too close. I reach forward and swiftly set it on the counter. "Let me do you the same favor? I'm a good guy. Promise."

His pleading "good guy" voice grates on me. It's almost a whine. I bet he has a soft spot on the back of his head; one crack and his brain would fold in on itself like a soufflé. The hockey stick I keep under my bed upstairs is too far away. Otherwise, I'd use it and call it self-defense.

"Thanks, Troy." I step behind the counter as I force the words out. Hope he doesn't see my hands curled into fists so tight I feel the burn in my palms.

"Spend a little time with me and there's plenty more treats

where that came from." When he hoists up his jeans by the waistband and adjusts himself, I'm sickened to see a telltale bulge in the crotch. He catches me looking and winks. "Now I'm gonna go think about you, Miss Stone. If you're picking up what I'm putting down."

I nod, wishing with my whole heart I could throw him outside by the scruff of his neck. Once he saunters out, I run to the front door, lock and bolt it, then throw the chocolates in the dumpster out back, where I make one last call for Keeper—where the hell is that cat?

Inside again, I run around frantically, checking the locks on all the windows, and for good measure, I yank down all the window shades.

Only then do I stop shaking enough to call the police.

"Chief Simpson, please," I say to the dispatcher who answers the phone. "This is urgent."

Sixteen minutes later, I'm engulfed in a whole different kind of icy rage when Shelton's chief of police picks up.

"Honey." He's too friendly and familiar, like he's known me all my life, which, to be fair, he has.

"Charlie," I say since he hates being called anything other than *Chief* at work.

"Do not disrespect me in the workplace, Honor," says Charlie in a warning tone. Like I haven't grown up seeing the old man stumbling drunk and puking off the back of his boat after too many Natty Lights. "You know I go above and beyond for you."

"Unlike my call-hold time, I'll keep it quick. Your nephew, Troy, who your department decided not to charge with murder—"

"Honor, what happened to Grace was a tragedy and an *accident*, and I will get off this line this minute if you keep throwing around false—"

"—is now harassing me at my place of work. So I'd like to file a restraining order."

Over the phone, Charlie blows a raspberry. "All right. I'm listening. What did he do?"

"He came into my shop and made me take his shitty chocolates and he tried to coerce me to go out to dinner with him." I don't add in the part about Troy's boner. I don't need Charlie to make some stupid joke or dismiss me and say it was a figment of my imagination.

"Chocolates and a night on the town with a friend who is grieving, too? Is that what passes for harassment these days?" The old cop laughs, a big, round, genial guffaw that is a fixture of the Simpson barbecues Gracie's taken me to over the years. "I feel like Nancy would be thrilled if I *harassed* her like that after thirty-three years."

"You're not listening to me. I want a restraining order."

"Against what? Pizza and a movie?"

"Troy should be held accountable, and you know it. You know he has a history of violence. He came to my place of work, and it's totally fucked-up that he's above the law just because he's a goddamn Simpson." I'm so frustrated it's almost impossible to tamp down the anger in my voice. "I'm truly scared."

"Honor, swearing like a sailor isn't the way to handle a complaint." Then Charlie's voice softens. "You've got no grounds for a restraining order, but I'll talk to him, okay? I'll tell him to give you some space for a bit."

This time it's my turn to laugh, though it comes out in a bitter snap. I've heard the "I'll talk to him" line before. The very first time I called Charlie after Gracie came home with a shiner.

"Fine. Thanks, *Chief,* for the usual . . . whatever." I end the call before I completely lose my temper. Alone, my thoughts are boiling.

There's a mewing at the door.

"Keeper!" I could burst into tears as I unlock the door and scoop him into my arms. "My sweetest buddy, I was worried about you! Why am I so paranoid, Keep? You always come home, dontcha, guy?"

Then I curl up on the couch and let my tears fall into his fur.

Something about the one-two punch of Troy plus Chief Charlie's gaslighting unravels me. I will give myself five minutes to cry. No more. Gracie and I made up that rule as a way to handle our worst days with our father.

Crying is less overwhelming if you know you have no choice but to stop.

But nothing hurts worse than crying alone.

"Hey, buddy. Now, why do you smell like tuna fish?" I take another sniff of Keeper's fur. Yes, it smells fishy. "Has someone been feeding you again?"

In response, Keeper tucks into my elbow, purring with pleasure as he nuzzles in. I wipe my face with my pajama sleeve and take a few calming breaths—then remember the VR set Paula entrusted to me as I left Ashburn.

It's on the kitchen chair, right where I left it.

I unpack the box, and a little thrill chases itself up my spine when I see the cover of the instructions pamphlet inside:

Property of DME. Not for Commercial Use.

The windows are drawn, and the only light is from the kitchen, but I check one more time for monsters in the closet and under the bed before I secure the headset with its strap and pick up the controllers. The game looks pretty self-explanatory. I punch in the codes and design my avatar to look like me. I call her PlayerXX.

With the press of a button, I find myself in a waiting room.

There's an elevator.

Inside the elevator are choices. I feel like a puppeteer choosing a set. I go with *Floor 3: Black Car*, which turns out to be just what it says, the plush interior of a large black car. Interesting that this choice exists. I'd been desperate for Strike to get in his car with me that first night.

When the game prompts me to create another player in the seat next to me, I assemble my coplayer, and twenty minutes later, I'm staring at . . . Strike. I've caught every detail. The tumble of his dark hair, the suggestive curl of his lip, the flex of his jawline. When I code half-moons of gray into his eyes, I feel like I've ignited his very soul. I name him PlayerXY.

My avatar is the driver, and soon we're in a big city—Vegas, maybe.

They—*we?*—can go anywhere. I choose the roof of the Wynn.

Now the whole city is below them, and in the next moment they're undressed, their bodies reflecting the neon glow of the Strip below. I wish I could find more sensation. Being up high, the wind in my face, naked on a rooftop—could these feelings be invented? It's not the intensity of the exterior experience, it's how much you can feel the intimacy.

Maybe that's the insight I can bring to the next meeting with Strike?

In the meantime, I let PlayerXY place his hands on my shoulders.

I'm re-creating that night. PlayerXY kisses me. A long, desperate, open-mouthed kiss. My stomach clenches in desire.

Suddenly I'm aware of what I must look like—a woman in pajamas and a VR headset, making out with the air. My face burning, I drop my handheld controllers and pull off the headgear.

Gracie used to say her favorite thing about me was my optimism. "You can't help being a glass-half-full girl, Honor. No matter how many times that water gets thrown in your face."

Foolish as I feel, the game made things seem a little brighter.

"Thanks for a fun date, Strike Madden," I whisper, "wherever you are."

TWENTY

HONOR

Now

Strike Madden checks out, Jo texts me Sunday. I'm sending you a PDF.

The file is slim, but it has the information I need. Strike Madden stays below the radar because DME is a holding company fronted by Ashburn. Paula Delgado is the de facto spokesperson and seems to handle the press inquiries. Strike might be behind the scenes, but he's not hiding there.

And so Monday morning, wearing a crisp white button-down with a navy skirt I ironed last night—along with Josie's loaned black slingbacks, one size too big—I jump into my Uber with a bounce of excitement. I am outrageously happy: I'm going to get to see Strike today.

For once, I will not be caught off guard.

Paula answers the door.

"Hi, Paula." I lift my portfolio. "Strike asked me to bring some of my art." With my other hand, I deliver the boxed VR set. "And thanks for this."

"Yes, of course," she says, her voice neutral, as she sets it on the hall table. Her coolness brings my excitement down a peg. "This way. I have instructions to get you all settled." She pauses. "Would you like some coffee before you get started?"

"No thanks." I'm way too jittery already. "No Strike?" I ask, my heart plunging, as I try and fail to keep the disappointment out of my voice. Paula shoots me a look, and my face goes full reaper chili.

Strike is my new boss. I need to remember that.

"Strike has a very full week. But he left a to-do list for you." I follow her through the foyer.

"Is that . . ." I pause a moment before a huge dark oil painting, all clotted, swirling reds and dark coppers.

"Yes," says Paula. "A brand-new acquisition. It was flown in from Antwerp yesterday."

The image swims up before my eyes—a woman, her hair black and flowing, her eyes half-closed, her lips parted, her flesh layered in dark gauze and . . . blood? Crooked under one arm and almost completely outside the frame is a dead man's severed head.

She's the victor. He's her trophy.

"From the Old Testament," says Paula. "*Judith Slaying Holofernes.*"

"I don't know that story," I say. I never try to cover up my lack of education. There's no point. I was raised without any religion, barely any school, and certainly no after-school sports or activities beyond keeping lookout for the cops while Grace worked the 7-Eleven, swiping every box of Toaster Strudels she could fit under her shirt.

Pretending only makes me look worse. Better to admit my ignorance and use it as a learning opportunity.

"It's a parable," says Paula, and I'm glad there's no judgment in her voice. "Holofernes was a military general—a stranger to Judith—who invaded and took possession of her home. So Judith and her maidservant decapitated him. Over the centuries, many artists have been inspired by its themes of . . . justice."

"And violence," I add, staring into Judith's face. I see anguish, triumph, exhaustion. A big dose of vengeance. I like this chick. Bet she keeps something more deadly than a hockey stick under her bed.

Paula stares at the painting. "I love it," she says softly, and I get an eerie sense of some unspoken past there.

I feel Judith's eyes track me the whole way up the stairs.

The studio is large and white and clean. Just like a canvas, it's nothing but potential. The fresh start I need.

"There's an off-site today—a couple of the designers stayed behind, but most of them won't be back until after lunch. Strike wants you here," says Paula, indicating one of the drafting tables; they're all set so far away from their neighbors, it feels like a display in an Apple Store.

It's open here, and at the same time, so private. "Make yourself comfortable." My stomach goes fizzy with her words.

Strike wants you here.

Once Paula is gone, I sit at the table, where I now see a small propped-up cardstock note in bold, letter block handwriting.

TODAY'S ASSIGNMENT FOR MISS FIREFLY:
DRAW YOUR FANTASY.
I EXPECT GREAT THINGS.
JUST REMEMBER—YOU'RE ON THE CLOCK.

I smile to myself. He's right, of course. No matter how attracted I am to Strike, I took this job to make art—and money.

"You got it, boss," I say softly as I select a pencil.

Great things coming up.

TWENTY-ONE

STRIKE

Now

She's here. I know it. I can feel her.

I got back to Ashburn in the small, secret predawn morning, and even now, hours later, lying sleepless in bed, my body is still pumping with adrenaline. I snap the sheet off and head naked to my bath suite and then beyond to my private spa.

Eucalyptus. Hot rocks. Blasts of dry heat and steam pound my tired body. The night comes back to me like jagged shards of broken glass through my brain. Did I enjoy it? In the moment, maybe. I feel born for it. The unique rush, the ultimate thrill. My every sense is raw and heightened.

Like every junkie, it's not until afterward that I feel clobbered by the crash. And that's when I think it's not so much that I was born for it; it's that too many others could never, ever do what I can do.

I pass on a session in my cryotherapy chamber, but I finish with an ice bath in the plunge pool. My body is used to these extreme rituals. But what I know from experience is that time is the best way to wash off the job.

With a little help from a visit to Axe to go over every detail and close the Martinez file.

No loose ends, no unfinished business.

My waist wrapped in a towel, I lean toward the mirror and give myself a much-needed shave. The walls are all soundproofed, so it would be impossible for me to actually hear Honor's voice. But I feel a bone-deep knowing. The sense of a twin flame that I've never experienced before.

She's walking up the central staircase. She's talking to Paula—and hopefully declining Paula's offer of shitty, medium-brew coffee if she remembers that a better machine awaits her in the studio.

She's nervous. First-day-of-work jitters. But she's excited, too.

Fuuuck. I wasn't counting on this feeling. It's like an unexpected trip wire. I told myself a thousand times that I have no reason to see her. I left her a note for the explicit purpose of assuring her that even though I wouldn't be with her for her first day, she was ready to dig in.

I need to maintain a professional atmosphere.

She's here to make art. That's it.

She does not need to see you today, buddy. You're not even on your A game.

But even as I hit up my cedar closet for a suit—another part of my next-day ritual is to wear a suit: clean up, clean page, all that—I can feel my resolve eroding.

Honor Stone is on the property. She's here.

The best-laid plans. I close my eyes. *Do not screw this up.*

Control has always been my best asset. It's my steadiest mental anchor, something I learned from my special ops days and that I value deeply. It empowers my best leadership skills.

Axe texts asking for my ETA. He's the only person in my orbit who understands what last night took out of me, and he always clears his day. Part of our ritual.

New plan. I've got to work. As soon as I text back, I feel control slip my grasp. For fuck's sake. Am I really doing this?

You sure? You good? I've never ducked a day-after meeting with Axe. This is a highly irregular breach of protocol, and I know he's clocking it.

But yes. I am sure. I have to see her today. Even if it's only for a couple of minutes. Just to check in.

My control might be extreme, but my curiosity is fucking insatiable.

All good. I'll catch up with you later, I text, and then I set my phone face down on my dresser and look for my lucky cufflinks.

TWENTY-TWO

HONOR

Now

Time burns up as I sit staring at Strike's note, examining his handwriting.

I don't open the stack of notebooks on the shelf.

Do not even consider opening the paints.

Definitely do not introduce myself to a couple of coworkers who come in and out of the room. I stare at them with the blankness of the shy new kid—which I am.

Draw your fantasy.

I've spent the last few years busting my ass getting Grace & Honor up and running. Before that, I was all about the survival instinct.

Those reflexes will never leave. They live deep inside, hibernating.

I will draw my fantasy for this paycheck.

I reach for the oil crayons and close my eyes. Strike's face, his trim, athletic body against a wash of night. I flash back to the VR game, where I can feel us on the rooftop. An excellent fantasy.

The press of his body against mine. No, that was no fantasy. That actually happened.

Strike's face again. On impulse, I sketch Paula at his side. Watching.

Hell, no. That's not my fantasy.

Okay, what if you imagine yourself from the outside looking in?

I move the crayon on the page in smooth strokes. I create an avatar who's full and luscious. My breasts cannot be contained by a T-shirt, my nipples are unapologetically aroused, my hair's in two cute space buns on top of my head with tendrils framing my face. Me, but not.

This is *fun*.

In a few minutes I've blocked in the background composition of the library where Strike interviewed me. It exudes a tantalizing blend of woodsmoke and leather and books and glowing lamps.

I sit back. My heart is palpitating. I take a laptop off the shelf and upload all my images to one of the animation design programs. I dress my avatar in a pink silk nightgown. When we were little, Gracie and I used to twist bluebells into each other's hair. I add a wreath of bluebells. I add a portal to a dense forest, and my avatar takes it. In the distance, pines and firs stand tall behind a cottage. It's all beautiful and safe here, peeled away from the brutal memories of Gracie's and my old hiding places.

Now my dashing hero appears, his muscles flexing as he springs to life. Under the soft light of the moon, our characters come together and lock lips in a fiery embrace, their tongues exploring each other's mouths, his hands expertly navigating to my most sensitive parts.

Ahem. *Her* sensitive parts.

I sit back, breathing hard.

Who am I kidding? This game is all about Strike and me.

Okay, but so what? I am getting lost in this art because it's good. Walls are falling away. My lust rises up in a tidal wave. My entire body wants to be touched. I've never been turned on by my own art like this. I've never *felt* so much from art before.

Then again, no one has ever said *draw your fantasy.*

I think about how Gracie used to disassociate when she was with Troy. This feeling is the exact opposite. I'm fully integrated— my brain, my body, my desire for this man.

I stop to get an orange that I brought with me in my purse for breakfast. It's ripe and fragrant, and I peel it into sections to eat, relishing the sweet and juicy bursts of flavor. My senses feel so heightened. This is definitely the wildest job I've ever had—and that includes when I was in high school and I'd dress up in latex and sequins as the entertainment for children's birthday parties on Saturdays. One week I was a pink Power Ranger, the next I was Minnie Mouse. (I had to keep baby powder in my bag for all the chafing.)

Orange finished, I sketch some more ideas and upload them. My next two characters wear leather pants and vests and have spiky rainbow hairstyles. Maybe this level is set in a world of musicians? Erotic rock stars with all the trimmings: the private jet, the tour bus, the stadium.

In another few minutes, I've got my gray-eyed, chiseled lead singer.

I wiggle in my seat, hoping to feel a tiny bit of friction and relief. *Eeeep*, no, I can't do this here. The few people who were in and out are long gone. I'm alone, thirsting for a hot guy who looks pretty much exactly like my boss. I'm not deleting him, though. *I'm drawing my fantasy.*

I make a series of thumbnail sketches: languorous limbs, open mouths, and sizzling entanglements. I'm not aware of the real-life mouth until it's right next to my real-life ear.

"Jesus, Honor," Strike whispers, and his voice feels as luxurious as a back scratch, as sexy as a lapping tongue. Even as I startle, I almost moan out loud. "Four and a half stars on your first day," he says. "That's a record."

TWENTY-THREE

HONOR

Now

Strike is wearing a suit, though the jacket is off and the tie is loosened.

He laughs when he sees me so obviously flustered.

"Sorry. Should have cleared my throat or something. But damn, you hit the ground running. No learning curve." Strike looks pleased as he casually leans over me, scrolling the images, then taking my pad to flip through my sketches, pausing to nod or point out something he likes.

If he has an inkling as to who inspired my art—along with some of the settings—he spares me the embarrassment of saying anything out loud.

Instead, he takes out his phone and sends off a quick text. A minute later, Paula arrives. As polished as she is, I feel like the soul of a pit bull lurks underneath. I wonder how she ended up working for Strike.

"There's some great stuff here, Paula, don't you think?" Strike clearly wants Paula to agree, but she takes her time. My palms sweat, waiting for her judgment.

"Interesting," she says, and shoots me a sideways glance. With one look I realize that she sees it plain as day—that Strike is my inspiration. Her boss—our boss—is my fantasy.

Strike was wrong the other day—there's naked and there's very, very naked. And in this moment? I feel very, very naked.

"Different sort of realism than what we've been doing," she says, her voice neutral. "But it's a start."

"It's more than a start, Paula. And you know it." Strike's voice raises as it deepens. "Look at that detail. I can feel the texture of this story. The formal precision. The untamed wild of the forest." He reaches down and rubs his finger over the picture, and I can't help it. I shiver. "Her . . . hunger."

"It's about fear and desire," I say. "The wolf at the door is one kind of adrenaline. But then she kills the wolf, and—"

"Claims the prince as her reward." Strike laughs. "It's cool."

"Thanks," I say. My voice cracks with relief.

"Perhaps you could use a refreshment," suggests Paula.

I nod; my fantasy session has left me famished in many ways. I hope it doesn't show in my eyes, but Strike is so good at reading me, I keep my head down.

"We'll do lunch in the garden, Paula," says Strike. "Just Honor and me."

She looks surprised—maybe I've upset some plans here? But she says nothing and leaves.

I shut down the laptop, and when I start to put away the oil crayons, Strike stops me by closing his hand around my wrist. "We have staff for that," he says, turning my arm over. When he catches sight of the scars along the inside of my wrist, I grab my hand back.

But I can feel his curiosity. "It's a nice day," he says into my silence. "Let's get some fresh air."

———

Ashburn's landscape is wild but not neglected, with fresh signs of spring in every spongy green bud and leaf. Strike leads me along a winding trail bordered by a dense tapestry of trees, some tall and towering, others young and slender, going all the way to that lake I saw from the library during my first visit here.

"How many acres do you have, anyhow?" I'm panting a little to keep up. His legs are so long.

"Two hundred," he answers. "Though most of it's woods. I let Ritter Farms—their property borders mine—use my back fields for their dairy cows in exchange for milk and cheese."

"That's so generous of you," I say. I'm tempted to run back to the studio as an image blooms in my mind: Strike as a farmer, in overalls, plowing my field.

"More like practical." He shrugs. He's shifted moods again; the heat that was between us in the studio has cooled. Or maybe I read the whole situation wrong? Maybe Strike himself is immune to erotic art and is using Dark Matter Entertainment as a gateway for spinning off products for maximum profit. It's all business for him. Like it should be for me.

We walk through an arbor and down the stone steps to a vast flower garden. In the corner, a table set formally for lunch is waiting for us.

"Whoa, fancy. Is that lobster?" I squint. I've never seen lobster on a plate, offered up as food. It looks predatorial.

"Would you prefer a steak?"

"No, this looks great." I'm lying. That lobster is giving me the stink eye. I sit and unfold my napkin. "The way I grew up, lunch meant Taco Bell or KFC if we were lucky."

"I'm no fast-food snob. A KFC bucket is great for a family night in."

I smile, surprised. What does Strike know about feeding a family? Hard to see him with a beer in one hand and a leg of crispy fried chicken in the other. Harder to picture little kids at his feet, although I like imagining it. I bet they'd have his eyes. You can tell those are some powerful genetics.

I stare down at my place setting. How am I supposed to eat this . . . boiled-red cockroach? With two forks, two knives, a tiny spoon, and a big nutcracker?

"How should I eat this?" I ask. I've never felt any shame about my lack of money, even when Gracie and I qualified for the free lunch line at school. Why should I? I've always been honest about it, the same way I'm honest about my lack of education.

"Watch." Strike uses his nutcracker to expertly declaw his own lobster, then uses his tiny fork to dunk the white lobster meat into a saucer of butter. "Next time, KFC," he says, giving me an almost-smile.

"The big treat back when I was growing up was cinnamon roll pancakes at Denny's on Gracie's and my birthday," I tell him. "Denny's beats everything."

"That right?"

"Yep." I shrug and pick up my nutcracker, imitating the way Strike handled it. "But lobster's . . . also . . . great." I've never had it. On my second try, a shard of claw shoots across the table.

Strike ducks.

"Oops! Sorry about that," I say. "You can't take me anywhere with these table manners."

"Claw-ful." He shoots me that sly smile that I feel deep in my gut. "They call that a dad joke, right?" His expression is as warm as one of my shop's flannel shirts, and I can feel my heart racing.

I'm not sure how I will survive working at DME with this intoxicating man as my boss, when every minute our relationship feels like it's teetering on something deeper. "So tell me about you, Honor." He indicates for me to pass him my plate of lobster, which he then begins to de-shell with surgical precision. "Who are you? Besides an incredible artist."

I feel a pattering of nerves in my stomach. "As in my life story?"

"Just some of the basics. Were you born here? Any other siblings? Grandparents? How's your family holding up after Gracie?" His eyes are more flint than smoke, watching me as he passes back my plate and the meaty pile of lobster flesh. It looks a little iffy.

"No family left." My throat is suddenly parched. I pick up my glass of water. If Strike wants to know who I was before I became who I am now, he won't find that girl here. "You've been to my shop," I say, keeping it carefully casual. "You've seen my paintings. You know about my sister. You probably know as much about me as anyone else I know. I have a cat named Keeper, my favorite person in the world."

"Cats aren't people."

"Oh, thanks. I didn't realize." Playfully I ball up my napkin and aim to bean him. Again, he's quick, catching it halfway across the table. "Keep is a person to me. If you can have a cat soulmate, he's mine."

"Not Josie?"

"She's the best, for sure." I nod. "I mean, we're friends and everything. We hang out. But I guess I . . . I tend to keep to myself."

"I do, too," he says. "Well, except for Paula. She's my ride-or-die."

I'm charmed that his ride-or-die is a gray-haired woman in her sixties who clucks around him like a mother hen.

"People can be complicated," I say. "Pets are way better."

He looks thoughtful. "People are complicated. But sometimes that's what makes them worthy."

"Yes," I agree. "Gracie was both," I add. "But now she's left me with half a heart."

"Not sure if I've ever said this to you—and I know words don't count for much," he says, "but I know exactly how you feel. I know loss."

"Thanks." Strike's expression is so compassionate that I don't doubt him for a second. Who is this man with surprisingly soft edges and empathetic eyes? I want to ask him more questions—*what was your loss?*—but today is not the day. "Tell me about you. Do you wake up each day and go, 'Son of a biscuit, I'm rich!' and then go nap in a pile of hundred-dollar bills? Do you take your cash and make it rain?"

"When I'm not using it for toilet paper."

"If I had another napkin, I'd throw it at you."

His smile lingers, then fades slowly as he cocks his head to the side, as if looking for something in my face. I'm not sure what. "Money doesn't make anyone more interesting. But you know that, right?" he asks more seriously. "If anything, it makes you boring. Life gets too easy. You can sidestep all the shit in your path if you want to. Never have to clean up after yourself."

"A very nice problem to have," I say.

"Don't be too sure." His tone is a little more clipped, and I bite my lip. Maybe it's bad manners—like lobster claws flying across the table—to talk about money to people who have too much of it. My life doesn't tend to overlap with superrich people—or even basic rich people, for that matter. But there are some repeat customers at the store who've parked their Teslas or Mercedes out front, and I've made it a point to observe them.

"The main thing I've learned about rich people from my time in retail is they love free samples just as much as everyone else," I tell Strike. "They don't like to be cheated. They like to think they're getting a deal. So, more same than different. But I still don't want your staff cleaning up my art materials." I arch an eyebrow, hoping I can thaw Strike back to my favorite version of him. The one where he looks like he's trying to suppress a grin.

Bingo.

"Fair enough," he says. "Though I felt like you deserved that one small luxury on your first day on the job. And don't forget, you're the talent." He sits back, arms crossed, and works me with that smirk. "Once this game sells, you're going all diva on me, right? I better start getting used to it."

"Yeah, that's me. Superdiva. I'll commute in by helicopter, and for lunch break, you'll to have to hand-feed me . . . caviar."

"You can't even say that without making a face."

"Caviar is gross."

"Maybe me personally hand-feeding it to you would elevate the taste?"

"Maybe." Our silence sinks into something deeper, more intense. His eyes actually smolder. Tension throbs between us.

Strike takes my hand, turns it over as if to touch the tender skin underneath.

Instinctively, I want to pull away, but Strike holds it, tight and sure, cradling my forearm in his fingertips, inspecting it like it's a map that holds the key to buried treasure. Gently, with his index finger, he traces the pale, welted, circular scars that make the faintest constellation across my palm. I hadn't expected him to notice them. I also hadn't expected his touch to feel so different from the way it did when Gracie and I touched the various marks on each other's skin.

Strike's touch is all wonder, as if I am offering something special with my body. Something unique and exciting and mine. I have to cross my legs.

How can he make me feel so aroused—by my scars? It's so unnerving and taboo that when Strike asks what happened, his voice the gentlest whisper, my answer is to shrug and pull my arm back, shaking my head.

In response, Strike jumps to his feet.

"You're finished?" I ask.

"Yes. I've got a meeting. But please, you stay. Enjoy your meal. You've earned it."

I look up at him, unsure if I'm supposed to insist on following. This whole situation is unbearably confusing. I'm exhausted from feeling out of my depth. And I can't help but think he's leaving out of some sense that he has overstepped and would like to redraw our boundaries.

"I should go back to work, too—"

"No. Stay, really. Relax. Like I said, you've earned it." He says this in a way that leaves little room to object, and so I don't. Not to mention, it is delightful out here, and I could use a moment to collect myself.

"Thanks."

"I'll be thinking about those pictures you drew for a long, long time, Honor Stone," he says, before leaving me alone with my lobster. And its claws.

TWENTY-FOUR

HONOR

Then
(Age 12)

The first time Daddy burns my palm with his cigarette, he tells me if I cry too loud he'll burn the other for a matched set. He winks as he says it. Sometimes the scariest thing about Daddy is how he can find a joke in anything—even torture.

But I also know he's serious.

My skin is sizzling. I press my lips together and jump in a circle. The pain feels like it'll turn me inside out. I search the pantry for honey—I read somewhere that it's good for burns—but of course, there's no honey in this house. Not even honey mustard packets from McDonald's.

"Miracle Whip!" says Gracie. "I heard it works on sunburns." She's standing in front of the fridge. Miracle Whip's just about all that's in there. I'm still hopping around the house, barefoot, in my nightgown. The pain feels like a scream from the base of my hand, up my arm, through my shoulder, into my neck. All I did was open the front door to see if the snow had started. I wanted to taste it on my tongue.

But I'd let in the winter cold, too. Daddy, sleeping it off on the couch, woke up in a rage. Mama, who's floating too high for her brain to care about anything except staying put in her bed, calls out from the other room that I should watch myself next time. Listen to Daddy.

"Here, Honor. Hold still a second and tell me if this helps." Gracie uses a plastic knife to slather my burns with the thick, creamy, white sandwich spread. "It's past the expiration date, but I don't think it matters."

Daddy, half-asleep and calm now, shakes his head and mutters, "Fucking Miracle Whip. I don't know which one of you girls is more stupid. You'd best both be quiet the rest of the morning and leave me to some goddamn peace."

Either I'm a cockeyed optimist or this Miracle Whip's helping, but the pain levels down a notch. I crawl to my bedroom and go to sleep. When I wake up, the day's done, the house is dark, and nobody's home.

"Gracie!" I holler. She's not here. Where is she? Hunger is raking its nails down my empty stomach, and my burn marks have welted up puffy like I've got measles or mumps. I run out the back door to Gracie's and my hiding place. She's not there, either. It's starting to snow, and I've left my coat—the warm one from Turning Point—at home. My hand throbs and I'm freezing. I curl up in the hollow. We've stashed blankets in here, too—this is not the first or the last time we've escaped the house without the foresight to worry about the cold.

I wrap one around myself.

Please, Gracie. Don't leave me.

Did she take Rusty with her? Sometimes it feels like she wasn't born afraid like I was. She's reckless and brave. When she got a D on her science test, she informed Ms. Warren that it was because she was a boring teacher, and when she got detention, she pulled the fire alarm, causing chaos for the next half hour. By then, she'd snuck out a window and gone home.

If she runs away and leaves me alone with our parents, I won't survive.

No. Gracie would never leave me behind.

"Show me."

I look up.

"Gracie!" She's been out in the snow for a while. She's soaked and grimy and out of breath. As she folds herself up and climbs into the hollow, I hold out my forearms. Wrists pointing upward, hands cupped.

Gracie says nothing. Packs some fresh snow on my hand and up my arm. I swear I almost hear those burns crackle. "Sorry I wasn't there when you woke up. Daddy and Mama went out, and I took Rusty over to the Brewers', and then I walked to the store. Look, I bought us dinner."

"'Bought'?" We don't buy, we steal. One day, when I'm older, with money of my own, I'm planning on writing a ginormous check to the 7-Eleven. Gracie says that's stupid because big corporations are doing fine without us paying for our Utz barbecue potato chips. She's probably right, though I like to think about the day when I have a wallet stuffed with my own cash and can make everything fair.

She pulls a bag of M&M's from inside her coat. "Peanut. For protein. There was a salami, but I figured you'd like this better."

The cold and the burn and the taste of peanuts and my beautiful sister suddenly, magically being here when I need her most, it feels like too much all at once exploding through me.

I start to cry.

"Five minutes," she says. "Then Normal."

"Five minutes for what?" I can't even wipe away my tears, because my arms are currently being held by Gracie. My cold face is now wet and snotty. My cheeks sting.

"Five minutes for crying, Honor. That's it. We need to be stronger than crying."

"And when we're done, we can play Normal?"

"Yep."

In Normal, we live in a cottage on a safe street of cottages that all look exactly like ours, but if you look closely, our front yard's got a tangerine tree. We have two parents, who own a tiny pizza place, and after hours they make us dinner in the brick oven. On Saturdays in Normal, we go to Target to buy new clothes, and we donate our old stuff to Turning Point. We have a grandmother who smells like cinnamon, with silver hair in a bun, and she babysits us when our parents go on date nights.

In Normal, Grandma keeps a bottle of rainbow sprinkles in her pocketbook, and she puts them on everything from French toast to scrambled eggs to make all our food into a party. This was Gracie's idea and one of her favorite parts of our fantasy, because Gracie likes sugar as much as she likes boys. Which is to say a whole lot.

Tonight Gracie is decorating our bedroom. She adds bunk beds with matching pink duvets and a ceiling full of glow-in-the-dark stars. We fight over who picked out all the marshmallows from the Lucky Charms. We have matching lunch boxes packed full each morning, and we trade granola bar flavors. We hang stockings in front of the fire because it's Christmastime.

In Normal, fire isn't a weapon; it's a comfort.

We fall asleep nestled together in our hollow tree like puppies in a children's book.

When we wake up, the sun is melting the snow.

Years later I read that Gracie was right—Miracle Whip does help a burn. The vinegar prevents infection and kills bacteria. But I'm not surprised. Gracie always knew how to love me best.

TWENTY-FIVE

HONOR

Now

From the moment I wake up, as I slide into my jeans and a T-shirt, grab an energy drink, and wait for one of Strike's black SUVs to whisk me off to work—another surprising perk—I'm on a cloud of tingling anticipation.

Plus there's that supercharge of an old-fashioned swoony crush. Even though I know it will never go anywhere.

But there's magic in this studio. I feel it like a whirl of starlight.

By now I've met Strike's design and coding team, and I can't believe I ever worried they wouldn't want to work with me. Right from the start, when Strike introduces me as an "original content creator," they accept me taking the lead. Every day, I feel more confident—though my impostor syndrome will never fully go away. I've got lots of ideas in the fantasy department, and I'm shocked by all the places my mind wants to go.

Especially when I've never done anything even close to as daring in my real life as some of the situations I conceive and storyboard.

When DME upgrades its VR system to beta launch a version

of my *Secret Garden* idea, I take it home on Friday after work. I think I'll wait until after dinner, but as soon as I've kicked off my shoes, I put on my diffuser and some soft music, and I don't log off until it's past midnight.

The next morning, the first thing I do after I open Grace & Honor is order a whole new line of sex toys for the shop: vibrating magic-tongue appendages with multiple stimulator settings, as well as a rainbow line of wearable sparkly butterfly clit massagers. The butterfly is a subtle strap-on device that gives a textured snuggle and discreetly buzzes and throbs.

Sure, they're more daring than our usual merchandise, but we'll tuck them in the back of the back.

I bet they'll fly off the shelves, no pun intended, laughs Gracie in my ear. She was always hoping I'd put more spice into the inventory.

Josie and Bryan are away in Atlantic City this weekend, and the empty day stretches bare before me.

Strike isn't at DME all the time, but yesterday afternoon he dropped by during a meeting to join a conversation about the human form. He offered some thoughts about why certain images turn people on and how to move DME away from stigma and misunderstanding. He talked about women's pleasure, about how historically porn—and now hentai—has been geared toward male fantasies and how our creations need to be the opposite.

"If there's one rule," he told the group, "it's that the woman's pleasure must be spotlighted and relished."

The room was silent, hanging on his every word.

In a way, I still am.

Girl, you have got it baaaad, whispers Gracie.

I shrug off her voice. Once I've sold a soy candle and an anal plug to a shyly curious couple of coeds, I open my laptop to look at what I've done this week. It's like I'm taking a crash course in sex-in-gaming animation. Here, a flick of a wrist can fundamentally change an image. Something that seems dark and foreboding can get erotic by adding a curve of a lip and an outstretched hand.

In focusing on what specifically arouses a woman, what arouses *me*, I turn up the wattage and push all my boundaries.

Ever since Gracie and I were kids, we'd find ourselves unwilling participants in male fantasies. On the bus, at the mall, when we worked at the Shelton Cinema or during our waitressing years—we rarely got through a day without some random man spying us and roaring, "Twins!"

"They say 'twins'—and what they really mean is 'I spent hours watching twins on Pornhub last night,'" Gracie would say, giggling. But it never felt funny to me. Dozens of men expressed this disgusting fantasy to us so often that my own idea of who I was and what I wanted felt like something I needed to keep guarded and separate from my sister.

Gracie lost her virginity in eighth grade, got on the pill the summer before high school, and went out with a handful of guys through our teens before settling for Troy, the worst choice of all. By junior high, I was fine with my own reputation for being a "prude." Maybe because it was true.

It took me a solid twenty-two years to unlock the achievement of losing my virginity—a sweetly forgettable summer romance when I reconnected with my high school chem lab study buddy slash prom date, Simon. We never had much spark, but Simon smelled like sugar cookies and wrote me romantic poems and never so much as raised his voice at me. I remember sex with

Simon as mostly looking at the ceiling of his bedroom, which smelled like lime deodorant and gym socks.

Just as I never bought into the sexy twins fantasy, I never paid attention to being known as Gracie's opposite. The frigid sister. But privately, I've always harbored a deep curiosity. I've certainly sampled every sex toy I ever ordered for the shop. I'm always ready to explore the wider world of sexual fantasy in my painting, even if I'm not having any sex. But it wasn't until I stepped into the art studio of DME that I felt like I was connecting this piece of myself to something bigger.

If Gracie was mostly interested in being desired, I was a lot more interested in what I myself desired most.

At 6 p.m., I lock up and go back to the apartment, where my loneliness kicks in like a punch. I've only spoken to customers all day—now the silence fills me with longing to hear Gracie sing Dua Lipa's "New Rules" while sitting on the toilet applying Barbie-pink polish to her toenails. Sometimes I like to pretend that she's just out on a date and she'll be home soon, and then we'll find something on Netflix and microwave a bag of Funfetti popcorn.

The bottle of "Grandma's Sprinkles," which Gracie liberally shook on anything from salads to buttered toast, is still in the cupboard. The photo of Gracie, Rusty, and me on the front steps of the old house, with an outline of where we cut out Daddy, still hangs on the fridge. Gracie's bejeweled flip-flops still sit by the front door.

I can't bring myself to throw away any piece of my sister.

It's just another Saturday night of me plus my sad frozen Healthy Choice dinner of chicken marinara with Parm, watching TV while Keeper lounges on the top of his cat tower. Then I lie in bed and mentally scroll through my Strike memories. The way he likes to twirl an Apple Pencil in his fingers like a propeller.

Or when he rakes a hand through his wavy dark hair.

How just yesterday he smiled at me and said in that low, decisive voice, "You'll lead the team, right, Honor?"

My fingers find a rhythmic pulse between my legs to get that sweet, exploding release as I imagine Strike standing behind me while he looks at my screen. His breath on my ear when he exhales. From bed, I reach for the selected toys I've stashed in my nightstand—a cherry-scented orgasm balm and a small magic wand with four different intensity settings and simultaneous clit suction and G-spot stimulation.

I take the wand, close my eyes, and guide it to my center. Behind my sealed eyes, Strike is here, tonight in his tux, and he's so real I can smell him. We're in the library—I guess I do have a thing for *Beauty and the Beast* after all—and he's got the back of my head cupped in his palms as he kisses me hard and urgently against the paneled wall. When I scrape my nails down his back, he moans. He rips off my skirt; one sharp pull and the fabric falls to the ground. I'm not wearing panties.

We slide to the floor, and now I'm fully naked, riding his face, his hands grabbing my ass and lifting me toward his mouth like I'm a juicy watermelon on a hot summer day.

He's getting off on me getting off, and it is so fucking hot.

I gasp when I climax—I swear I can feel the rough sweep of his tongue right where I want it as I continue to pulse—and then after a couple of minutes, I smile. I feel like I'm beta testing the game from the privacy of my own bed.

I'd love to send Strike a bill. This is work research, after all.

TWENTY-SIX

HONOR

Now

Those first weeks of working for DME glide by in a haze of sensuous delight. I love the work, especially with the daily potential of seeing Strike. Whenever he's around, everything is a thousand times more exciting.

But when he's gone, no one knows his whereabouts.

While Strike's policy is to open his door to interviewees, it's also a formality. Once you're hired—except for his annual DME holiday party—Strike's home is off-limits to all Dark Matter Entertainment employees.

I'm not the only one curious about him. Rumors abound.

Paula once let slip that Strike has a room in his house stocked with a priceless collection of antique knives from all over the world. I've also heard that Strike eats and showers at odd hours, takes unexplained trips for "business," collects ancient Roman surgical tools and first-edition classic horror novels, and that once he sewed up his own ankle—it took seventeen stitches—when he cut it on broken glass.

These strange bits and pieces of watercooler gossip only make me more curious. I want to know all the tiny details that add up to a person. What were his parents like? Was he a lonely kid? Happy? What does he wear to bed? What music does he like? Does he have a best friend? What does his voice sound like when he wakes up in the morning? What would his fingertips feel like linked with mine? What does he taste like?

Sometimes I sketch him in meetings—I'm always sketching through meetings, and for the first time, I'm in a job where doodling is encouraged. I know every bone and hollow of his face, the serious set of his features, the slight downward pull of his lips, which break open into a grin easily and often, especially when the conversations get spicy. When I draw his large, powerful hands, I take my time with each and every one of his long, tapered fingers, the pads of his thumbs, the crescents of his nails. I imagine his strength, how easily he could lift me. If I were ever called upon to do so, I could 3D print him or sculpt him from clay.

I didn't know it was possible to feel someone else's smile inside your own body, but I do. I feel everything about him from a deep place.

One late afternoon, Strike strolls into the studio, catching me rinsing off my brushes. I'm the only one left. He was MIA all day, and the rumor mill has been on overdrive because he had marked out several hours on his calendar as "personal." Most people took it as an opportunity to head home early.

He's here now—my whole body jolts with surprise, but after we exchange a brief smile of greeting, I keep washing up, my head down and my hands busy, as he prowls around. He's in his usual work uniform: dark pants and tailored shirt, sleeves rolled to that hint of tattoo—a series of straight lines. I feel like I'm always scanning an indecipherable bar code. He's got a shadow of stubble, and I sense the day's been long, but he's alert as he inspects the work on the boards and monitors.

"You could go further with this," he says as he stops to look at my work spread out on the drafting table.

Only now do I turn my head. "How so?"

"You're holding back," he says. "You know what turns *you* on. But I think that you need to get into other people's heads. Find what makes them tick."

"I don't want to think about what makes *everyone* tick," I say as my insides suddenly clench. Thinking about Strike might be my happy place, but Troy, whose name often rises like unexpected bile, makes me feel sick. When he pushed Gracie, I imagined it was in a fit of rage, but since then, I've wondered to the point of obsession whether he'd been planning it. Did Troy feel a surge of power hearing her scream? Did it arouse him? Does her death still get him off?

I close my eyes. It's so hard to fight the specter of Troy—his leering face, his tight jeans, his fists like cannonballs. Every time my phone pings, every time I hear a noise outside, I'm terrified. Will I ever breathe freely?

"Hey." Strike is right next to me—I've let the water run too high in the sink. He turns off the tap. "You okay?"

"Yeah." I smile. "Daydreaming. Sorry."

"Stop cleaning up." He hands me a paper towel. "Let's talk art."

Together, we walk to the table to inspect my sketches and storyboards.

"You're climbing into someone else's head as well as into their bed, right? You're imagining how everything that's happened to them has shaped what they want sexually. You're searching for a core desire. Things that can't be found cruising Pornhub. You're inventing things."

"Right," I say, aware that we are only about a foot apart. Everything else falls away. It's only the two of us. He's so close.

Easy, girl. You need this job. Lose these silly feelings. Look what happened to me. Gracie's voice in my ear surprises and sobers me. I know it's my own conscience, but the longer she's been gone, the more I imagine her regret for a life so needlessly taken.

"Honor, I feel like you're someone with lots of stories to tell." He pauses. "I saw your arms. Whatever happened there, I bet it's changed who you are and how you want to be loved." I sense he's hesitant to even use the word *love.* As if it's been out of circulation in his vocabulary for a while.

"Maybe."

He smiles. "You always tap your fingers to your lips when you want someone to stop speaking."

"I do?" But he's right and he knows it. "There's a vein at your temple that pulses very faintly, almost invisibly, when you're annoyed," I say.

"That right?"

"Yup." His hand reflexively brushes through his hairline.

"Well, you blush when anyone looks at your art."

I'm blushing just to be called out on it.

"My blush always gives me away," I say. "Lifelong issue." The length of our gaze speaks volumes. We've confessed a fraction of the details we've observed in each other. These tiny distinctions that make us unique, and as much as I crave to learn more, so does he.

"Hey, want to grab a drink in the library?" he asks. "It's been a long day. I think I could use some tequila to unwind." The invitation to his home feels innocent enough, but Gracie's voice is sharp in my head and, again, uncharacteristically sensible: *Nope, no way, Sunday. You've got a sweet gig happening here, and you need to hold on to that paycheck. So let's be real, if you slam back some tequila, you might be tempted to spill the beans to Strike about how he's the muse to your creative genius. Cool your jets, girlfriend.*

"I'd love to, but, um, I've got to get back."

Gracie's warning also reminds me I've got four loans that need repaying, and Jo's relying on me. I'm making real progress, and I don't need any setbacks. I love this job more than any work I've ever done.

The thing is, I learned long ago never to get involved with someone if you're the only one who has something to lose.

Bottom line, I need Strike a lot more than he needs me.

Even if every bone in my body wants to down all the tequila with this man, I know better. I'm going to make better decisions than Gracie used to make.

I will not sleep with my boss.

Even if what I want most in this world is to sleep with him and to wake up next to him.

Shit. Where did that thought come from?

I'm in dangerous territory. In way over my head.

Now Strike rubs his own fingers slowly along his jawline. Another of his tells, but I don't point it out. That's what he does when he's hoping someone will change their mind.

"Back to . . . what?"

"My cat," I lie promptly. "I worry about him. Keeper's been prowling outside since morning. He gets anxious if he's alone too long. I've come home many times to that cat howling like a wolf at the back door."

"Right, well, your cat *is* your favorite person," he says. "One drink? My driver will take you home right after. Thirty minutes, tops."

"Last time I heard that one, I ended up in a gothic fortress drawing erotic animation," I joke.

"And see how well that turned out." He takes a step closer. My hair is pulled back into a bun, held in place with a clean paintbrush. Strike tugs it loose, and as the heavy tumble of my hair falls around my shoulders, I feel him staring at me like he's just opened the Christmas gift he's been wanting all year. His eyes shine with something like awe. And hunger.

My breath stutters. I can't think.

Not with Strike here. Right in front of me.

"You're my boss," I say. I clear my throat. My pulse is racing. "And while I'd love to have a drink, I . . . I can't."

He nods, steps away.

"I understand. I never meant. I wouldn't—I mean, I would have. But not if you didn't." His smile is rueful. "Fuck, you get what I'm saying, right?"

I nod. "Loud and clear." This might be my favorite of the Strikes. Perplexed. Sweet. Human. Concerned more about me than about himself.

"You know what? It was probably a bad idea." He says this so casually—as if he'd given the invitation minimal consideration.

"Right," I say. But then it's like my feet are glued to the floor. Thankfully, he's stronger than me—or maybe he can simply downshift easier. He moves to go. "Great work today, Honor," he says from the door on his way out. "Really."

As I lift my hand, it takes a huge effort for me to disguise the disappointment on my face. No need for Strike to know how badly I'm thirsting for that drink together—or how badly I'm thirsting, period.

Lavender dusk has fallen when the SUV pulls into my driveway. As I get out, I wave goodbye to Max, the driver, and head for the mailbox. My favorite hour of my favorite season. Spring always feels like a clean second chance at the year, a chance to recommit to resolutions—*I will not fuck my boss.*

It's only when I open the mailbox to find a handful of coupon circulars that I look up at my front door.

Something is on the step.

I walk toward it. Slowly, tentatively. Ever since Troy appeared in the shop with his crappy chocolate and his revolting suggestion to take me out for dinner about a month ago, I've been half-terrified of an encore visit.

But it seems my call to his uncle Charlie actually did the trick. Charlie knows in his bones that his nephew is rotten. Even without a legal restraining order, I'm assuming Charlie issued Troy an unofficial warning to toe the line.

I look at the stoop. I see it, but I don't see it. I let my imagination transform it into something else, a reprieve. Something I ordered and can't remember. My mind is racing.

What did I buy? A sweater? A pair of slippers?

The package is lumpy and shapeless, suggesting something soft.

The hairs on the back of my neck stand up, the horror engulfing me fully as my brain struggles to process it.

It's not slippers.

I know, in the same way I knew the second my doorbell rang that Charlie Simpson was here to tell me they'd found Gracie's dead body.

Loss is my sixth sense.

A cry rips from my throat as I sprint across the lawn and race up the steps to the door. A lump of all-too-familiar softness. Lifeless. I see the telltale calico markings. I collapse to the ground.

This is not the ragged work of a predatorial raccoon or a dog. This is evil. Human evil. This is murder.

Keeper is dead.

A pink Hallmark card is propped up next to my baby. The front, preprinted and covered in metallic hearts, is scripted "I promise to always be with you" in bold red ink.

A tremor moves through me from head to toe, and I bite back my nausea.

I open the card. Inside, handwritten in a scrawl:

> *Honor,*
>
> *I found your sweet lil Keep dead at the bottom of a ravine. I'm real sorry. Figured I should bring him back to you for a burial. It sure does hurt to lose the things you love. xo T*
>
> *PS I wish you wouldn't tell my uncle about our private business.*

TWENTY-SEVEN

STRIKE

Now

"It's going to be okay." It's all I can think to say, in a soothing, gentle refrain as I smooth Honor's hair.

Even if I know these words won't bring that cat back from the dead.

For the past half hour, Honor has been trembling next to me on the small couch in my den, shaking like a Yorkie at the vet, and I've been trying desperately to make her feel better. I'd do anything to stop her tears. My military training—verbal de-escalation, nonverbal empathetic communication—seems hopelessly inadequate.

At first, Honor was so hysterical on the call I couldn't understand what she was saying. Something about Keep and blood and her doorstep.

Twenty minutes later, keeping her on speakerphone as I raced my car, using the speed limit as a mere suggestion, I was at her building.

Honor was on the front stoop of the shop, sitting with her shoulders drawn forward, her spine curved into a protective arc, as if trying to shield herself from an unseen threat. Her arms were wrapped tightly around her knees, close to her chest, as if she was attempting to make herself as small and inconspicuous as possible.

Even when she saw me, her eyes looked nervous and frightened, on watch for danger, and her breath was shallow and rapid.

We couldn't stay at her place. She was too shaken to even go inside.

I scooped her up and took her to my home, straight through to my inner sanctum, where I go to unwind after a particularly shitty day. The den has wood-paneled soundproof walls, thick rugs, oversized pillows, and soft furnishings in various shades of navy and midnight blue, the color of sleep.

I step out to text Paula that she should deploy the DME security detail to clean up what remained of the cat, start surveillance on Honor's property, and keep a set of eyes on Troy.

Axe texts me assurances that he'll personally see to the digital sweep.

When I return to find Honor in the sanctum, she's tucked where I left her, on an ocean-dark velvet couch where I've taken some of my best naps. One of the kitchen staff brought her the hot toddy I requested for her.

"You're safe here. I promise," I tell her now. I already showed her my state-of-the-art alarm system, and now I remind her of the eight-foot finial-spiked iron gates that surround the property. And the fact that I've got a twenty-four-hour patrolling security team.

I don't know how to explain to her that she doesn't have to worry simply because she's with me. No one can get within one hundred feet of her—if, by some dark magic, the security of the compound were breached, I'd have the perp disarmed, on his back, and begging for his life in five seconds flat.

I have no idea why I took her to a room where I've never invited anyone, but then again, I have no idea why I was Honor's first call after she found that her cat had been killed. But I'm not complaining about the opportunity to be near her.

"Get a couple of sips down," I command.

She nods, and with shaking hands, she brings the steaming mug of hot lemon water and honey with a splash of whiskey to her lips—I'm glad Axe isn't here to watch me break my ironclad rule against water and whiskey, and for a woman, no less. "Listen to me, Honor. My private surveillance team is the best in the business. That lowlife piece of shit won't hurt you tonight. He can't."

"But what does that even mean?" Honor's voice cracks. "Last time I called the police about Troy, I got laughed at. He *murdered* my sister. He *disemboweled* Keep. He's a psychopath. Who the hell knows what he'll do next? He's so sick. He sees me as some replacement for Gracie. He'll never give up until I'm . . ."

She can't finish the sentence and she doesn't have to.

Dead. He'll never give up until she's dead.

Honor's not wrong.

That's what men like Troy do. They kill. And then kill again.

"I'll keep you safe. I promise." Her body vibrates, shivering, and after a moment, I sit next to her, drawing her toward me, then I cover her with that handwoven blanket I bought at her store.

Her head rests against my chest. "Your heart beats so slow," she says quietly. "It's calming."

I smile. "Yeah, that's the goal. I wait for damsels in distress to come around, and then offer them my heart." Fuck. I didn't count on the double meaning there. If she clocks it, she says nothing.

"Troy's been our tormenter since Grace and I were kids," she says after a couple of minutes. "At school, he did horrible things. Like he'd get us alone in the coat room and force-kiss us and tell

Gracie she was the better kisser. But then once he wrote me a note telling me I was prettier, and when I showed Gracie the note, and she showed him, he kicked me so hard I had a bruise like a storm cloud on my skin. The teachers always said it was because Troy had too much of a crush on us. Like us being twins was something we had done to him."

"Jesus," I say, finding and squeezing her hand. I remain calm—no need for her to see that I'm fantasizing about annihilating this sewer maggot. "'He hits you because he likes you'? That's some toxic shit."

"The worst is that Grace really thought she was in love with Troy. But, of course, it wasn't love. It was fear. Part of the pattern she saw with my parents. Even if she could never connect it." Tears spill hot and quick down Honor's cheeks. "Growing up, being pushed around and tormented . . . it was . . . what we knew. *All* we knew."

"I'm so sorry, Honor," I say.

"I probably shouldn't be telling you this stuff. I shouldn't even be here tonight."

"I want you here," I say—it might be the truest thing I've said all week.

"Keeper was the only person I had left in this world."

"Hey," I say. "I'm here, right?" I tuck a stray piece of her hair behind her ears. Cup her cheek with my palm. "You hungry? I know a very highly rated restaurant near here. Apparently they've got the best spaghetti and meatballs in Shelton."

"I'm not too presentable right now—but sure, if you want. Let me wash my face and we can go." I don't tell her she's stunning just like this—her cheeks blotchy, her eyes tired. She's always stunning, and, looking at her, I feel like she's keeping me anchored to reality despite the dark chaos of my world.

But I don't tell her any of that.

Instead, I stand and take her hands in mine to pull her up. It occurs to me that her hands themselves are two works of art, considering all the creativity that flows through them.

I don't tell her this, either.

She tilts her face to look into my eyes—and I feel like she can read my thoughts anyway.

Impulsively, I kiss her forehead, keeping it as quick, chaste, and professional as I can, given the circumstances. When she called me, and I answered that call, we crossed a line—and we both know it. I'm not sure what territory it puts us in. As much as I intended to maintain careful control, I can't figure out a way to turn back from this.

"It's around the corner," I say. "We don't have to go far. Promise."

TWENTY-EIGHT

HONOR

Now

Strike leads me out of the den, through the giant labyrinth of his downstairs. Everything feels even larger in the shadow of darkness. I catch tantalizing glimpses of a billiards room, a large formal dining room, and what I'm pretty sure is an indoor swimming pool. His hand is large and comforting, enveloping mine in warmth and security like a weighted blanket. After the shock and horror of discovering Keep, my heart is full of gratitude for Strike's compassion.

An hour ago, when I called him hysterically crying and deeply terrorized, I wasn't sure why, exactly, I turned first to Strike to get me through this nightmare.

But I did.

And there he was.

And here we are. In his kitchen.

In sheer square footage, it leaves me speechless. In Strike's world, size definitely matters. I look around, amazed at this professional chef setup, with its gleaming stainless-steel appliances, bronze pull handles, and open shelving so you can see every perfectly stacked dish. Knives of various sizes hang on magnetic strips crossing one entire wall. The effect is both mesmerizing and disturbing, but maybe I only think it's the latter because of tonight's events. I don't normally associate knives with the killing of beloved pets.

Unlike the knives Paula said Strike collects, these don't look like they might have once belonged to Spanish Conquistadors. No, these knives are bladed to slice meat from a carcass.

What's more, they look like they're in use. In rotation.

I flash to the book in Strike's library: *The Guide for the Home Butcher: How to Slice Any Animal for the Dinner Table.* With a set of knives like that, what would Strike hunt? Wild boar? Dragons?

I shiver. Actually, I haven't stopped shivering since I found Keep.

"Are we eating here?" I ask, unsure but mostly relieved. I was not feeling up for a restaurant tonight.

"Hottest ticket in town," Strike says, his voice briskly cheerful; I know he's trying to get my mind off Keeper as he leads me to a banquette tucked into the kitchen's far corner. The red-checkered tablecloth and wine bottle candle holder give it a fun, casual bistro vibe.

The table's already set for two, and for the hundredth time I'm amazed at the efficient way Strike runs his household, arranging things backstage so that they are perfectly, flawlessly organized.

Someone even lit the long white tapered candles, but while Strike is distracted getting things ready in the kitchen, I blow them out. I'm happy to sell candles, but I don't ever like to see them burn.

If Strike notices, he doesn't say anything.

"You do realize that your home sweet home is one hundred percent real estate porn," I say, and he laughs.

"Now there's the Honor I know." Strike opens a drawer and pulls out a white cotton chef's apron, tying it securely at the waist.

"So you're really cooking for me?"

"Yup." He pulls a small knife from the wall. "This is my signature dish. Sit back and get comfortable."

"Sounds like a plan."

A tingle rolls up my spine as he flips the handle in his fingers with the deftness of a Benihana chef. It's such a practiced move that it entices and unnerves me. He picks up an onion, and within minutes it's diced into tiny, perfect squares.

Next he pulls a bottle of wine from a hidden pantry. "Red okay?"

I feel the whiskey from earlier branching out from my gut, through my limbs, numbing me from the inside out. I want more of that feeling, but my stomach feels sour, ill-equipped for alcohol tonight. I shake my head. He pours himself a glass, and a glass of water for me.

But when Strike turns back to cooking, I recall the small tin in my purse. Jo gifted me weed gummies a few months ago, and though I've never tried them before, I wouldn't mind putting a little bit of a hazy filter on this night.

I loop the table for my purse and stealth-pop a gummy into my mouth. That'll take the edge off.

"Do you make a habit of cooking for women?" I ask, surprising myself as I return to the kitchen counter and slide onto the island barstool. It's obvious he's a practiced cook—the room is scented with an intoxicating balance of spices and roasting garlic.

"Yeah, it relaxes me," he answers. "Keeps my heart rate low." He winks. The tattoo on his bicep is on full display tonight, and my gaze is drawn to that mysterious series of lines. I count seven, or maybe six.

Strike starts telling me about an upcoming DME VR-Con in New Delhi, and I know it's all about getting my mind off Keep, and I appreciate it. His voice is so deep and comforting, soothing the jagged edges of my anxiety. Nothing feels better than sitting here watching him talk and move about his pristine kitchen. He's graceful and adept and so objectively goddamn sexy. I bet tomorrow I'll be brave enough to draw this exact scene in anime form for my next storyboard. But in it, he'd lift me onto the counter and run an ice cube up and down my body, licking along its path until anime-me sees literal stars.

In fact, I wish he'd do that to me right now. Now *that* would get my mind completely off the fact that there's a violent criminal on the loose who is likely fantasizing about me and what he wants to—*Don't go there, Honor.*

Too late. Sweat pricks up my neck.

When Strike isn't watching, I pop another gummy.

"Last thing, we'll julienne some zucchini," Strike says as he takes down a terrifyingly long, narrow knife with a blade as thin as a cat's whisker, then masterfully slices a zucchini into uniform, matchstick-sized segments. He's as precise as a surgeon, but more forceful.

"Wow, I wouldn't want to be a zucchini in your house. Who taught you to cook?" I ask.

A shadow crosses Strike's face, and then he shrugs. "Self-taught," he says. "It's good meditation for me. It works best when I'm angry. A great way to blow off steam."

When Strike speaks of his anger, it sends an electrifying shiver right through my bone marrow, igniting a mix of fear and my undeniable attraction. I want to tell him I know other ways to blow off steam, but I don't feel enough Dutch courage. Though I do think I might already feel the gummies working their way through my system. I sense a soft heaviness in my limbs.

"Strike," I begin. "Thank you for picking me up tonight. It's really nice not to be alone. Especially tonight, but actually, most nights I feel . . ."

Shh, Honor! Don't tell him about how lonely you are! That is such a turn-off! Gracie is hissing a gale-force warning in my ear.

Strike stares at me. "You feel how?"

"Oh, I just mean I like being in a working kitchen. Where onions are sizzling. The sound reminds me of a soft rainstorm."

He nods. "Yeah, yeah. I get that."

Stoners should be seen and not heard, says Gracie. *Watch your mouth, Sunday. You're high as a kite.*

She's right. I press my lips together and keep my gaze fixed intently on Strike as he lowers the heat under the saucepan, then adds a simmering mixture of tomato paste, Worcestershire sauce, and seasonings with the same masterful ease he does everything with. My body feels boneless, slumped in relaxation.

Meatballs appear—homemade, pre-batched, and absolutely delicious looking—and Strike fires up a skillet to brown them. Then he brings a pot of water to boil. No gesture wasted, not even an unnecessary flick of the wrist.

"Take a seat at the table," he says. "We're a minute out."

I feel like I've fallen under a deep spell; this phenomenal, mysterious man is making dinner exclusively for me. I want to post a photo on Instagram, set him to music on TikTok, and announce it to the world: "Friday nights at home with my boyfriend."

Good grief, Honor, he's not your boyfriend, reminds Gracie. *He's your boss and he feels* sorry *for you. And probably a little worried now that Troy has decided to make an enemy of you. That's worse than being Strike's girlfriend.*

I move carefully to sit at the table, where I reach for the wine bottle, forgetting that I wasn't going to drink tonight, but my arm falls short.

Too much effort while under the spell of the weed.

"Hey, hey, hey." I blink. Strike is here. He crouches in front of me as he touches the side of my face, staring into my eyes. My face is cupped in his giant, beautiful hands. "What's going on? You look like you're going to pass out. Here, drink your water. If you fall asleep, you won't be able to properly rate this dinner."

"All the stars in the whole Yelp sky," I say.

He quirks an eyebrow. Okay, I just said a dumb thing.

Don't say any more dumb things!

I can't tell if it's Grace's voice or my own conscience. My head is pinwheeling.

Man, these gummies are strong. Why did I take two of them?

Now Strike is here with steaming bowls full of spaghetti, and it's so good my eyes are wet.

Gummy tears? I am feeling too many feelings. We eat silently; I'm starved and the food is delicious.

"Thank you," I tell him when I'm finished. I am staring at his lips and thinking how if he kissed me now, we'd both taste like sweet tomatoes. Kissing Strike would obliterate all the ugly thoughts in my head. Kissing Strike would obliterate everything.

If our lips met, we'd melt into each other, and I wouldn't know where I ended and he began. We'd merge into one being.

Oh shit. I am very, very high. "You're a great cook."

"I enjoy cooking for people I enjoy," he says, his gaze lingering on my face.

"The way you look at me," I say softly, taking his hand, "makes me feel like you think I'm worth something." *Nooo.* I am sabotaging this whole night. I need to drop his hand, but instead I'm holding it up, examining it like it's a beautiful sculpture. *Honor, don't say anything else out loud. Don't tell him what you want his hands to do. Do not speak a word about finger-sucking.*

"Of course you're worth something, Honor. You're worth everything."

The moment is so intense that I can't hold it; when I stand up to clear the table, the floor tilts away from me and Strike springs to his feet and catches me before I fall. I wish I felt even a quarter as sharp-edged as he is.

"Oopsie-doopsie," I say, giggling as I throw my arms around his neck. "This is the part of the night where you pick me up and take me to bed, right?" The weight of my yearning feels like it could swallow me whole, amplified by how my world's gone fuzzy around the edges. My body feels stretchy and loose. I think about all the positions Strike can fold me into, as if I've become my own avatar. Who knew gummies turn you into human Silly Putty?

A distant awareness tells me that I've lost too much inhibition. I'm being ridiculous, embarrassing myself. I might even have said *oopsie-doopsie.*

Out loud.

But the more pressing thought is that Strike needs to find my tongue and let it play with his and then rip off my clothes and fuck me all night long in whatever giant Strike-worthy bed is up-stairs.

I don't care what room he chooses. Maybe we should christen all of them, bed and after bed, like Goldilocks.

Yes, this is all I want.

Naked animal sex with Strike until the sun comes up.

TWENTY-NINE

STRIKE

Now

Since I haven't seen her drink anything more than a splash of scotch in honey-lemon water, I suspect Honor's popped a very strong edible, and I'm glad to see it's working. For the first time tonight, she doesn't look hunted. Her features have relaxed, and her face is serene and peaceful.

"Time to take you up to bed," I say, scooping her into my arms.

"Okay," she says sleepily. When she nuzzles her nose against my cheek, I'm immediately aroused—even this tiny point of contact is an insistent reminder of what her whole body might feel like against mine. I sense that she wants me, too. Or at least Stoned Honor wants me.

Which is why there's no way I'm going to take advantage of this situation.

Contrary to what people might think, I'm a fucking gentleman.

I swing us through the kitchen doors and down the hall.

"You know what?" Heavy-lidded and gorgeous, Honor studies me as she traces a finger along my jawline. "You're the best-looking man I've ever seen in my life. Six out of five stars."

When I laugh, she nuzzles in closer.

"Six out of five? I'm flattered," I say as we head up the staircase. The pragmatic side of me has made the decision to keep her here because she's in no shape to go home—and Simpson presents a clear and present danger.

The only other time I remember using the guest bedroom was when Axe barreled through an entire bottle of scotch on the night he successfully fought off a hostile takeover of his company. And it was more like Axe fell over onto the bed like a drunk but mighty oak tree than slept in it like a proper guest. But the staff keeps it at the ready, and tonight the shades are drawn, the lamps lit, with the guest pajamas and toiletry kit at the foot of the bed.

"Less imposing than I imagined, but it'll get the job done," Honor says as I set her down lightly on the bed. She slaps a hand to her mouth as she realizes that Saucy Minx Honor has collided with Conscientious Employee Honor. "I said that out loud, didn't I?"

"What do you mean, imposing? Were you expecting a weight-lifting bench?" I smile. "Whips and chains?"

She giggles. "What's gotten into me?"

I fold my arms across my chest. She looks so tousled and soft, my cock aches. "My guess is something fun and possibly illegal," I say.

"I'll have you know, weed gummies are now medically legal in the state of Pennsylvania. At least I think they are? That's what Josie told me . . ."

Her words slur as she leans up off the bed toward me, her eyes closing, as if maybe she's going for a kiss? But she misses wide, and almost falls sideways on the carpet—I have to grab her arm to steady her.

"Yup. I'm good. Nothing to see here," she says as another giggle escapes. Truly, I've never seen this side of Honor, who arrives every morning at DME the epitome of cool and collected and never lets the fact that we're working in the adult anime fantasy market blur into personal territory. I don't know if she's dating anyone or even if the fantasies she shares with the team are even hers.

This is a different flavor of Honor.

And she's ridiculously cute when she's high and messy.

"You need a good night's sleep," I tell her, and I give in to my impulse to smooth her hair, which has gone all wild and radiant around her face like an unruly halo. But as far as I can tell from her art, this woman is no saint. And thank fuck for that. Saints are boring.

She takes the stack from the end of the bed and weaves her way to the bathroom, reemerging a few minutes later swimming in a crisp white cotton pajama set, the sleeves and waist both triple rolled, and climbs under the sheets.

"Need a tuck-in?" I offer.

"A what?" Honor sounds like she's floating away. She'll be asleep in two minutes. Those must be some good gummies.

"Like this." I bend down and tuck the comforter around her so she's snug like an egg roll. Against my better judgment, I stroke her cheek, and when I feel a tear trickle down, I brush it away with my thumb.

"Nobody ever gave me a tuck-in before," she says.

"Been a long day, Firefly," I say.

She nods, then snuggles deep into the covers, sighs as if this bed is the softest thing she's ever known. I lean down and kiss her squarely on the forehead. I keep it platonic, almost joking.

"Good night," I whisper.

"Good night, Stri—" But she's fast asleep before she even finishes saying my name.

THIRTY

HONOR

Now

Troy must have jimmied the window of Gracie's bedroom open again. It's a trick Gracie taught him when she asked him to pay her a late-night visit but didn't want his footsteps on the stairs to wake me. When he throws himself over me, his body is as heavy as a safe, the meat of his tongue slimy and sour in my mouth, forcing my own mouth open by plunging so far into the back of my throat that I start to choke.

"Draw your fantasy, Firefly," he whispers thickly, but it's all wrong, his hand finding my nipple and pinching it hard as his other hand forces me to feel his thick, swollen—

My eyes fly open as I sit up in a single lunge. I'm screaming—no, I'm not making a sound, because both of my hands are clamped over my mouth to stop Troy's phantom tongue. The night floods through me—spaghetti, gummies, Strike carrying me here to his guest room. I'm fine.

But now I also hear a noise that is a kind of screaming, and it's coming from somewhere inside the house.

An old-fashioned alarm clock reads 3:42—I've been asleep for hours. The sound didn't wake me—the nightmare did—but now that I'm fully conscious and aware, I hear it, a low and angry shouting, and it's coming from right down the hall.

My heartbeat quickens to a scamper. Oh my God, what if Troy's here? Attacking Strike? Strike has at least six inches on Troy, and maybe fifty pounds of muscle, but Troy would have the element of surprise, or, God forbid, a weapon.

I slip from the bed and leave my bedroom without thinking, running toward the noise. I sprint down the long dark corridor, my bare feet slapping against the cold hardwood floor, fear slicing through my body. Any residual effects of the gummy are burned off by jets of adrenaline and fear. A sudden, primal scream leads me farther and faster toward the dark—there's absolutely no light from anywhere, and now I'm groping along the walls, stumbling blind.

The cuffs of my too-long pajamas nearly trip me up, and the sleeves hang long past my hands. I am as defenseless as a child. That doesn't stop me. I will beat Troy with my bare fists if I have to.

After this, I'm definitely buying a gun.

The door is cracked open a fraction, and I slide through.

In the shadows, my eyes strain to piece together the scene playing out in front of me. My heart trips.

No fight.

No Troy.

Only Strike tossing and turning in the center of an enormous bed. He's been thrashing around so much that his duvet has fallen to the carpet and his silky sheets are tangled around his ankles. He's half yelling, half crying in his sleep, a low guttural sound that's so heartbreaking, I act totally on instinct.

He's having a night terror.

"Strike?" I whisper, as I slide into his bed, edging closer and closer until I'm a shadow alongside his body, my arms tentatively reaching for him as I attempt to calm him. "Strike, you're having a bad dream. Wake up. Wake up, sweetheart." The word escapes me shyly but instinctively, even though I've never used the word *sweetheart* in my life and I'm shocked that the first time I've spoken it, it's for a man.

And not any man, but this one.

But I want Strike to stop hurting. Whatever is happening in his dream right now must be even worse than the horrors I've experienced in real life.

Strike's body twists and suddenly lunges upward, gasping, as if he's been drowning and now has abruptly washed onto shore.

His eyes blink open to stare up at me through the darkness. He's still twitching and shaking so hard that holding him is like trying to wrestle a crocodile.

"Kate," he gasps.

Kate? The mention of another woman's name sends a shocked twinge up my spine. As far as I know, nobody by that name works for Strike or DME.

I have no idea who Kate is, but I instantly hate her.

Kate, the woman of his literal dreams.

He thrashes for another minute and finally seems to come to, shifting back, exhausted, into the crook of my arms.

"Shh," I say, rubbing his back. "Shh."

"Honor?" he asks, panicked confusion in his voice—but he sounds more awake. He exhales as he drags his hands through his hair. Stares around the room, reorienting himself.

"Yes, it's me—you had a bad dream, so I came running. Everything is okay." *And who is Kate?*

Strike shakes his head a few times as if to rid himself of

thoughts swirling inside it. He takes a few more deep breaths and wipes at his eyes.

Then I ask, "Do you want to talk about it?"

Strike gives me a quick no, but then in a sudden change of heart, he sinks back and buries his face into my neck, his muffled cries so heartbroken that now my own eyes flood—because how can I not cry tonight? For my sister and Keeper, and even for Strike, because it breaks me that this strong, good man would be so tormented.

And Strike is crying for . . . what? Who? What monsters are visiting him at this unholy hour?

"Sorry," he says roughly, shaking his head as if to rid himself of his thoughts. But his tears don't stop, and soon my hair is damp along my neck.

After a little while, Strike's breathing slows, and his head feels heavier. His arm stretches across my back and pulls me in so that the cloth of my pajamas is all that separates our skin, and before long, Strike is fast asleep in my arms. It feels so right and good, and for the first time in my adult life, I feel safer in a shared bed than whenever I've slept alone. Troy can't get to me here.

I let my eyes shut.

And this time, with my arms and legs entangled with Strike's, I sleep so hard that I don't dream at all.

THIRTY-ONE

HONOR

Now

The next morning, I feel like I'm surfacing from the bottom of a dark lagoon. My head is still murky. I wonder if Gracie's hangover cure, Flamin' Hot Cheetos and tomato juice, helps with weed? When my eyes finally crack open, it takes me a minute to remember that I spent the early morning hours in Strike's bedroom.

In Strike's arms.

But Strike is gone.

He told me last night that he had a morning call with some game developers in Shanghai. Still, my stomach squeezes in disappointment.

Enough sunlight filters through the bottom gap in the heavy blackout drapes that I can take in my surroundings. Whoa. I was wrong. I'd assumed his bedroom would be either all Victorian kink or a modern loft.

Nope. Strike's bedroom, now that I'm in it, is perfectly suited to him—and it's nothing like I imagined. I stretch out on my back and take in the elegance of the high ceiling, a stone accent wall, the rich cream and nutmeg textiles, and a fireplace accented by a marble mantel. Of course the walls are covered in beautiful—if slightly menacing—modern art. Yes, this is one hundred percent the bedroom version of Strike, and I love that I'm in it, wearing his pajamas—sexier to me than any lingerie I could ever own.

The scent of him lingers everywhere. I want to capture whatever whisper of his touch remains. I remember the feeling of his heavy, muscular legs taut against mine, his arms pulling me closer. I luxuriate in the silky sheets, the way my toes feel rubbing along the fabric. It helps crowd out the visions of Keep.

And the mysterious Kate.

But now, in the sobering light of day, I moan with frustration that Strike is no longer here. My longing feels insatiable. I'd give anything to spend today in this bed with him.

Instead, I force myself to face a few terrible truths. Troy killed Keeper. He's tormenting me, enjoying my total fear of his next move.

Strike, on the other hand, is not an actual option for me, no matter how strange and vulnerable last night was on both sides. We've already crossed an employer-employee line that neither of us wanted to. Strike is too much of a gentleman to have sent me home in the state I was in last night.

But he didn't invite me into his bed, either.

And what was that horrific nightmare all about, anyway? I've heard him talk about his time in the military with his friend Axe almost fondly. He's never mentioned PTSD or seemed guarded about it. What secrets is he hiding from me?

It's not until I sit up that I see a bottle of Gatorade on the nightstand, with a Post-it note stuck to it.

DRINK UP. YOU NEED TO HYDRATE.

I've held on to Strike's "Draw your fantasy" card as much for the message as because I love Strike's handwriting. He writes in all caps, as if he's yelling his words. It's all part of that crisp, commanding, suffer-no-fools-gladly presence.

I'll save this card, too.

Now I drink deeply and gratefully. Wiping my lips with the back of my hand, I cringe, thinking about last night from Strike's perspective. I've been the only sober person and designated driver in a room of drunk or high people more times than I can count. I know how I must have looked to him.

Shame spills through me. I said *oopsie-doopsie*. I went for a clumsy kiss. I assumed Strike was taking me to bed. And now it's morning, and I'm wearing my boss's pajamas. My next thought: *I cannot walk-of-shame out of here.* If any Dark Matter Entertainment employee saw me exit Strike's house, I'd be the center of gossip for weeks. I just know one of Strike's staff—or worse, Paula, DME's in-house cool cucumber to my hot mess—is going to be around the corner as soon as I step out of this room.

Sweat prickles under my arms.

Fuck. Fuck. Fuck.

One thing at a time, Honor.

"Okay," I tell myself. "First things first. Shower."

But when I walk into Strike's bathroom, I cannot suppress a gasp. The room has got to be at least fifteen hundred square feet, bigger than my entire store. A carved wooden bathtub centers the space, and it's a literal piece of art. The counters are, of course, spotless. Not a single product litters their surface, except a razor hanging from a stunning hand-carved ivory holder. My toes curl a little as I imagine Strike, a towel knotted loosely at his waist, gliding the blade smoothly against the contours of his cheekbones.

One wall is devoted to a framed, blown-up, black-and-white photograph, but I don't really understand what I'm seeing at first. Studying it, I realize it's a close-up of a man's jaw lathered with shaving cream. The cutting edge of a barber's blade is a millimeter from the jugular.

On the opposite wall, a shadow box showcases a collection of vintage razors, blades angled open from their guards. Each is meticulously labeled with its own name, a patent number, and a year. The oldest one in the bunch dates back to 1762 and is called "The Perret." This is almost as weird as Gracie's collection of Pokémon plushies.

Along the lip of the bathtub is a wooden tray that holds an assortment of bath oils and salts. I don't even have to cross the room. My heart fills with joy that they are from Grace & Honor, and I'm warm at the idea of Strike in the bath using them.

Okay, get your head out of the clouds. You're here to shower, not romanticize.

The room is laid out like an L, and around the corner is another small room, covered floor-to-ceiling in Moroccan tile. The only indication that this is the shower is a round digital dial on the far wall.

Reluctantly, I strip off my borrowed pajamas and fold them neatly. I press the button, and a series of options pops up, preset sequences and temperatures. I choose *A.M.*, and a waterfall showerhead descends from the ceiling. A second later, additional jets emerge from the walls. I see now they've been hidden by sliding tiles.

Oh my God, that feels good. I lean my head back and let the hot water wash over me from all different directions. I push down on some of the many dispensers, feeling like a bartender mixing up a fancy cocktail. A few pumps, and soon I'm sudsy and lathered in a fragrant concoction that I recognize as Strike's own signature scent—that distinct mix of cedar, woodsmoke, and lavender. A forest oasis blended into a fresh unity. I inhale deeply—I can't get enough.

After my shower, I grab an oversized white towel from a fluffy pile and wrap it around myself. I pull my hair into a messy, wet bun on top of my head. I turn the corner, going back the way I came—even his bathroom is like a maze—and see that on the counter someone has laid a simple cornflower-blue cotton sundress.

Another note:

WEAR IT. FROM YOUR STORE, SO I ASSUME YOU LIKE?

My cheeks flame. When did this get here?

Clearly, my exit plan won't be as smooth as I hoped.

But he's right. I do love this dress. I don't carry much inventory of clothes at G&H, but I do have a small rack of easy feminine pieces. I slip the dress over my head and see that a pair of cute boy shorts have been folded underneath.

Tags still attached.

These are not from my shop. The only panties we sell are lacy thongs, cutouts, and edibles. Did Strike send Paula on an emergency undies run? Even weirder: Does he have a drawer somewhere in this house full of brand-new women's panties? These are black silk, both sexy and practical.

I slip them on under the dress. They're mine now.

I can't imagine what it will feel like to face Strike today. My stomach swirls. Does he blame me for Gummygate? I'm sure I'll feel shy and not play it as cool as I hope. There's also the very real possibility that I might break down when I see him. My first day without Keep is tugging hard at my heart.

Back into the bedroom, I peek and check around, curious to see if I can learn anything else about this mysterious man. On the other side of the bed is a side table; on it, I spy a framed photograph.

I close in on it. The picture is of a beautiful red-haired woman; next to her is a handsome, smiling man, and in front of them, a little boy no more than three. His paper graduation cap tamps down ginger curls a few shades lighter than his mother's. Both parents have their hands on the kid's shoulders, and it's obvious they are bursting with pride. Some sort of preschool graduation, I assume.

Is this Strike's brother and sister-in-law? No, he's an only child. So . . . who's this?

I pick up the picture. The man . . . is actually . . . Strike himself.

Holy shit. What? How? I touch my finger to his face in disbelief. The sculpted physique and geometric jawline are exactly the same. It takes me a second to pinpoint why I feel so confused. Why isn't this Strike *my* Strike, exactly? It's not just because he looks younger.

The eyes, I realize. Past-tense Strike's eyes radiate such joy. Not at all the eyes of the man I first met in the morgue. I feel my heart crack, and my knees give way as I sink to sit on the side of the bed.

What is the story? Is Strike married? To this woman? Is she Kate? Are they divorced? Is he a father?

I look more closely at the little boy and force myself to admit that Strike is quite obviously this kid's dad. Same face shape, same gray eyes. More than that, it's the way Strike is looking at him, his large hand on the boy's little shoulder, that tells me this child belongs to him. I can feel his protective instinct, like he'd slay a thousand monsters if that's what he needed to do.

Over these past twelve hours, I've broken down in this man's arms, shared a meal with him, let him put me to bed, shared his own bed, comforted him, enveloped myself in the soft fabric of his sheets, luxuriated in his steam shower, and been utterly consumed by endless fantasies of his hands and mouth exploring my body . . . and still, Strike remains a stranger to me.

I have no idea who this man really is.

THIRTY-TWO

HONOR

Now

I want a photo of this family, but my phone is in the other room.

Quickly, I put down the framed picture and leave Strike's bedroom. My ears are pricked as I creep along the long hall, retracing my steps—with a few false starts—to the room where he first deposited my gummy-dummy ass last night, which feels about five weeks ago. When I finally find it, the bed's been made up. All of my clothing, along with my flats and bag, make a tidy square pile on the chair.

I pick up the stack and sniff. My shirt has been washed, pressed, and folded. There's even a small canvas DME tote for me to drop everything inside.

When I check my phone in my bag, it's got a full battery.

It was down to a sliver last night. Are these invisible hands considerate or controlling? Not that I have anything on there I wouldn't want Strike to see, but I exhale with some relief that my phone is locked and password protected—and with a real password. Not Gracie's ridiculous 1-2-3-4.

No way Strike would snoop and look at my phone. He has a

million more important things to do. A member of the Ashburn secret-agent spy squad must have stepped in.

I slip back down the hall to Strike's room.

The door to his bedroom is now locked.

Crap. No way I can take that photo of Strike and his family now. Though it was a sneaky idea, a Gracie idea, and maybe I shouldn't operate so far outside my normal MO. I'm not sure Gracie ever went to a party without opening the bathroom medicine cabinet and dropping a few pills into her handbag.

If Strike has an ex-wife and a young son he doesn't want to talk about, that's his prerogative. It's none of my business. Maybe she ran off in protest of a joint custody agreement or something. Who knows? Things only feel secretive until someone lets you in on the story. Every narrative has multiple perspectives. It all comes down to who's telling it. What's that famous quote? "History is written by the victors."

I'm sure Strike will tell me when he's ready. Perhaps there's no big, juicy secret at all. Maybe Kate lives on the other side of town. Maybe he visits his kid at her house instead of bringing him here to hentai headquarters. Could be he doesn't want his child exposed to violent video games and erotic anime. I heard Steve Jobs wouldn't let his kids have iPhones.

I don't let myself dwell on the fact that Strike has never once mentioned this wife and child. Or that a few weeks ago, I sketched out some panels starring a redheaded character and Strike suggested—firmly—that he'd prefer to see a brunette.

"Redheads are too niche," he said, which struck me as odd at the time, but I didn't push it. Hentai is all about niche tastes. Some of our characters have tails or the bodies of horses or massive appendages.

A cute ginger didn't feel even slightly far-fetched.

I've got to get out of here. I call Jo and ask her to pick me up—
we have plans this morning to get over to SugarLips Wholesale
to check out some new supplies for the store. Though I don't welcome the barrage of questions she'll have for me about why I'm
at DME this morning, she's my only option. Breath held, I scamper down all the back stairs and through one of the many side
doors, until I'm safely outside on a path that winds down the
driveway away from the DME building to the front security gates.

When I punch in the code, the door buzzes and I walk out.

I slip my trusty can of Mace from my purse and keep it
clenched in my hand. Jo said she'd be only a few minutes, but still
I feel exposed. I take out my phone to keep me distracted while I
wait. I absorb myself by googling "Strike Madden family," "Strike
Madden wedding," "Strike Madden wife." Of course I turn up
nothing. I try an image search. Different spellings. As uncomfortable as I feel, I search "Strike Madden death of family" and "Kate
Madden obituary."

Zilch. When Jo did her initial Strike search, she affirmed my
hunch that Strike, like most high-profile figures, kept his online
profile scrubbed and sanitized. But wedding registries and deaths
are public domain.

"Madden wife dead."

Nothing.

"Madden estate."

Nothing.

"Dark Matter Entertainment."

A horn beeps. I look up and wave at Jo, who is smiling at me
through the windshield of her Beetle. She cranks down the
window.

"I'm totally freaked out," she says. "I pulled the Five of Swords
this morning." She looks more delighted than freaked. I have no

idea what she's talking about. No matter how much she swears by it, I can't follow her down the rabbit hole of her tarot card predictions.

As I go to open the passenger-side door, something across the street catches my eye, and I freeze. My panic buttons start firing all at once. Oh my God. It can't be. No, I'm hallucinating. Maybe I'm still in Strike's bed and this is a nightmare.

Him. It's him. I know Troy instantly even though he's recently grown a patchy beard. He's standing on the side of the road. No truck. What's he doing here? Has he been casing the property?

He is staring at me with unsettling cheerfulness, his bugged-out gaze sending a freezing chill up my spine.

Trembling and defenseless, I stand frozen in fear as I realize the grave mistake I've made by underestimating Troy's threat. How could I be so dumb? How could I not have realized his obsession was only going to escalate? Troy once put a tracking app on Gracie's phone, and then he'd show up random places where she was and pretend it was a coincidence.

At least he's too far away—for now.

My brain tells me to run or to jump in the car, but I'm rooted to the spot.

My sister's and Keep's murderer is just across the street.

Troy smiles and lifts up his hand in a friendly wave. Like we're neighbors. Like I'd be happy to see him. I can tell he's already drunk, too—even though it's still morning. Or maybe he's *still* drunk from last night.

"Hi, Honor," he calls. "Did you get my card? I'm so sorry about Keep. I loved that cat like an in-law." He laughs like he said something particularly witty. "Man, when your hair is like that? You look so much like her. Like that hologram they did that brought back Tupac. I really love looking at you. It's like she's still here.

Anyhow, let's stop playing games. I want us to spend some time together, like we used to."

It's only when he steps toward me that I finally, *finally* unfreeze. "Lock the doors," I scream, as I hurl myself into the car beside Jo. "Lock them, lock them, lock them!"

Jo looks at me—*behind me?*—her mouth an O.

"Jo, that's Troy!" I press the lock button. "Drive!" But then I see Strike striding across the street. He's barefoot, in jeans and a cotton undershirt. He's got a metal baseball bat in his hands.

"You fucking piece of shit," Strike says, advancing.

Troy puts up his hands.

"What the fuck, man?" he asks.

In answer Strike takes a swing then slams the bat so it cracks right against the side of Troy's head.

Troy yelps an unearthly hyena-like sound as he buckles and goes down. To my horror, Strike isn't finished yet, even as the blood pours in twin red rivers from Troy's nose and mouth. Strikes swings his bat again, this time so that it connects with Troy's crotch like it's a piñata.

Howling and writhing, Troy shields his junk with both hands, and through the fog of my shock I wonder if balls can burst— God, I hope so.

Now Strike stands over him, a foot planted on either side of Troy's body as he lifts the bat again, a baseball player on the mound. He measures his mark, steadying himself to destroy Troy with a single—probably fatal—blow to the skull. He holds the bat at his shoulder like he's waiting for the pitch. He's gone to a dark place in his mind.

This isn't only about Troy.

"Do something, Honor!" Jo is screaming at the top of her lungs, her fingers clawed into my shoulder. "Tell him to stop!"

She's right, of course—Strike is going to kill him.

Against all instinct, I jump out of the car.

"Strike, wait!" I yell, surprising myself.

I've spent so many nights fantasizing about killing Troy. Dreams where I, too, am holding a baseball bat or a brick. Where I have all the advantage. So I have no idea where this mercy is coming from. And then it hits me: I feel no mercy at all. All I feel is protective.

I don't want Strike to kill Troy in plain sight. I don't want Strike to have to pay for protecting me.

Strike glances up, his pupils blown, his eyes so dark. He looks nothing like the doting father in that picture I saw earlier. He's certainly not the handsome chef who made me spaghetti and meatballs and then swung me in his arms and took me upstairs, where he tucked me into bed. I see no trace of the man who let me hold him after his nightmare.

This man is *eager* to attack.

He's . . . *enjoying* this.

THIRTY-THREE

STRIKE

Now

"Give me one good reason," I growl at her. I want to destroy this motherfucker. My voice is guttural, and I can tell by the way Honor is staring that I look terrifying. An animal hunting prey.

"Because you'll kill him," she answers. Her breath is shaky. Our eyes connect, and that white-hot energy zips between us.

"And . . . ?" I ask. I'm curious why she'd stop me. He killed her sister. He has been stalking her nonstop. He gutted her cat. She's not safe until he's dead. There's a short, straight line between problem and solution. "Why shouldn't I kill him? He obviously deserves to die."

Troy, who is writhing on the ground like a pussy, moans in protest. I'm torn between giving him another kick and not wanting any more of his blood to splash on my feet.

"Because"—Honor's voice so quiet it feels like it's for me alone—"you'll be punished. You'll be the one to go to jail."

"She's right. It would be manslaughter. Maybe first-degree murder." I turn at the sound of Paula's voice as she steps out from behind the front gate. It's times like now that I'm glad I keep her well compensated on the company payroll. Paula assesses the weight of my actions only in terms of how they'd impact DME. She's a voice of reason.

Whereas Honor—she's coming to it from a different place entirely. She thirsts for vengeance. It burns hot inside her.

I see it in her eyes. She wants him dead, too.

"You've got your reasons, Strike—and I'm not doubting them—but you're smarter than this," says Paula.

"Not sure smart has anything to do with it. Also, we had this guy on surveillance," I say. "What the fuck happened?"

"And he is on surveillance," says Paula. "He's fully locked in."

When I glance up at the house, I see that my security team is, in fact, in place on the roof, the balcony, and the ground. Down the road, the same—an unmarked car that has presumably been tailing this little shitbag since he got the ten-dollar idea to hunt Honor down. Likely by following Josie.

"They're a little slow to react, no?" I ask.

"Hey, you started it, Derek Jeter," says Paula. "He's unarmed."

"Don't kill me, man," Troy wheezes, words garbled. He looks scared. Good. I hope he shits his pants. "Honor, you gotta tell him," he whines. "Tell him how we're old friends."

"Get. The fuck. Out of here," I say as Troy finally manages to get up on his knees, then he staggers on shaky legs to his feet, backing away. "And if you come within five hundred feet of this property again, or anywhere near this woman, I will kill you. But first I'll slice off your dick with a razor blade. Do you understand me?"

Troy is finally speechless. That, or his mouth is bleeding too hard for conversation. His jaw hangs loose and broken, and he's got it braced with a hand. He starts limping as quickly as he can down the road, and now I see his pathetic beat-up truck parked farther up ahead, hidden by trees.

My team gives me the sign they've got him covered.

I give them the finger because they should have removed him from the property immediately. He should never have gotten this close.

Honor takes a step toward me, but I hold up a hand. She'd better not come any closer. I'm too wound-up, too furious, too . . . everything. I take the bat in my hands, wind it around a few times, and then throw it so hard it marks my gate. I point to the mark. "Fix that," I tell Paula.

"Yes, of course," she says.

"Strike," Honor says tentatively, but I brush past her. I have a security team to chew out.

"Later," I say over my shoulder as I head back inside. "We'll talk about this later."

I have no intention of discussing this with Honor. There is nothing to discuss. That sniveling little bastard deserves to lose so much more than some of his blood smeared on the end of my baseball bat.

I will not apologize for defending her.

I storm through my house, ignoring the curious looks of my cleaning staff. I head straight to my kitchen, where I wash my hands in the sink with the precision and composure of a skilled surgeon. I don't want even a tiny piece of that motherfucker's DNA under my nails.

THIRTY-FOUR

HONOR

Now

Jo drops me home and stays with me for a cup of tea, but the moment she's gone, my jitters sweep through me like a roller coaster, ascending and plummeting. I've got to move. There are some woods behind the house that lead to a main road—my usual jogging route—and after I change into my running clothes and sneakers, I slip my can of Mace into one pocket and a switchblade into the other.

I hit the trail, restless, my heart pounding, and I know why.

Being raised by wolves means I can't escape my own wolf. The wildness has seeped into my body like toxic chemicals in the water supply. I was raised to feel that every day is another fight I have to survive. I should have recognized myself mirrored back in him. But mostly I was fixated on the fact that I've never been as physically attracted to Strike as I was in that moment.

The moment when he wanted to kill for me.

If my inner alarms were ringing with a sense that Strike Madden is scarred and warped by his wounds, I wasn't paying too much attention. But that's not to say I didn't hear. Maybe all along I sensed the savage wildness within him.

Maybe that's what attracted me to him in the first place.

Maybe I liked that he's a study in balance—there is good in Strike, for sure, but his darkness is equally real. Maybe I saw something of myself in that.

There was murder in Strike's eyes this morning. He would have bludgeoned Troy Simpson to death if we hadn't stopped him. And a big part of me wishes we hadn't. That Troy had been wiped from the face of the Earth with Strike's baseball bat.

Jogging along the path, I feel the sunshine on my body, and I hear the crunch of pine needles beneath my sneakers. I try to let go of my anxiety, but Troy feels like a zombie hand reaching out of the mud to grab hold of me and drag me down, wrestle me into the dirt and deliver me to the same fate as the rest of my family.

Ashes to ashes. Dust to dust.

Home again, out of breath and dripping with sweat, I find Gracie's hot pink gardening spade and matching plastic bucket, and I dig a hole out back for Keeper's grave. Paula texted me that DME staff came to the house last night and put the body in a hemp sack and then put the sack in the cellar. She's also sent me my new alarm code.

Apparently, Strike had a state-of-the-art system installed overnight.

A little invasive, but in this case, I'll take it.

I pop a quick text to Jo letting her know. I'm glad Strike's people thought to have Keep's little body covered and stored. I was too distraught to do it myself.

I bury Keep, marking the spot with a large rock. I use my switchblade to scratch a large *K* on its face.

Although it feels faintly ridiculous to give a cat a proper funeral, I say a few words. "Keeper, my friend, from the day Gracie found you half-starved behind a dumpster, you brought so much laughter and beauty to our lives. Your green eyes and your purring warmth got me through those first months without my sister. I wish I could have protected you better. I will miss you forever, my precious little buddy."

I toss in his catnip mouse and his salmon snacks before I cover him in topsoil, then I sit on my knees and lift my face to feel the rays of afternoon sun. I let it dry my tears.

Everything's going to be okay, I tell myself.

You're a survivor, I tell myself.

But really what I mean is this: *You are all alone now. Nothing left to lose.*

The next day at work, I feel less like a survivor and more like a nuisance. Paula is her usual professional self, served straight up and chilled. As for Strike, after holding a brief staff meeting about the upcoming Game Developers Conference in San Francisco, he tells me he's too busy to review my work.

When I ask him for a little more guidance about the presentation, he stops me midsentence. "Keep going with whatever you're doing, Honor. You should know the ropes by now."

"Except there are a few different directions that—"

"So pick one. I'm sure it'll be fine."

"I want my work to be better than fine. That's why you hired me," I say, following him down the hall—I'm as annoyed by the pleading lilt in my voice as I am by the fact that he's making me talk to his back as I trail him through the courtyard. What I really want to say is: *What happened to you, Strike? Why can't you sleep at night? What torments you? What enrages you? We're not so un-alike. I have my secrets, too.*

I can think of plenty of reasons why Strike is avoiding me. Starting with yesterday. If there's one thing I know about Strike Madden, it's that he doesn't like to feel out of control.

And with Troy, he was wild.

But there've been other issues, too. We've been alone together in such vulnerable moments. I've pushed past the traditional employee limits with him—calling him up and leaning on him like a goddamn damsel in distress. (How many times did I tell Gracie we would not ever be goddamn damsels in distress? How many times did I tell Gracie we would always save ourselves? But then again, how many times did Gracie pinkie-promise she'd read my favorite female empowerment book, *Untamed*—only to leave it untouched in her beach bag, its cover stained with tanning oil?)

Strike might want some distance from me, but in just this brief span of weeks, he's ballooned into my whole world.

He's also bought me some peace from Troy. I still packed Mace, and I've made an appointment to take some pistol shooting lessons next week, but I feel safer today than I did a few days ago. Troy knows that Strike is a dangerous enemy.

This afternoon, I sharpen my colored pencils and pour my emotions into my art. Let my work speak for me.

I sketch a Regency courtyard full of people milling about in gowns and waistcoats. The water fountain becomes the centerpiece of a slow seduction scene that begins with a woman pleasuring herself in the pump of a gushing fountain. As she is joined by other figures, image-by-image, their fine clothing melts off their bodies, colors pooling like a slippery pastel rainbow into the water.

At the base of the fountain's pool, they embrace in a passionate dance of love and desire. Their limbs intertwined like delicate vines. Their intimacy is fleeting yet intense as they savor every moment before reluctantly breaking away.

One of the coders starts to transcribe and upload the images into RapidArt, and by the end of the morning, we've got a dreamy, sexy story—*Whispering Wet Vines*. I am so lost in work I don't even notice that Paula is here.

"Strike wanted me to relay a message," she says. "You need to stay home for a few days."

The coder moves away, embarrassed to overhear what sounds like punishment. My cheeks burn.

"Why? What's going on?" I ask. My anxieties double down. "Have I been fired?"

"He'll be in touch," says Paula. Her face is inscrutable as always. "Car's waiting."

It's obvious she's been instructed to say as little as possible. I was looking forward to moving into the RapidArt program to add in my own glow-ups—but now it seems like I'm being banned from DME.

Why? What did I do? My heart jerks with a new thought: am I being blamed for Troy showing up on the property? Because it compromised the safety of the corporation? When Troy found himself on the receiving end of Strike's fury yesterday, I'm sure there was no shortage of talk about it throughout Ashburn. And if these past couple of days are anything to go by, I've created my fair share of gossip. My surprise sleepover might have disrupted the peace in DME's HR division more than I know.

But is he really sending me packing?

"When can I come back?" I ask. My voice is a girlish squeak.

"We'll let you know," Paula replies. She's as polished as marble. Not fair. This is my playroom, my creative space, and my happy place, all rolled up into one.

"Your pay stub," she says, handing me an envelope.

It's a formality; my payment is direct deposit. My heart sinks. What is Strike trying to tell me?

Outside in the car, I unroll the window of the SUV to feel the breeze on my cheeks, and the cold air hits my tears.

Five minutes, Honor. That's all the crying you get.

As always, my apartment feels too empty without Gracie, without Keeper.

Today is Jo's day off, and I know I should open the store—it would be a productive distraction. I've really let Jo take over so much of the day-to-day since I've become involved with DME, and there's a mountain of invoices to sign off on and new stock to approve. But I just don't have the energy. I can't even face the customers. I don't want to smile or be friendly or pretend that I'm okay. When I am pretty fucking not okay.

I hold the envelope between my nervous fingers.

What if it's a note telling me to stay far away from Dark Matter Entertainment? That my brand of mess isn't welcome there?

I wouldn't blame Strike. I don't know why I've always been a magnet for trouble, especially when I've worked so hard to keep my nose clean. Officially, I'm a good girl; I can count on one hand the number of times I've been drunk. I've never tried a drug unless you count caffeine and those gummies. Other than some low-key shoplifting during childhood—necessity, not greed—I keep myself on the right side of the law.

I've never even gotten an extension on my taxes.

Gracie was the wild one. Not me.

But what did it matter in the end? On whatever new path I've tried to follow, chaos and tragedy stuck close. We were both raised by wolves, anyway.

I make myself open the envelope. No paycheck, only that recognizable cardstock. His classic all-caps. My heart squeezes.

STAY AWAY FROM MONSTERS. INCLUDING ME.

The message is reliably cryptic. What does that even mean? I want to text Strike. Tell him he has it all wrong. He's a wolf, like me. Not a monster.

I've known monsters all my life. I was born to one, burned by one, brought to my knees by one. I've hidden in the woods so I wouldn't be hunted by one.

Strike is an altogether different animal.

I'm not scared of you, Strike. I know what
you are.

I type the text on my phone, and my fingers hover.
When I go to bed later, I still haven't hit send.

THIRTY-FIVE

HONOR

Then
(Age 13)

Gracie and I continue to play Normal. We share the comfort of our imaginations, and as we've aged, we've folded our dreams from Normal into the shapes of actual plans.

At the heart of our game, we cut loose from our parents.

They are gone so we can fly.

"Our boyfriends will be brothers," Gracie says. We picture them, dark-haired and brown-eyed, skin as pale as moonlight, and as worshipful as Robert Pattinson in Twilight.

"Twins," I say.

"Duh," Gracie says.

"And they will be so Normal! They'll play soccer and guitar, and when they invite us to their Thanksgiving, their table will have a tablecloth and place mats," I add.

"Yeah, and they'll give us rings with our birthstone," Gracie says.

"And we'll live with them in their apartments, which are next door to each other, and our fridges will always be full of food."

*"And Rusty will go back and forth between our places," Gracie
says.*

"Duh," I say.

*We are bigger and older now. Harder to beat and harder to
catch. We run through the forest howling, knowing our parents
can't find us. Not that Mama would ever come looking. We steal
one of Daddy's beers and pass it back and forth in our hollow tree,
and we talk about ways we can save up for an iPod.*

*At home, we have to shield Rusty from our father. If our little
brother's not at TJ's, he hides in a leaf pile out back or he's in his
room under a heap of blankets. Sometimes he won't say anything
to anyone for days or only mumbles words I don't understand
under his breath. If he's in a mood, he'll scream, fists flailing when
we touch him. He's too scrawny to hurt anyone, but he might hurt
himself.*

I don't know how to give him a safe outlet.

*There are no safe outlets for the Stone family. Only self-destruct
buttons. Gracie and I know it's only a matter of time before one of
us pushes ours.*

Now

Blinking, out of breath, I wipe my eyes with the back of my hand
as I stare down at the small gravestone: *Russell "Rusty" Pacer
Stone 2005–2017.*

Thoughts of my family have backflipped me through time so
that this morning when I find myself here at St. Martin-in-the-
Fields Cemetery, I'm surprised. I can't even remember when I
decided to run this way.

It's been a lot to absorb. My mind has been such a jumble these past days.

And now I'm here, for whatever reason—but there are no accidents. It wasn't until Strike Madden strode into my life that I felt like I might have a real shot at happiness. A path toward him that picked a straight line through this mess of my life.

If he only knew.

What a joke. What five-star fucking irony.

You didn't have to banish me, I finally text him quickly and impulsively before I pocket my phone.

I'm still crying, but my cheeks are also wet with the start of rain.

Five minutes to cry, Honor.

I'm way past five minutes. I pluck some wildflowers from along the stone wall, and I set them to rest on the little headstone. Gracie and Rusty never even crossed the Pennsylvania state line. I haven't broken the Stone curse, either. I'm also doomed to die here, probably. It's a thought that feels too big and frightening.

My phone pings. Him.

> You deserve a prince. Not me. Don't ever
> forget that.

I blow out my lips in frustration. How can Strike not realize he *is* the prince? I think about how he moved on Troy so quickly, with such brash, sure, whiplash force. He would have taken Troy down without a second thought. For me.

No other man has ever made me ache like this. I always assumed I was incapable of those sorts of feelings. And now here I stand, imbalanced, overwhelmed, my whole body on fire.

So, fine. Strike doesn't want to drag me down into whatever

his shit is. I don't want to drag him down into mine. But we were fated to meet.

Even if, perhaps, we were also fated to fail.

The rain is a downpour by the time I've jogged back to the apartment, no little Keep at the window to greet me.

I open my pantry to find a pile of ramen blocks, like a tidy stack of lonely nights waiting for me.

But when I put the pot on to boil, I just stand there, a package in my hand. *Are you really going to spend another night alone on the couch in your sweaty jogging clothes, eating another ninety-nine-cent dinner, listening to the rain, and playing the world's tiniest violin?* Gracie asks. *Girl, take charge!*

But how?

I get that Strike is so desperate to keep me from his real self that he's chosen exile for us both instead. But should I accept it, too? Am I really resigned to this broken goodbye without a fight? Will I let this one golden chance at happiness slip out of my grasp because I doubt my own worth?

Whether Gracie was making her own small-batch bath salts and sugar scrubs for the store or spending her weekends hiking mountains or working for the animal rescue, she always knew that I encouraged her to chase her own star, to run her own life.

It's too late for poor Gracie. But maybe not for me.

I put the package of ramen back in the cupboard.

And I know exactly what I'm going to do next.

THIRTY-SIX

HONOR

Now

I stand at Strike's front door, holding a casserole dish in my hands, protected by a pair of blue-checkered oven mitts, brand-new from the shop. I've showered and changed into a cropped T-shirt and jeans, and I'm hoping I give off an I-was-just-in-the-neighborhood vibe.

Who the fuck am I kidding?

I'm wearing my only matching bra-and-panties set, delicate scalloped lace in soft pastel blue. I'm holding a likely terrible but extremely earnest attempt at lasagna. I took an Uber across town.

I was explicitly told to stay away.

There's nothing casual about this visit.

A minute passes, then two. I peer into the eye of his Ring doorbell. Getting through the front gate was no problem—all Dark Matter employees are given the code after we sign the non-disclosure agreement—but this door is usually locked during normal working hours.

It didn't occur to me that Strike might not be home.

Oh shit. I don't know what I'm doing. Nothing and everything has changed. Am I here to beg for him to let me get back to work? To put the last few days behind us and start fresh?

Am I here to tell him that nothing else matters but him and me?

Mostly you're here to bang your boss, you sly little minx, teases Gracie in my head. *Seducing your superior? Pretty scandalous, Sunday!*

She's right, of course. But I'm done worrying that I work for Strike. The idea that I might not get to see him has only intensified my feelings for him. It's like he unlocked something in me that I never knew was there.

Now I can't be sated until I see him again.

But I'm getting nervous out here. So exposed that I check over my shoulder a couple of times, though I doubt Troy would dare mess with me. Not this week. I'd be surprised if he wasn't immobilized by at least a cracked pelvis.

But you never know.

It's dark, and the street is quiet. I guess that's part of being rich—your life is never polluted by other people's noise. For a moment, I consider turning around and calling another Uber. Pretending this never happened. I'm being irresponsible. Strike doesn't need to know I was ever here. Unless he watches his Ring home-security video later? Fuck.

You deserve a prince. Not me.

How can Strike see himself like that? He's gone out of his way to protect me at every opportunity. Monsters don't do that.

And I'm not inventing our chemistry. I can't be.

I've changed my mind. Be brave, Sunday. Be reckless, even.

Gracie's voice. And mine. A duet.

I gather my courage and press the doorbell again.

When I hear footsteps, my stomach drops. Is it too late to run?

Then the door opens, and he's standing in front of me, framed by the door, the house's dark interior vast—almost menacing—behind him.

"Hi! I brought you dinner." I have no idea where this new confidence comes from. Maybe knowing that not even Keeper is waiting for me at home. That other than Jo, I am one hundred percent alone in this world except for this beautiful stranger in front of me.

His jaw drops; he looks truly surprised. "Honor?" He moves slightly into the light over the doorway. He's in a well-worn UPenn T-shirt and sweatpants, and he looks like he's just stepped out of the shower. I notice a long vertical scrape etched down his neck, like he's been scratched by an angry cat. As clean and scrubbed as he looks, I sense a wildness in his eyes, like a man who's just come back from the woods—I don't know what to make of it.

"I have homemade lasagna," I blurt, my words rushing to get out. "I cooked it just for you and I hope it's perfect. I always make it on Gracie's birthday. It's a recipe from a neighbor we had growing up. Gracie liked sprinkles on top—which doesn't really make it taste any better; it was a Gracie thing, to make everything into a party—but I didn't add sprinkles to this. I mean, what I'm trying to say is, sprinkles or no sprinkles, I wanted to see you." I press my lips together. To stop more silly words from spilling out of my mouth.

"You shouldn't be here." His tone is a growl, dark, borderline angry. He is talking in all capital letters. "I was very clear that you should stay away from me."

"No," I say, moving past him into the house even though my heart is beating like a rabbit and my impulse is to turn and run. I've got to see this through. Ride this small wave of courage.

"Your warning was bullshit and you know it, Strike Madden. It's time to stop passing notes like high schoolers."

"Honor, wait . . ." he says, sidestepping me, blocking my path to the kitchen. "This is a bad time."

"Oh." I stop, unsure. A bad time? Is there another woman in there? "Okay, well . . . if you're working, take a break." I falter. "You need to eat."

"I'm not working. I . . . You should go."

"I'm not going anywhere." There's no woman. No way. I'm who he wants. I'm who he thinks about. Even if a tiny voice niggles me—*is Kate here?*—I have to bet on myself. I lift my chin and grip my confidence with both hands.

"No?" His lips curve with the start of a smile. Maybe he's amused by my new assertiveness, but now I feel my hold strengthen—here's the real Strike.

"Nope." The casserole dish is starting to feel as heavy as a kettlebell, and I am second-guessing not only my presence here but also TJ's mom's lasagna. It's entirely possible this recipe will taste like baked glue sticks to a man who employs a full-time private chef. "Strike, I—"

"Honor, listen—"

As we each move an inch toward each other, the dish suddenly slips from my mitts and goes crashing down, creating an instant crime scene in a slop of bloodred sauce that splatters everywhere. Noodles shimmy like thick, wet worms, rolling in all different directions over the silk carpet.

"Oh, shit!" I drop to my hands and knees, using the mitts to wipe up the floor, but all I'm doing is widening the spread of red slime.

"Hey, hey, hey. It's no problem." When Strike reaches down

and pulls me to my feet, I notice that his hand is wrapped in gauze. "We'll deal with it later. And you know what? You win. Let's eat. Your lasagna did—somewhat dramatically—remind me that I haven't eaten anything all day." He allows a small laugh; it's like a splash of whiskey, warm and strong, a salve with a kick to it. "Sometimes I can be abrupt. I apologize," he says. "But, yeah, let's behave like adults and share this meal—ah, such that it is— that you took all this trouble to make."

I'm nodding. "Yes, that's all I—"

"And then you'll need to go." His words are as sharp as any blade on his knife rack. I can only nod; I'm covered in sauce, and I've ruined his carpet, which feels pretty foolish. I don't have much bargaining power.

He scoops the dish from the floor and pivots, leaving me to follow him down the hall, around the corner, and down a short flight of stairs into his private, garden-level kitchen.

It's not until he tosses me a roll of paper towels that I realize just how much of the dinner has landed on me. My cropped T-shirt is ruined. I no longer look cute and casual and festive. I look like a toddler after a big, messy meal.

I glance around. Something's up. Last time I was here, this kitchen was so welcoming, but tonight it feels clinical and cold. I'm suddenly aware of the stinging odor of bleach, and that drop cloths have been placed over the island, the booth, the oven, and the sinks.

"What happened here?" I ask, cupping my nose with my hands—the bleach is industrial-strength. "What'd I miss?"

"First of the month, I get the staff to do a thorough disinfection and cleaning. Old habit." He shrugs.

"Right." Then I say, "Today's not the first of the month."

His brow knits. "I didn't mean it literally. They do a monthly super-clean. What can I say? I run a tight ship."

He sounds both completely convincing and somewhat guarded. And now I feel bad again about that mess I made of the foyer. His staff will be cleaning up that sauce forever.

Strike pops the dish in the oven to reheat it and then snaps off the various drop cloths. Opens the window to clear the smell.

The booth is revealed with its candles and cushions and has me tingling with adrenaline—okay, maybe this night is not going the way I planned, but I did it! I'm here. For now. I sit and watch, wiping traces of sauce from my shirt and jeans as Strike briskly restores order. He tucks the drop cloths into the pantry and rearranges his magnetic knife rack with a few that were in his sink. He washes his hands with precision, getting under each fingernail and scrubbing carefully.

I look around at the spotless setting, the thorough cleanliness, and wonder if Strike has a little bit of OCD. It's a thought that makes my heart squeeze tighter. I like seeing evidence of Strike's occasional imperfections, especially when I'm in such awe of his power as the head of a vast international corporation. And, of course, as someone who has rescued me more than any knight in shining armor ever could.

Strike disappears for a moment and returns with a bottle of red and a fresh white T-shirt for me that he leaves folded on the table. "There's a bathroom down the hall if you want to change," he says. I nod in thanks. Strike tells Alexa to play SM Favorites and pulls out heavy plates that are as gray as his eyes, along with some napkins and utensils.

I feel a light ripple of déjà vu. Another dinner in Strike's private sanctum, only this time I'm not sobbing over Keep.

And this time gummies won't abruptly end the evening.

I take the place settings to arrange on the table as Strike busies himself with the wine opener. Despite the obvious tension between us, for a few moments we fall into a rhythm, somewhere between an electric first date and our natural ease as colleagues at DME.

"Gracie and I had this game we called Normal," I say, "where we'd live in this soft, kind, easy world, and we'd pretend the plastic plates were ceramic and the paper napkins were cloth. She'd say to me, 'One day, Sunday, we'll live in a house where everything feels like someone picked it out.'"

"Sunday?" He lifts an eyebrow.

"My middle name."

"That's beautiful. Is there a story behind that?"

I suck in my breath and then play it off as if I've never imagined this moment, though it's so delicious, I want to capture it in every way I can.

"I was born two minutes after midnight on Sunday, and three minutes and twenty-seven seconds after Gracie. The nurse named me."

"The *nurse*?"

"My mom didn't know she was having twins until the delivery, and so she'd picked out only one name, Grace Marie."

Strike raises an eyebrow. "How did your mom possibly miss the memo that she was carrying twins?"

"Because she didn't see a doctor until she was in labor. None of us saw doctors when I was growing up." I shrug. "My parents were a little backwoods."

"Well, I've never met another Honor. Nor a Sunday. Both suit you, Honor Sunday." He says my name with such reverence that I suddenly grasp, all at once, that that's why I'm here. No one has ever looked at me the way he does. No one has ever taken my name and turned it into a prayer.

Our unspoken thoughts are a force field.

"I've always loved my name—and Gracie loved hers. But we didn't grow up with the kind of parents who put any thought into things like names or clothes or if our nails and hair were cut. My dad was so controlling over my mother, and day by day, month by month over the years, he sort of broke her spirit. She loved him so much, but her love was a weakness. We kids were collateral damage, and we ended up mostly raising ourselves."

"That's how you learned to care," says Strike. "By caring for each other."

"I guess. I did my best with Gracie," I say. "But in the end, not having our parents' love—it ruined something in her. She couldn't dream any bigger than Troy. She couldn't find the worth in herself."

"You're her identical twin—and you're nothing like that. I see it in your art every day," he says, looking at me with something that feels like hunger. "You've got so much sparkle and life, so much fight."

"Listen to you, being so complimentary," I say, and then, more seriously, I add, "I want to be everything Gracie couldn't be. While I'm still here, she's still here, you know? I want to live for us both."

"You never should have lost her," says Strike, his voice hard. "You'd already lost so much."

Our eyes meet, and time stands still as we both stare at each other, transfixed. I chew my bottom lip, feeling a rush of antici-pation as I feel Strike study me with unfiltered intensity. His pupils are as dark as a lynx's, his jaw set. If I spoke every thought in my head—but no. I'm not ready yet. I'm here, but I'm scared there will be no going back, so I take a beat, change the subject.

"What did you do today?" I ask. Strike's tendency to up and disappear is a favorite watercooler conversation at DME, and I'm sure today was more of the same. I've heard every guess from mastering fighter pilot training in Pensacola to a covert life as a CIA operative.

Who knows? It's not the wildest theory. Maybe he *is* a spy.

"Nope," he says.

"Nope, what?"

"Nope, we're not going to do that," Strike says. "We both know you didn't come here to chat about what I did or where I was today or middle names or lasagna recipes. We're not here to play . . . Normal." He allows a trace of a smile. "Tell me why you came here."

"Because. You." I clear my throat. Try to form a full sentence. "Because I wanted to see you. *Needed* to see you."

"I'm not good enough for you, Honor." He says it like it's a fact. No room for disagreement. "I love what I recognize of myself in your art. But we both know that's not the whole picture."

"Then show me," I say. "Show me the whole picture."

He shakes his head. "It's not possible. And this can't go any further with us. Not when I'm your boss."

I shrug like his being my boss doesn't really matter to me. Though of course it does. It's just that this—the lightning magnetism zipping back and forth between us—matters more now. I want *him* more.

"You might be my boss, Strike," I say quietly, "but we both know you're not always in charge."

At that, he looks surprised, but he doesn't deny it. Doesn't move. I can feel the tension coming off his body. I can sense the wild thoughts in his head.

"Listen, I can't deny it—I love to see you. You enchant me. Which is also the whole fucking problem. After we eat, you really will need to leave," Strike says. "This has gone way too far."

We are both motionless, eyes locked.

I nod even as I feel my lips tremble. I fight against the tears of frustration that spring to my eyes. *Don't cry, Honor.* When I press the palm of my hand against my mouth, this motion seems to release Strike from whatever had him in its grip.

"No, no. Don't," he says, as he quickly takes my hand from my face, turning it upward and bringing it swiftly to his lips, his nostrils flaring. As if the scent of my skin has briefly drugged his senses. As if he is utterly helpless to it. When he sees my scars, those raised, welted moons, his expression gentles, and he softly brushes the lightest, gentlest kiss there—and then, with fervent urgency, his tongue darts across my skin right in that damaged and sensitive place where his lips just touched.

I inhale sharply.

Even as I'm shocked by the surprise of this intimate contact, his tongue alone is a heady sensory overload.

This kiss is his confession.

Just as my fate is in Strike's hands, now I know his fate is in mine. I'm already submitting to it: a deep-down, dragging-under pull of desire low in my stomach that I have no power to fight. My heart races, and my body shivers to the bone. We've been dancing around each other for far too long, moths to each other's flames.

But now it is happening.

With this one brush of his lips to my palm, Strike has lit the match and all but admitted that I'm right. That he is not, in fact, in control of what happens tonight.

"You know what? You need to change—now," he says, and there is no room for argument. "I brought you a fresh T-shirt. Take that one off."

He's issuing a challenge. I see his chest move up and down as he breathes deep, in and out.

"Here?"

"Yes."

I nod. Challenge accepted, even though I'm quaking—but if Strike wants to hold on to some of his precious control, fine.

I'm brave enough to play. I came here, after all.

I lift the bottom edge of my sauce-spattered T-shirt, pull it over my head, drop it on the pristine floor. Now I'm standing in front of him, shivering in my bra and my jeans. Strike's gaze is direct, taking in the rosy pink of my nipples, all too visible through the lacy pattern.

I make sure to position myself so that I'm facing him directly. Even if I'm feeling my boldest self tonight, I also feel shy, and I want to be careful that every bit of me isn't revealed and exposed to Strike just yet.

He is fully absorbed, drinking me in. And yet he makes no move. I take the fresh white T-shirt and pull it over my head. It's one of Strike's, and it smells like him, too. It envelops me, loose and light. My eyes flutter closed.

"Jeans," he demands.

Startled, I look down. The T-shirt hits me mid-thigh. Skimpy, but I will be revealing no more of myself than what other women wear to bars and clubs on a Saturday night. I nod again. Tug off my jeans and step out of them. Kick them over to join my stained T-shirt in the soft heap on his pristine kitchen floor.

"Sit."

Obediently, I do so as Strike stands and crosses the room to pull the dish from the oven. I watch as he scoops a helping of lasagna into each of our pasta bowls. I know this man. He is reclaiming his domain, his control of this situation. "First, Honor Sunday, we eat." His smile is slow, quirking up the corner of his mouth. "And then . . . we'll see."

My stomach is roiling with nerves. Now that Strike has decided to cross this line, I feel that he's reasserting himself, deciding the rules.

Ha. There's no way in hell I can eat now.

But Strike does. Almost making a show of it. He enjoys his meal slowly, with deliberate ease. Reaching for the wine bottle and refilling his glass. Grating some extra Parmesan cheese over the lasagna. Adjusting the volume of the John Legend song that is piping in softly on surround sound.

But I know what Strike's doing—he's performing his control. He will keep me sitting here—shivering and nibbling the square of pasta that's speared on the end of my fork and feeling way too conscious of my nipples perked through the cotton of this thin white T-shirt—for as long as he likes.

First, we eat. And then . . . we'll see.

I can hardly dare to steal a glance at him.

Only minutes ago, Strike kissed my palm and ignited a white-hot fire between us. There is no going back from that moment; it puts us right at the edge of changing everything. My heart is skittering wildly.

"What happened?" I manage to ask, indicating his gauze-wrapped hand.

"This?" Strike sets down his fork and raises his arm as if he has to remember. "Ah, nothing. I box," he says. "With Axe."

That would explain his perfect physique, plus his comfort with beating someone to a pulp with a baseball bat. Axe, who I've seen around the office, looks like he'd be the perfect sparring partner for Strike. He's equally cut.

"Is boxing also how you got . . . that?" I ask, drawing a line with my finger down my own cheek at the place where Strike's is lacerated.

"Yup," he says with a flinty smile. He's taken his last bite, and now he leans back in his chair. "Delicious. I'm full. But you've hardly touched your food, Honor Sunday."

"Maybe later," I counter.

"Sometimes it's better to be left wanting more." He says this lightly, though his words send exquisite shivers down my spine.

But I won't let him control every move. I lean forward. "Can I ask you something?"

"Anything."

"Does the work we do ever affect you?"

In the silence, I let his eyes scrutinize me. "Affect me?" Strike tilts his head to the side, as if he doesn't know what I'm asking. "Affect me . . . how?"

I feel a flush come on. Because how could I not blush when he looks at me that way? His expression is intense, the same expression he gets whenever he's caged me with his arms to look over my drawings.

"You know what I mean. The pictures I draw. Do they . . . turn you on?" Brave Honor is back. Powerful, or at least testing my power.

Taking initiative. Wolf, not sheep.

Strike pushes his plate to the side, leans forward on his elbows, and captures me with the force of his gaze.

"They turn me on when they look like you," he says, his voice husky with want. His eyes are laser-focused. He's a seductive predator who has decided on his next conquest.

"They do?" I whisper. Strike nods slowly as he skims the edge of his tongue along his bottom lip. I feel the throb and heat between my legs as if that tongue has already found me.

"And the ones that look like you and me? Now, those . . ." Strike grips the table, almost unable to finish his sentence. "Those fucking kill me."

THIRTY-SEVEN

HONOR

Now

We move to the library, where Strike pours us both more wine. We're tucked into opposite ends of his leather couch, facing each other, continuing this performance, every moment on a razor's edge and every word weighted. Strike tells me about the *Whispering Wet Vines* presentation, and his plans for expanding the DME brand in Europe. I ask the appropriate questions. But we both know this is a kind of controlled, erotic foreplay. Just a glance at Strike's silhouette by the soft light of the single table lamp, and my mind goes dizzy. Occasionally, I cross and uncross my legs so he gets a flashing view of what I know he wants most.

Neither of us pounces, but I can feel the energy thrumming between us, immediate and fierce. The anticipation is only intensifying the pleasure. We are almost at the breaking point. I can hardly look at him; I swear I might come just from eye contact. When I move to set down my wineglass, my T-shirt rides an inch higher up my thigh, and I don't even attempt to tug it back down.

But this proves to be too much for him.

"You." Strike's voice is low, a growl of ownership. *You*—this word could mean *mine*. But it could also mean *now*. He leans forward and pulls at my T-shirt, bringing me roughly toward him. Inches from my face, he stops just short of kissing me. His proximity is magnetic and maddening and sets my body ablaze with longing. My lips part involuntarily, a silent plea.

Please, I think.

"Honor, please." Strike echoes my thought aloud, his breath in my mouth, his scent of woodsmoke making my head spin.

I look at him questioningly.

"Take it off."

Such a simple request, and yet—it's everything. Obediently, I slip out of his shirt and drop it next to me on the couch, but then as my shyness kicks in, I instinctively cross my arms in front of my chest.

"No, don't," he says. "I've thought of this moment so many times. You're as perfect as I knew you'd be. Let me look at you, Honor. Stand up. Let me see."

His voice is intoxicating, and I refuse to let my nervousness control my desire. This is all I want, too. Slowly, shyly, I rise to stand before him. I watch his face take in the view I am allowing him—my nipples at points, the lips of my pussy through the scrap of soft cotton and lace—until I'm blushing so furiously that I have to look away. And still I feel him zoning in on me so long and deeply, it's as if he intends to memorize me. For all I know, he is. I hear his breath, a creak of leather as he adjusts his body so that I am now centered between his legs.

"You are so incredibly gorgeous," he whispers. "You planted a craving in me, Honor Stone. I've wanted to do this ever since the first unforgettable night when I met you. Countless times I've imagined you this way. Right here, right in this room."

Suddenly I feel so dizzy with it all—Strike's power and precision, the luxurious beauty of his library, and my own sense of being Strike Madden's most coveted prize. His eyes rove my body, top to bottom and then back up again. I'm so disarmed and vulnerable that it's excruciating, and yet I'm also trembling with life.

With slow deliberation, Strike's hands move to cradle my ass, his fingers strong and sure, moving me even closer to him and angling my center toward his face. I gasp with surprise—gasp again, more sharply, at the first brush of his lips between my legs. As many times as I've dared to picture this moment, when I feel the heated contact of Strike's mouth through the fabric, it is far more shocking than anything I've imagined.

First, we eat . . . and then . . . My eyes flutter closed.

Strike's very first kisses are soft and warm; his closed mouth is almost chaste. The tease of it all and his unrelenting restraint begin winding me up into a coiled spring. My fantasies could never conjure this. It's all far too real, too intense—and yet when his lips finally do part, it's only to print the warmth of his breath on me. His confidence has never been more obvious. I sense his focused desire to turn up my pleasure incrementally, notch by notch, so that the promise of release will deliver me an almost unbearable sweetness of surrender.

He is taking his time, as only Strike could, with his characteristic meticulous mastery.

In the past, I've been rubbed and clumsily fingered, but anytime a boyfriend ever went down on me, I couldn't help but feel that we were just rushing through some appetizers. Tonight is nothing like that. My heart is pounding as I realize that Strike is planning to devour me.

When I feel the specific pressure of his tongue, I whimper. It feels so good, so expert, but at first Strike uses his power sparingly, pressing his tongue's tip against the lace, letting the fabric soften, creating gentle friction. Different sensations of heat and wet as it rubs against me. Flattening his tongue, he pulses it just briefly, a butterfly kiss to the clit, bringing me to a moment of such exquisitely pure ecstasy that I cry out—the notch tweaked up yet higher. I hear my own breath, ragged in my throat as Strike now centers his mouth over my pussy and begins the slow drag of his full tongue, which is more intense than I ever could have anticipated.

My cheeks burn as my back arches and my fingers grip handfuls of Strike's thick dark hair to hold my balance, bringing him closer, cinching his connection. I am close and getting closer with every slow pulse.

When he stops—maddeningly, teasingly, and with that mindbendingly precise timing—to look up at me, my wordless gasp is one of shock.

Nooo. Don't stop. Don't stop, don't stop, don't stop.

"So fucking beautiful, Honor," he says, his words an animal growl. He rises effortlessly from the couch to a stand, his body pressing against me as his mouth finds mine, his kiss hungry. When I feel the pressure of his erection, strong and stiff and enormous, I realize with a nervous tingle that I might be in way over my head, but it's much too late to go back now. His mouth leaves mine to trail gentler, cloud-soft kisses in a slow path down my throat, then continues its journey to each shoulder as his hand traces the curve of my ass.

I suddenly remember a drawing I made that depicted exactly this scene, and now I feel wildly exposed. Strike knows exactly what I like, what I want, what I crave—because he's seen it. I've drawn this fantasy. The anticipation is intoxicating.

Strike's fingers blaze their own path, grazing my navel and then lightly trailing from hip bone to hip bone. My moan is mostly breath as Strike hooks my panties to the side and begins slowly tracing my wet, velvety folds before inserting that same finger, his thumb moving in gentle rhythm over my clit, all the while staring down at me, his eyes holding me in place. "You know how much I want this. I have wanted you for so long. What do you want?"

The words are out of my mouth before I even have time to think them through.

"I want to fuck you in your bed," I say.

THIRTY-EIGHT

STRIKE

Now

Honor Stone is my own fault.

That light, honeysuckle-clean scent of her skin has tortured me from the moment I met her. And yet I let her in. Not only into DME but also into my private rooms, my sanctuary. I never in a million years could have predicted that I'd sense her everywhere now—even when she's not here. Even when it makes no sense. Even when I've got to be imagining that lightest, sweetest whiff of her presence around every corner or—far too often—in my dreams.

I am addicted to it.

I'd have to burn down my own house to get rid of it.

I've never wanted a woman as badly as I do this one—from the moment I let her inside my life, I knew I didn't stand a chance. I feel like a half-starved animal as I take her to my bedroom. It's been attended to and arranged, with a low fire crackling in the fireplace, the shades and curtains drawn. The candle on my night-stand casts the barest glow. I'd throw on all the lights right now if I thought it wouldn't scare her. My eyes do not want to miss a minute of this show.

If we are going to do this—and we are—I want to examine every dimple and freckle, every bend and swell and curve of Honor's beautiful body.

At the door, I lift her, and her legs quickly wrap around me. I remind myself to take things slow. Honor has always felt elusive—it is part of her allure that she feels impossible to grasp, and I don't want her running away like a frightened deer. I feed gentle kisses to her mouth and then move to lightly bite her shoulder.

Then I toss her onto the bed, and for a moment, I just look at my prize: my sweet, lovely Honor, splayed and blushing on my bed. My overwhelming desire is to touch and kiss and know every part of her body, to sink myself inside her, to pin and possess her with all the force and urgency inside me. I've felt it since the moment I laid eyes on her, and now it's an inferno, a storm, a roar in me that fully blocks out all my other thoughts. Honor Sunday, this surprising contradiction of a woman—as feisty as she is gentle, as spicy as she is sweet, as brave as she is delicate, as luscious as she is guarded—is all mine tonight.

I pull her toward me and then crouch over her, my thighs and arms locked on either side of her soft, creamy body. I trace kisses across her collarbone, drop my head, and take one round, firm breast between my lips, my tongue licking the nipple to a point, then shifting to the other. The soft, breathless noises that Honor makes are as utterly delicious as the warmth of her hard nipple in my mouth.

Slow, I remind myself, but my body isn't listening.

"I want you," she says.

As impossible as it is to believe, I'm even harder.

"How bad?"

"You know how bad," she says. "Please, Strike. What are you doing to me?" Her breath through her teeth is ragged, passionate.

"What we're doing is taking it slow, Firefly," I tell her. "No need to rush. We've got all the time in the world."

I can see how hard she's trying to slow herself down, to match my control, but then she bucks her hips to rub against the full length of me. Her body feels so peachy-soft, so ripe and ready, that I don't know how much longer I can control my slow pace. I want to devour her now, to fill her until she cries out.

"You make me crazy," I whisper as my tongue traces down the stem and contours of her neck.

The light from the candle flickers, throwing her face into and out of shadow. I kiss her lips again, and this time I let my body drop so she's pinned under my weight. I groan; it's intoxicating to feel all the butter-soft warmth of her skin. When my fingers brush the inside of her thigh, then lightly touch the wetness between her legs, she arches, and I know that I'm tormenting her with my touch.

"The fucking scent of you," I whisper, burying my nose in her neck. "Every time you walk by me in the office, I get rock hard. It's fucking absurd what you do to me. But I think I've been patient enough."

She whimpers as I slide a finger into her tight wetness in anticipation of what's to come; when I kick off my shoes, I hear something knock over—a book, I think. Honor's own fingers are pulling at the drawstring of my sweatpants, and I shimmy her out of her soaked panties as fast as I can while I press my mouth to hers, then lift my face so that I'm staring at her. Our bodies are as close as they've ever been, and the knowledge fills me with heavy, liquid desire.

I need everything now. It's a roar through my body. I'm so swollen I ache—and yet I also want to savor every moment.

Then her eyes fly open. And everything changes.

"Something's burning!" Her voice emanates a primal fear, conveying a depth of terror that I've never heard from her before.

I glance over. The candle. "Aw, shit—hang tight." I leap from the bed to my feet and grab the carafe of water on my nightstand. I must have kicked over the candle, not a book, and now tiny campfire flames are eating the thin silk of my antique Turkish carpet. It takes fewer than five seconds to put the thing out—no big deal—but the moment I return to Honor, she's a changed being, way over on the far side of the bed as if the fire might be growing instead of tamped out, cringing and shrinking.

"I put it out," I say helplessly. "There's nothing to be afraid of."

But still she keeps moving away from me, leaving the bed to cower in the corner, her shoulders up, her head ducked. She's whimpering, speaking in soft, indecipherable, panicked phrases— I hear the words "everywhere," "fire," and "it's all burning"—as she wraps her hands around her knees, hyperventilating.

It's obvious PTSD. I saw it all the time in the military.

I walk toward her carefully. My hands in the air, palms out, as if approaching a wounded animal. If she's reliving her trauma in some sort of an acute paroxysm, I don't want to startle her.

"Honor, baby—it's fine. No fire. Hey. We're all good. You're safe." Though it probably doesn't help the dynamic that I'm standing, fully dressed, while she's practically naked and looks like a child who's been sent to the corner. Honor seems to be able to hear me, as if from a distance, as she rubs at her arms like her skin is burning. "No danger here," I assure her. "Accidents happen."

She mumbles something to the effect of "I'm fine."

But she's obviously miles away from fine.

"Don't cry." I keep my voice gentle, hoping that my words soothe her and help get her back to reality. Sometimes these psychic breaks just need to run their course. It pains me to see the tears streaming down Honor's face in rivulets. I kneel before her, brush my thumbs to her cheeks to stop the tears.

Fuck, I hate seeing her like this.

And I hate being powerless to stop it. "Let me get you a blanket."

She nods, barely. I grab the throw from the bottom of the bed, then quickly wrap it around her body, tucking it tight so that she feels secure.

"Honor. You're safe. It was nothing," I say, my voice calmly commanding. I, too, have slipped into some dark places. I, too, know how easy it is for the world to trip a trauma response.

When Honor nods again, I think she's within reach. The horror of her memories is seeping out of her; she's gradually resurfacing, her breath slowed, her tears stopped. I scoop her up, carry her back to the bed, and hold her tight in my arms. She turns and buries her face in my neck as I stroke her hair.

"You're okay, baby. I've got you," I murmur. I can sense her focusing on that goddamn cut on my neck, tracing it with her finger. I fight the instinct to flinch. The slice is fresh and it hurts like hell, but she doesn't need to know that. I can't believe I let that piece of shit get close to me—a lapse in judgment on my part, and a moment that's still surprising and disconcerting for me. My work is usually so clean.

"I have a thing with fire," she murmurs quietly.

"Yeah, next time, no open flames."

At the words *next time*, Honor tightens her arms around me a little. As if in agreement. But she doesn't elaborate on her fear of fire. Fine by me. We're both entitled to our difficult secrets.

Fuck knows I've got mine.

I kiss the top of her head and gently release her.

"Be right back." I head for my walk-in closet and return with one of my cashmere sweatsuits—a comfort and luxury I indulge in by having a set in every one of my preferred colors.

"This feels incredible," she says once she's wriggled into my clothes, swimming in them like a tiny boat adrift in a sea of cashmere. "Thank you." Even tearstained and red-nosed, Honor wrapped up in my pajamas might be the cutest thing I've ever seen. I roll cuffs for her wrists and ankles before I pull her into my lap again so that her back is resting against my chest.

"This is so nice," she says softly. "I could stay here awhile . . ."

"Of course." I kiss my way down her neck—I'm no longer trying to seduce her, only to offer comfort and distract her from her fears—and I watch as her eyes flutter closed, contentment soon replacing her skittishness.

I turn to her mouth and catch her bottom lip with my teeth, and she makes the sexiest little sound. She's into it.

I'm unhurried, glad to start again. There's no urgency; we've got all night. From the other side of the room, Honor's phone buzzes, but she ignores the ring. She shifts toward me, giving me better access, her mouth now hungry on mine. I angle myself so that she feels me hard against her, and suddenly I don't feel like taking it slow.

But the phone goes off once more. It seems somehow insistent this time. Fuck. I try to block out the noise. The ringing stops, only to begin five seconds later, and this time Honor breaks our kiss with a sigh of frustration.

"I think—" she whispers.

"Nah, let it go," I say, pulling back. I tap her nose with my finger. "They'll get the message." *We need more time.*

Ping, ping, ping, ping.

"Don't answer it," I say.

"Just let me . . . it'll only take . . ." She breaks free and crosses the room, and I admire the curve of her round ass all giftwrapped in cashmere.

"I'm blowing up," she jokes, and then takes out her phone.

I keep my face inscrutable, impassive. My thoughts are a tornado, but of course Honor doesn't hear any of them. She frowns at the screen, and then—*fuck*—up at me. Then back at the screen. "Oh my God," she whispers, and my heart bottoms out. "Oh God."

And then I watch as she sinks to the floor.

THIRTY-NINE

HONOR

Now

I blink at the words, but I can't make sense of them.

TROY WAS KILLED CALL ME

My skin is ice. I read the sentence over and over.

TROY WAS KILLED CALL ME

I'm conscious of Strike watching me and equally conscious of the fact that I'm slumped to my knees on his carpet. In his bedroom. In his home.

What happened?

They're saying it was brutal. A 🔪 to the neck or something? They're hinting he owed 💰 for some gambling debts??? It's all over the 📰 I am freaked out

"What's up?" asks Strike abruptly from bed. "Who're you texting with?"

I turn to look at him.

"It's Jo. Troy Simpson was murdered." My voice is a whisper. Shocked by this news, I feel nauseated—and yet, at the same time, a lightness washes over me, a thousand white-hot skin-pricking stars lighting up my skin.

This is—yes, a very complicated relief.

Troy Simpson cannot hurt me anymore.

Strike hasn't moved. When I look at him, his expression doesn't change. He's as hungry for me as he was before the call came in.

As if nothing has happened.

I don't see even a glimmer of surprise.

I want him to say something. Anything. The word *murder* echoes in my mind. I'm struggling to be present in this moment with Strike, and yet tonight has been overwhelming, and my mind and body are exhausted. It's too much to handle. I can feel myself shutting down.

"I need to go home," I tell him.

Disappointment flicks across his face, but Strike seems to get it. With a nod, he moves into efficiency mode, texting Max and getting me downstairs and out the door in a way that feels both protective and careful.

"Stay," he says once we're outside. "I can set up the guest room so you have your own space."

I shake my head. I can't get a handle on my words.

"I'm sorry to be leaving you like this," I say.

"You don't have to be sorry. It's . . . a lot."

My heart skips a beat as his lips meet mine, but the spark has changed. I can feel his mind probing mine for all the thoughts locked inside, but I'm afraid of what he might find.

Murder.

Minutes later, waiting for Max to drive around with the SUV, I'm still reeling, intently chewing the edge of a cuticle to keep from having to engage in any talk. Even the air feels different, the summer heat a little thicker and more brutal since I first arrived.

"I'll check in with you tomorrow," Strike says gently.

"Thanks. It's just . . . I want to be in my sister's room tonight," I say.

"There's a way to see this as good news, Honor," he says softly as the car glides up. He opens the back door and I get in. "Troy Simpson was evil. In the end, it's one less monster in the world. That's what matters, right?"

I nod. Right. Of course. But my eyes sting, and as I rummage for the packet of Kleenex in my bag, I feel my can of Mace. Except now I don't need protection—or do I? I'm rushed with a sense of monsters hiding in every dark corner.

"You're sure you're okay to be alone?" he asks one last time.

"Yeah, I'll be fine."

Troy is gone. That's real. I could get out of this car and return to the house with Strike. Lose myself in his arms. Shake off everything until tomorrow. I could take a gummy, even, and let the world be a little floatier. Hell, I have a whole tin.

But no. I won't do that. Something in me needs to leave this house.

Strike wants to say more. Maybe I do, too. But I don't trust the words I'd use. The car pulls out and away. I stare out at the black nothing of the interstate whipping past, and I hear myself ask Max to take me to Jo's instead of home.

As if I'm making an impulsive decision.

As if I hadn't been planning that all along.

Gracie used to say I was too quick to see the worst in others. That I was born suspicious.

But if growing up with parents like mine taught me anything, it's that not everyone deserves the benefit of the doubt. Most people don't like to believe there is evil in the world. That is another privilege I've never been afforded.

I've looked evil in the eye. I've watched evil burn.

I don't want to go home—to my lonely apartment, with my kitchen-window view of Keeper's little grave and my twin sister's closed bedroom door. And I didn't want to stay with Strike, either. He feels so fundamentally unknowable right now. What lies behind his calm, controlled facade?

"Of course you can hang with me," Josie said when I made the call, quietly, from Strike's bathroom after she texted me. I locked the door, ran the water—I didn't know what to think.

I didn't explain myself to Strike when I left. How do you say *You turn me on and terrify me in equal measure*? How do you say *I am feeling too much to be here*? How do you say *Can I ask you something, even when I really don't want to hear the answer*?

The garage apartment is at the back of Jo's mom and stepdad's house—a cranky couple I've only met once, but that was enough for me. Jo, who has a nice word to say for just about everyone, has never said anything to me about her parents. What I do know is that she'd even marry Bryan to change her situation.

Still, her apartment is pretty cute, with vinyl records glued on the wall, and every flat surface—desk, dresser, bookshelf—devoted to Jo's bedazzled knickknacks, dream catchers, and crystals. As soon as she opens the door for me, we lock in a fierce hug. We are at the end of Troy Simpson's reign of terror. We are free.

But when Jo pulls back to look at me, she sees something else in my expression. "Cheetos Christ, Honor! You look like death yourself."

"Yeah, it's been . . . a lot." I collapse on her pink-checkered couch, and she grabs me a can of Malibu peach rum punch from her mini-fridge.

"I mean, it's probably super triggering," she says. "Though it's not *all* bad," she adds, studying me. "That piece of shit is dead."

"The shitpocalypse did happen," I say, trying to match her mood.

"Right? I mean, this is a celebration zone."

"I know, I know," I say. "Maybe it's just that my exhaustion is finally catching up now that this battle is over."

She nods. "It's surreal. When I heard, I got goose bumps—and they haven't left." She shows me the raised skin on her arm, and then she reaches her Malibu can toward mine. "But it's justice for Gracie, that's the big thing. And even little Keep. We've been through a lot, and now we're on the other side of it. Cheers!"

"Cheers," I say quietly, and we clink drinks.

Jo finds a stash of Slim Jims in her desk drawer, peels off three, then throws me the pack. "Bryan's so relieved. He was always a little freaked out about the whole thing—especially when Troy started visiting after Gracie was gone." Fear briefly takes hold of Jo's face. "He liked the baseball bat story. He was like, 'Yo, Honor's boss is a beast.'" Jo does her best impression of Bryan, which always makes me laugh, because she sounds exactly like him— douchey bro with a slight sinus condition.

"Where's Bryan tonight?" I ask.

"Out with the boys." Jo uses her back teeth to pull off the end of her beef jerky. "God, the more I think about it, the more I want to throw a goddamn parade. That asshole scared the living crap out of us for months. Actually, if you count when he was dating Gracie, entire years. Now he's gone forever."

"Yes, but . . ." But it's not like Troy fell off a ladder or crashed his truck. Murder is different. Why does violence endlessly circle my life like something that I can't seem to help attracting? I exhale; my breath catches.

"Hey, hey." Jo puts down her snack and leans forward to take my hands in hers, and she stares deeply into my eyes with an exaggerated palm-reader expression. "Girl, what's up with those cashmere sweats?"

I smile. "Borrowed."

She strokes a finger up and down the baby's-cheek softness of the sleeve. "Supersized and super luxe," she says. Her eyes narrow. "Where've you been tonight?"

"No place special." My heart starts pounding. I examine my fingers. There's a dot of lasagna sauce under my pinkie nail. It looks like blood.

"You're doing that thing with your face when you want to tell me something and don't know how," says Jo. "I'm here to listen. But whatever. On your own time." She picks up her phone. "Bryan's ETA is forty minutes."

I nod. She's right. I want so badly to tell her, but I can't. I can't make myself say it out loud. My mind replays Strike's blank reaction to Troy's death.

The bandages on Strike's knuckles.

The stinging scent of cleaning bleach in his kitchen.

That fresh, serrated cut down his neck.

His meticulous handwashing.

Something was up with him tonight, too. Something that, in hindsight, feels ominous. The wild hunger in his eyes when he opened the door and saw me. When he put his mouth on my scarred palm, I knew that tonight, the hunger of his desire for me outweighed his caution.

Jo is staring at me. "Don't tell me."

"Don't tell you what?"

"That's got to be Mr. Baseball Bat's very own cashmere set, right?"

I'm startled. "Don't call him that."

It's obvious from my face that she's guessed right. But Jo looks worried, and I can feel her placing her thoughts carefully, the way she arranges the shop's display window. "Look, Honor, I've been around long enough to know that Shelton boys—they aren't exactly great candidates. You float above so much of their shit. Gracie never played it safe, but she never questioned anything, either. The thing is, as her twin, maybe it left you having to question everything."

I nod. "That's probably true. And your point is . . . ?"

"My point is, Strike is about as far from a Shelton boy as it gets. He's so mysterious. He's crazy intimidating. He also sees how special you are—I could tell the minute he came into the shop that day. He was full-on hypnotized by you. But . . ." Jo blows a breath through her lips. "But he comes with a whole other set of question marks, right? That afternoon, the way he attacked Troy." She wraps her arms around her body. "That look in his eye. He was like something from a sci-fi movie. Like, he didn't even feel human."

I take a very large sip of my drink. My stomach gnaws with anxiety. "We both know Troy was a huge danger to us. Strike knew it, too. He knew what he was doing that day."

"Okay," says Jo. "But he's also your boss. So, are you seeing him? Like, personally? 'Cause that cashmere makes me think you're in pretty deep."

I shake my head. "No, of course not. And he's a good boss. He's brilliant, and he holds my work to such high standards, and I'm learning a ton—which is all I ever wanted from any job. I'm only in these sweats because I was working late, and I spilled some lasagna—Strike wouldn't think twice about lending out some clothes."

"So that's probably fine," says Jo doubtfully. "As long as you trust him, I'm all for it. Your boss with wardrobe benefits."

"Jo!" I find one of her innumerable shaggy pillows—the kind that remind me of tiny, pastel circus dogs—and hurl it at her.

She ducks, but it hits her anyway. "Well, you have to admit, Strike Madden is not exactly till-death-do-us-part material. And Bryan's always saying a local girl makes the best kind of wife because she . . ." But once Jo mentions Bryan's name, I completely tune her out.

A whole other set of question marks.

Didn't even feel human.

I wish I hadn't had a single drink tonight. My thoughts are too muddy. I put down my can.

No. Jo's being ridiculous. I'm being ridiculous. The man who just wrapped me in a blanket is not the sort of person who could extinguish another person's soul. But Jo's also right—my whole entire life here, I've never connected to anyone. It wasn't until I met Strike Madden that I realized how totally shut down I've felt, from as far back as grade school. Like I was just put here to be Gracie's guardian angel, her chaperone, and the voice of reason she mostly ignored.

Not that I could save her in the end.

But Strike has unlocked something in me. A private self I didn't even know I had. I've been so used to playing the introvert.

Who he is matters so much less than who he is *for me.*

When Jo takes a call from Bryan, I pull out my own phone. Dash off the text before I chicken out.

Please. Tell me you had nothing to do with it.

Clenched, silent, I watch the three dots bounce and pause, bounce and pause.

Then, nothing.

He is not answering me.

Answer me, goddamn it.

My dread and suspicion churn together. He needs to answer me.

Nothing.

"Ugh, turns out Bryan's not coming home tonight," says Jo when she gets off the call. "He's doing some trades with his fantasy NHL team and crashing at a friend's. He's so serious about it, you'd think it was a real job." She looks at me. "You good, Honor?"

"Just tired," I answer. "Long night. Hey, could you give me a lift home?"

"Yeah, sure." She stands and grabs her keys.

I wait until I'm in my apartment before I type out a new text with shaking hands.

Prince AND monster. Maybe you're both.

This time he writes back immediately.

Maybe I am.

FORTY

HONOR

Then
(Age 13)

"Rusty!" Gracie calls as we search our small house for him. Daddy's working overtime at the water tower, so it's a good night for Normal dinner at the table. Rusty does this sometimes. Disappears like vapor. His differences—the things Gracie and I love most about him—infuriate Daddy, who triggers Rusty's grunting and his twitches and tics. It's like Daddy winds him up as if to prove how unmanageable he is.

Rusty might be the hardest to raise, but none of us was wanted much. That's just the truth. Our parents are obsessed with each other. As kids, we've mostly been in the way, footnotes to their poisonous romance. So when Mama tells how Rusty came out backward and that's why he's "messed in the head," it's more like a throwaway story.

Or when Daddy calls him a "goddamn freak" it's more like an opinion. In other families, there would have been a diagnosis, or at least an evaluation. Some well-meaning efforts to figure him out.

But not with Mama and Daddy.

So Gracie and I are his real parents. We watch over him. We threaten to beat up the kids who pick on him and rough him up at school. We listen when he goes down his rabbit holes. We go to the library and try to find terms to describe him: Autism? Asperger's? We don't know. What we do know is that he's smart, despite the Ds on his report cards, and he reads better than most first graders, even if all he wants to learn are encyclopedia facts about wild animals.

Rusty's in his room, under his blankets with his wrapping papers. I don't remember when he started the collection—this is not a house overflowing with gifts or materials to wrap them in. He keeps the papers in a canvas tote he got free from the library. Scraps of striped, flowery, or foil wrapping paper, which he carries everywhere like other kids carry their blankies. When he's overwhelmed he smooths the paper squares out on the floor, lies on his stomach, and flattens his pieces all around him. Sometimes he rolls onto his back and holds them up to the light like they're baseball cards.

"Oooh, is that one new? It's pretty," I say, pointing to a silver square. "I've never noticed that one before."

I love how Rusty looks at his papers.

I love that he has something that feels precious to him.

"Got it from TJ's house," Rusty says. "His mom saved it for me." Thank God for TJ, whose own tics and twitches remind us of Rusty's. TJ's mom looks out for us in small ways. She's the one who hooked us up with shoes and backpacks from Turning Point. She sends Rusty home with enough leftovers for three wrapped in tin foil. The dishes are simple—green bean casseroles and lasagnas—and so appreciated.

"TJ's mom says everything's better homemade," Rusty tells us, a note of hope in his voice.

"That's true. That's why I made dinner," says Gracie.

"We're sitting at the table tonight like a real family."

"That's why I'm bringing my riches." Rusty smooths his paper scraps carefully into his bag so they won't wrinkle.

Rusty doesn't like to be touched, so I shape a heart with my hands. "You take good care of your things, Rusty."

"I don't like when they get dirty."

"I know, buddy," I say soothingly. "I know."

Gracie microwaved four Stouffer's dinners—two turkey and mashed potatoes, two Salisbury steak—which she lifted from the 7-Eleven. She puts them out for each of us on the table, along with plastic forks on McDonald's napkins. We let Mama sit at the head of the table, and when she says she wants the steak instead of turkey, I trade.

Mama doesn't ask where these dinners came from. She doesn't know Gracie's tricks, wearing a double layer of clothing so she won't feel the press of a frozen dinner against her bare skin and needing to stay under Adolfo's radar at the 7-Eleven. I'm convinced he turns a blind eye to our stealing food, realizing we need it more than his boss needs the sale. Gracie thinks Adolfo's too distracted by her ass in tight jeans to notice when she's pregnant with a couple of bags of potato chips. Before she goes "shopping" she intentionally leans across the counter so he can see down her shirt. A sneak peek as currency.

Rusty doesn't like noises, and so while we eat, we make sure to keep things soft—no scraped-back chairs, no metal utensils, no banging pots.

"This is delicious, Gracie," I tell her even before I swallow. The house feels happy when it's just us four at the table, the radio playing softly in the background. "Like a real family," I say out loud.

"Aren't we a real family?" asks Rusty.

"'Course we are. Chew with your mouth closed," Mama reminds him, as if she suddenly wants to play Normal, too. "Napkin goes on your lap."

Gracie and I look at each other. Even if most of what we learn about being a family comes from what we've seen on television shows, it always makes us happy when Mama remembers her part. She looks pleased with herself. She pours some water from the pitcher and then she refills our cups, too.

"Did you know wolves have forty-two teeth?" Rusty asks, and Gracie and I trade another look across the table. This is what we hope these dinners will bring: Rusty confident and talking to us. "And they eat ungulates, which are hoofed mammals. Like, say, bison. Even caribou. TJ's dad hunted bison and brought it home to eat. I don't think humans should eat ungulates unless they hunt them themselves, like wolves do."

"Or TJ's dad," adds Gracie. TJ's dad hunts deer, too, and sometimes he brings us bags of venison jerky.

"Yeah, yeah! Exactly. Like TJ's dad." Rusty's smiling.

In moments like this, I think the world will find room for our Rusty and his beautifully different brain. In moments like this, I can feel how the world might one day be bigger than this house.

We're almost finished when we hear the car. Mechanically, we jump up to remove all traces of this dinner and make ourselves scarce. Daddy expects a quiet house. But tonight, he comes in the front door with a bang, startling us, shifting the energy.

"What, no dinner for your hardworking husband?" He's leering at Mama, with beer on his breath and that too-loud voice that means he's been in a bar. "I'm the one who pays rent in this house, but there's no hot plate for me?"

"Sorry, Daddy! We didn't think—" Gracie begins.

"We got plenty. Have the rest of mine." I push my plate over.

"And what special occasion brings you out, Margie?"

Mama blinks at her lap. Her mind switches off so quickly, it's like someone cut the power. Daddy's staring at her, hoping for any last little spark from her. When we were really little, it was nothing but fighting between them. Now it's just ashes. His fingers prong a slice of my turkey, and he drops it into his mouth.

"Tastes like ass—aw, not this shit again," he says as he spies Rusty's bag of wrapping papers on the spare chair. He picks it up and crushes it in one hand like a tube of toothpaste. "You still holding on to this? What are you, retarded?"

Rusty has gone as still as a block of ice.

"Give it back, Daddy," says Gracie, but her voice is a whimper.

I stand up and try to think of the best course of action. "Daddy, let me take Rusty's bag and fix you a drink. We got some Pepsi." It's Gracie's Pepsi, which she's been saving, and I avoid eye contact.

Daddy blinks to focus on me. Sometimes I feel like Mama's all he really notices; the rest of us are ghosts or shadows crossing through. He's drunk, as usual, and he's also riding some high I can't see. There's no way he's coming from work, but to argue it would be to invite a bigger fight that only Daddy could win.

"I'll get myself a beer," Daddy says, and when he opens the fridge and stares into it, I signal for Gracie to go.

She slips out the back door, heading to our tree.

Daddy spies the Pepsi and cracks it open, and I exhale. I'm about to ask him if I can take Rusty's stuff when he grabs a handful of the wrapping paper, throws it into the sink and then pours the soda on top.

"No, Daddy! You put the wet on it!" Rusty jumps from his chair, frantic.

"Rusty, it's okay, I'll dry it off," I say.

"'I'll dry it off,'" Daddy mimics.

I motion for Rusty to make himself scarce, but he's frozen, staring at his damp collection scattered around the dirty sink.

"We'll get a hair dryer, Rusty."

"Yeah, we'll dry it off, Rusty." Daddy's laughing. He pulls a lighter from his back pocket. He finds the silver square, Rusty's favorite, at the bottom of the bag and holds the paper high between two fingertips so Rusty has a front-row seat. He sets the silver square aflame and drops it onto the pile in the sink.

The flame catches, paper curling and burning.

"Noooooo!" Rusty cries. "My riches! Noooooo!" He drops to the floor and covers his ears with his hands, keening and rocking on his heels.

Daddy, always ready when someone shows their softest belly to the world, kicks him in the ribs. Rusty screams, then curls in on himself and goes silent.

"You got to be a man sometimes," says Daddy. "All of you are so fucking disrespectful. I need to knock sense into each and every one of you ingrates."

A fog of rage clouds my vision as Daddy's angry spit lands on my cheek.

I imagine I'm a wolf, with forty-two teeth ripping through Daddy's cartilage. I imagine I have claws. I imagine a world of wrapping paper and ribbons. I imagine reversing the clock an hour and sending Rusty to TJ's house with his tote bag. I imagine anything but this moment: watching my seven-year-old brother cry—not even in pain; we've grown used to pain—but for the only thing he has ever known how to love.

Gracie has been right all along. Tonight I can feel it in my bones. We can't continue to live this way. We live in dread that at some point, Daddy's going to kill us—but we can't just sit here waiting for the night when he really snaps and takes us all down *with him. We need to act before it's too late. We need to find a way out of this nightmare. Our lives depend on it.*

    I pick up the frying pan—maybe I can end this right now, once and for all—but it takes Daddy no effort to snap it from my hand and knock me out cold.

FORTY-ONE

HONOR

Now

My eyes fly open into darkness. My body is hot and damp, ignited by a nightmare I've had too many times to count. As the dream ebbs, I try to hold on to it. My memories are bone-chilling, the kind you work to bury forever. But my siblings are so alive in them. It's an exhausting trade-off. With no win.

When I look down at my open palms, the half-moon- and circle-shaped marks are bright red—my body remembers all of it, as if it happened yesterday. Over the day, the marks, like the nightmare of the trauma itself, will fade as I reset. I'm not in that little house of horrors anymore.

It's early morning, the sun's just breaking over the horizon, and I'm safe in my apartment. Safer than I was yesterday.

The sun is up, and Troy is dead.

Because Strike, *my Strike*, killed him.

I think.

You know.

The news alerts across Jo's iPad last night were sketchy about the cause of Troy's death. *Found by a neighbor. Fatally stabbed in his home.* I prop up on an elbow and blearily grope for my phone, which is recharging on my nightstand. I want to see if any new details were released.

I tap on a headline, which links to a video story on Apple News.

First, one of Troy's old mugshots from an assault charge.

"The victim had a criminal record and a history of violence," the reporter says flatly, as a younger, bearded Troy stares at me with his goldfish eyes.

"Numerous complaints have been made against Simpson over the last decade, though charges have always been dropped. Last year, his girlfriend of several years, twenty-six-year-old Shelton resident Grace Stone, died in a camping accident. According to sources, many in the community held suspicions that Simpson was involved in her death." The reporter is standing outside the dilapidated apartment complex where Troy was killed. I'm taken by surprise at the quick dissolve to Gracie's high school photo.

My eyes brim as all this information sinks into me fresh.

My sister's murderer is dead.

And you know who killed him, Honor. You know it.

"Police are asking for any members of the public who might have information about this crime to please come forward," the reporter says.

I make myself think it all the way through. Make myself feel what it means if the same strong, warm hands that caressed my body might have, only hours before, wielded the knife that slit Troy's throat.

He deserved it. An eye for an eye.

The voice in my head refuses to be silent. I give myself permission to allow my thoughts space and freedom. Because I do believe that Troy deserved no less than what my sister got. I hope he suffered. It would bring me true peace if I knew he met her same grim end.

From downstairs comes the sound of a quick, hard knock. I bolt upright in bed and peek through my curtains. Strike's vintage Jaguar is in my driveway. Shit. Strike always takes that car, and its racing-green color feels like a metaphor for the man who drives it. Rare, elegant.

Stop it, Honor. Stop romanticizing this person you hardly know. Monster.

He did warn you, Honor.

He is everything you've been running from your whole fucking life. Strike is danger. He is the fire. You can't live in fire.

If only it were that easy.

If only my heart could sync up with my brain.

I slide from bed, tiptoe down the stairs. Should I be scared? Because mostly I'm not. What does that say about me? I'm still wearing Strike's cashmere.

"Honor. I know you're in there."

Should I even open the door? If I turn this knob, I am welcoming a killer inside my home. I'm welcoming a killer inside my life. I almost welcomed a killer inside my body. Who am I kidding? I still want him inside my body.

"Honor." Strike's words are gruff on the other side of the door.

I press my cheek against the wood, and my eyes squeeze shut.

"I can't leave until you know the truth."

"I already know it. You killed him, didn't you?" I ask. My voice shakes.

"You know I'd never ever hurt you, right?"

This is one thing I do know, and it's why I finally open the door. The cool morning air hits me immediately, and from the way Strike appraises my body through the clinging cashmere, I'm self-conscious of what he sees.

It's clear that, in spite of everything, I've stayed wrapped up in his clothes.

Strike paired his jeans and work boots with a flannel shirt with the arms rolled up, his tattoos exposed. His face looks like how I feel. Haunted. Shadows hug his cheekbones, and it's obvious he hasn't slept. He's got a to-go coffee cup in each hand, and as I take the cup he offers, I step aside so that he can come inside. I sip—it's my usual order: double espresso, large splash of oat milk, two pumps of vanilla.

But he doesn't move. "Come with me," he says. "I want to show you something." I feel that piercing gaze at my hard, pointing nipples, the V between my legs. "You might want to change—as much as I love you in my clothes."

Embarrassed, I duck my head. "Give me ten minutes."

"I'll wait in the car." He knows I might be afraid to have him in my house.

Upstairs, I gulp the coffee and then take an icy, punishing shower and change into my jean shorts and a T-shirt—under the chill of the morning, it feels like today might be another scorcher. My body feels unsteady with anticipation.

What does he want to show me?

Back downstairs, I step outside to find Strike leaning against his car, his arms crossed, his chin lifted. Morning sun alights on the planes of his face. Bone structure like his usually means a professional photographer is working behind the scenes, finding all the right shots. The reality is that Strike doesn't have a bad angle.

His eyes suddenly connect with me as if he can read my

thoughts, and he smiles briefly in what I can only think of as his "cashmere" smile—as beautiful and tailored as every other thing he possesses. This man. I slip on my sunglasses—in some small way, they feel like a barrier to protect me from the sense that he's reading my mind.

As I cross the lawn, Strike crosses in front of the car to open the passenger-side door. Always the gentleman.

"You haven't told me where we're going," I say once he's back behind the wheel.

He shifts to look at me. "You'll have to trust me on this one," he says.

I push my sunglasses higher on my nose and stare ahead. "I'm here, aren't I?"

Strike reaches out and covers my hand with his own, firm and assuring. "Yes. You deserve to learn everything. I see that. But then you can't unknow it. It's a risk."

I nod, though my heart leaps to hear it. "I understand."

"Okay." Then he throws the gear shift into reverse.

Strike drives fast, with a decisiveness that sends a prickling down my spine and under my arms as we get on the highway. Trusting him is also opening a Pandora's box. I know that grief and abuse have warped me.

Perhaps love has warped me, too.

"Bad news, by the way," Strike mentions as he puts the car in park on Wheeler Street. "Since we were here last, they've lost a star. They installed a coffee machine, but I'm sorry to report the brew tastes like piss."

He's trying for some lightness, but when I see where we are, my heart skips a beat. *What fresh hell is this?* My panic signals are flashing as Strike gets out and then walks around the front of the car to open my door. Suddenly I feel lightheaded. I catch his fingers harder in my grip as I bring myself up to stand right next to him.

"Wait," I say, then inhale. "I need a minute."

"I can take you back home." His fingers twine through mine, palm to palm. The press of his skin feels warm and solid.

"No, I'm fine," I say, suddenly resolute. If he takes me home, I'll lose him forever. "Whatever you want to show me. I can handle it."

We walk across the street to the building. Through the front door, I see the coroner, a little Druid of a man waiting to greet us.

"Just make it quick, if you don't mind," he says, pocketing the bills Strike casually hands him as we pass. "I got everything you asked."

When I look up at Strike, his gray eyes are a calm harbor, though the moment is taut with tension. We're back at the morgue—and I think I know why. We follow the coroner down the stairs and into the room where a metal gurney with a body lying on it, fully covered by a white plastic sheet, has been rolled out from its refrigerated cabinet.

I feel a wave of nausea; my hands are clammy.

The coroner gives Strike the autopsy report, which he then hands to me. "We'll need a few minutes," Strike says, dismissing him.

Once the coroner is gone, I exhale slightly, though my hands are gripped into fists.

"As I bet you've already guessed, under that sheet is the body of Troy Simpson," says Strike. "Your sister's killer. I read Gracie's autopsy, and while she technically died of concussive injuries sustained by a fall, she also had multiple inexplicable wounds all over her body—old and new. She was a longtime victim of abuse. There's no doubt Troy routinely abused her and eventually murdered her."

I feel the last of my breath leave my lungs. "I know."

"Justice came for him."

"Yes."

"You don't have to look, Honor. But I think you want to."

My silence doesn't deny this.

"Now I'm going to show you exactly what happened to him." Strike's voice is calm, almost soothing. He stands behind me and rubs my arms as if to warm me up. Instead, his touch feels electric. "Are you ready?"

I hadn't realized I was cold, though of course I am. My heart is racing with anticipation and uncertainty; more than this, I know I can't let this chance slip through my fingers. This opportunity will never come again, and I refuse to allow my nerves to hold me back. This is when I can face my fears and find the closure I so desperately need.

"You are stronger than you think, and you are braver than you know," Strike says, his voice so deliberate that it's almost meditative.

Yes. He's right.

I feel myself relaxing. Or maybe succumbing. I'm not sure which. My spine presses against his chest, anchoring me to his strength. "I hope this will help you sleep at night." He pauses, and then whispers into my ear. "It will help you to understand."

"Then show me."

Strike leans over me and tugs back the sheet.

I gasp. I'm not sure what I expected. But it certainly wasn't this.

FORTY-TWO

HONOR

Now

Troy Simpson is naked, his flesh crisscrossed with the fresh marks of multiple knife wounds, like so many tire slashes over his body. Some are large, others more like deep scrapes or shaving nicks, blood-caked and bruised. The gash across his heart tells the story of his cause of death—it's a volcanic eruption of thickly hardened blood and yellowish pus, exactly what I'd think Troy's twisted heart would look like. His skin is gray and hangs loose and slack—it reminds me of an old man without his dentures. His exposed tats are some of the ugliest I've ever seen, a gallery of busty mermaids and skeletons riding motorcycles or dancing with the devil. I've seen a few of them before, but not the *BORN TO DIE* that's lettered in prophetic all-caps across Troy's groin or the equally ironic *Live Hard* that's scripted down his inner thigh.

His bug eyes are closed, thank God. I allow myself to enjoy the power of staring at him without the fear of him staring back at me. But even still, I ache to think that the last person Gracie saw and touched and smelled was this worthless human being. I hate him with a vehemence I didn't known was possible. I hate him even though I once knew him as a little boy with two front teeth missing and a bowl cut. I hate him even though he's a limp sack of meat and bone, a lifeless object.

And I hate him even though he can no longer hurt me, because I am left with the scars of who he was and what he did during his time on this planet.

A dead Troy Simpson can't erase the fact that he existed.

I'm trembling with rage. It floods me and leaves me wordless. Strike looks at my face and understands what's written across it. And then he begins to speak in a voice that is as soft as it is hypnotic.

"He was asleep when I found him. So the first thing I did was wake him up and explain that I had come to kill him and that it would take some time, so he needed to be quiet, and that's why I'd had to tape his mouth shut. Then I restrained his arms and legs with jute rope." Strike speaks low, directly into my ear. I feel a melting, pulsing curiosity stirring deep inside me. I want to hear more of this story. I need all of it. Every last detail of this murder.

Holy shit. Holy shit. Holy shit.

"You tied him up," I say.

"Handcuff knots. He didn't fight me much. Except for . . ." With a finger, Strike gestures to the still-faintly-visible slash across his face.

"And your knuckles?"

"Yeah, a little warm-up. I punched him a couple of times in the face," Strike tells me, calm, so very calm. "To be honest, I considered making it fast. If I'd slit his trachea, he'd be dead in two minutes." He pauses, considering. "But this one—it felt personal. Why give this monster an easy death? Was that what he deserved? He'd tortured you and Gracie both from when you were little girls. After he killed your sister, he made your own life a misery. He taunted you endlessly; he mutilated Keep. You lived in daily fucking fear."

This is a dream and a nightmare. My nipples tighten; my whole body, inexplicably, is on fire.

"But even more importantly, the moment my fist connected with his face, when I saw him buckle to his knees, when I saw that fear in his eyes because he knew he would not survive, I had to ask myself"—his words drop to a whisper—"what would Honor want?"

In the silence, Strike uses his index finger to trace his way, slowly and gently, from the notch behind my right ear to down around my neck. My eyes close; my skin tingles where it's met by his warm breath.

"What I want," I repeat, but then I can't speak, because all that I really want is this: Strike's finger like a bolt of electricity jolting through my skin. What I want is for it to be his tongue. Strike draws me in closer, his arms locking me to him. In my mind's eye, I can feel exactly how I would draw this moment. How I'd connect the lines of our bodies. How can this feel so perfect?

Is this what I would have wanted?

Troy Simpson, meticulously destroyed by this man who has enveloped me so fully in his protective embrace?

Yes. Yes. A hundred times yes.

"I will never forget the way you were staring at Grace in this same spot that day we met. It tore me apart, Honor. I felt it like a physical force, a cyclone through me, feeling this intense attraction to you along with the knowledge that your sister's murderer was out there somewhere, capable of inflicting even more harm, even more pain."

I close my eyes as Gracie's last moments flow through me. It must be a twin thing. Sometimes I can feel exactly what happened to her, abandoned and alone in the vast dark, broken and terrified, crying my name as her life drained from her.

I'd do anything to get her back, but in a world where that's not possible, Strike has given me what might be the next best thing. Standing here, the truth of his darkness is revealed, and I let it consume my senses.

The taste of revenge.

It's fucking delicious.

My entire being is so white-hot with rage and desire, I feel like I might explode. I can feel Strike against me, the length of him rock-solid against the curve of my ass. "Tell me that he suffered."

"Oh, he suffered, I promise," says Strike. "I knew you wanted that."

I nod, barely. There's no use denying it. To say otherwise would be cowardly—and a lie.

"I started on him with my favorite knife—an antique Gerber eleven-inch. Beautiful fillet knife. The truth is, I wanted to carve up that meat sack with the precision of Michelangelo—but I couldn't get too flashy because of the police." He shrugs. "So I also used kitchen knives. It needed to look messy—a debt collection situation."

We are standing so close that I feel the reverberation of his voice. It rolls through my body, and there's a warm ache between my legs.

"I told you before—I warned you, Honor—I'm not a nice man."

"But why? Why did you do it?" I whisper.

"Vengeance," he says. "Vengeance is justice."

"You sound like you think you're God," I tell him.

"I don't believe in God. How can I believe in a greater power that would allow someone as beautiful as Gracie—someone you loved—to be murdered? How can I believe in a greater power that allows so much suffering to go unpunished?" His beautiful gray eyes are as soft as mist and seem to bear the weight of his emotions, a sense of loss and sadness so profound it draws me in. "No, Honor, you've got me all wrong. I don't think I'm God. I protect women and children from monsters like him. A drop in the ocean, maybe, but it's my ripple." Strike stands tall, his feet rooted to the ground, his voice clear and strong. There's conviction in his eyes, too. A steely resolve. Not a shred of doubt.

"But what gives you the right?" I ask.

The muscles in his jaw tighten, and he shrugs. "Nobody gave Simpson the right. There is so much evil in this fucking world. No one needs to give me the right to do what's needed to protect you. To give you what you want."

Suddenly I feel the power of this place, of what Strike has done. Every time I came to this morgue before, I was a grieving victim. But not this time.

"This isn't your first . . . ?" Strike will tell me the truth. He always does.

"What I do is brutal," Strike says after a moment.

The heat between my legs surprises me. "How many?" I ask softly.

In answer, Strike rolls the sleeve of his flannel shirt a little higher, and I see the fresh mark on the end of his tattoo, another strike.

Seven.

He has murdered seven killers. My head is spinning like a top.

You're wet, Honor. This is your fantasy—the one you didn't even know about until Strike showed it to you. I don't know how I've gotten to this point. I'm in love with a killer—because clearly that's what this madness, this *disease* is, love.

"You did this for me," I say softly.

He shrugs. "I took his life because he didn't deserve it. But you, Honor—you deserve the best life. With Christmas mornings and a couple of cute kids, and a hammock out back and a man who knows how to work a barbecue grill and talk bullshit to the neighbors. But that's not me."

"What makes you think you know what I want?" I ask. Pain is sawing through my heart. I used to want nothing more than Normal.

But that was before I met Strike.

"Maybe I don't," Strike concedes. "And I sure as hell know that I love you, Honor. But loving you doesn't change who I am or what I do—and what I will continue to do. I can't change for you, and I'm not going to let you live in my darkness."

He loves me. My heart catches. His words should feel as sweet as sugar, as fizzy as the pop of a champagne cork, but I can see in his eyes that it's agony for him to admit. The moment hangs suspended between us. There's a tension building, as forceful as the tide. I will not stay away from this man.

"I'm not asking you to change," I whisper. My heart is beating a trillion beats per second as I move toward Strike at the same time as he steps toward me. His mouth crushes against mine, a collision of passion, rough and unyielding, devouring. My lips part as I reach my hands to the back of his neck, grip his hair, pull him closer. His tongue is a revelation in my mouth. So many times, I've fantasized about this. I feel a deep rush in my ears as Strike's hands move to take full possession of my body, gripping me so hard against him I know he'll leave bruises.

"I did it for you," he groans, breathing between his teeth. He nips at my neck. My shoulder. I want him to draw blood. "For. You."

"I know, I know," My eyes flutter closed as the space between my legs throbs and pulses. Every square inch of my body is primed for the gasping thrill of his hand as it pushes into the waist of my shorts, pulls them down, and slides right into my panties, where he finds my clit and begins to rub in tiny, wet circles. He's rough—no delicacy, no gentleness. But I'm ready—ready for him to take what's already his.

"I told Troy that he needed to die so that you could live, Honor," he whispers, his lips against my ear, and now my knees buckle. *Fuck.* I've never felt like this—overwhelmed with lust, with need. He killed my monster to set me free. And now he's saying goodbye.

"Please. I want you inside me," I tell him, as he tugs down my panties, too, fingers building pressure between my legs, and his grip tightens around my waist. I'm so overcome by him, by his wet fingers and my pulsing clit, that I'm having trouble concentrating. "Please don't stop."

He presses me close, then drags his free hand through my hair, kissing me at the temple.

"I can't stop," he says as his tongue licks a vertical line from the base of my throat to my chin. When his fingers between my legs stop moving, we both know he's leaving me right on the edge of surrender. I try not to whimper as he removes his fingers from my still-pulsing wetness, and then I squeeze my thighs together; it's all I can do not to use my own fingers to finish the job. I feel a trickle of moisture down my leg.

He takes a step away, looks at me. A hunter.

I'm a mess. My jean shorts and panties are soaked and pooled around my ankles.

How can he stand there so still? So in control?

And yet he waits—for what? I don't know. The strength to

leave, I think. I have no strength left. He feasts on me with his eyes. Our gazes lock as he runs his tongue along the length of his wet fingers.

Up and down, and then into his mouth. He tastes me. No. He relishes me.

"Fucking delicious," he growls, and I see it happen—and I see I was wrong. He's not in control, he's decided to finish me off as he crushes me back into his arms. His kisses are fierce and burning—oh God, yes. The pulsing and pooling between my legs is aching so hard for release; I groan in anticipation of the sheer length of him, hard and huge, and holy shit, I've never wanted anything as much as I want this man.

"Oh my God," I say, and throw my head back and moan, as I grip Strike's thick dark hair, as his expert fingers find the perfect spot and build me to the orgasm I've been so desperate for. At the very edge of release, I drop to my knees, unbuttoning and yanking at his pants—knowing full well that I've created this entire scene in *Whispering Wet Vines*—and yet it's different somehow, because I didn't expect it to come wrapped in so much desire now that I know what he's done for me. I take Strike in my hands, stroking his swollen shaft with one hand while the other grips its firm base. I imagined this scene exactly, though I didn't anticipate the sizzling rush of power. The overwhelming need to feel him in my mouth.

When I look up at him, Strike closes his eyes and he groans, pulsing for release. I slip the head between my lips, teasing and licking and kissing him, opening my eyes briefly to watch the tension through his forearms. I love the feeling of his fingers twisted through my hair, the sense that his desire is locked within every fiber and cell of his being. Inch by inch, I take him wholly into my mouth. The sound of my own pleasure is muffled by his thickness. He is already so close to the point of climax that he barely moves. I feel him tense, and my pussy tightens in response. His cock is stiff and heavy against my tongue as I suck on him, as I fill my throat with him, wrapping my fingers like a cock ring at his base. Knowing how much he wants this causes an indescribable, eddying pleasure to flow through me—I can tell that every second is just as excruciating and intense for him, too.

"Fuck, you're incredible," he says, panting as the pleasure keeps ratcheting up. I back off and slow down a couple of times, just to keep him on the edge until he can't take any more.

With a low, guttural moan, he grips the back of my head as he erupts and spills into my desperate mouth. I swallow him greedily—something I've never done before, but feels so right in this moment, with this man. Then Strike pulls me up so that we are facing each other, and he closes one arm around me.

"I want you to come for me, baby," he murmurs, his breath hot on my ear, as his fingers slip inside me again, playing me like an instrument. My orgasm hits so fast that if Strike wasn't encircling me, I'd slide to the floor in blacked-out bliss. Instead I bury my face into his chest. He brushes a soft kiss at my temple, then holds me, his own cheek pressed against the crown of my head as he breathes me in.

Slowly, we touch back down to Earth. Find our clothes in silence. A tear streams its way down my face.

I take one last look at Troy's body across the room, decaying on its gurney, witness to our ecstasy. I'd completely forgotten about him—a first. I smile inwardly. Because he is nothing now.

And I have never, ever felt so alive.

At the car, Strike opens my door and reaches across to buckle my seat belt, then slips into the driver's seat. As we head home, I sense something has shifted between us. The orgasm that overwhelmed me, filled my senses to heady overload, is ebbing, receding like a faint and fading dream. Questions gnaw at me, silently tormenting my thoughts: *Where do we possibly go from here?*

We don't speak the entire way to my place, and even after I get out, I'm still half hoping he will tell me that there's got to be another way forward for us. But I can't find the words myself. Just outside my inner turmoil are all the words I want to say to make him understand how nobody has ever made me feel so cherished.

That just as I was twinned with Grace, Strike and I are also inextricably connected.

Say it, Honor. But I remain silent.

When I finally reach my front door, I turn, my eyes brimming with tears. "Goodbye, then."

"Goodbye, Honor Sunday Stone," he says.

I look down and take a shaky breath. Is this really it?

But I know that it is. I don't look up again until he's gone.

FORTY-THREE

HONOR

Now

The next morning, the first thing I read on my phone before I've even had my coffee is a lawyer's note, telling me my employment contract with Dark Matter Entertainment has been officially terminated and that I will be receiving severance pay. That the rights to all the drawings I completed in-house have reverted back to me to use however I wish.

I'm devastated, of course, but I'm not totally surprised.

The tears flow down my cheeks, and I let myself cry it out—even though there's nothing more depressing than the haunting echo of my own uncomforted sobs in my lonely, empty apartment. Not since Gracie died have I felt such a sluggish urge to never leave my bed.

Strike doesn't want me to be part of DME because I know too much. Fine. He loves me—it's a giddy thought—but he can't be near me because he is dangerous—equally dizzying. I understand that, even if every molecule of me protests it. But what I can't fathom, what slices as painfully as every knife mark across

Troy Simpson's body, is that Strike doesn't want any memory of me through my drawings.

I know my art is good. I know I poured my soul into my work. I loved taking my desire seriously—creating characters who turn away from being shy women faking their pleasure and their orgasms and toward a world where they can run free, where women come first, both literally and figuratively.

I was getting better every day, too. As I gained confidence in myself, I could take risks. But if confidence is a tightrope, I've fallen. My hopes for the future are now shattered, the shards of doubt piercing me, leaving me amid the scattered pieces of my broken dreams. I wonder if I was only kidding myself, before.

Maybe my paintings really do belong in the basement.

A few minutes later the doorbell rings. Jo is early, and I bet she brought donuts as usual—we have a breakfast date this morning to run through some wholesale lookbooks and make final decisions on what we're stocking up on for fall. The bank loans don't care if my life is upside-down, but Jo's stepped up and found some really cute possibilities—seasonal umbrellas, pumpkin-shaped votives, plaid and checkered flannel-lined pajamas, and a new small-batch caramel company that sent a dozen ribbon-tied muslin bags of free samples in assorted flavors like rum, butterscotch, and espresso.

I'm looking forward to burying my sorrows, for this morning at least, in some coziness.

But it's not Jo with a box of Boston cream donuts at the door.

The man who stands before me wears a DME driver's uniform and is holding a giant cardboard box. "Delivery," he says, as if it isn't obvious.

"Thank you." I take the box—oof, it's heavier than it looks—and set it on the front table.

The man slides an envelope from his breast pocket. His face is inscrutable—a typical DME employee who gives away nothing. "Have a good day, ma'am."

Once he's gone, I'm so unnerved that I'm frozen in place. My gaze shifts back and forth from the envelope to the box. Do I open it? Ignore it? Send it back?

Dismiss Strike the same way he's dismissed me?

Yeah, right.

Box first. I tear away the tape and cardboard.

"Oh!" I gasp, my heart skipping at the sight of so many neatly packaged treasures inside: a cornucopia of pristine paintbrushes, paint boxes, and watercolors and a thick pyramid of sketch pads. It's such an excess at my fingertips, and I feel giddy at the thought of what I can create with it. A childish delight rushes through me—this feels like receiving all the birthday gifts I've ever imagined, all the Santa wish lists I ever made, all at once.

The cardstock square at the top of the box is in Strike's telltale all-caps handwriting.

FOR A FRESH START. YOU'LL KNOW WHAT TO DO.
X S

My heart can't take all these mixed messages. I was just fired by email. Now Strike is sending me the most thoughtful gift I've ever received?

I tear open the envelope. Inside is a final, generous severance check that's about equal to four months' salary—about twice as long as I've worked at DME. My stomach drops. I've never seen so much money. I have never had a bank balance higher than three digits. Is this a bribe for my silence?

Surely he knows I'd never say a word.

It can buy me relief. It can pay off more of my mortgage and pay down those other loans. There will be enough left over for other expenses. Of all the emotions flooding through me, my gratitude for this simple act of generosity is overwhelming.

There's another note card slipped in with the check. Even the letters of his monogram, *SCM*, melt me. I read greedily:

BET ON YOURSELF.
MAKE BEAUTIFUL ART. SHINE ALL YOUR LIGHT.
DON'T LET THE DARKNESS IN.

After all the crying I've been doing lately, I'm shocked that I still have more tears left in me. I cry for all the monsters I've loved and lost.

I cry for me, the biggest monster of all.

FORTY-FOUR

HONOR

Then
(Age Sixteen)

I smell the fire before I see it. Daddy's done it before—nodded off with a cigarette between his lips, nearly burned the whole house down.

Stay low, cover your mouth—didn't they teach us that in school? Quickly I tie my pillowcase into a face mask like a bank robber, and I nudge Gracie awake. "Wake up! Wake up!" I share a bed with Gracie. She sits up bleary-eyed. The house is filled with smoke.

Our house is tiny, with Grace's and my bedroom off the kitchen, our parents' and Rusty's down a short hall on the opposite side of the living room. "He's set a fire again," I say to Gracie, who is sitting up, whimpering. "So you need to get Rusty, I'll get Mama. Mask up and stay low, remember!"

Gracie springs from bed. "Fire!" she screams. "Fire!" Once we had a smoke detector, but the batteries in that thing have been dead for years. Is there a fire extinguisher under the sink?

In Normal the fire engines would already be sounding.

In Normal help would be on the way.

We live too far outside the zip code for Normal.

Daddy's passed out cold, his body beached and immobile. His hands are suspended—forefinger and middle finger dangling—as if to hold his cigarette butt.

Flames are skimming the bottom of the upholstery like fairy lights while longer tongues dance up the living room curtains. I am paralyzed, staring at my father like I'm looking at a painting: Portrait of a Man on Fire.

Gracie appears, carrying Rusty. He's a runty ten-year-old, and his legs are wrapped around her waist like a spider monkey's. They're both coughing, smoke is billowing, and the flames are catching quickly now.

"Go, go, get help!" I tell Gracie as she opens the front door.

"Save my riches!" Rusty screams.

"I'll get them, Rusty!" I promise. "Go—get out. Now!"

I inch around to my parents' bedroom, where Mama leans in the doorway. She's wrapped in her same yellow cardigan, her hair matted and her eyes owlish.

"You gotta save your daddy, Honor," she says, and this seems to be the only thing piercing through her conscious mind.

He's waking up, not quite activated. But the fire is. Flames leap across the rug and spark up his leg. I smell the acrid, nauseating tang of burning flesh. He moans in agony.

It's all happening so quickly.

"Don't worry about Daddy—you gotta follow me." I beckon to her as she takes a small, terrified step toward me. "You can do it, Mama," I wave her forward. "Hurry now—we can save ourselves."

"Honor!" Gracie is calling from the front door. She's come back for me. "Rusty's safe, and the Brewers say the fire trucks are on the way—but you gotta run." The relentless heat and smoke suffocate her voice. "The walls are burning. You can't just sacrifice yourself—"

But now the flames consume my father, and his howling screams of terror and agony fill the air. I watch his eyes bulge with horror as he is engulfed in an inferno, fighting and losing to death within a blazing cage. This is what I wanted. This is what he deserves. But now that it's happening, the conflict between my yearning and the starkness of this present moment grips me in a whirlwind of agonizing emotions that are nearly as tormenting as the circumstances that have led us to this fiery hell.

"Mama, come on!" I yell, tugging at her.

But Mama pushes me away hard, and I scream as my back is slammed against the roaring-hot surface of the wall. The rip of searing pain across my shoulder blades is mind-melting torture, so intense I feel like it could seep into my soul. If I survive, if I don't turn to black ash tonight, this scar will undoubtedly haunt me forever.

"No!" Mama cries, transfixed by the flames. In just her underpants and stained, ratty cardigan and tattered old T-shirt—the one Daddy got free from the water plant—she looks feral, a woman staring into the mouth of madness. Defiant, teeth bared, standing her ground as if determined to protect what's hers. "I'm not leaving without you, baby! You can't go without me, either!"

"Mama!" I scream. But she doesn't hear my voice. Tears are streaming down her face as she walks, arms outstretched, right toward Daddy, the only one she ever loved. He's led her right into his flames. Her T-shirt fabric catches first, lighting her up like an enchanted circle.

In my last image of my mother, her face is contorted in pain, and yet I also see—in her trancelike state—what I could only describe as resolve.

In death, as in life, she chooses him.

"Honor!" Gracie calls, breaking me from my shock as she yanks

me with ferocious strength through the living room and out the door, where I fall to the ground on my hands and knees, coughing and choking.

What surprises me later is not that it happened. Or even my own role in it. What surprises me is the fact that Gracie and I do not run farther away. We stay right there, unable to remove ourselves from the scene. Our smoke-blackened hands make a single, solid fist as we listen to our parents' faint and fading screams.

I watch the only home I've ever known blacken to smoldering char. An apocalyptic ending. A fitting goodbye.

But I have to watch.

I need proof that my parents are gone.

And I need to know they aren't coming back.

FORTY-FIVE

HONOR

Now

My twenty-third morning without Strike Madden has been no easier than the first. Even though I'm really trying. I want so badly to heal my heart from this wound—and it scares me to think I can't. When I'm with Jo, the only person I'll let into my pain, I listen deeply when she explains my fate doesn't align with Strike's—although Jo thinks it's mostly because I'm a Libra and Strike's a Scorpio.

Whenever I'm alone, on a jog or working on a painting or in bed at night, I remind myself how I've been here before. I've got these scars already.

Because I know how it feels to yearn for love and not get it.

Until the moment they died, all I wanted was for my parents to love me.

If there's one thing my life taught me, it was to know better than to beg for scraps. Still, I'm living through each day hopeful that eventually Strike won't consume my every thought. That I won't know if it's the sixty-eighth day or the ninetieth, because I'll have stopped counting. I might not even remember how his love was a bright, buttery sun beaming down on me. How I felt chosen and seen and adored.

But right now, my life is as cold as the morgue.

I dream of him. I paint him.

None of it fills me in any way. I've never felt so empty.

I've known grief—deep, abject grief—but I've never felt this. Time when I'm not painting feels like a flat, gloomy monochrome of hours barely lived. Nights are different—I snap from dreams, my heart pounding fiercely with sudden, jarring awakening, the remnants of my nightmares clinging like shadows as I transition to my somber reality. As terrifying as they are, at least my nightmares provide a brief distraction from grappling with the sadness that haunts my waking life.

Some mornings, even the smallest things—showering, eating, collecting the mail—feel like entirely too much of an ordeal.

Live for yourself, Honor. Live your life for you.

I keep trying. I tell myself how grateful I am for the little things. Grateful that I even got to know a love like Strike's at all. Every morning, I walk outside to feel the dappled-gold late summer sun on my face. In an old coat pocket I find a pack of Gracie's Winston Menthol 100s—and so I start treating myself to one with my coffee, just the way she did. Even though I hate smoking, I can feel a memory of Gracie, and the memories are all I've got.

At the shop, I convince the rich ladies of Shelton to buy hand-painted scarves and leather-bound journals and artisanal cocoa and our new sensual clove-infused massage balm. Jo and I string colored lights, and we try out the new lavender-scented diffuser, and we even burn sage to banish any vestige of Troy's karma. The shop has never looked more charming or been more bustling, but my mind never sticks here. I'm always eleven miles down the road. I'm always at Ashburn.

I ache for his touch. I crave seeing the lust rising in his gray eyes. I twist my own hands together to find the memory of pleasure in our entwined fingers. I daydream for hours, imagining the touch of his mouth on my body.

Just an hour. Half an hour. It would sustain me for a month. A year.

In the afternoon, I paint like my life depends on it. With desperation and a survival instinct. Jo never wants to be anywhere but the shop—another fight with either Bryan or her stepdad always sends her running here, and she knows I'm too careful with her feelings to ask embarrassing, probing questions. I relish time at my easel, lost in the privacy of my own imagination. Brushstrokes dance across the canvas, telling a story only I can hear. I'm in a white-hot fever of creativity as I create one piece after another.

This is my only escape. My chance to contribute real beauty to the world.

But I feel something else in me, too. I've spent a lifetime wrestling demons, struggling to bury memories deep within me. Then destiny intervened, introducing me to a man unafraid to confront the darkest horrors head-on. His presence activated a dormant spark in me, igniting a belief that some evil could, indeed, be vanquished. In Strike's absence, I'm forced not just to bury my wounds but to suppress that newfound ember of hope—and that has become a battle all its own.

One afternoon, when Jo says she's got some news and asks for girl time on the back porch after closing, I try to keep my dread at bay.

We test out the new electric tea kettle, steeping glass mugs of loose-leaf peppermint tea. When Jo adds a stick of peppermint candy to each and then swipes a bag of salted caramels for our snack, I have to laugh.

"Sometimes you remind me so much of Gracie," I tell her as we each settle into a porch rocker. "I'm so glad you've been here with me, Jo—especially during these past weeks." Even though I know Jo privately thinks it's for the best that I stay away from Strike. Ever since the baseball bat incident, he has made Jo uneasy.

"Hey, you know how glad I am for this shop. It's like a haven. Besides, you work too hard, and I like keeping an eye on you," she says. "I'm also super grateful for the overtime, since I'll need to take some time off in spring."

When I look at her, my eyebrows raised, she smiles coyly and stretches out the fingers of her left hand so that I can see.

"Oh!" I stare at the ring. "Is that . . . ?"

"Yup!" She grins. "Bryan put a ring on it! Well, sort of. This is a temp. He's still saving for a real, cut-stone ring, but in the meantime, he got this pin made into a band—you know, because we both love the Philadelphia Flyers, and Bryan always says that one day we're gonna have our own Itty-Bitty Gritty."

I am speechless. The ring is silver and orange, and on closer inspection I can see that melted into a little heart is the face of the Philadelphia Flyers mascot, Gritty. I know it's supposed to be endearing and a personal joke—and it does feel exactly like Bryan's sense of humor—but I despise everything about it. Jo tries so hard—she's such a saver and a rainy-day planner, such a careful watcher of people's moods and always hoping for the best in everyone. Something about this tacky toy ring reminds me that Bryan is doing what he always does, taking advantage of Josie's goodness.

"He's had it for weeks," she tells me now. "But he said he wasn't going to give it to me until we had make-up sex. Sure enough, Friday I asked him to come with me to an open house—oh, Honor, it's the cutest little split-level out by Route 422 near Pottstown, but Bry got pissed because—bah, never mind. Dumb fight." Jo looks a little wistful. "Anyway, we wound up horny and naked, thankfully, and afterward Bry gets down on one knee— on the bed—and says, 'Babe, will you be my forever linemate?'"

"Ah, good one, Bryan," I say, pushing my mouth upward in a smile. If Josie wants this, then I want it for her. Still, I can't imagine any version of happily ever after that involves Bryan.

They've reserved the ballroom at the Holiday Inn for mid-April, and the honeymoon will be a road trip to Dollywood, which has been on Josie's bucket list for as long as I can remember.

According to Josie, their astrological charts align enough to add some intrigue: "We're a celestial commotion that highlights some fascinating interplay." I'm not sure that Jo totally believes it. Celestial collision is more like it.

"Hey, we can have your wedding shower here, if you want," I tell her. "We'll close the shop for a private party and make it a potluck."

Josie clasps her hands. "Oh my gosh, Honor, that would be the cutest!"

Later, after I've walked her to her car, I let go of Gracie's five-minute rule and cry. I close the front door and press my cheek against it and let it all shudder through me. For Josie's undeserving fiancé, for Gracie's shit luck, and for all my losses, too. Who knew I had so many tears inside me? I thought I was tougher than this.

Or maybe it's time I choose a new definition of tough. After all, I'm still here. Still standing. Surely that counts for something.

———

The next morning, I wake up feeling a glimmer of optimism, and I know what to do. I jump on the local bus to the animal shelter outside Shelton, where I adopt a creamsicle-orange-and-white cat with gray eyes and a chunk of flesh missing from her left hind leg.

"Most likely a coyote did this damage," the guy at the shelter explains as we both examine the angry, ridged scar that grew over the wound.

In response, the kitten hisses and then mews the anguished cry of the underloved. My heart catches. We speak the same language.

In other words, she's perfect.

I name her Fivestar.

"Like the notebook brand?" Jo asks when she comes in Monday morning.

"Yep," I lie. "You know how I love notebooks."

"You'd be safer with a dog," she says when Fivestar jumps up on our home goods table, loudly displacing a festive jar of pencils so they all go clattering to the floor. "Someone to protect you when you go running."

"I don't need protecting," I say. "Dogs demand a lot." Whereas a cat is gentle empathy and quiet companionship the same size as my lap.

A cat's enough for me.

As I gather the pencils off the floor, Fivestar jumps up on the bath and beauty table to nuzzle a loofah. It's so sweet that Josie races for her phone to post it. What I do need is distraction, and my curious kitty provides plenty of that. She's also a comfort.

My little survivor, I whisper into Fivestar's fur that night as I settle in for another movie night—this time, it's *The Hunger*

Games. Her rhythmic purring, her ridiculous softness, and her nonjudging gaze lull me. This was a good idea. I can tell that Fivestar understands loss. And maybe more importantly, what it's like to have once been feral. She's a comforting presence—even if Strike occupies my thoughts constantly—and a quiet solace for my heart.

FORTY-SIX

STRIKE

Now

"We can choose courage, or we can choose comfort," Axe says. "But we can't choose both." He's been crushing me at eight ball and drinking my best scotch while slinging Brené Brown quotes at me all night, and I feel like he's just getting started.

"Back off, prick," I say as I position the cue to line up a bank shot.

"What I'm trying to say is you're a big fucking idiot," he says.

"Thanks. Point taken." Of course I realize I am a big fucking idiot, but Axe wants to keep hammering me with it. We're also halfway through a second bottle of Macallan M, and I can barely taste it. Tonight I'm dealing with the darkness by numbing it, but I've tried a number of other different tactics this past month, throwing myself into my work, my workouts, my meditation, a couple of motorcycle rides—hell, last weekend I took the chopper up to New Hampshire for a day trip to climb Mount Washington. Alone at the summit in the bracing air, with spectacular views of the Great Gulf Wilderness and the Atlantic Ocean, I still couldn't find any reprieve from losing Honor.

Missing her feels like the sun forgot to rise.

I'm just flailing here, and frankly it disgusts me.

When I hit the cue ball, it cracks too hard against the cushion, overbanks, and goes wide, striking balls at random angles. Rage rushes through me in a liquid tide—suddenly I want to lift up the entire billiards table, feel the bolts in its legs uproot like some kind of monster sequoia, and then send it into a seismic crash against the wall.

"Though I do wonder how many workplace sexual harassment laws you've broken," says Axe, casually salting my wound while he expertly sinks the next shot.

"I didn't sexually harass her," I say through gritted teeth.

"So why did you fire her?"

"It was the right thing to do."

Axe snorts, sinks two more shots clean. "Keep telling yourself that, champ."

"Like I'm going to take love life advice from you," I say. "How long has it been?"

"Fuck off. This isn't about me." When I first met Axe, he was fifteen years old, his glasses mended at the bridge with masking tape and an Adam's apple the size of a lime. The scrawny little fucker wasn't more than a hundred pounds soaking wet, not that I had much more to offer. Sure, I was taller and more jacked, but my brain was better geared for Dungeons & Dragons than dating and dances. Axe and I became friends online in a hacker chatroom on the dark web—we were on different continents at the time—and then bonded after college when we teamed up in a personal challenge to hack into the Pentagon. This got us a lot of attention from the CIA, who recruited us both, which was far better than the alternative: prosecution.

You wouldn't know if you looked at him now, but the dude

was a late bloomer, and though we can hardly go out to dinner without some cute waitress or hostess flirting up a storm, Axe has been single pretty much since I've known him. He's also known the me from Before, which gives us a lot of history.

"This is about you and self-sabotage," he tells me now.

"It's not self-sabotage. I'm protecting her."

"As Brené Brown says, 'Vulnerability is not winning or losing; it's having the courage to show up,'" says Axe as he pockets the last solid, then the eight ball, his third win in a row.

"Brown also says, 'You cannot shame or belittle people into changing their behaviors.' Which is kinda what you're fucking doing to me, dude," I tell him.

But Axe is undaunted. "Did Honor ever once say, 'Stay away, you frighten me'?" Axe puts on a high voice that sounds nothing like Honor. "No, she didn't. And pretty much every other woman in the world would have. I think that tells you something."

"That she's emotionally unstable?" I snap, and then soften. "Actually she's pretty much the exact opposite. I'll never know how she managed to build up an actual life on a scaffold made from shit."

"Exactly. She loves you. The real you. I don't know anyone you've let get close enough to see the real you. Not in years, anyway." When I tense at the reference, Axe slings an arm over my shoulder. For a second I think he's gone full Brené Brown and is about to give me a hug—but instead he slips his leg behind my knees me so that I instantly buckle.

"What the fuck?!" But my words are garbled; Axe has me in a full headlock.

"Aw, remember my world-famous noogies, miladdie?" Axe takes his knuckles and grinds them hard into my scalp.

"We were fucking teenagers!" I roar, but Axe goes in for the press. I twist and turn, then reach over his shoulder, grab his ear, and pull down forcefully while twisting my body hard in the opposite direction. Axe yowls but keeps me locked. The guy is built from titanium.

We also trained together, so he knows how to deflect my every move.

"Get offa me, you ape!" I growl, grabbing his ankle to knock off his balance at the same time as he releases me with a shove, and we stagger back from each other. I know that Axe is only half teasing, but he's also so goddamn frustrated with me and how I've been acting this past month. Clobbering me probably feels like the best way for him to deal with it. "Last Brené, best Brené," he says, his Scottish brogue thick with whiskey, one finger raised, his navy eyes hard on me: "And never forget it: 'If you own this story, you get to write the ending.'"

Fuck. Those words hurt worse than the scalp-pounding or the hangover I'm gonna get from consuming a bottle of scotch. And still, I could bash my own head against the wall to stop this ache that's warped my entire body since the day I said goodbye to her. All I want is to go find that woman and claim her as mine.

But Axe is wrong.

I don't get to write the ending because I don't own this story.

What happened to me and my family still owns me.

"Best outta ten," I say as I go to rack up another game.

FORTY-SEVEN

HONOR

Now

Alone in my kitchen after a long day at the shop, I'm finishing the last couple of slices of cold leftover pizza and contemplating a night of watching *Vanderpump Rules* with Fivestar when my phone buzzes.

I don't recognize the number but pick it up anyway.

"Honor Stone? This is Benny Mendez," says a man's voice, light and quick. "We've never met in person, but I own the Willis-Holmes."

"I know! I'm a huge fan!" I say, then immediately regret that I don't sound more self-assured—probably because I'm speaking through a mouthful of pizza. Do-over, please. I swallow. "I love your gallery—I used to take art classes in the Annex," I add, adopting a voice I don't recognize, two octaves lower than usual. "I was just there a few weeks ago." It was a pure whim to bring over my portfolio, and the only reason I didn't turn around and walk straight out was because the gallery assistant looked disorientingly like a nineteen-year-old Gracie—or, I guess, a young me—only with sky-blue hair and a nose ring.

She took down all my information and was excited about my work when I showed her—though I chalked it up to youth. After a week or so, I figured Benny Mendez would never see it or didn't like what he saw and that I'd be getting a polite brush-off email soon enough.

"Ha, well, your visit is why I called," he says now, "so I'll cut to the chase. Our intern showed me the portfolio you dropped by, and we'd love to represent you and schedule a showing if you're game. We're thinking maybe between twenty and twenty-five originals."

A showing? I'm shocked and silent.

As it turns out, you can just walk into the place that has intimidated you your whole entire life and pitch your work.

Turns out, an act of bravery like that can pay off.

"Honor?"

"Yes, of course," I say, my eyes stinging, my heart exploding. "I'm game. I'm—I'm all game!"

Benny laughs brightly. "We'll be in touch soon," he says.

Off the call, I do a happy dance in my kitchen, scooping Five-star up with me—she even obliges me for a few seconds before she jumps free.

I am going to have my own art show. At a real gallery.

I almost call Strike right then and there.

I almost call Jo.

It's not until later, alone in bed and surrounded by all my usual doubts, that I start to panic. What if my art isn't good enough? Why am I inviting the world to weigh in? Briefly, I consider gathering all my work into the backyard and starting a bonfire. A conflagration of self-sabotage.

Start a little fire? How on-brand of you, Honor.

Instead, I keep my secret tucked away, open the shop, and fix on a poker face all morning until Jo arrives, at which point I retreat upstairs.

Some days, I just have too many feelings.

Painting usually calms me. It's a huge meditative reset button. Today I'm mixing up my colors, adding my linseed oil, finding my palette. I have nervous energy to burn, so I take it out on the canvas, and with each passing hour, I find meaning and purpose, as if I've had a vision.

When I'm done, I step back and try to make sense of the mess of paint. My fear has burned off like morning fog.

I look at my work.

Strike stares back at me from my canvas. His eyebrow is cocked like a dare. Somehow, through my art, we've had a whole conversation, the way Gracie and I used to with a single look. His lips curve as if to say: *You can do this. Of course you can.*

Is he right? Can I?

I'd do anything to hear him say so.

FORTY-EIGHT

HONOR

Now

A week later, in bed and watching my digital alarm clock flip from 1:59 to 2:00 a.m., I finally give up and pick up my phone to scroll the Paperless Post e-vite for the show that I'm cohosting with the Willis-Holmes Gallery. The show is in ten days, and while I've added a few of my contacts, there's one person who hasn't received an invitation. And not for a lack of my thinking about it.

I type in Strike's email address—

Do it, Honor!

—and I press the send button.

I expect to feel regret, but instead, relief and fatigue kick in hard together. I lie back on my pillow and feel my bones melt. Done.

Once upon a time, Strike wanted this for me, too. He knew this was my dream—and in spite of everything between us, I can't imagine not having the man I love present for the biggest night of my life.

If he comes to the opening, I'll make sure that it's different. I won't let him know that I think about him from the moment I wake up, sleepy and aroused from dreaming about him, to my hot, fantasy-infused shower, to indigo midnights when I stroke myself between my legs and pretend that it's his perfect tongue.

He won't see my desperation. My painful longing.

I'm glad I sent his link without an RSVP option so I can't obsess over whether he will be there or not. Still, Strike's so spotlighted in my mind that two days before the reception, when Jo tells me she saw Strike and another woman at Sambuca Grille while she and Bryan were celebrating the second anniversary of their very first hookup, my heart nearly stops.

"Was it a date?"

"Probably?" says Jo. "He was being very attentive. And Sambuca's pricey. It's for the best, Honor. He's moved on. It's time for you to move on, too. Want me to do a quick reading to learn your best days for something new?"

"No thanks." Then I have to ask. "Was she cute?"

"She had cute bangs," says Jo. Her teeth gnaw at her lower lip. "And I'm just gonna blurt out this part because there's no easy way to say it. She was really young."

"How young?"

"Like younger than me."

"Like eighteen?" I ask.

"Like maybe twenty? Sorry," she adds earnestly. "Don't kill the messenger."

"It's fine, it's fine." I could get an Oscar for how hard I have to work to hide my feelings as I put a double knot on a bunch of dried chili peppers that I've hung from the top shelf of the section I've labeled *The Spicy Corner*. Dried chilis, along with some very cute, crocheted chili pepper emoji pillows that just came in, feel like the best invite to this section of the shop. No more hiding this part of the store. "I hardly ever think about him anymore," I add.

It might be the biggest lie I've ever told. If he comes to my show, it will be the first time I've seen him in eighty-three days.

The night of the exhibit, I'm in revenge-dress mode. Black, of course, with a deep sweetheart neck and a nipped waist. It makes me feel like Audrey Hepburn. I don't think I've ever bought my-self anything nearly this extravagant before—I almost threw up when I saw the price tag.

But it was too late. I'd fallen in love.

And if there was ever a night to invest in myself, it's this one.

When I look in the mirror, even though there's more exposed skin than I've ever allowed myself to put on display, I know that I'm ready.

I pile my hair on my head, letting a few loose curls wisp free to frame my face. I hope I look sophisticated and also the slightest bit tousled. I wear Gracie's favorite ring; it fits my index finger perfectly. From the box marked *Rusty*—which I keep next to my box marked *Gracie*, both high up on my closet shelf—I find a small silver square of Rusty's wrapping paper from the second bag of "riches" he began collecting after Daddy destroyed the first.

I slip the square into my bag like a tiny concealed shield. Now both of my siblings are with me tonight. When I give myself a last once-over before I head out the door, I can almost hear Gracie behind me.

You look as pretty as a Sunday breeze, sis.

Rusty doesn't say anything. In my mind, he just presses the heel of his small hand to the bow at the dress's waist.

I don't allow myself to think of my parents. They deserve no part of this moment. I did not get here because of them. I'm here in spite of them.

You're not gonna sell nothing, anyway. Daddy's voice. *You're a shit painter. You're an all-around piece of shit.*

"Shut up shut up shut up," I whisper to my parents' ghosts as my Uber drops me at the corner. It's twilight—my lucky time, my special shade of lavender-to-gray. I'm a tiny bit late, and my heart catches in my throat as I walk through the front door of the Willis-Holmes Gallery.

So many people are here. I stand very still for a moment. Take it all in. Ten thousand hours captured, beautifully matted and hung, and lit with perfect, museum-quality uplighting.

And yet it all feels like a blur, too. There's so much to absorb.

If I'd shown up naked at this event, I wouldn't feel more vulnerable. The place is packed with Shelton's elite. All of them are here for my art.

A blown-up black-and-white photograph of me stares down from the wall opposite the door. It's a snapshot taken by Jo after the store closed one day. Something about the natural sunlight and my carefree smile makes me glitch whenever I see it, because it could be Gracie.

Or maybe it's just that I feel her in spirit, cheering me on.

I feel too shy to pause and look at it or to read the bio next to it that makes me sound like a legitimate artist.

Lacquered fingers flutter little waves at me—I didn't think I'd know anyone, but there are a few familiar faces in the crowd that I recognize as customers at Grace & Honor. The mysterious woman who buys my body oil by the quart is here, and as soon as she sees me, she pulls me aside.

"Honor Stone, I didn't know you painted! You're a marvel!" Her liquor-soaked breath puffs in my face. "Do you take commissions?"

"Umm." *Do* I take commissions? Thankfully, I don't have to

respond, because suddenly Jo is at my elbow, marshaling me through the crowd.

"Let's get you a drink, superstar," she says. "And put some space to breathe between you and your adoring crowd."

Adoring crowd? Who, *me*? My heart is fluttering.

But it's sort of weirdly true. Everywhere I turn, another interested pair of eyes is beaming right on me. I'm glad I'm protected by the robin's-egg-blue pashmina wrap draped around my shoulders—a borrow from the store—that also covers my back and bare arms. But my heart skips a beat the moment I see Strike all the way across the room, and I quickly draw it tighter, more protectively over my skin. I am already far too vulnerable to be exposed.

Strike is tall and imposing in a tailored black suit, his commanding presence unmistakable even from a distance. He's not alone, either. My heart quickens, my skin flushes, and my stomach plummets a thousand floors when I see the poised woman at his side. She's tall, with bangs, and she's very young. Exactly as Jo described.

So it's true, then.

I've been replaced.

Did I know him at all? Did he ever love me?

I watch them talking. A subtle smile graces Strike's lips; his charisma is drawing her in effortlessly. Pain washes over me in a wave of loss and nostalgia for all the moments he and I once shared. It's just too much, to be expected to stand here.

As if he can read my thoughts, Strike looks up, and as our eyes briefly meet, I feel myself immediately transported to those memories—still so raw—of when I intimately knew this man. In one glance of mutual recognition, we share all the unspoken emotions of that time, and a rush of feelings swirls within me. The start of tears stings the corners of my eyes. *Don't cry. Don't you dare cry on your special night, Sunday.* But I feel like such a fool. I've been so stupid to be a little bit hopeful. Did I really think to-night could be a new start? What does Strike want me to think by showing up with a date? Is this his casually cruel way of friend-zoning me?

Strike is being so attentive to this woman, too. She tilts her head, nods at whatever he's said. She's captivated by him. My stomach clenches.

What kind of a sadist brings a date to his ex-girlfriend's art show? It's not too respectful to the new girlfriend, either.

You were never his girlfriend, Honor. You were his employee. A watercooler flirtation. A few explosive hookups that never should have happened. Temporary feelings. Nothing more.

"That's her?" I ask, and Jo nods.

"It's so icky. I'm getting weird paternal vibes between them." She takes my hand so that I'll turn. "I'm incredibly proud of you, Honor. And Gracie would be, too."

"Thank you," I say, my eyes filling, but Jo shakes her head vehemently.

"Happy thoughts only! Or you'll mess up your makeup." Jo hands me a napkin and I dab carefully under my eyes before I find myself scooped up into strong arms.

"Congratulations," says a deep, gravelly, sexy voice. My heart lifts and then drops when I hear the hint of an accent. Not Strike, but Axe, Strike's best friend. We met a few times around the office. Tall and ruggedly handsome with a well-groomed beard and piercing navy-blue eyes, he always brings with him the warmest, kindest vibe despite looking like he could bench-press both me and Josie with one arm.

"Axe! You came!" I say, genuinely pleased. I also sent him the invite but figured he had better things to do. Josie looks up, and

I watch her eyes widen and register the bulk of him as they sweep him from head to toe.

"Excuse me, are you a Scorpio rising?" she asks, unable to conceal the wonder in her voice. Axe turns to her and looks her up and down in much the same way she did him, though his lips are quirked, as if what he sees amuses him.

"Scorpio rising? What are you bletherin' on about, woman? Please tell me you don't believe in that shite," he says, his Scottish brogue rich with amusement.

"Not shite, or shit, or whatever," Josie says, indignant. "Astrology has been around for centuries as an accurate framework for how time of birth influences personalities and choices. It's very real, even if you are too small-minded to believe in it. Also, I don't *blether*, whatever that means, thank you very much."

"I am a man of science. Not constellation-ology," Axe says, chest puffing.

Jo looks like she might deck him if he weren't built like a bull. "Excuse me, Honor," she says, "I'm getting another drink."

As she storms off, I laugh to myself. Axe might be twice her size, but Jo can definitely hold her own. Don't believe in astrology? Not a problem for her. *Laugh* at astrology? Jo will take you down.

"What was that?" Axe asks, genuinely bewildered. He watches her move across the room with the awe of a kid meeting Santa for the first time and discovering he is real after all.

"That was a Josie," I say.

Twenty minutes later, I've toured the exhibit, talked to almost everyone, and now, alone, I don't know what to do with myself—beyond avoiding Strike. Actually, I haven't seen him in a while; if he's left, I'd bet anything that tomorrow I'll get a bouquet of flowers with a card in his blocky penmanship telling me how great tonight was—even if he thought it was awful and couldn't wait to get out of here with his leggy young girlfriend. Ever the gentleman. Would he really just leave, though? My spirits sink when I can't find him in the crowd.

Okay, chin up, Honor. You still need to mingle, talk shop, and shake off this torturous impostor syndrome for good.

The smiling Honor in the photograph sure thinks she has the right to star in a one-woman show.

Caterers glide past, bearing trays with champagne and tiny morsels of food. Beautiful bites of smoked salmon, beef tenderloin sliders, and tiny quiches. It occurs to me that the rich are good at either miniature or mansion scale. Very rarely do they play in between. But even doll food would be too much for my nervous stomach to handle right now.

I scoop up a flute and down a honeyed pour of champagne.

The truth is, I do not belong among this gilded crowd. It's a lot more than I bargained for. More people. More glitz. I'm a shopgirl. A part-time artist who never even went to art school. Who decided that I should be the toast of the town, anyway? I feel like a fraud.

"Ah. The guest of honor."

Strike's voice sends a bolt through me. I turn.

"I thought you'd left."

"Before giving you my regards?" Strike raises an eyebrow, and in his thoughtful expression, I see that he understands how he has inspired this entire show—and that he might even feel a touch of pride in his role as my muse. After all, as the program shows, the title of my exhibit is *Dark Pastimes*.

Suddenly I feel way too naked, my heart hanging out there for all to see. The complete awkwardness of my obsession is up on every wall, and Strike is here with another woman. At least he is alone right now, detached from his date, who's now standing with Paula. I hadn't realized Paula was coming. She and the other woman are on the other side of the room, looking at one of my favorite paintings, *Comes the Wolf.* The six-foot canvas is, even for me, a work of unbridled imagination. A humanesque wolf stares out from the stuffy trappings of a nineteenth-century botanical garden. He's in a three-piece suit, choked by a necktie.

Yet the wolf is wild. His expression is so provocative, he might leap out of the canvas to grab his observer by the throat. I painted Strike into the gray of the wolf's eye. In the scruff of his jawline. What does Strike's new girlfriend think of it? Can everyone here see what I did? It's all so mortifying.

Strike follows my gaze to Paula.

"Paula's daughter's doing an internship at DME," he says. "She's a hard worker. Nice kid. She's majoring in gender studies at Penn State. Has lots of thoughts on equity and hentai."

Relief bowls me over as my consuming tension over this young woman's presence here melts away. Now I see her resemblance to Paula. That serious face and touch of cup-handle ears.

Not a date. The weight lifts off my shoulders, dissipating into thin air.

"And congratulations," he adds, lightly pinging his champagne glass against mine. "It's stunning to see it all here at once."

"Thank you." I take the compliment. Let it tingle and flow through my body like the champagne.

"And those green dots!"

"Green dots?" At my puzzled expression, Strike grins. "Whenever a piece has been purchased, the gallery marks it on the wall with a green dot. You didn't notice?" Now he breaks out his full-wattage smile. "Only you would come to your own gallery exhibit and not know that every piece sold out within the first hour."

The hairs on the back of my neck stand up.

Sales. Sales, *plural*.

"Honor!" We both turn to see that Benny Mendez has just arrived. He's bald, with a trimmed goatee, multiple earrings, and a billowing printed blouse. "This is amazing," he says, giving me a kiss on each cheek like they do in France. "Isn't this amazing?" Benny poses the question to Strike.

"Absolutely. The art is truly original, one of a kind. Much like Honor herself," Strike says, and the sound of my name in his voice sends a trembling surge through me as I remember how he's spoken it before, on other nights, in different contexts. But nothing in his face betrays him now.

"Exactly! Your work is truly special, darling," says Benny. "The way you merge dark and light. The mundane and the savage. The themes of innocence and guilt. Sex and passion. Hyperrealism mixed with occasional absurdity, especially around themes of shame. The moment I saw it, I knew it was spectacular!"

"Um, thank you?" I'm trying to process his compliments, but my skin is prickling with heat and my head swims with all those words. To be honest, I'm worried I might pass out. It's too much.

"This show has been an unequivocal hit. Not that I ever had a doubt. It's so hard to find a fresh new voice. You must let us do your next exhibit."

"Thank you. Of course. I'm always working on new stuff," I say. I infuse my voice with confidence. If Benny thinks I belong here, then I belong here.

Oh, Gracie, if you could see me now!

Maybe she can. Maybe she's right beside me, smiling along

with me. An echo, a whisper, the faintest ghostly doppelgänger. I hope so.

And now that I'm looking for them, I can see that the room is a sea of green dots. My work has value, like Gracie always said.

Later, after I've done my best to work the room—a concept wholly foreign to me until tonight—Strike joins me again.

"I like the new pieces," he says, motioning to the corner. My exhibit has been broken into two groups on opposite walls. On one side, the erotic work: nude bodies, limbs entangled, desire stamped across the women's faces. And on the other, the portraits I painted after I left DME. "That one in particular: *Strike and Burn*? Was that a . . . little revenge?"

"If I was guilty of anything," I tell him, "it's that I missed you."

"You're blushing."

"I'm not." I raise my chin even though I could be auditioning for the role of a tomato in a school play.

He smirks. "Tell me more about these revenge paintings."

I drain my champagne. "All right. Well. Two things I know about Strike Madden? He values his privacy as much as he values control."

"True."

"Making these pieces felt like I was peeling back your layers and exposing you to the world," I explain. "In a beautiful way, I hope. Because I love your multitudes. Prince Charming. Entrepreneur. Titan of Industry. Monster. Warrior. Wolf. Lover." We are walking slowly through the gallery, and I feel the warmth of him. His pull is as magnetic as ever.

"I like *Comes the Wolf* best," he says.

"I wasn't sure how you would react to these. Part of me thought you would be absolutely furious."

"No. They're just too damn good." That smile. I don't know how to deal with this version of Strike who lets me see how genuinely excited he is about my success.

"So, you . . . you really like them?" I ask.

"Honor, I love them." When he looks at me, the heat rises through my body like Strike's own best whiskey. "I'd have bought every single one, but I was too late. They'd all been sold. You're brilliant, Honor. Every person here thinks so."

"So none of those green dots . . . were you?" I had halfway assumed they were all Strike—another P. G. Delgado situation.

"I wish they were," says Strike. "But none are me. Or Paula."

"Oh." Strike wasn't my benefactor. My relief is washed with pride.

"Which was a bummer, until I remembered I do have an in with the artist. So I'm hoping I can commission something from her directly."

"You want to commission a painting of yourself?" I ask teasingly. "I'd think there was enough of you on these walls to satisfy you."

"'Satisfy,'" he repeats. "Interesting word. I'm not sure a piece of art could ever truly satisfy me. Not when the artist always leaves me wanting more."

"But you've never tested this theory." I say this lightly, though I feel anything but light. I feel hot and full of desire—brimming with a new confidence that doesn't feel entirely like me.

"Honor," Strike's mouth is only an inch from my ear. "That's not fair."

"Not even once?" I ask. "Just once?"

"Once would never be enough."

"Or maybe, in this case, it would be exactly enough." I lift my chin. "Tell me you haven't thought about me."

"Are you kidding? You're in my head every goddamn second of every goddamn day. I can't seem to get you out of there," he says. "And believe me, I've tried."

"I'm not in your head now," I tell him. "I'm standing right here in front of you. And things are different. After all, I don't work for you anymore." I smile. "Apparently, I'm a successful self-made artist."

Hunger burns in his eyes, and in this moment, Strike hasn't just inspired *Comes the Wolf*—he's become the painting.

My nostrils flare with all my memories of him. Our specific, magnetic intensity has always felt like destiny.

But now, surrounded by my own art, I feel bold with bright and shiny new self-assurance.

Occasionally, I do know exactly what I want.

"I'm so hard I can't think straight." He half smiles ruefully as he steps away from me. As if physical distance will make this easier. It doesn't. It intensifies what's between us. Magnifies the pull.

"I'm so wet," I whisper. Only now does my evening wrap slip from my shoulders. In this bright gallery light, the faded burn marks that striate my upper back are like tiger stripes, clear as day.

I've never shown these scars before.

But something about this room makes me different.

Or maybe it's this dress.

But I couldn't be more exposed than I am tonight—it's like that awful dream of walking naked through your high school. And yet tonight is anything but awful. Even though the gallery is still bustling with gawkers, I'm not ashamed.

If Strike is surprised, he doesn't show it, but there's a coal-bright intensity in his eyes as he slowly walks around me for a better view. My heart is fluttering harder than a firefly trapped in a jar as he stops behind me.

Then he turns me to face him; he traces a finger along my jaw, and then presses it to his lips. From my peripheral vision, I am aware that we are being watched—and I don't care.

"You want me? Despite everything you know? Despite everything you yourself have been through? You've known violence, Honor. You've known monsters." Strike's quiet voice is harsh with frustration. "I killed that man with pleasure, Honor."

"Don't you get it? I'm glad—I *rejoice*—that you did," I say. "Nobody else was going to protect me from Troy. Nobody." I swallow the sob in the back of my throat as my voice catches. "We don't get to decide who we want or need. Desire makes the decisions. Even the bad ones."

"Maybe especially the bad ones," he says. His eyes are dark, ravenous. We are standing so close I feel the heat off his skin, hot as sunshine.

"I love you, Strike Madden," I tell him. No matter what happens next, I can't imagine that I would ever regret saying these words. The truth. "Now fuck me one last time or lose me for good."

Strike does not hesitate. He takes my hand, and we head for the door.

FORTY-NINE

STRIKE

Now

Neither of us speaks as my Jag leaps down South Street. The car feels alive; I take every turn too fast, and I could not give less of a shit. I'm not worried about my precious rims. I feel Honor next to me, her uneven breathing, the way she's squeezing her thighs together, and I'm so hard it aches. If the choice is between fucking her or losing her, I am one hundred percent down to fuck.

Besides, I already know how it feels to lose her. Shipwrecked, that's how.

When I valet park outside the Keystone, Honor smiles.

It's the same place where I had to say goodbye to her the night we met—a night that was doomed in so many ways.

But tonight is a start, not an ending.

One swipe of my AmEx, and we've got the entire penthouse. I shoot the concierge a look, and he knows better than to escort us to the twentieth floor. Part of what I pay for—part of what money guarantees—is my absolute privacy.

The VIP deluxe suite is breathtaking, with wraparound windows and an unparalleled view of the city below.

Honor gasps when she sees it all, and her face is pure girlish delight. Even though I'm used to this suite, this view—the Keystone penthouse is where I put up my out-of-town clients—tonight, it's another kind of magic. Our private Eden. When I look out over downtown Shelton I see our shadowed reflection, which reminds me of one of those trippy VR games Honor designed.

Knowing that tonight is no game, not some fantasy drawing or anime, gets me so hard again I feel like my cock could rip through my pants.

But I'm not going to touch her. Not just yet. I haven't even reached out my hand for hers. Instead I let the tension escalate, let it vibrate between us like a force field as we stand together, staring out at the city.

Tonight, finally, I get to take what is mine.

So why not make her wait a little? The same way I made her wait when she came over to Ashburn. Knowing how bad Honor wants it, how she's initiated this, gives me a feeling of control—as temporary or delusional as it may be, since I'm battling the impulse to tear off her dress right this second and fuck her raw.

I cut a look at her, her skin soft and pale against that black dress. Her scars are etched deep across her back and shoulders—I've long known that Honor's skin was marked by some sort of scar or birthmark, since seeing her body by candlelight that night when I almost accidentally set my bedroom on fire. By the light of the moon, her scars are both worse and more beautiful. Worse because there are so many of them and beautiful because they have faded to make an intricate pattern that looks as natural as an etching of twisted vines.

Still, with her scars in full view, part of me is immediately enraged and restless with an all-too-familiar feeling, wanting to hunt down and destroy the coward shitbag—wherever they are—who marked her forever.

But I'm on Honor's timeline, waiting for when she wants to talk about them.

Tonight belongs to us.

I watch as Honor tucks a piece of silky hair behind her ear and chews a corner of her lower lip. "I've never thought of Shelton as beautiful," she says, shyly breaking the silence. "But looking down on the lights, the landmarks, even the view of the mountains in the distance—it feels like a symphony. Everything fits together so perfectly."

"It's all a matter of perspective," I say. "You're the artist. You should know that." Then I finally reach my hand across to hers, and catch her pinkie, hard, with mine. It's a tiny movement, a snake capturing its prey, and she gasps. The electric shock slices through my body.

"Strike," she says as she glances at me, her voice soft but serious, "I need you to know something. I lied before. I don't want this to be a one-time thing. Even if I said—" But I don't let her finish. I move quickly, reeling her in, crushing my lips against hers as I press the back of her body against the window. Her breath catches in her throat, and I can practically hear the switch flick in my own brain as I leave that other self behind.

Honor told me she accepted the real me.

She swore she could handle it. I want to believe it.

But we won't know until we try.

And I can't hold back any longer. I need to consume her, to feel every inch of her skin's softness against mine, to taste her lips again and again, to feel the powerful electricity that will surge through both our bodies when we come together.

My kisses are punishing, an explosion of pent-up lust, but she meets my tongue with equal violence as her head tips back, exposing her throat. Does she know I've thought about that beautiful throat of hers? How it would feel when I've got her on her knees again, her mouth unhinged and gargling my cock?

I want this woman. All of her.

I lift her up, keeping her back pressed against the cold glass, and her legs reflexively wrap around my waist. Fuck. I need her closer. I need her naked. I need every last inch of me buried *inside* her.

As she pulls at my shirt, ripping it, a button goes flying across the room.

"Off," she whispers, but it's not my shirt that's coming off first. I lower her to the ground, and with a single hand, I unzip that beautiful dress that's been taunting me all night. I loosen my grasp for a split second to let it fall to the floor where it belongs.

She steps out of the puddle of dark fabric and stands before me in only a sheer black bra and a matching thong.

She's . . . gorgeous. A goddess. I swallow.

If anyone in the city cared to look up twenty floors, they could see us. My own desperate animal hunger.

Let them look.

There is no other woman in this whole fucked-up fucking world who is like her. I trail kisses down her neck, loop her delicate satin bra straps around my fingers, and tug hard. My mouth takes her nipple, and I scrape it with my teeth. She groans softly in response, and it sets me on fire.

She grabs at my belt and swiftly unbuckles it. She pulls down my pants, along with my boxer briefs, and I spring out into her open hand. My erection finally uncaged, there is no denying how much I want her. The pooling of precum already glistens at my tip. I pull her up into a hot, wet kiss. She catches my bottom lip between her teeth and moans into my mouth.

"I like when you make those noises," I say.

She's panting now, and I haven't even reached between her legs.

"You're killing me—no fair," she says.

"Life isn't fair," I say, and then drop to my knees. I inhale the smell of her innermost parts. I'm all wolf right now, ready to eat. She's so fucking wet.

I shimmy her soaked panties down over her hips, and she kicks them away. I kneel in front of her like she's an altar and I'm saying a prayer. She is naked and trembling, and I lean toward her slowly. Carefully. The growl in my throat erupts as I trail kisses along the inside of her thigh until my tongue is centered between her legs, tasting the sweet tang of her, and I cannot get enough. I circle my tongue, and she grips my shoulders, her fingernails digging so hard into my back, as if she wants to leave marks. Her toes are clenched, holding on to the sensation exactly like that painting I bought and keep in my bedroom. So tightly coiled, on the brink of explosion.

She makes a little sound, wanting and wordless—I'm incapable of words at the moment, too. Only desire and revelation.

"You're so fucking delicious. I cannot wait to see you come," I finally say, looking up briefly. Her eyes catch mine, and I can see she's on the edge. I sneak a finger inside her as I continue to feast on her like she's an all-you-can eat buffet. I grab her ass and pull her greedily to my face. *More.* She's shaking with pleasure now, her legs shifting back and forth—*this goddamn woman will be the death of me*—as she releases into a shuddering climax, a plunge of pleasure against the cold night sky.

Now I feel myself on the brink, and she's barely even touched me.

Fucking has never felt like this before—so shattering, so extreme.

I stand and kiss her slowly, and her taste lingers on my lips. With one hand, I gather a hank of her hair, twisting it hard so it wraps around my wrist as I pivot her so that I can explore every inch of her skin. I stroke and coax her orgasm along, lingering on her perfect hard nipples, her navel, her collarbone.

She is a work of art created for my pleasure.

FIFTY

HONOR

Now

As my climax ebbs through me, so powerful that I'm leaning my arms against the glass to hold myself up, I hear Strike tear the wrapper off a condom. I'm whimpering for him. I've waited so long, and now the only thing I need in this life is to feel the strength and pressure of him inside me.

I cannot get close enough.

He lines himself up with my entrance and teases me for a second.

"My beauty," he says. "You are beautiful." I want to correct him. I am not beautiful. Beautiful people do not do the things I have done. But then I realize: if there's anyone who understands my brand of broken, it is this man. Maybe it's true; he can look at me and see who I really am, the beauty that exists in my soul.

Because that's exactly how I see him.

"Please, now. Fuck me now," I say, not caring that he's reduced me to pleading.

"Listen to you, ordering me around," he says, amused, but he doesn't wait. He fists his magnificent cock and pumps once, hard, before he turns me, thrusting into my pussy from behind, and the sheer force is everything I wanted. Forceful, unyielding, opening me up so quickly I cry out. I didn't expect him to be gentle, but his strength makes me gasp. We are finally locked together. Strike's growl is a deep, satisfied sound from the base of his throat.

"Honor," he says, his voice rough with lust, "I can't tell you how many times I've dreamed of this moment."

Him and me both. My head falls back, and my eyes flutter closed. His thrusts are deep, firm, and full, and it's not long before I feel myself starting to wind up again, circling through ever-spiraling rings of desire.

"How can you be even better than my dreams?" he asks as he pushes me up against the glass, the cold searing my breasts. His fingers easily find my clit and begin their expert work.

"You, you," I whisper. It's going too fast. I want to slow us down, I want to feel this thrill forever, but I know it's already too late. I'm too far gone.

"You own this city, Honor," he whispers roughly, his other hand twisting back up into my hair as his lips leave a trail of kisses along the nape of my neck. "But I own you, too. You are mine, aren't you?"

I can only moan a yes. My breath is shuddering in tiny gasps of exquisite pleasure as I place my fingertips on the window's glass, my panting breath fogging our reflections as Strike sets his hands on either side of my hips, easing me into his rhythm. I stare down at the city below us, the cars and pedestrians reduced to doll-sized figurines. This whole city always felt so intimidating when I wasn't sure of my own place in it. Now I'm here, on top of the world—and yet all I can think about is what I feel for this one extraordinary, ferocious man.

Strike's breath is hot in my ear as his teeth lightly nip and nibble at me.

"Every inch," he whispers as he slams into me hard. "All for you."

"Yes," I manage to whisper.

"Tell me what you like. Tell me what you want."

"All of you," I gasp. "How wet you're making me. The way you fill me. The way you're owning me with every stroke. The pulse of your fingers on me."

"I'm bringing you to the edge. Jesus Christ, I can feel you tightening around me. I can feel every bit of you. You're fucking killing me." His fingers continue their magic as he pumps in and out, like he's a master-class maestro.

"Yes. I'm here," I manage to gasp. "I'm . . ."

And then, just short of my next crescendoing orgasm, Strike stops, sliding out his shaft to its thick tip.

I buck against him, but his flexed hands easily keep me from him, and his strength is suddenly almost laughably obvious; it takes him so little effort to keep me exactly where he wants me.

"Let me look at you, baby," he says. "Please let me look at you."

"What are you doing? Don't stop now. I'm so close." I'm begging him. Practically sobbing. I honestly feel like I'll die if he doesn't get back inside me right now.

"Ah, I know how close you are," he whispers. "But I needed to take a moment to enjoy *my* view." And then his hands lift me up by my ass cheeks so that I'm on tiptoe. My body burns, feeling Strike's eyes following every curve and dip of my body.

"Please," I whimper. "I've never wanted anything so badly."

These words are all the magic I need. Strike makes a guttural sound and pushes into me again. This time burying himself inside me so deeply that I cry out. The only other sounds are the thrust of his body and the slick, slippery, wet noises of my sex.

He's given me everything I've ever wanted all at once, and together we ascend. He seems to know exactly when to pause so I'm right at the edge; he draws me back and then moves again before finally, finally he takes me to the climax. I come hard and fast, and I feel him release inside me. The rich, shuddering collapse is so exquisite that tears stream down my face.

"The little death," says Strike, his whisper rough in my ear.

"Yes," I say. "It feels just like that."

"It's what the French call the orgasm. La petite mort."

The term rolls off his tongue. "La petite mort," I repeat shyly. I took Spanish at Roosevelt High—and only two years of it at that. The closest I've ever come to France is Benny's double-cheek kiss earlier tonight.

I press my legs together to calm the warmth juddering through my body. Yes, that's exactly what this feels like: the most delicious little death.

Does that make Strike your killer?

I'm too spent to care if it does.

I close my eyes and lean back against him. I let him hold me up.

I'm very happy to die a little.

FIFTY-ONE

HONOR

Now

As morning light streaks through the windows, my eyes open, and I remember all the goodness in a rush. My spent and tingling body. The night of my life. My crowded art exhibit. Every piece sold. The man currently sleeping soundly in my arms, his eyelashes curled upward and as thick as Bambi's, one muscular arm thrown over the pillow so that his fingertips are threaded in my hair. The fact that my entire life has seemingly changed overnight.

I'm overwhelmed with conflicting emotions. The thrill, of course, and I'm basking in the seductive sensations of last night. But now also the apprehension. How ironic that feeling truly alive is so inextricably linked to my fear of all I've got to lose.

When Strike begins to stir, I stroke his hair and kiss his forehead. He looks so beautiful asleep—a peaceful warrior—and there's a serenity in his face that I've never seen when he's awake.

Last night was unforgettable. Not only the sex, though I never knew it could be like that. My body ignited like wildfire, blazing hotter than I'd ever imagined as Strike pushed my pleasure to its limits. It's always been more than that with us, every moment of contact with him has been seared into the very essence of my being—this indelible, electrifying connection. It's an overwhelming force and an irresistible magnetism, like being suspended within a bubble of pure, electric enchantment.

The way Strike touched my body like every part of it was a gift he'd won.

The way he kissed my mouth like he was making a wish on my lips.

The way we seemed to fit, not seamless and smooth but perfectly jagged. A zipper.

The way we came together again and again.

"Hey, you," Strike says, his eyes fluttering open. He reaches out and rolls me back toward his body, my ass pressed to his hardness, my back against his chest, his long lashes tickling my neck as he brushes his lips against me.

"Hi," I say softly.

"You're magnificent," he says, pressing the lightest kisses along my throat. His mouth turns insistent, parting my lips, his tongue pushing, then plunging, then feather-light and flickering. It's as if he's reminding me of everything that devilish tongue has done and can do.

Time falls away. All I know is this gorgeous man's mouth, and I feel—in that way I've come to know so well with Strike—that we are having an entire conversation in this soft, wet, unending story of kisses that are spinning me into giddy eddies of desire.

Strike is kissing me, yes. But he is also somehow taking possession. Claiming me while I claim him.

Finally he lifts his head, and as we smile at each other, the mood shifts and the intensity dissolves. He presses his face into the joint where my neck meets my collarbone. "I'm inhaling you," he says, his voice muffled.

He's so burrowed in, it reminds me of Fivestar nosing around for a snack in the couch cushions. I giggle.

"Don't forget to leave a review," I tell him, and then he reaches forward and grabs my foot and tickles me till I shriek.

After we go still, I let the moment sink deep into my bones. I've lived long and hard enough to know that this sort of perfection is fleeting, that I have to absorb every second of goodness to fuel me when it's gone. I will take this memory treasure and put it in a box—like one of those beautiful wooden keepsakes we sell at the shop.

He shifts so that my body tips and rolls deeper into the crook of his arm. "Hey, I think this is called making Honor roll," he says, and I'm still smiling at the corny joke when he adds, his voice quiet against in my neck, "We do need to talk."

My skin prickles. "Not now," I say. I want the moment to last forever. And if not forever, at least another couple of minutes.

"Okay. Not now," he agrees, and then I lift my body onto his. I rise and slowly, so slowly, sink onto him so that he's fully inside me. An image I've painted so many times in the studio come to life. And before I begin to rock, to ride this wave of pleasure, I hold him, and the moment. Press it deep into me to cherish.

We shower together, soaping and sudsing each other, our bodies sliding against each other, our kisses as wet as our skin. Then Strike orders us a breakfast of fluffy scrambled eggs, juice, pancakes, and coffee. We wrap up in big white bunny-soft hotel robes, and when the food comes, all perfectly presented on silver trays, I eat ravenously.

My whole body feels like spun sugar, smugly sex-drunk, and yet I'm still hungry despite last night's excess. Strike takes me again, on the floor, and this time he's so hard and our movements together are so perfect they feel choreographed, a synchronized duet right up to the moment of release. It's wild how we already understand each other's bodies, how we anticipate the other's needs, and yet that's how it feels. Like we're talking and answering without having to say a single word out loud.

I didn't know making love could be such a smooth, intuitive dance. Maybe it's because he's already seen all my desires on canvas. Maybe it's because in every instance he puts me first; he's the apex of discipline and control as he holds off finishing until I climax so we come together.

Maybe it's because our souls speak the same strange language.

We're still lying together, all damp skin and heaving breaths, when there's a knock on the door. Strike jumps up and throws on a robe to open it.

When he returns, he's laughing.

"The concierge sent us a bottle of champagne," he says. "Guess we were a little loud. Want a mimosa?"

"Sure." Sex mimosas? Why not. He pops the bottle and we clink glasses. Is there such a thing as too much joy? I run my fingers through his wet, freshly washed hair, and he purrs like a jungle cat in pleasure. We're on the couch now, resting our bodies.

"You sound like a giant Fivestar," I say.

"Who's Fivestar?" he asks.

"My new cat," I say, and Strike barks out a laugh.

"Perfect name. Two thumbs up. Dare I give it . . . five stars?"

I laugh.

"I'm glad you got a new friend. I didn't like thinking about you all alone in your apartment," Strike says.

"You've never even been upstairs to my apartment," I say.

"Having seen your store, I can imagine it. Cozy blankets?"

"Check—though you've got the best blanket."

"Lots of overflow knickknacks?"

"Check."

"A bounty of sex toys."

"Not quite a bounty, but yeah."

"Yum. And I bet it also smells like you." Strike's nose is deep in my neck again, as he takes another whiff. And then he sits back, and his voice turns serious. "Honor, I need to tell you a few things. If we are going to do this—and God knows I hope we are—I need you to understand me. For you to go into this with your eyes open."

"Hey, my eyes are wide open," I say, turning to flutter my eyelashes at him. He chuckles.

"I've shown you who I am by taking you to see what I did to Simpson. I've trusted you in a way I've never trusted anyone. But I need you to understand how I became who I am."

"I'm listening," I say. "Tell me about Kate."

FIFTY-TWO

STRIKE

Now

Hearing Kate's name on Honor's lips, my muscles tighten as if braced for a blow. "You know about . . . Kate?" I ask. I do my best to keep my tone neutral, detached, as if it's no big deal that she knows her name. But of course it's a big fucking deal.

Who told her? Did Axe screw up his internet scrub?

No, Axe doesn't make mistakes.

It doesn't matter anyway. This conversation is inevitable. In fact, I'm the one who started it in the first place. I hadn't planned on getting this specific, though.

"I just know her name. You said it when you were having that nightmare. And I saw the picture on your bedside table." Honor's eyes meet mine, and they are soft with compassion I don't deserve. "They're your . . . family?"

Like it's a simple question. Like there's an easy answer. But can I call them my family when they are no longer mine?

When I wasn't able to protect them and keep them?

I lean my head back against the couch and gather Honor so she's tucked under my chin. This will be easier if I don't have to see her face, to see the pity that will soon be written across it. She laces her fingers through mine. I squeeze once.

A yes in answer to her question. *They were my family.*

"Tell me everything," she says.

"Kate was my wife. And Henry . . ." I clear my throat. I start again. "Henry was my son."

"Was," Honor says, softly. This time there's no lilt. She's not asking. The *was* is really all she needs to know.

"They were murdered," I say. Honor does not react to this bombshell. She doesn't even flinch, and if I wasn't sure I loved her before, I am one hundred percent certain now. "Cops still have no idea who did it. I've been searching on my own for years. One theory is that the guy might have gotten fixated on one of the early combat-focused Dark Matter games. Which, if that's true, means it's all my fault."

"Big if, and either way, it's not your fault," she says, but I wave her words away. We're not going to debate my culpability. There's no point. We both know I've done much worse since. If Hell exists, I know where I'm headed.

"The only other possibility was an obsessed ex-boyfriend of Kate's who she dated in college. That guy fell off the planet—we've never been able to locate him—so we don't know for sure, but statistically he's the most likely suspect. We managed to keep it all out of the news—didn't want a copycat getting any ideas if it was work-related. And I discontinued the game soon after. I wasn't going to take any chances. Pivoted away from all of it, to be honest."

"And now you are building a sexy VR feminist hentai empire instead," Honor says, and I can hear the giggle in her voice. I can't help but smile.

"Anyway, he's out there, whoever he is. Possibly destroying other people's lives like he destroyed mine."

"And so now in addition to sexifying the metaverse, you protect other people's families. That's why you do . . . what you do, right?" Tentatively, she traces her finger along my tattoo.

I nod, cup her face between my palms, and kiss each of her eyes softly. "Yup, that's why I do what I do. We can't get back what we've lost, but if there's any way that I can help survivors transform pain into power, I'm all in. Sure, I'll go after the abuser—they are so clearly the bad guys, no gray area—and it's my nature; it's the skill I was trained in." His jaw flexes. "But I never want to forget the victims."

"Like that first time . . . when I met you in the morgue."

I nod. "After Esperanza Martinez was killed, Turning Point managed to locate an older sister living in Guatemala—Esperanza had been sending her money every month, hoping to bring her to the States. We got the sister here, safely and legally, and we set her up with an apartment and a job plus night classes in business admin in exchange for being the legal guardian of her orphaned niece and nephews. Otherwise, three kids would have been split up and sent off to God knows where."

Honor is hanging on my every word. "That's incredible," she says, her eyes full. "A rescue like that would have been lifesaving for Grace and me after . . ." She swallows, shakes off the thought, and I gather her in even tighter,

"We can't save them all. But a place like Turning Point heals hearts, reclaims lives, and even helps to build out a few dreams, too," I say. "At least, that's what I believe. That's why I show up."

"So tell me about them," she says softly. "About Kate and Henry."

Can I do this? I wonder. It's always been too difficult to talk about them, to share out loud without feeling like I'm handing over too much of myself. Honor waits patiently, like she can tell I need a minute to gather my courage.

"Kate was . . . a force," I begin, and once I start, I find that the words are easy, even if talking means I'm letting this woman see my vulnerabilities. I showed her who I am at the morgue, but this is me stripped bare. Strike the Loving Husband was shattered and has been buried and locked away behind Strike the Vigilante Killer. "Kate was Irish, fun-loving. She loved nothing better than a big birthday party or an open-air concert—but she'd also stop to watch the sunset. She was a hands-on mom, too, who loved our boy—she was always dressing him like a little man and singing sea shanties and lullabies to him. She made forts with the couch cushions, and she'd read him twenty books at bedtime. But she could be a mama bear. I remember once a kid threw a rock at Henry at the playground, and I thought she'd get arrested, the way she went after that family." I stop. If this woman can still be with me after seeing what I'm capable of, she deserves nothing less than the truth. I take a breath and say it: "I loved her."

Honor's eyes go dark, and I don't see any jealousy there. Only vicarious pain. We both know what it is to love and lose, to play the terrible gamble that's part and parcel of real living.

"She was kind and funny," I continue. "She had a quick temper and unreasonable obsessions with olives and the weather. She was messy—she drove me up the wall because she never fully closed the tops of the cereal boxes. She loved the beach and drinks with umbrellas, and she made everyone rum cake at Christmas, and I still can't get my head around the fact that someone that vibrant can be here one day and gone the next . . ." My voice cracks, and I clear my throat. "Anyhow, she was mine, and I was hers. For a while."

"And Henry . . ."

"Henry." What can be said about Henry? "He was fucking perfect. A joy. So beautiful it hurt to look at him. I didn't know something that pure could exist. Maybe it can't."

Honor moves closer into me, as if she's trying to turn herself into a blanket. To keep me rooted in place.

"He had a little sprig of ginger hair when he was born. And he loved to talk. Babbled all day long like he was the narrator in a story. 'Dada, this is a tree. Dada, ice cream is a sometimes food. Dada, Mommy was mad at preschool pickup today. Dada, did you know caterpillars turn into butterflies?'"

I swallow hard and close my eyes. For just a second I can see and hear him—*Dada, Dada, Dada, Dada*. What would Henry think about the fact that the man who was his father no longer exists?

My heart squeezes, and it all hurts so fucking much it's like someone is carving my fucking guts out with one of my antique knives.

Henry.

He once asked me: *Dada, did you know kids can die?* And I lied straight to his face. *You will never die*, I promised. *I will always protect you.*

"I don't have kids yet," Honor says softly, and I surprise myself by not clenching at the word *yet*. Instead, I draw her closer to me. "But I know exactly what it feels like when you can't save the one thing you were put on Earth to protect."

"I say his name," I admit, which is something I've never told anyone. Not even the therapist I went to for a while after the murder. The one who told me to meditate, like that would change a single fucking thing. Like that could tame even one molecule of my infinite rage. "I say it all the time. Because the rest of the world has already forgotten him. But he existed. He was real. So I'll say it while brushing my teeth. Or driving to the store. Henry."

"Henry," Honor repeats.

"Henry Patrick Madden," I say.

"That picture in your bedroom," Honor says. "You were all so beautiful together. Like the gorgeous stock photo that comes with the frame."

"Sometimes that's exactly what that photo feels like. Not quite real," I say. "A fantasy life."

She braids our fingers together.

"Maybe I didn't know them, but I promise I will help you keep their memory alive. You loved them, and so I love them—Kate and Henry."

Her cheeks are wet, and so are mine. I kiss her tears away. A damp press of skin on skin.

"Now it's my turn to tell you something," Honor says. "Because the truth is, you and me? We are not that different."

FIFTY-THREE

HONOR

Now

I reach for my purse on the table and open it. Hand Strike the tiny silver square of wrapping paper. Then I retreat to the corner of the couch, my arms folded over my knees, so that I can look at Strike face-to-face.

Strike takes the paper. The midmorning sun catches its twinkling metallic surface. "What is it?"

"It belonged to my baby brother, Rusty."

Strike's expression is both curious and concerned. He prongs the paper carefully between two fingers and lifts it to catch more of the light, the way Rusty used to. It kills me a little. "You have a brother?"

"Had," I say. Strike closes his eyes for a beat.

"Rusty Stone," he says, and I smile in appreciation.

"That's him. My little brother, Rusty Pacer Stone. My mom had a Pacer, and she said nothing ever made her feel freer than that car. Anyway, Rusty was quirky. He collected scrap paper like this. I'm sure if he had more time or we had more money or if my parents were fundamentally different people, he'd have gotten some sort of help or tools, maybe a diagnosis at some point. The world was always too confusing and too loud for him. But we weren't that sort of family. We weren't . . . a family at all." The emotion wells up and thickens my voice.

I take the paper from Strike, and smooth it, the same way I saw my little brother do a thousand times.

"Tell me the rest," Strike says.

And so softly, hesitantly, I tell my whole story. I am unwavering, unsparing of the details. The little house of horrors. Daddy's rampages, Mama unwilling—or unable—to put up a hand. Gracie's and my hollow tree. I hold out my arms, the scars I know he's touched, but now I match them with their stories. I stand up and show him the dozens and dozens of thin, flat, white scars, slightly lighter than my skin, that crosshatch along my calves from Daddy's belt buckle. Then I drop the robe halfway down my back and lift my hair, so he can look at the worst scar. The one from the fire. Pale raised ridges like a tire's tread marks. The lasting imprint of the scorching press of my skin against a flaming wall.

I remember that quote "History is written by the victors," and I wonder if that's true. Because I didn't etch these stories on my skin. And yet here they are, written on my body. I am passing them on. Or perhaps letting them go.

I am victim, villain, and victor all at once.

Strike has gone so quiet that I can hear all the other kinds of quietness in the room—the distant traffic, the hum of the air conditioner.

"My parents. My dad was—" I don't know how to finish the sentence, because there is no word for what he was. A sadist? A sociopath? Evil? An abusive asshole? He doesn't deserve the comfort of a generic label.

"Yeah, I know," Strike says, letting me leave it undefined. Which is another perfect Strike kindness. A secret, quiet gift.

"They died in a house fire. Gracie got Rusty out. And I tried to save my mom. But not my dad." As I say it, that night floods back. Mama, Rusty, Gracie, all in their rooms, sound asleep. Daddy passed out on the couch.

"The rest of us escaped, except for Mama. She chose Daddy. She always chose Daddy. But I chose Gracie, Rusty, and me. It was a house of pain and rage. We had to get out." Strike nods. "Daddy deserved much worse. As a kid—because that's what I was, an abused, terrified kid—it seemed like a solution. He was gone, we were free."

I hold up the wrapping paper. A sad scrap of nothing.

My eyes fill. My Rusty.

"But there were consequences. Rusty had night terrors. He stopped speaking. He stopped being anything, really. He was placed with a foster family who didn't have the resources to take care of him, either, and they couldn't help him. Gracie and I were also separated into different homes, but we would visit him as much as we could. Still, something in him had shifted. He'd just gone so deep into himself, there was no finding him. And then," I continue after taking a moment to steady my voice, "for his twelfth birthday, Gracie and I were going to take him to Six Flags. He'd been talking about it for years, and we had it all planned. We were going to take the bus, grab lunch. The morning we went to pick him up, we found his body. He'd hung himself in his foster family's garage."

I close my eyes and remember. The way I had a sense he was gone even before we opened the door. The inhuman sounds Gracie and I made when we saw him there, swaying, his small body gone slack. The despair and the heartbreak, the mourning, and the bone-deep knowledge that he hadn't escaped after all.

"He left us a note that he couldn't live in this world. He wasn't strong enough for it."

"Honor." Strike reaches forward, catches my hand in his.

"If I had any innocence or childhood left then, it was gone. Any prior version of me decimated. Every time I think about it—that he thought that there was something wrong with *him*, and not with everyone else . . ."

This is the hardest part. How I failed my little brother. Strike places the palm of his hand on my back.

"Rusty must have been in so much pain and felt so lost and alone to leave us like that. Even in the best of times, and there weren't many of them, he was hard to reach, but once Gracie and I were out of his daily life, he lost his best support . . ." I stop, catch my breath. The guilt burns like stomach acid. "He really believed he was supposed to be tougher, not that everyone else should have been softer. And I think about that all the time—how in the end, he was probably right. The world doesn't soften for those who need it to. There isn't enough room for people like my dad and my brother to coexist. Rusty deserved so much better than he got from any of us, me included."

"Your father was a sadist. He would have killed you. Just like you knew Troy Simpson would have killed you." I feel Strike's fingers tracing my skin, the ridges of my scars. A gentle affirmation.

"Yes." It's true.

"You were a little girl. And you did what you had to do to get out. And what you did was so brave." He moves close, and our bodies lock together immediately. If I could, I'd crawl into the warmth of his skin. Burrow in and hibernate. "You are the strongest person I know."

"But there's something else," I say. I've never told another living soul. Not even Gracie. She never knew. Never even suspected, as far as I know. But my need to confess—to spill my truth to the one person who'd understand—is undeniable.

I look Strike directly in the eyes. If I am going to hand over my biggest secret, the one that I could leave buried with Gracie and Rusty, I need to do it like this.

"I did it on purpose. I intentionally murdered my father." I take a breath. "I lit that cigarette myself. I knew I'd be able to get the rest of us out in time. I wanted to kill him, Strike, and I did. I took the cigarette from the pack in his pocket, and I lit it, and then I just . . . let it fall."

I can see it now, the dark burn of the lit cigarette on the carpet by Daddy's empty beer glass, the one I gave to him, laced with the crushed powder of Mama's sleeping pills. The tiny sparking flame started to catch from the same green matchbook I had kept as a kid. How I ran to bed to wait, almost giddy with excitement. The beginning of the end.

I can feel it now, too: Lying on the mattress counting to a full minute, waiting for the smoke to rise. That intense feeling of relief, of power soaring through my veins. The grin on my face at the possibility of success.

It wasn't the first time I tried to murder him.

It was the first time it worked.

"Slaying a monster doesn't make you one," Strike says.

"Do you really believe that?"

"Yes," he says. "Absolutely. You want to pretend you made a bad choice, but it wasn't a choice at all. Sometimes there aren't any good choices. You wanted to get out of that house alive. And there was only one way to do it."

Then he reaches out with his fingers and lifts my chin, drawing me into his focused, piercing gaze.

"Honor. You are . . . everything," he says. "I've never wanted any woman as much as I want you. And yes, this world is fucked-up, and yes, we've lived through our own personal hells—and somehow we found a way to rise from the ashes, right? Scar tissue is beautiful because it's tough and strong and reminds you that healing is possible. So maybe that's also what makes this whole . . . you and me . . . possible. The fact that we see and understand each other's scars. The fact that all of our jagged edges fit. If there's even a chance that might be true, I'd like to take it. Would you?"

Every beat of my heart is a fire inside me that rages for this man. I have no idea where this passion will take us. If it will consume us. But Strike is also right—our challenges, our experiences of pain and grief, suffering and loss, are also what unite us, in strength and compatibility, along with a deeply felt empathy and compassion for each other's flaws.

There is only one answer.

"Yes," I say.

"Yes," Strike repeats. A slow smile spreads across his face. "I love you, Honor Stone. If we burn, we'll burn up together."

FIFTY-FOUR

HONOR

Two Months Later
Fall

I'm in my kitchen, squeezing some lemon juice into a Tupperware container of sliced apples so they don't turn brown, when Strike catches me around the waist, causing me to jump.

"You scared me!" I laugh as I swat at him with a dishcloth. "I didn't hear you come in."

"You look good enough to eat," he says. To prove it, he bites me on the shoulder. It takes all my willpower not to grab his hand and pull him into my bedroom and straddle his gorgeous face. But we have plans today.

"Everything's all ready." I smooth a gingham cloth over the food, close the picnic basket, and fasten the clasp.

Today is Strike's birthday, and the man who has everything doesn't want anything except for a romantic picnic lunch with me.

No arguments here.

"Let's do it."

We lock up and go—though I don't know where we're going,

and I don't bother guessing. Strike knows all the best spots, the tiny corners of delight no one else seems to notice. Sometimes that's how I feel when he looks at me—like I'm another surprise corner. When he stares at me like that—with awe, as if I'm this unexpected moment of beauty he's discovered—my heart is a fountain overflowing with love and joy.

The sun is out, and Strike hands me a fancy-looking sunglasses case; inside are a pair of sleek designer sunglasses that match his.

"These are incredible—thank you!" I've needed new sunnies since I lost the crummy old plastic pair I'd bought from a gas station floor spinner for $6.99. These are a bit of an upgrade. "But it's not *my* birthday," I say, slipping them over my face. A check in the mirror confirms they look badass.

"Every day is your birthday to me, Firefly," he says.

"Aw, if that's really how you feel, I guess I'll take it."

In the Jag, the wind in my face, I look over at Strike, in his sunglasses, looking better than a movie star. It's fun to match with him, to feel the power of this couplehood. I've finally stepped away from the loneliness that's been my steady companion my whole life. For the first time, I feel cherished.

My own gift to Strike is in the picnic basket—an almost-naked self-portrait of me that I painted from a morning selfie I took a few weeks ago, where I'm tousled and tired after a long night of lovemaking. In it I'm wearing Strike's beloved threadbare UPenn T-shirt, but it's slipping so far off my shoulders that my breasts are revealed, my nipples peachy and erect. A painting that stars myself for a change, to balance out the number of portraits I've done of Strike.

I know he'll devour it.

We've been taking the back roads, but it's not until he turns the bend that I get it. We're at St. Martin-in-the-Fields.

"Oh," I say. How in the world could Strike know where Rusty was buried? My heart is a sudden pony stampede. Strike slips a hand over mine as we drive through the cemetery gates.

I've never been to Rusty's grave with another person before. Not even Gracie. No way could we have adhered to our five-minute rule if we had come here together. In fact, after he died, we couldn't even bring ourselves to talk about him. Too painful, too shattering, too everything.

In those days, our survival demanded an unwavering focus on moving forward.

Gracie's buried over at Forest Hill Cemetery, the only one that would let me pay with a roulette of my various maxed-out credit cards. It's way less pretty over there—fewer trees, tombstones as crooked as an old man's teeth.

"I know it's my birthday," says Strike as he glances at my puzzled face. "But I have something to show you. I guess it's kind of a gift."

"Another gift."

He smiles enigmatically, and I have a feeling that what he wants to show me is more meaningful than designer sunglasses. We park at a small lot behind the church. Strikes pops the trunk and takes out a huge bouquet of lilies along with a canvas bag. "Can you grab the last thing?"

"There's nothing . . ." But when I check the trunk, there is, in fact, a last thing. A Mojave woven blanket identical to the one I sold Strike the very first time he came into the shop—only his is gray, and this one is blue. "You didn't!"

But of course he did. "The first of many picnics, I hope."

Another gift—but the blanket isn't what he wants to show me. He walks with purpose—he's been here before.

"Rusty's grave is on the other side," I say, pointing.

"Let's walk," he says, slipping his hand in mine. "What I want to show you is also over there." We smile at each other and then wind along the lane and pass beneath some more oak trees, bright with leaves creeping toward orange.

"This one's always sweet," I say, as I stop in front of a short rectangle of slate engraved with *Indiana Bones 1984–1989. A good dog.*

"Kate had a dog," says Strike. "Penny. Little terrier mix. It's with her parents in Ireland now."

Strike has started talking a bit more about Henry and Kate lately, bringing them into conversations on days like today. I know sweet Henry loved pranks and chili sauce and wearing his rubber rain boots and his Batman cape every day. I know Kate collected stuffed owls and could make a mean lemon meringue pie and wrote old-fashioned thank-you notes and could recite reams of Irish poetry—Yeats was her favorite. Henry loved the movie *Frozen*, and Strike still watches it the way I do *The Hunger Games*, Gracie's favorite. One day we plan to do a double feature.

"I've established ten scholarships at Turning Point dedicated to their memories," Strike says now. "But no actual stone or plaque. They were cremated."

"You could dedicate something here," I suggest. "A bench, maybe? Where you could go to think about them or talk to them."

"Talk to them." He smiles thinly. "I guess I do talk to them in my head."

"I talk to Rusty all the time when I visit. Not that I think he can hear me, but I'm not sure that matters. We could come

together. Though I wouldn't make you run here like I usually do."
I elbow him playfully.

"What? You think I can't keep up with you?"

"Oh, I *know* you can't," I say.

Rusty's grave is on the outer reaches of the property. It's lucky
he got a space at all; Gracie and I couldn't afford the headstone.
But his foster family took up a collection for us. "You won't get
over it, but given time, pray you'll get through it," his foster mom
told Gracie and me. She'd been an unpleasant woman with a
chain smoker's cough, but she'd looked shattered at the burial. A
twelve-year-old boy hanging himself in your garage will do that
to you.

Within a few yards of Rusty's grave, I can tell something looks
different. It's not that the cemetery never changes—new plots are
added, new bushes are planted, and seasons turn, of course—but
there's an enduring familiarity that I tend to take for granted.

When I see it, my body feels like someone's lit a match inside
my soul.

Rusty's stone stands as it always does. *Russell Pacer Stone,
2005–2017.* But now he has a new neighbor.

"Grace Marie Stone, 1998–2024," I read.

I glance up at Strike, my heart in my throat. "How did you
know? How did you know that this is what I dreamed of?" My
voice breaks, and tears stream down my face, a bittersweet mix
of sorrow and sunshine.

"I knew you wanted your siblings together," Strike says simply.

We're all together again: Rusty, Gracie, and me. Here, under
this clear sky, a happy, peaceful day in Normal. We are protected.
We are safe. I can cry as much as I want for Gracie, for Rusty, for
the people I loved and lost, because Strike is here, too. In it with
me. Holding me up.

He'll help me share the weight of my grief, and I'll share his. Maybe we'll even find a way to teach each other, bit by bit, how to let go.

Strike lays the bouquet of lilies by Gracie's headstone, and then he gives me the tote bag. "I thought you could pick."

I look inside the bag—it's filled with all different colored squares of plain and printed wrapping papers. "Oh!" For a moment, I am just completely overwhelmed. More tears prick the corners of my eyes. "Strike," I breathe. "This is . . . so right . . . it's exactly . . ." But then it's just too hard to speak, and so I keep my head ducked as I look for the one my little brother would pick. Then I see it—all different colors mashed together like glittery ice cream sprinkles.

New riches.

I pull it out, along with another Christmassy one, red-and-silver-striped like a candy cane. "He'd have loved these so much." But I'm not looking at what's in my hand. I'm looking at Strike. "Thank you."

He kisses me on the top of my head before he releases me.

"You might be right. You're not nice. Not even a little. But you are so very kind," I say.

Strike lifts his chin; the hint of smile on his lips is matched by the hint of smile in his eyes.

"I think that kindness is a way to heal," he says. "We've both lost so much—too much—and the only way I know how to not bow under that is to find hope where I can, to find peace, to find love."

He looks straight into my eyes.

"I love you, Honor Stone. God knows I've tried not to and have tried to believe you'd be better off without me. But I can't help myself. I'm utterly, completely, totally in love with you."

"I love you, too," I say, reaching up to wipe away his tears. I wish there were a way to pull him in tighter, to stitch him to me, to know that I will never lose him, that we will be side by side, unbreakable.

I want to believe all that, and at least in this moment, I do.

FIFTY-FIVE

STRIKE

Late Fall

The news comes with a frost that transforms all of Ashburn into a frozen landscape of ice crystals. I stare out my office window, listen to the hushed stillness that feels like a warning, and debate whether to read the local news story that just popped up on my phone. Before Honor, I would have clicked right away. No, before Honor I would likely have already made all the calls, would have had my dossier in hand before the body made it to the morgue. I don't normally get my information from the newspaper, but I told my sources I'd be lying low for a while. To contact me only in case of an emergency.

Guess no one thought a dead kid was an emergency.

This fucking world.

The headline is short and to the point: *Eleven-Year-Old Boy Found Dead.* I scroll past it, rub at my morning stubble—all I want is a blade in my hand. The temptation is almost seductive. I know myself—I'd be a dog with a bone.

Honor and I are happy. In love. No need to mess shit up.

I open an earnings report. Close it. I put on my VR headset

and poke around Honor's newest game. Nope. Even that doesn't distract me, though I make a mental note to tell her I like that the avatar is wearing snakeskin stilettos, exactly like the pair I recently bought her.

Damn it. I click. Then google. Soon the information blankets my monitor. I devour the articles, scan news reports, then move to the dark web, where I message my contacts for more information. I'm like a furious knight charging in and stabbing my sword through a dense thicket of data.

"An eleven-year-old child is dead today."

"Dubbs County is mourning the loss of a young fifth-grade boy."

"A child from West Shelton . . ."

"Pronounced dead . . . was killed . . . foul play suspected."

The little boy has a chipmunk face, spiky eyebrows, hair cut as short as golf grass. He is half smiling from his fifth-grade school picture. Henry was killed before he got to attend elementary school, so we never got the joy of his school portrait. But there's something about this kid's picture, in a generic rectangle with the standard blue background—the fact that he is so himself, with crooked teeth and a goofy haircut—that makes me sick to my stomach.

I play a video in which a sad-eyed reporter interviews the neighbors.

"They seemed like a nice family," one elderly lady says. "I can't believe this was happening right next door."

The boy's name, Jaxon Gower, runs in the chyron at the bottom of the screen. He died tied to a chair after being starved and beaten by his father. The police think it was the dehydration that ultimately killed him. They estimated he was in that chair for roughly seventy-two hours.

Seventy-two hours. Three days.

After a few calls, I discover it might have been longer. He had ligature scarring around his ankles. Bite scars all over his malnourished body.

Jaxon's dad is currently in jail, awaiting trial; meanwhile, his other two children have been removed and put into foster care. The reporter says this in the same way he reported a recent small increase in local gas prices. Nothing is officially stated about the mother, though another neighbor mentions that she seemed "like a nice enough lady."

"A real sweetheart. What's nicer than keeping your boy tied to a chair and beaten?" I'm almost shouting at the screen. I rub my throbbing temples. The news frames it as a local story about the failure of Shelton's Child Welfare Services—apparently a teacher made a complaint years ago.

After only one home visit, a social worker had cleared the family.

"It won't even be picked up by the national news," I tell Honor later when we're getting ready for our first formal event as a couple. Long after I closed my tabs and pushed through my workday, the image of Jaxon floats in my peripheral vision.

"Probably not," Honor says, turning around so I can zip up her green silk dress. I kiss the back of her neck. Inhale her scent. Let Honor help me slow my roll. "Child abuse happens too often to be considered news."

"Still," I say.

"Later," she says. "Let's get through tonight."

Ugh. Tonight I'm being honored at the Catch-22 Club in town for my support of Turning Point. I will have to make a speech and shake hands and pretend like we don't live in a world where a boy is tied to a chair and tortured to death and nobody can do anything about it. I wanted Paula to go in my place, but instead I got an earful about how these sorts of events are not only good for my public profile but also good for me socially.

"It's time to step into the spotlight," she told me. "Your life is so much steadier now with Honor at your side."

She isn't wrong about that. And Honor does look beautiful tonight in that flattering green silk, a color I associate with her as a lover of nature and tranquility.

At the banquet I slip into the role of CEO, forcing that school picture out of my mind for now.

"You two are a couple of power players," remarks George Forthlarkin from one seat over, a buddy of mine who's also the CEO of the West Shelton Financial Services.

"Bank Bitch's boss's boss," Honor whispers gleefully in my ear. I met Bank Bitch when I went with Honor to pay off her loans in full using the earnings from her art show. I offered to pay them myself—I'd never be asshole enough to say it to her, but her life-changing funds are my pocket change—but she refused. Bank Bitch is such a low-level functionary that it's hard to believe she ever had the power to upset Honor, so I made a point of mentioning Forthlarkin just to watch her sweat and grovel and essentially plead for her crappy job. The only reason I didn't insist he fire her is because I know she just had a baby.

"I have one of your paintings hanging in my foyer," says George now, and even though he's a sixty-year-old man, my ears are supersonic for the edge of flirtation in his voice.

"You do?" Honor asks a little shyly, and I remember how much I hate it when Honor underestimates herself. I will make it my life's mission for her to realize just how fucking talented and brilliant she is.

"I stop and look at it every morning. I always find something new to enjoy about it," says George. I give him a smile to make him remember she's great, but she's also mine. George gets it. "Anyhow, Honor, Strike, have you met the mayor?" he asks, smoothly pivoting.

I have, of course, but Honor hasn't. I smile and shake hands with the mayor, and then the mayor's husband, and three more people whose names I don't remember, and then stand back as Honor dazzles them with her small talk. I do not stop touching her. My hand rests on her lower back, and I draw lazy circles, a promise about what I will do to her when we get home.

I only leave her side for five minutes during the reception when I laser in on the sad-eyed reporter from the news who I've chatted with a few times before. His sources are usually good.

"Saw your report earlier. What's up with the Gower case?" I ask.

I don't mention that I've already read the police file. That I've seen the pictures. That my information is only a few hours stale.

"What's up is it's a sick joke. Dad's going to walk," he answers. He seems numbed to his job, and I don't blame him. I choose action, but I can see how someone could go the other way. "We're waiting on the final word from our source, but there was some sort of accidental Miranda rights violation. Off on a technicality. This shit happens all the time, but it still sucks."

He pulls his performance of a sad face. Now I want to punch him in the mouth. My source at the DA's office didn't mention the possibility of the dad walking.

"But that man killed his own child. Jaxon is dead," I say.

"Cops are human," the reporter says. "They make mistakes. And our AG keeps a clean house. Likes to play strictly by the rules, even when that means justice isn't necessarily served."

Justice.

My body seizes with a blinding rage. I want to roar, to smash every piece of glass, to lock the doors and keep everyone hostage until the governor signs a bill that would protect a boy who could not protect himself from the one person who was supposed to protect him the most.

But nobody will do that.

Judith Slaying Holofernes. There's a reason I keep her on my wall. Vengeance isn't pretty.

"Keep me updated," I tell the reporter, but as I walk away, my fists are clenched and my breathing is rapid-fire. I need to feel the curve of Honor's waist. I need to get lost before I lose control.

I look around the gala. Spot my favorite girl talking to the mayor and looking as sweet as an orchid in green, and I'm as aroused as the first night we met. I swipe a glass of champagne from a passing caterer, and as I approach and hand it off to her, I speak one word into her ear: "Now."

FIFTY-SIX

HONOR

Now

We're barely inside the front door before Strike peels my dress from my body like it's a candy wrapper. In the darkened entrance, he picks me up, pulls down my silky thong, and presses me hard against the wall. My gasps become growls as we kiss hungrily— together we are a drug that we're both hooked on.

This, I've realized, is an even better release than painting.

Doctors should prescribe orgasms.

As soon as Strike settles me back onto my feet, I yank down his zipper, and he springs rock-hard into my hand. He's so god-damn ready. He uses my own wetness to graze my clit with his thumb. I arch toward him, on tiptoe, guiding him inside me. No foreplay tonight. In only a few short seconds we've revved from zero to sixty.

We don't even stop for the condom—I have health insurance, we're both clean, and I'm on birth control—and in another moment, I'm meeting his every thrust, and his strong, heavy hands grip my hips like I'm his best prize. We fuck hard against the wall, fast and rough and desperate. I can tell Strike's got something on his mind—usually I can take his strokes fairly easily, but tonight he drives deeper, deeper. It's delicious. He goes so hard I have to tense against his thrusts.

He wants to claim me as much as he wants to rid himself of the rage in his body, and even though Strike cups the back of my head so it doesn't bruise—but honestly, I wouldn't care if it did— I feel the strength of his force in the heavy press of his mouth on mine, in the way his other hand squeezes my breast, in my incredible fullness. When he sinks into me in one last impossibly deep push, we come together in a final explosion. My heart is pounding and I feel electric, every part of me lit up.

I can no longer keep standing, not even another second.

When I sink to my knees, Strike laughs.

"We didn't even make it up the stairs." He snorts.

"We didn't even make it out of our clothes," I say. My dress is hiked up to my waist; his pants are still crumpled around his ankles.

"That's what next time is for, my love." He kisses my cheek, tenderly now, and it feels like an exquisite treat. He reaches down to help me up, pulls me in for a quiet hug. My body presses against his. "You okay? I hope that wasn't too much for you," he whispers roughly. "Next time, we'll take it slow . . . and in a bed."

"You are so demanding," I joke. "Tonight was almost perfect. I love being out with you. I love being on your arm. I love feeling like we're a team."

"Because we are," he says.

It's not until later, in his promised bed, that I say it again, this time inviting further conversation, "Tonight was almost perfect."

"I know," Strike says, rolling over onto his elbows so he can look me in the eyes. "You're thinking about Jaxon."

"I am. And you are, too." He nods, agreeing. We do this now. Read each other's thoughts.

"The dad's going to walk, isn't he?"

Strike nods again in short, reluctant confirmation.

"I could feel it in your body tonight." I trace my finger down his cheek, along the lines that bracket his mouth. "Let me see the dossier."

Strike absorbs this with some mild incredulity. Yes, we often know what the other is thinking, but this is one step further. This is me seeing into his soul.

After another moment he sits up, leans over to his side table, presses a button. A drawer opens and he slides out an iPad.

"Come closer."

I lean in. He touches the screen, and it's all there. Douglas Matthew Gower of Dubbs County. Files of his criminal record, his parents, his partner, his kids, his everything.

Pictures of sweet little Jaxon.

The coroner's pictures of Jaxon's bruises. They are graphic, grotesque. Images you can't unsee.

"He'll be released in the next week," says Strike.

"So what now?" I ask. "What do we do?"

Strike's gray eyes are level on me with unblinking intensity. "What do you want to do?"

FIFTY-SEVEN

HONOR

Late Fall

At first I'm not sure. What do I want to do? To know. To help. To understand. To stop Gower from ever hurting anyone else. For good.

"I want to know everything," I tell Strike.

So he gives me his passwords. The keys to Strike Madden's castle are child's play compared with the keys to the double-encryption codes, the button-activated mechanisms, and the fingerprint safe hidden behind a wall. In minutes I have Doug Gower's entire criminal history in my hands. A dossier, I learn, that was compiled by Axe.

The punishment, no doubt, will fit the crime. This is how Strike operates. With deliberate and careful consideration. And I am all in.

Except that he doesn't want me there.

"I can't allow you to be implicated in any way," Strike says. The papers are spread around us on the bed. I turn over the pictures of Jaxon's body that the coroner slipped to Strike. I cannot look even though they've already been seared into my brain. "It's too fucking dangerous, Honor. This isn't a spectator sport."

"You've carried this alone for too long," I say. I get out of the bed and walk around to the other side, staring him down. I need him to see me right now. To see how determined I am. I take his hands in mine like I'm making a vow. Maybe I am. "You and I both know this has nothing to do with sport. This is not recreation for you. You are not playing a game; you are fighting a war. Enlist me."

"Private Stone?" Strike asks, his lips almost curving into a smile as I sit on the edge of the bed.

"Yes, Captain."

"Honor." He tucks a piece of my hair behind my ear.

"Strike." I trace my finger along the furrow between his eyebrows.

"Seriously, no."

"Seriously, yes. The universe conspired to bring us together. We figured out how all our broken edges fit. Your damage and my damage speak the same secret language. You know all of my secrets. I know all of yours." I kiss him on the mouth, my lips parted, sighing into it and enjoying the shivery sensory input that his touch brings. He returns the kiss playfully, his tongue touching mine, an invitation that's also a way to remember we are here for each other. "Let's make some new secrets together."

It's been brewing in me ever since I heard about that poor boy. Or maybe since I witnessed Troy cut up like a quilting pattern. Or maybe it was even before, when I saw the raw, animal fear in my father's eyes. I was frightened by the exhilaration before. I couldn't bear to think I could be capable of it. But I am. I can feel it inside me—I don't want to be a spectator. I want to wield a weapon like a paintbrush. I want to plunge a blade straight through Gower's heart. He has stolen too much.

Strike considers me. Shakes his head once, twice.

Like he can't believe what he's about to say. But then he nods.

"Okay. If we're doing this together for real, we need to make a plan."

"You can start by showing me your knife collection."

"Don't even think of borrowing my Gerber," Strike says. "That's my baby."

"If only I could use that Hattori that just sold at auction." Life with Strike means keeping up with his antique knife and razor obsessions, and I know that last week, a slender, scalpel-sharp Hattori knife that Strike had his eye on sold to a private buyer for approximately the same cost as an Airstream trailer.

Strike stares at me in awe, and then his eyes narrow, and I can tell what he's thinking—that he wants to throw me back on the bed and devour me whole. "You're an expert in both knives *and* sex toys? Holy shit. You're the perfect woman."

I laugh, pull him to his feet. "Tell me. Was it you who bought that knife?" My voice drops. "For me?"

Strike doesn't answer, but smiles, quirks an eyebrow, and takes my hand in his.

And I follow him eagerly to his weapons room.

EPILOGUE

HONOR

Two Weeks Later

I try not to think about the needle. Or the fact that I am deliberately adding another scar to my body.

Instead, on the entire drive to Philadelphia, Strike and I sing along to his Spotify playlist, which has a surprising number of the sort of crowd-pleasers you'd hear at a school dance. "Party in the U.S.A." "Uptown Funk." Even "Happy." Strike wants to take me to Paris, Tibet, Sydney, all the most beautiful places in the world, but I already know I like this travel best. Road-tripping. Feet on the dash. A bag of snacks at my feet. Iced coffees in the cup holders.

Rusty, Gracie, and I dreamed that one day we'd drive across the country. Strike wanted to take Kate and Henry to Disney World to ride Space Mountain. Today, it's just Strike and me and I-95—and the ghosts we bring with us everywhere we go.

There's the Shelton city limit, Grace, I think. *I'm finally crossing it. Rusty, look how the sun makes the buildings shimmer.*

Strike wanted us to stay at the Four Seasons, of course, but I convinced him we should book a sweet, charming B&B on Pine

Street. When we arrive, we notice a little plaque next to the check-in window.

"Look at that—five whole stars!"

He laughs, an easy laugh that I hear more and more these days. He spins me around in a circle and then brings me close. "Rated by some website called PhiladelphiaSecretSpots.com. Not sure how official that is. Though, come to think of it, this place does look like it got all of its stuff from Grace & Honor." I look around, and he's actually right. The lamps, the cushions—it's a haven.

"Maybe that website is onto something."

After we check in, we decide to walk to our destination. Along the way we take a quick detour to the art museum, where I get my photo taken on the stairs like Rocky. Then Strike surprises me with a trip to Denny's.

"It's not lobster," he says when our stacks of cinnamon roll pancakes are delivered.

"So much better than lobster."

From there, we head for South Street. Recently, Strike bought me a pair of black boots that match his, and I love the way we walk in step, hard heels clomping like badasses. They have completely seamless flat soles. I haven't asked, but I bet they leave behind no identifiable footprints.

Strike's friend Pat waits for us outside even though there's a fall wind and he's not wearing a jacket. He's big and burly, with a curly thatch of ginger hair. He greets Strike with a broad smile and a back-slapping bear hug.

"This guy," he says to me, and then he can't quite speak. His eyes are shiny, and on someone who's so big and burly that he looks like he could have a side hustle as a bouncer, his show of emotion disarms me.

There's something in his face that looks familiar. And then I know, and my heart aches with the realization of why Strike was so insistent we come here.

Pat is Kate's brother. Henry's uncle. Strike used to live here. He is *from* Philadelphia. This is the closest he can come to bringing me home.

"I understand we got a double today," Pat says, smiling and holding open the door to 215Ink.

"I'm a little nervous," I admit.

"Breathe," Pat says, and I look over at Strike. I wonder if he remembers how that was his first word to me. From the way he beams back, I know he's thinking the same thing. How this all started with that strange command at the morgue a year ago.

"Yup. I will."

"Better make it a good one, Pat. She might look sweet, but she's tougher than a well-done steak when it comes to her ratings on Yelp."

I swat at Strike. "I've seen the work you've done on him. I'm not worried about that part."

Pat nods at me with a friendly smile and then pulls Strike a few steps away.

"Sorry. Need to talk to the big guy," Strike says to me apologetically. I don't mind. I like seeing Strike here, seeing echoes of the world he used to inhabit. The two men whisper in the corner, and though I can't hear what they're saying, I catch a few words. "Kate . . . fucking shitbag . . . cops think . . . dead end."

Strike hasn't stopped looking for the man who destroyed his life. Of course, Pat hasn't stopped, either.

I take out my phone and fiddle with the screen. Pretend I can't hear a word. When and if Strike ever needs to involve me, I know he will.

The two men thump each other on the back, and Strike throws a "Thanks, man" over his shoulder.

"Strike said you wanted something similar to his tat?" Pat asks, when he returns to where I'm standing.

"Please," I say.

"Show me," Pat says. I hand over the scrap of paper in my pocket with my hand-drawn sketch.

"Two lines. The first in the shape of a match." Listening to Strike talk about his tattoos ignited a spark within me. While some of the canvas of his skin functions as a scorecard to mark his kills, other tattoos—inked mementos in dates, monograms, and insignias—are a testament to his life's narrative. I yearn for the same attention and thoughtfulness in my own life's journey—my intentions firm and my milestones boldly etched in ink.

"And Strike, you want one line added to yours?"

Strike nods in affirmation, and he and I trade a look.

I climb into the tattoo chair, resting my arm so Pat has easy access to my inner bicep. He shaves my arm, blots it with alcohol, and shows me the ink-filled needle.

"For some people, the pain is nothing," he says.

Across the room, Strike mouths, *I love you.*

I hear the buzz, and when I feel the tiny sting, I want to laugh. It's less than a mosquito bite. I've endured far, far worse pain than this. With each zap of needle and ink, I'm more euphoric. As a girl, I lived my life being surprised by pain and danger where I was supposed to feel happiness and safety. My tattoo is the opposite, and the ink permanently etched on my skin will remind me of my ability to choose my own scars and to shape my own destiny.

"You good?" Strike asks me softly.

"I'm good."

I'm so much better than good. After all the twists and turns that marked this wild journey—and even with so much ahead still unknown—I did it. I'm here. I survived. I bloomed. I even found my soulmate, and together, whatever happens next, we will be the victors of our story. We'll get to write our own precious and unexpected Normal.

We're home.

ACKNOWLEDGMENTS

First and foremost, thank you to our fabulous readers who buckled in with us for the whole wild ride. You made this journey so exhilarating! We also want to give a great big, delicious hug to the romance community. Your passion and enthusiasm inspired us to deep-dive headfirst into the world of dark romance. As longtime fans and readers, we're thrilled and honored we now get to enjoy some of this space on the shelf.

To our earliest readers, Rose Brock and Catherine McKenzie—thank you so much! Nothing made us happier than your green light to keep going!

We are also very grateful to our agents, Erin Harris, Jenn Joel, and Emily Van Beek. We are so appreciative of your wisdom and support as we embarked on this new, uncharted adventure.

A very special thank-you to Kristin Cipolla, Abby Graves, Kim-Salina I, Megha Jain, Christine Legon, Jessica Mangicaro, Chelsea Pascoe, and especially our editor, Liz Sellers, who shaped this document into a book with such vast capability and clarity—along with a spicy, spirited sense of fun.

We also wanted to give a special shout-out to all the life-affirming jokes, snacks, memes, and GIFs that helped make our collaboration such a joyride—and without which this book might still be only a fever dream. Whether it was another perfectly timed rainbow unicorn sticker, cup of coffee, or guac-and-chips writing break, we loved the magic and sparkle of the entire process.

STRIKE
and
BURN

TAYLOR HUTTON

DISCUSSION QUESTIONS

1. Strike and Honor's morgue meeting sets an immediate dark tone for their relationship. How does their first encounter reflect the overall mood of the story?

2. In what ways does the chemistry between Honor and Strike evolve throughout the novel? Why do their secrets continue to spark the connection between them?

3. Honor's new job at DME's erotic animation studio is symbolic of her sexual awakening. How does Honor change as she explores her sexuality, both in her work and in her personal life?

4. Honor's shop sells a wide range of wares, from cozy cardigans to sex toys. It contains multitudes! How do you think this eclectic mix of items symbolizes the complexities of Honor's personality and her journey throughout the novel?

5. How does Troy Simpson escalate the tension in the story? What are your thoughts on the authors' portrayal of this antagonist, and how do you think Troy's psychological impact on Honor compares with her response to Strike's own ethical ambiguity?

6. In what ways do the dynamics of Strike's and Honor's friendships with Axe and Josie provide deeper insight into their own personalities and motivations? What do these friendships reveal?

7. Honor's traumatic childhood profoundly impacts her actions and decisions. How do these deeply scarring experiences influence her choices, good and bad? How does her tragedy affect her interactions with Strike? Do you think she and Strike find true healing by the end of the novel? Can justice be considered a form of healing?

8. How do the authors explore themes of power and vulnerability through Honor and Strike's interactions and individual backstories?

9. Honor repeats the adage "History is written by the victors." Do you agree with this statement? How do you think this saying relates to the telling of Honor and Strike's love story?

Author photo by Indy Flore

Taylor Hutton is the pen name for bestselling coauthors Adele Griffin and Julie Buxbaum.

Adele Griffin is the acclaimed author of more than thirty books. Her works include the National Book Award finalists *Sons of Liberty* and *Where I Want to Be*. She lives in Los Angeles with her family.

Julie Buxbaum is the *New York Times* bestselling author of novels for adults, young adults, and middle grade readers and is an Edgar Award finalist. Her work has been translated into twenty-five languages.

VISIT TAYLOR HUTTON ONLINE

⊙ ♪ TaylorHuttonBooks

Ready to find
your next great read?

Let us help.

Visit prh.com/nextread

Penguin
Random
House